LTYP GARLOCK

Garlock, Dorothy

Nightrose

MAY 29 1997

APR 15

W9-BOS-622

3 3008 00656 6802

NIGHTROSE

G·K
Hall
&Cº.

Also by Dorothy Garlock
in Large Print:

Annie Lash
Wild Sweet Wilderness
Almost Eden
Forever, Victoria
Home Place
Ribbon in the Sky
Sins of Summer
Tenderness
Yesteryear

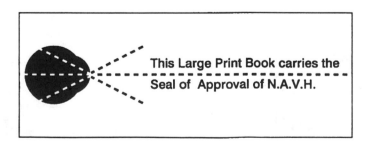

This Large Print Book carries the
Seal of Approval of N.A.V.H.

Dorothy Garlock

NIGHTROSE

G.K. Hall & Co.
Thorndike, Maine

GLENDORA LIBRARY AND CULTURAL CENTER
GLENDORA, CA 91741

Copyright © 1990 by Dorothy Garlock

All rights reserved.

Published in 1997 by arrangement with Warner Books, Inc.

G.K. Hall Large Print Core Collection.

The text of this Large Print edition is unabridged.
Other aspects of the book may vary from the original edition.

Set in 16 pt. Plantin.

Printed in the United States on permanent paper.

Library of Congress Cataloging in Publication Data

Garlock, Dorothy.
    Nightrose / Dorothy Garlock.
       p.   cm.
    ISBN 0-7838-8098-7 (lg. print : hc)
    1. Large type books.   I. Title.
    [PS3557.A71645N54   1997]
    813'.54—dc21   97-1516

To Gary Rowe for that great evening
when he gave me the idea for
this story,
and
to his wife, Beth, who puts up with his
shenanigans —

CHAPTER

<u>One</u>

"He's out there again! Come look, Katy."

Katy's head jerked up. "What's he doing?"

"I don't know. He moved so fast I only got a glimpse of him."

Katy got up from the rocking chair, stepped over the child sitting on the floor at her feet, and went to the window. She didn't want to act too concerned about the mysterious man whom they had glimpsed from time to time moving amid the deserted buildings. It would alarm her sister even more. Married to that feather-head Roy Stanton caused Mary enough worry.

"Where?"

"He went behind the blacksmith shop. Now he's pounding on something," Mary said as if Katy couldn't hear the sound of a hammer on iron. "His dog is there in the grass by the building."

"I see the big ugly beast. They're a strange pair. From what I've seen of him, he's about as hairy as the dog," Katy said with disgust.

"He hasn't been out in the road since that day he rode in. I wonder why he only moves around behind the buildings."

Katy looked over her shoulder when the child began to rock the chair. It made a loud hollow sound against the rough plank floor.

"Be careful, Theresa, you'll rock over your toes."

"No, I won't," Theresa said stubbornly and continued to rock the chair.

Katy's blond hair was swept away from her forehead and hung down her back in a single thick braid. It slid along her spine like a golden rope as she turned to peer out the window over the shoulder of her shorter sister.

The bearded man had ridden into town five days ago. Since then they had caught only glimpses of him. At first they had hoped that the miners were returning, but when no one else rode in, and the stranger failed to present himself at their door, or even acknowledge their presence, he became a cause for worry.

Katy looked down the rutted, deserted street of Trinity, Montana Territory. Weeds had sprung up in the road since the heavy spring rain. The town looked peaceful, a contrast with the boisterous days of eight months ago when they had first arrived. Then, Trinity had been a mining town filled to capacity with men seeking to fulfill their dreams of making the big strike. The tall, false-fronted saloons with rooms upstairs, the store, the boardinghouse for single miners, the washhouse, and the eateries, all had done a thriving business.

Across the street and farther down was a square

log building known as "the girlie house." It, too, had enjoyed five years of prosperity. When the hopes of Trinity's becoming another booming gold-mining town faded, and the miners left to pursue their dreams elsewhere, the good-time girls had followed.

"It's scary knowing he's here and having him ignore us. Oh, there he is. He's carrying a big hammer. The dog follows every move he makes."

"I should go over there and ask him to help us get out of here."

"Oh, no! If he were a decent sort of man, he'd have come and paid his respects." Mary sat down in the rocker. Theresa climbed up into her lap. "He might think we have men working downstream."

"Fiddle!" Katy snorted. "He knows the men deserted this town like rats fleeing a sinking ship once the mine started petering out. And as far as his being *decent* — we're more likely to find a cow in a tree than a decent man out here."

"Roy will be back, Katy. I know you don't think he's much of a man, but he'd be back here like a shot if he knew everyone had left."

"Wherever Roy is, he must have gotten word that the mine played-out here." What Katy wanted to say was that Roy would be off like a shot to anyplace he had heard of that had a gold strike, no matter how small. His wife, daughter, and sister-in-law were his least concern.

Katy glanced up at the rifle that hung on the wall out of the reach of Theresa. She had placed it there when they had moved down from the shack on the hill into this building — the most solidly built in town except for the small stone jail. The man who had built this structure had been a carpenter and funeral director. The big, black-lettered sign in front said: GROG'S FUNERARY. Here, Grog had put together tables, chairs, wardrobes, beds, burial boxes, and laid out the dead when they were brought to him. He had left a box behind when he moved on. It was now Theresa's bed.

"Deliver me from a man with gold fever," Katy said crossly. "We can't wait here much longer. If not for the supplies we bought from the store man before he left, and for our scavenging the deserted houses, we'd starve. Thank goodness we've got ammunition for the rifle."

"How can we leave? We don't have a horse."

Until recently, Mary had always looked younger than her twenty-five years. Now, the years of following her husband from mining camp to mining camp, and the loss of two children who had not come to full term had taken their toll. Faint lines of strain had appeared between her brows and at the corners of her eyes and mouth. Her face often had a pensive look, and shadows of worry ringed her eyes.

"We have the cow the Flannerys left behind when they rushed off to the next gold strike," Katy said. When she saw big tears flooding her sister's eyes, she attempted to lighten her mood by adding, "We'll hitch Mable to the wagon."

"Oh, poo!" Mary hugged her daughter to her. "Your Aunt Katy can say the silliest things."

"Mable ain't a horse." Theresa looked at her aunt with a puzzled expression,

"Isn't a horse, honey," Mary corrected absently.

"We may have to walk. That would mean leaving everything behind except what we can carry. If we go due south, we *may* reach a stage station. If we go northwest, we *may* reach Bannack."

"We *may* run into Indians," Mary said softly, her hand over her daughter's ear.

"Sister, we're in a hell of a mess."

"Oh, Katy! Let's not allow ourselves to be *crude*."

"Crude, my foot! I'm twenty-one years old. I've the right to be crude if l want to."

Katy's wide mouth, its lower lip fuller and softer than the upper one, turned down at the corners as her blue-gray eyes, deep set and slightly tilted at the outer corners, roved over her sister and niece. It hurt that her gentle sister, with her love for reading, writing, and music, should come to this. Here they sat in a deserted town waiting for Roy Stanton to remember where he had left them.

"We'll have to bring up more water tonight. We can't allow the cow to go dry."

"We can lead her down to the stream and let her drink her fill."

"We could, if not for bushy-face."

"Do you think he's waiting his chance to . . .

11

have his way with us?"

"If he is, he's in for a surprise." Katy patted her pocket. She had used the little pistol more than once to discourage amorous, woman-hungry miners.

Katy looked around the funeral parlor they had made into a home. It was as comfortable as the rooms they had in Laramie, thanks to all the discards left by the gold-seeking crowd. They had two beds, a sheet-iron cookstove, table, chairs, a rocker, a round potbellied stove for heat. They had a good assortment of nice, heavy china and a variety of cooking pots. At first they had been hesitant about taking anything from the deserted buildings. But after they had been alone for a month, seeing what they could find became a game. They had even found a sack of potatoes that Mary eyed and planted in a little patch. Gathering firewood and bringing water up from the stream was an everyday chore, because the rope and pulley were gone from the well.

Katy held her hand out to Theresa, and the child jumped from her mother's lap. "Come on, ladybug. Let's go out and pull some grass for Mable. She's been feeding us; we've got to do our best for her."

"Do you think you should go out with *him* out there, Katy?"

"He's been here all this time and hasn't bothered us."

"Maybe he hasn't been here all this time. Maybe he goes someplace and comes back."

"Where would he go? There isn't a town within fifty miles of here. Don't worry. I tied Mable near the side door. The front door is barred and the rifle is loaded in case you should need it. You can watch out the window, and if you see him coming, you can yell."

"Leave the door open."

"I don't think he'll bother us. He's probably some old prospector scavenging for what he can find."

"He didn't look like a prospector when he rode in. He had a good horse."

"He also had two pack mules."

"Why are we scared of the man, Mamma?" Theresa's small hands cupped her mother's face and turned it toward her to get her attention.

"We don't know him, honey."

"Maybe he's seen Papa. Can I ask him?"

"No. If he had a message from Papa, he'd have come and told us. Papa will come for us soon." Mary looked at her daughter with a sympathetic smile. "Maybe he'll bring you a pretty."

"I want a music box."

"You've got your sights set high."

"Cow in the tree again," Katy muttered and turned her face away, knowing the dislike she felt for Roy Stanton was mirrored there. "Why don't you write in your journal while we're gone?"

"I don't know why I keep writing in it: There hasn't been anything good to write about for a long time."

"Someday you can write a book about two

beautiful sisters and a golden-haired child who were left in a deserted mining town." Katy threw her arms wide in a dramatic gesture, bowed to her audience, and began to speak. "Friends, let me introduce myself. My name is Katherine Louise Burns, and I'm here to tell you a tale written by Mrs. Mary Theresa Burns Stanton."

Mary and Theresa clapped their hands as they always did when Katy was play acting.

"Alas!" Katy continued. "The ladies were the only residents of the town of Trinity in Montana Territory." Katy clasped her hands to her breast with an expression of deep sorrow on her face. "One day they heard the sound of a bugle, and lo" — she shaded her eyes with her hand and turned from side to side — "a knight with a purple plume on his helmet came riding into town on a white steed. Behind him came a coach drawn by . . . six pink cows."

"Cows aren't pink," Theresa shouted. "You're silly, Aunt Katy."

"Who said that cows can't be pink, ladybug?" Katy stood with her hands on her hips and glared at her niece. "I can have pink cows if I want to. Just for that I'll not let you ride in my coach. So there!"

"I will too ride in your coach."

"You will not. You can ride on one of the cows. Come on, we'll practice on Mable."

"Be careful," Mary called as they went out the side door.

Mary went to the window again. Her soft

14

brown eyes searched up and down the rutted street where already the weeds were growing. At first she failed to see the dog who lay as still as a rock in the shade next to the stone building that had served as a jail. She saw him when he snapped at a pesky fly and knew the man was nearby. If he was in the jail, she reasoned, he would not see Katy and Theresa pulling grass for the cow.

Mary was still wondering about the bearded man when she lifted the lid of her humpbacked trunk and took out the journal. The book was an inch thick, and more than half the pages were filled with small, neat script. It was one of Mary's most precious possessions. The first entry had been made eight years ago when she and Roy Stanton were married in Montgomery, Alabama. She had recorded the first few happy months of their marriage. Later in the journal she had mentioned her husband's inability to adjust to the New South. Another entry told of the Stanton Plantation going on the auction block and falling into the hands of a Northerner. That was the final blow to Roy's pride. His dream of making enough money to go back and reclaim the house and land had brought them to the gold fields. All of this was neatly recorded in the journal.

Pulling the chair close to the window, Mary sat down with the book in her lap.

"Oh, Mamma, you wanted me to marry into a fine Southern family, and look what it got me into." She did not realize that she had spoken aloud until she heard her own voice. Roy was not

15

prepared to take responsibility for a wife and a child. He'd always had everything he wanted without lifting a finger. He had even paid for someone to fight in his place during the War. Now he was off chasing a dream of finding riches, and she and Theresa would be here alone if not for Katy.

Mary seldom let herself think about how disappointed she was in the man she had married, or how different her life might have been had she married another man or remained a spinster. She had chosen Roy, for better or for worse, and her marriage vows were sacred to her. She could thank him for Theresa. Her child was worth all the heartache she had suffered. Mary turned from those dark thoughts, opened the journal and began to read an entry she had made almost five years ago.

Cripple Creek, Colorado Territory, June 14, 1868.

Today I received the news that Mamma is gone. Oh, but I wish I could have been with her at the last. Katy said she didn't suffer as Papa had. I'm grateful for that. Katy and I are all that is left of the family. My dear brothers, Roger and Clifford, died at Gettysburg, a place I never heard of before, and Papa died of apoplexy brought on by a broken heart. Katy wants to come out here to be near me. I'm so ashamed to have her see this hovel we live in. But, oh, I want her to

16

come. I'm so lonesome that at times I could die.

Black Hawk, Colorado Territory, May 5, 1869.
Katy has arrived at last. It is so good to see her that I keep looking at her and touching her to make sure she is really here. She is so fresh-looking and beautiful. Some of the men here in the camp have shaved and even put on clean shirts hoping that she will notice them, but she pays them no mind. I know she is shocked by the living conditions here, but, bless her, she hasn't let on. Roy was angry when he found out my bleeding had stopped. I hope he will stay here at least until the baby comes.

Mary continued to thumb through the journal, reading entries she had made in places called Breckenridge, Bonanza, Myrtle Gulch, Laramie, Virginia City, and finally Trinity.

Trinity, Montana Territory, September 5, 1873.
This is the wildest place we have ever been. There are two saloons and a girlie house. The women parade themselves out front all hours of the day and night. As many people are on the street at midnight as at noon. I don't understand why Roy brought us here. We should have stayed in Laramie. Katy had a teaching job at the orphanage. Mrs. Gal-

17

lagher said I could stay and help with the children. Roy was embarrassed that his wife would work for wages. He insisted that Theresa and I come with him. I think it was because he didn't want to go back and face the Gallaghers after Pack told him the mining camps were no place to take a family. Katy came with us, although I know she is seething with resentment. Roy found a place for us in a crude log-hut up above the town.

Trinity, December 25, 1873.
I'm lying abed. I lost another babe. Oh, the poor little thing. It is so cold here that I don't know if it would have lived anyway. Theresa has to stay in bed with me to keep warm. Roy gave me a blue-ribboned bonnet and Theresa a pair of slippers for Christmas. When will I ever wear a ribboned bonnet? Theresa will outgrow the slippers before spring. Roy is so impractical. He and Katy had cross words again this morning. She is angry at him for spending so much time and money down at the saloon. We're almost out of firewood. It isn't fair that Katy must do so much. Oh, I wonder where we will be when another Christmas comes around again.

April 5, 1874.
Roy used the last of our money to buy supplies to go into the hills and look for gold.

He's sure that he'll find it this time. I'm so ashamed. I know now why he wanted us to come with him. He knew Katy would come. She has a little money, and he knows that she'll not let me and Theresa go hungry. He says the mine here is playing out and that he wants to get the jump on the others. He has promised to be gone only a few weeks. He is like a small boy looking for the pot of gold at the end of the rainbow. He wants riches without working for them.

Mary turned the pages, scanning the entries where she told about their first few days alone in the deserted town, and how frightened they were when they heard a cougar scream in the night. When she came to a blank page, she moistened the lead of the pencil with the tip of her tongue and began to write.

June 5, 1874.
    Roy has been gone for two months. I'm afraid that he will never come back, although I don't let on to Katy. I don't want to think that he would leave us here deliberately, without even a horse to pull the wagon. Now I'm wondering if something could have happened to him. Oh, I know he's selfish, but he wouldn't leave his baby daughter. At least I don't think he would. I feel terrible about Katy being stuck here with us. She has devoted the best years of her life to me and

Theresa. As far as I know, she has never had a serious beau. She could have had her pick of men this past winter, but she wanted nothing to do with any of them. She said she would stay single for the rest of her life before she'd marry a miner. Today we saw the stranger again. He is big with a coal black beard. I can't tell if he's young or old. I've not seen his horse or his pack mules since he rode in, but we've smelled his cookfire several times, and the fresh meat he was cooking smelled so good. We've not had fresh meat since Katy shot a baby deer. She cried because the mother was so frantic. We didn't know anything about skinning it, so we cut off a leg. Something carried the rest of it off in the night.

Mary closed the journal and sat for a while, gazing out the window. She could have written more, but she had to be saving with the paper. The prospects of getting another book to write in were small, if not nonexistent; that is, if they ever got out of this lonely place. A mouse scurrying across the floor drew Mary's attention, and she wished for a cat. Rats and mice were becoming a problem, but a minor one, she admitted silently, compared to their other concerns. She got up to make sure the lid to the flour tin was in place. She was returning to the chair by the window when she heard Katy shout.

"Mary! Get Theresa. I'm bringing in the cow!"

"What in tarnation — !" Mary ran to the back and out the door. She grabbed Theresa who was standing with her finger in her mouth as if she were thunderstruck. Mary darted back to the door, shoved the child inside, and went to help Katy tug on the rope around the neck of the bawling, frightened cow. "Is *he* out there?"

Katy was too busy to answer. "Get in there, damn you!" she shouted and whacked the cow on the rump with the palm of her hand. "You stupid, brainless creature, I'm trying to save your flea-bitten hide!" She got behind the cow and shoved. The cow lifted her hind foot threateningly. "You kick me and I'll brain you," Katy yelled.

The frightened cow had become tame during the last two months, but she was reluctant to go inside the building. The doorway was narrow and the sound of her hooves on the plank floor terrified her. She balked, bawled, shook her head, and tried to break free.

"Yeeeow!" The primitive scream of a cougar came from close behind them. Ingrained fear of the beast caused the cow to lunge, her forelegs collapsing, and she sprawled half-in and half-out of the doorway, almost knocking Mary off her feet.

Katy looked over her shoulder to see the large, slick cat move with effortless grace along the rim of the slanting cliff behind the building. Its head jutted forward; its long sweeping tail hung close to its powerful hindquarters; its yellow eyes

21

gleamed as it viewed its prospective prey.

"Oh, blessed Father!" The words came from Katy's stiff, dry throat. The cat's huge eyes glared fixedly at her. The big body arched, and a powerful growl exploded from its huge mouth.

"Yeeeow!"

Blocking the doorway, Mable was scrambling to get to her feet. Katy cowered against the side of the building, her eyes fixed with horror on the stalking beast. Fear raced through her; her knees felt like water. The cat prowled a few steps closer, then froze in immobility. Screaming again, it bunched its powerful muscles to spring.

The sharp crack of a rifle penetrated Katy's stunned senses as she had begun to lift her arm to her face. The sound of the shot rebounded from the mountains. As the bullet found its mark, the cat dropped from the ledge. It landed in the brush a few yards from where Katy stood.

"Don't move!"

The gruff words hit Katy like a slap in the face, and she came out of her near-hysterical trance to see a buckskin-clad figure in a round-brimmed leather hat approaching the cat with his rifle ready. Katy's eyes were on the cougar, expecting it to spring up and attack the man. He nudged it a time or two with the end of his rifle, grabbed its tail and pulled. When he was sure it was dead, he turned and trotted away without so much as a look in her direction.

"Mister!" Katy choked, then called. "Hey, mister! Thank you —" She followed him to the

22

front of the building, watched him lope down the road and disappear between the jail and the black-smith shop.

Katy hurried back to the side-door. Theresa was crying and Mary was calling to her frantically.

"Katy! Katy!"

"I'm all right. Bushy-face killed it. Glory! I'm going to sit down. My legs are trembling."

"I was never so scared in my life."

"I see that you got Mable inside. The stubborn beast. It would serve her right if she broke her leg."

"Her legs are all right. She cut her udder. It's bleeding on the floor."

"Tie a bandage around it while I get my breath. That was just a whisker too close."

CHAPTER
Two

"Damn woman's gutsy; I'll say that for her." Garrick Rowe spoke aloud to the dog who lay flat on his belly, his big head on his crossed paws. "Didn't scream or faint. I can't figure out what the hell two gentle womenfolk are doing here without men. Jesus! It's a wonder they haven't been carried off by a Cheyenne war party or some half-civilized, woman-hungry fur trapper."

Rowe turned the squirrel carcass on the spit. His cookfire was built beside the eight-foot-square stone building where he had decided to take up residence. He didn't need much space for now, just a place where he could store his supplies and hold off an attack if the occasion arose.

He viewed the meat critically. It was browning and the juices were dripping. He'd had his fill of fresh meat. Right now, he would give a silver dollar for a biscuit with butter on it. The women in Grog's Funerary had butter. The day he arrived, the brown-haired one had been sitting on the porch working the dasher up and down in a churn. She scrambled inside when she saw him corning, a sure sign there were no menfolk around.

"After we eat, Modo, we'll get one of the mules and drag that cat off down the gully. In a day or two he'll stink so bad the ladies will be cussing me for shooting him. You can gnaw on him if you want, but first I'll take his pelt. No sense in letting it go to waste."

Rowe fingered his beard. It had protected his face from the cold during the winter, but now that it was getting hot, he would have to shave. He slid the teakettle close to the fire to heat some water. Usually, he shaved with his hunting knife, but with a winter's growth of whiskers, he'd need help or he'd not leave any skin left on his face.

Why were the women here? They were not Grogs. He had set up shop in Bannack. As far as anyone knew, this town would never revive. Rowe didn't have time to play nursemaid. Their men should be here looking out for them unless they were widows. If that were the case, why hadn't they left with the others? Big John Beecher, the blacksmith, had been one of the last to leave Trinity. John hadn't mentioned any permanent residents when he and Rowe met in Virginia City. In another week Hank would be here with tools, Big John, and a couple of wagon-loads of men, Hell, Rowe hadn't counted on two lone women to complicate things.

While he ate, his mind went back to the woman with the heavy rope of blond hair hanging down her back. It irritated him that he hadn't been able to get her face out of his mind since he first saw it five days ago. It was etched there as if he had

25

looked upon it a million times. Her profile was classical, her neck long, and her eyes blue. How did he know that, he wondered. He hadn't been within a dozen yards of the woman. Her eyes could be green or brown, or black like his. He stopped eating and held the meat in his two hands. No, they were blue. He could see them clearly in his mind.

Rowe now had that same strange feeling he'd had when he'd first seen her walking to the creek to get water. She had seemed to float over the ground without so much as a bob of her head. It was as if he had known this woman before, known her well, as if he could have picked her out of a crowd of hundreds had she been strolling amid the ruins on the flat-topped hill known as the Acropolis in Athens.

He cursed in Greek, the language of his mother, as he always did when he was frustrated. He didn't like blond women. He'd never bedded a blond woman, had shunned them when possible. Hell and high water! Hadn't he had enough of the fair race to last a lifetime? He was sure he had never set eyes on this woman before, yet today, when he had heard her talking to the little girl, her voice had sounded familiar. He heard the child laugh and call her Aunt Katy. He was not surprised that the child was not hers. When he heard her call out, somehow he found his rifle in his hand and his feet had moved automatically. He saw the cougar on the ledge — as if it had all happened before — and shot it, knowing that he wouldn't miss.

Damnation! Was he losing his mind?

Darkness comes suddenly in the mountains. The town lay on a long bench that bordered the creek on the far side. Actually, the creek curved around the bench. The town was backed up against the mountain; behind and above it was a thick growth of trees. Rowe had been pleased to see that the town had at least a dozen buildings and a scattering of houses and shacks on the slope above it, including a long bunkhouse that offered bunks to those less discriminating than the hotel patrons. Behind the livery was a stone reservoir some ten feet across and about eight feet deep. Water ran from the rocks into it. Now a thin stream made its way to the creek below. Within the rail fence surrounding the tank he had left his mules and his horse.

During the final minutes before dark, Rowe leaned against the side of the building and fingered his newly shaved chin. He scarcely recognized himself in the small square of mirror he carried in his saddlebag. His hair, cut with his hunting knife, was no more than two inches long. After it was washed it would curl up even shorter. His face had felt so bare once the hair was off his cheeks and chin that he had left the hair above his lip. He stroked it now, first on one side and then the other.

It was still light enough for him to see the great empty eyes of the windows of the vacant buildings and the swaying of the sign in front of the boarded-up eatery. The day after he arrived, he had smashed the hasp from the saloon door and pushed it open. The mirror behind the bar was intact, but the space above it was strangely lacking the usual picture of a naked woman lying on a couch. The owner had taken all the whiskey but left a supply of glasses. Tables and chairs stood in the room, and a thick layer of dust covered everything. In the back of the saloon a stairway led up to a hall where doorways opened to a half-dozen small rooms.

Eager to profit by a boom such as the one at Virginia City, money-hungry men had flocked to Trinity. When the crash came the people had fled, leaving behind all they could not pack on a horse or in a wagon, hurrying to the next strike, carrying their dreams and ambitions, knowing that success was just around the corner.

Rowe realized that he had gotten a lot more than he bargained for when he bought the town. Suddenly he saw a dim light appear in the window of Grog's Funerary. Almost as soon as he saw the light, one of the women approached the window with a quilt or a blanket and the light was gone. It was a smart move to cover the window. Any drifter who came into town would have headed directly for the light. Rowe knew that wasn't the reason they covered it. It was because they feared he could spy on them. The sound that came from him was almost a chuckle. They were like two babes in the woods. He knew almost every time they went out the side door to empty the chamber pot.

After he made his rounds of the town and was satisfied that the population was still only two women, a child, and himself, Rowe took a bar of carbolic soap and clean buckskins and headed for the creek. Modo padded silently behind him.

"You'll be getting a bath one day soon," he told the dog. "You gather fleas like a bee gathers honey."

Cleanliness was almost a fetish with Rowe. He used the carbolic soap in case he had picked up a flea from Modo. Before he left the building, he sprinkled his bedroll with kerosene should the building be infested with bedbugs. He shed his clothes and stepped naked into the icy cold water that came down from the snow-covered mountains above. He ducked until the water flowed over his head, then stood knee-deep in the stream and lathered the hair on his head, chest, and groin with the soap.

Modo lay on the bank beside Rowe's discarded clothes. Suddenly he stood, his head slung low, his tail extended straight out. Rowe started toward the bank. A second later he heard the sound of something coming down the path from town.

"Shhh . . ." The hissed sound was a command the dog obeyed.

Rowe moved toward the bank and into a screen of willows. Knowing automatically that his master wanted him out of sight, Modo slunk silently amid the drooping branches.

The blond woman came quietly down the

path, a rifle in one hand, a lead rope in the other. It was the cow she was leading who had made the noise. She led the animal to the stream not a dozen feet from where Rowe stood shivering in the icy water. While the cow drank, she knelt down, and with her free hand splashed water on her face, then stood waiting patiently, turning her head slowly from one side to the other, watching and listening. She was fully alert. Rowe found himself nodding his head in approval. This was no empty-headed woman. He had no doubt that if he made a move toward her, she would shoot him. He glanced at his clothing on the bank. Because the buckskins looked like a rock in the darkness, he doubted that she would notice them.

After she had led the cow back up the path, he moved out into the stream, sat down on the rocky bottom, leaned back, and let the swiftly moving water rinse the soap from his hair. The women were being cautious and he couldn't fault them for that. Katy had not taken the cow to the tank behind the livery because she would have to pass the stone building. By cutting across the road above town, she could reach the creek without being seen from the jail. Because of him they had been carrying their water up that steep path.

He was sitting on the grass putting on his moccasins when Modo raised his head and looked toward the path again. Rowe and the dog moved swiftly into the willows. Katy came down the path with a bucket in each hand. He frowned. This time she had not brought the rifle. He watched as she dipped the cool, clear water from the stream, paused to look around, then headed back up the path. He motioned to the dog, picked up his rifle, and followed closely enough to keep her in sight.

At the edge of the woods she stopped. Rowe motioned for the dog to stay and moved up closer. She had set the buckets on the ground beside a bush of yellow flowers. Her light head was bent over them, her nose buried in the blossoms.

"Ouch!" The small muffled cry escaped her when she reached down to snap off a stem, and her fingers were pierced by the thorns. She stuck her finger in her mouth for a moment, then picked up the buckets and walked on.

Rowe and Modo stood beneath an aspen across the road from the funerary and watched her until she disappeared inside.

Nightrose. The word dropped into his mind. Was it a name or a place?

"Nightrose." He said the word aloud. It rolled off his tongue as if he were saying "darling" or "sweetheart" to a lover. Once again he had the eerie feeling of having said the word before in connection with *this* woman.

Rowe believed that when a person died, his soul wandered until it came back to earth in another body. He had discussed this theory with a professor at Harvard University and again with his mother's old friend, Victor Hugo, during a visit to Paris last year. The dramatist, poet, and novelist was a firm believer in reincarnation, and they had spent several enjoyable evenings together while Victor's still-beautiful mistress of forty years, Juliette, was away visiting relatives.

Had Rowe known Katy in another life? Had her name been Nightrose? Were he and this woman destined to live out their days together? An indescribable feeling of elation came over him. He shook his wet head; water from his hair trickled down the side of his face. Here, in the darkness of this vast wilderness, he was experiencing the feeling of coming home.

Modo moved up beside him and nuzzled his leg, bringing him back to reality. He turned back down the path only to pause when he came to the wild rosebush. He stood for a moment, then drew his knife and cut a cluster of blossoms from the bush. With a few quick strokes of the blade he removed the thorns from the stem and held the flowers to his face. As if drawn by an unseen hand, he crossed the road to the funerary and placed the sprig of roses beside the door, and then moved silently away.

"You'll never guess what," Katy said, as she came in the side door carrying the bucket of fresh milk.

"Shhh . . . Theresa's still sleeping. What? What's happened to get you so excited this morning?" Mary's cheeks were flushed from the heat of the cookstove.

"There's a tub of water out there for Mable."

Mary slid a pan of biscuits onto the top of the iron range before she spoke. "Well, I do declare! *He* must have put it there."

"It was either Bushy-face or the fairies, and I never did believe in fairies or goblins or 'haints,' as Posie used to call them." Katy set the bucket of milk on the floor and draped a cloth over it to keep out the flies.

"That was really sweet of him. Do you think we should offer him some milk? We have more than we can use."

"Give Bushy-face milk? He'd laugh in your face, Mary. He probably went right from his mother's breast to the whiskey barrel."

"Oh, maybe not. You can't always judge people by the way they look."

"If we did, he'd win the prize. Wheee! It's going to be hot today. Let's go down to the creek and do some washing. Bushy-face has done us two good turns. I don't think he has murder or fornicating on his mind, or he'd have tried it by now. But I'll take the rifle along just the same."

"The cook-stove heats this place like an oven. I hope it'll do the same if we're still here this winter. That cabin we lived in last winter was almost like living out of doors."

"This *winter!* Heaven forbid, Mary. We've got to get out of here, and back to civilization. I don't think we're going to get any help from old what's-his-face." Katy's spontaneous laughter rang out as it did at the most unexpected times. "He acts

33

as if we have the cholera or smallpox."

Theresa sat up in her makeshift bed. "Who's Bushy-face, Aunt Katy?"

"Well, look who's awake and listening to every word."

Katy lifted the child from the box. "Do you need to use the chamber?"

"I . . . already did —" Theresa's lips began to quiver and she held her wet gown away from her legs.

Katy flipped the gown up over the child's head. "Don't worry about it, honey. We're going to wash today. You've not wet the bed in a long time." She slipped the child's arms into one of her shirts and buttoned it down the front.

Mary opened the front door and a cool breeze swept through the building.

"Well, for goodness' sake." She picked up the branch of yellow rose blooms. "Look at what the wind blew up onto the porch, Katy."

"Wind, my hind foot. There wasn't a breath of wind stirring last night." Katy, remembering her thorn prick the night before, saw at a glance that the tips of the thorns had been sliced off. She began to smile. "Why, Mary, I do believe you've got a suitor. Bushy-face is courting you."

Mary's eyes became large and questioning. "Tarnation! What in the world are you talking about?"

"He left them at the door. Look at the stem. It's been dethorned." Katy began to laugh when Mary's face turned a fiery red.

"But . . . but —" she sputtered. "I'm a married woman."

"He doesn't know that. Didn't you say he gave you a long hard look when he rode in?"

"Well, yes, but — oh, Katy, you're the darndest tease!"

Katy watched the soft line of her sister's mouth curve into a smile. With the color in her cheeks she was pretty, really pretty, and she was wasting her life waiting for a good-for-nothing like Roy Stanton.

"Maybe we should invite him to supper." Katy's blue eyes danced with pure mischief. "But maybe not. He may not be able to find his mouth beneath all that brush."

"We should do something for him. I think I'll leave a pan of hot biscuits on the porch. He saved you from the cougar and put water out for the cow."

"The cougar might have been after Mable, not me," Katy said stubbornly. She was still angry with herself for not taking the rifle when she went out to pull grass for the cow.

Mary slid half of the pan of biscuits onto a plate and went to the porch, her back straight and defiant, as if she expected Katy to call her back.

"Mister!" she called toward the stone building. "Oh, Mister!"

"Call him Bushy-face," Katy prompted. "He might think you're calling someone else."

"Oh, hush, Katy," Mary chided, then called again. "Thank you for killing the lion, or whatever

35

it was. And thank you for the water for the cow. Here's fresh biscuits if you would care for them. I'll leave them here on the porch."

Mary went back inside, pushing Katy and Theresa ahead of her, and then closed the door.

"There! At least we've tried to pay him back a little. Stay away from the window, Katy, or he'll not come to get them. He may have been in the mountains for so long that he's shy around white women."

"He needn't be. I can't think of a single white woman who would give him a second look with all that hair on his face, unless it would be Winnie Fennel back home. Remember her, Mary? She'd have taken anything walking on two legs. She did everything in her power to attract our brothers, and they were a good ten years younger than she was. Finally she got old Dan Brower, but he was desperate for someone to care for seven youn-guns. He up and died on her after six months. His oldest boy said she just plumb wore his pa out." Katy went into gales of laughter.

"Oh, you! Sit down and I'll pour the tea." Mary washed her daughter's hands with a wet cloth and lifted her up onto a stool. "Eat your breakfast, honey. Then we've got to do something about that hair of yours."

"I'd give a nickel for a slice of ham," Katy said. "Remember when Posie cooked ham and made red-eye gravy?"

"What I remember most is peach pie and straw-berry tarts."

"I remember roast turkey and dressing."

"Chicken and dumplings with suet pudding and raisin sauce —"

"Laced with rum. Remember?"

"I remember that you ate nothing but the sauce." Mary dipped milk from a gray crock and set it in front of Theresa's plate.

"Drink your milk, ladybug. It'll put hair on your chest." Katy gazed fondly at the child.

"I don't want hair on my chest, Aunt Katy!"

"She's teasing, as usual," Mary said patiently. "Only men have hair on their chest."

The sound of something clanking on the porch brought Katy to her feet. She rushed to the window, looked out, and burst into laughter.

"His dog has eaten his biscuits." She opened the door and rushed out onto the porch. "Here, dog! Leave the plate."

"Well, I never!" Mary crowded out the door behind her. The dog was going down the road. The empty plate had fallen into the weeds beside the porch. Katy stepped down and picked it up.

"I can just hear that dog saying, 'Those were the best goldurned biscuits I ever et!' "

Musical laughter floated down the empty street. Coming down from the old mine, Rowe paused to listen. He didn't understand his attraction for this woman. Her features were clearly etched in his mind. He knew her and the realization was purely instinctive that she had the power to make his life heaven or . . . hell.

37

Determined to get his mind off the crazy notion that she was important to him, he went into the saloon and spread his maps out on the bar to study them once again. His partner and friend, Anton Hooker, had been right. Anton had taken a sample from the mine months ago, had it assayed, and decided the mine was worth opening. Running through the heavy iron deposits was a vein of silver. It would be a hard job getting at it. At first, the ore would have to be hauled in heavy freight-wagons to the smelter in Bay Horse where the pure silver would be extracted. Later, if the vein proved to be long-lasting, they would continue to operate the mine along with their other project.

The former mine owners had only been interested in quick riches. When the gold petered out, they were ready to cut their losses and move on. As a matter of fact, Rowe mused, he might have purchased the mine and the several hundred thousand acres of land adjoining it for a mere fraction of its eventual worth. He had, however, given the owners their asking price.

Rowe scanned the map, noting every mountain, stream, and trail in the area. His eyes lingered the longest on the spot that lay to the north, along the Madison River. This was his land. He would make his home there and start a ranch someday. He had no reason now to go back to Paris. His mother was gone. And it would please him greatly if he never set eyes on his only living kin, his half brother Justin, again. The same went for the

Rowe mansion on the Hudson River and all it entailed; it could drop into hell for all he cared.

Everything in its own time, Rowe thought. He rolled up the maps and tied them with a string. This afternoon, he would ride south and see if there was any sign of Hank and the wagons.

At noon Rowe chewed on a strip of jerky and ate a can of peaches, dreaming about lobster tails dipped in melted butter and tender, thin pancakes filled with raspberry jam and sprinkled with sugar. God! He hoped Hank had found someone who could cook something more than corn bread, beans and grits.

Rowe had stayed on the far side of the town while the women were at the creek. They were getting braver, he decided. After he had killed the cougar and put water out for the cow, they must have decided he wasn't going to attack them. How little they knew of men. If he'd had that on his mind, he would have done just what he'd done — try to win their confidence and when they let down their guard, pounce. He walked down to the edge of the stream. He chuckled to see the array of women's garments spread on the bushes to dry. The unmentionables had been hung in such a manner as to disguise their purpose, should he happen upon them. But drawers were drawers, and during his travels he supposed he'd seen every kind imaginable.

It was a quiet afternoon except for a whippoorwill, which swooped down over the swiftly running water, and the bluejays, which scolded from the upper branches of the cottonwood tree. A robin, perched on a swaying limb of the willow, sang as if it didn't have a care in the world. One of the bluejays, attracted by the shiny buttons on a pair of drawers, flew down. As Rowe watched, his mouth twitched in amusement. The bird pecked at the button and pulled in vain. Finally, frustrated, it rose into the air with an angry screech, circled the bushes, then swooped and dropped his calling card on a pair of drawers trimmed with lace and blue ribbon. Unable to stop himself, Rowe laughed aloud.

"Mr. Jay, you've been eating berries and Katy isn't going to like what you just did one little bit."

Rowe wished he could be around when Katy discovered the bird droppings on her clean drawers. Although his face wore its usual somber look, he was still laughing inside as he saddled his horse and rode out of town. Since Apollo was anxious to run, Rowe let him race three miles before he drew up in a small cluster of cottonwoods, where water seeping from the rocky cliff had made a tiny pool. He allowed the horse a little water, then remounted and headed south again. The air was clear and bright, the sky almost cloudless. He saw no Indians, although there were plenty of tracks. He traveled slowly to keep down the dust, staying off the trail when possible. He came to a shelf that jutted out over the valley. Keeping to the trees, he walked the horse to a spot that had a clear view for at least five miles.

No train of wagons appeared on the trail below,

but there were four riders. Rowe dismounted, pulled his horse back out of sight, and tied him to a bush. He motioned for Modo to stay with the horse and took the spyglass from his saddlebag. Walking hunched so that he wouldn't be outlined against the sky, he crept to the edge of the shelf and dropped down on his belly. His first thought was that the men were a detail of soldiers because of their uniforms. He studied them, then changed his mind when he saw the way they slumped in the saddles. Also, any detail this far from the fort would have had a packhorse to carry supplies.

Suddenly, the two riders ahead stopped, spun their horses around, and faced the two men riding behind. One of these drew apart leaving his fellow rider to face the other two. He was gesturing with his arm. Although Rowe couldn't hear what they were saying, it was evident to him they were having an argument. The lone man turned his horse as if to leave.

The sound of the shot was no more than a pop by the time it reached Rowe. Hit in the back, the man fell from his saddle and his horse danced away. The man who had fired the gun shoved it into his holster and dismounted. He kicked at the man on the ground with his booted foot, then stripped him of his holster, gun, and the contents of his pockets. One of his companions caught the dead man's frightened horse, and they proceeded up the trail toward Trinity.

"The bastards didn't even bury the man,"

41

Rowe murmured.

He closed the spyglass and hurried back to his horse. The men were deserters, or they had killed for the army uniforms. Rowe figured that he would get to town fifteen or twenty minutes before the trio. After what he had seen, he had no doubt about the kind of men they were. Any decent human would have buried the man he killed, regardless of the reason for killing him. To leave a man's body for the buzzards and wolves and calmly ride away was the act of the morally depraved.

Rowe put his heels to the big black horse. The Arabian loved to run, and where the trail was smooth, he let him. If Rowe had only himself to consider, there wouldn't be the urgency to get back. He could hole up in the stone building until the trio left town unless they decided to set fire to the buildings, in which case he would have to stop them.

The women and the child were his concern. They would be totally helpless against such men. Rage at the thought of a man forcing himself on Katy or the child's mother knifed through him. Rage made him reckless, and he found himself letting Apollo run full speed over a rocky, twisting course. He pulled up on the reins and slowed the horse down. Now was not the time to take unnecessary chances. He was all that stood between the women and that trio riding into town.

CHAPTER

Three

The sound of a horse running hard caused Katy to snap shut the book she had been reading and hurry to the door. A big black horse was coming up through the center of town at full speed. She reached for the rifle and checked the load before stepping out onto the porch.

"Who is it?" Mary, with Theresa in her arms, stuck her head out the doorway so that she could see.

"Stay inside." Katy backed into the building and prepared to slam the door.

The rider came directly to their door and jumped from the saddle.

"Stay back!" Katy shouted. "Put one foot on this porch and I'll blow it off."

"Put the gun down, Katy. You've nothing to fear from me."

Katy's mouth dropped open when the man said her name. There was something familiar about the buckskins, the wide shoulders, the flat-crowned leather hat, and the way the gun belt clung to his narrow hips.

"Who . . . are you?" The thought hovered in the back of her mind that the man's battle-scarred face was that of an ancient warrior.

"Garrick Rowe. I shot the cougar." The big brown dog came and lay at Rowe's feet, his tongue hanging out. "I've been here damn near a week. You've seen me —"

"The man who shot the cougar had a beard."

"Good Lord! I shaved!"

The eyes that looked into Katy's were as black as midnight. The hair that curled down over his forehead, his eyebrows and mustache were as black as his eyes. Hard cheekbones, a wide firm mouth, an arrogant nose, a square chin, and stubborn jaw completed his face. He stood still, looking at her in the same intense way she was looking at him.

"If you're Bushy-face, why've you been sneaking around?" Katy snarled, and lowered the rifle. "Why didn't you come tell us who you were and what you're doing here?" Her eyes clung to the dark craggy face of the man who towered over her.

"Pay you a social call? Would you have served tea?" he asked, his voice heavily laced with sarcasm. "This visit isn't a social call, either. You've got to get out of here. Go down to that stone building and take your valuables with you."

"Is it Bushy-face, Mamma?"

"Shhh . . . Theresa —" Mary scolded, then hugged the child, who began to whimper with fear and hid her face against her mother's neck.

"What are you talking about?" Katy turned the

44

gun on him again. "We're not going anywhere on your say-so."

"You stubborn little mule! I knew you'd be like this," he said softly, then barked irritably, "Put that gun down before you shoot somebody. You don't have much time. Within the next fifteen or twenty minutes three men will ride into town who'll make me look like a saint. I just saw one of them kill a man in cold blood."

"You saw it, and you did nothing to stop it?" Katy asked contemptuously.

"Goddammit, Katy! I was a quarter of a mile away and saw it through my spyglass. Are you going down to that stone building, or am I going to throw you across my shoulder and carry you there?" He stepped upon the porch, shouldered his way past her and went inside. "Do you have any more ammunition for that rifle?"

"Yes," Mary answered. "Four boxes."

"Get it, and anything else you value that you can carry, and go to the stone building. It's the safest place in town." He directed his remarks to Mary. "I'll close this place and throw some trash up onto the porch so they'll think it's as empty as the rest of the town."

He went through their living quarters to the rear and shut the door. On his way back he checked the firebox on the cookstove. Katy was still standing beside the door, stunned motionless. Mary put Theresa on the floor and spread a blanket on the bed. With the child clinging to her skirts, she went to the trunk for her journal.

45

She placed it and the clock her mother had given her for a wedding present in the center of the blanket, added the boxes of shells, and tied the four corners.

"Mary! Why are we trusting him?" Katy blurted. "Maybe it's Roy coming back."

"Ma'am, would your husband be wearing parts of an army uniform?" Rowe asked sharply.

"No," Mary answered, then to Katy, "We've got to trust him. We have no choice."

"That's right you don't. Now go, unless you plan to stay here and be raped by three killers when they get here."

His dark eyes bored into Katy's blue ones, a hint of repressed savagery behind them. There was impatience in such a man, impatience that would cause most women to obey his orders without question. But Katy was not one to follow blindly.

She turned her back and spoke to her sister. "I say we stay here. We may be in just as much danger from *him* as from the men riding in."

"Don't push me, Katy," Rowe said angrily. "I'll not permit you a choice now or ever when your safety is concerned. Climb down off your high horse and behave. You're going to that stone building — whether you like it or not."

"Come on, Katy," Mary pleaded. "We've got to trust him."

"I don't like him. He's got shifty eyes."

Katy didn't know why she had said anything so stupid! His gaze was as steady as a hawk's.

The only excuse she gave herself for the untruth was that she was determined not to knuckle under completely. Was that laughter she saw in the depth of his midnight eyes just before she thrust her arm under the knot Mary had tied in the blanket? What really infuriated her was the inescapable feeling that she could buck him every step of the way, but in the end she would do as he said. For Mary and Theresa's sake, she told herself.

"Can you carry all that?" Mary asked.

"I'll have to. You'll have to carry Theresa."

"What about Mable?" Mary turned back as they stepped off the porch.

"Mable? Good God! Is there another woman here beside you two?"

"Mable's the cow."

"Ah . . ." He said several words in a language they didn't understand, but there was no mistaking the frustration in his tone. "I'll put the cow behind the livery if there's time. Don't fool around about getting down there. I want you women out of sight."

Katy and Mary hurried as fast as they could through the middle of the deserted town. Katy looked over her shoulder to see the man who called himself Garrick Rowe throwing dead brush and broken boards up onto the porch of their home. Then he took a branch and began to sweep away their footprints. He was trying to help them. She had known it from the first, but his arrogant manner had forced her to rebel against his orders.

"Walk in the grass," she told Mary. "He's trying to erase our footprints."

The two women were out of breath by the time they reached the stone building. The interior was cool and dim. Katy dropped the bundle inside the door as soon as they entered; her arm was numb from carrying it.

"Does he expect us to just sit here and wait?"

"He's trying to help us," Mary said firmly.

"He said the men were wearing army uniforms, Mary. How do we know that it isn't a legitimate patrol? How do we know he doesn't want to keep us here and is scaring us into staying out of sight?"

"Do we dare take the chance? Why are you so suspicious of him?"

"From past experience. I've been pushed, pulled, pinched, fondled, and propositioned ever since I came West. I'm sick of men who slobber, spit, and stink. All they know is mining, brawling, drinking, and whoring. Old Bushy-face may have killed the cat, carried water to Mable, and shaved; but he's still a scallywag looking to get rich without working."

"Oh, Katy. I didn't realize you were so bitter. It's because of me you're here and I'm so sorry."

The pain in Mary's voice slipped through Katy's anger and into her mind. She turned and put her arm around her sister.

"I'm sorry for being such a grouch. The way he looked at me and the way he bossed us around got under my skin. I knew we'd do what he thought best, but I wasn't going to fall whole-hog into his plan like a mindless feather-head."

Mary set Theresa down on one of the two slabs, built out from the wall, that served as bunks. Rowe's bedroll was on one of them. The bedding was folded neatly and the bags containing his belongings were stacked beneath his bunk. A narrow slit was cut in the rock wall on the south, used as a lookout and for ventilation.

"He's taking Mable to the corral behind the livery," Katy said from her position beside the door.

The bawling cow was protesting in the only way she knew how. The lead rope was stretching her neck as she was being pulled along behind the black horse, her heavy udders swaying with each step. They disappeared behind the livery and a few minutes later Rowe was loping down the road toward the jail, the dog at his heels.

The first thing he did was to scatter the cold ashes where he had cooked his food. Then he scooped up an armful of dead brush, and covered them. Katy stood just inside the building, looking out the doorway.

Rowe came to the door. "They'll be here anytime now," he said looking toward the south. "Do you know how to use that rifle?"

"I wouldn't be carrying it if I didn't."

Her answer seemed to satisfy him. "I'll draw them away from here if I can. Keep the little girl quiet."

"Where will you go?"

"To the saloon. They'll see my horse and the

mules and know that someone is here. It's better to face them down before they find out the town's completely deserted."

"I could help —"

"No. Stay here. I don't want to worry about you."

"But —"

"Don't buck me now, Katy. I don't have time for it. Do as I tell you and you'll come out of this all right. Shut and bar the door and don't leave this place regardless of what you hear. There's water and food to last for several days. Understand?"

"No." Her retort was quick. "Why should I follow your orders without question? You're as much of a stranger as they —"

He cut into what she was saying. "Do I seem like a stranger to you, Katy?"

Under the steady gaze of his dark eyes, her heart began to hammer. No, right at this minute he didn't seem like a stranger, but damned if she'd admit it to him! To evade the question, she asked one of her own.

"Is there a chance they're not as bad as you think?"

"There's always a chance, but not much of one. They shot a man in the back and left him for the wolves. You don't get much worse than that. Like I said, shut and bar the door and don't come out until I call to you. And . . . cover that slit in the wall so they won't be tempted to come look inside." His voice was low and even, but the tone left no doubt that he expected to be obeyed.

"All right."

For just an instant, his hand touched her arm. "If anyone tries to come in, shoot him."

"I will. Be careful."

"You, too." A whisper of a smile touched his mouth. Then, with a gesture to the dog, he ran across the street to the saloon, his shaggy pet at his heels.

Katy watched him go. The man and the dog were a team. Who was he? From the look of his plunder, he was here to stay a good long while. A distant part of her mind told her to steer clear of personal involvement with this man. He was the kind of man who would take over a woman's life, and she wouldn't have a prayer of holding out against him.

Rowe opened the double doors of the saloon and pushed them back against the wall. He took a full bottle of whiskey from his private stock beneath the counter and set it out on the bar along with several glasses so that they could be seen through the open door. It just might make the men riding in think there were several men inside. He checked his gun. The pistol was a Smith & Wesson, the best gun built. After trying the balance of it in his hand, he checked the load and shoved it down in the holster. His cartridge belt was full, and he had extra ammunition for the rifle. He tilted his hat back and surveyed the road leading into town. With the rifle in the crook of his arm, he stood just inside the building, waiting. He had no plan except to tell them to leave. After that, he would play it by ear.

Modo came and sat down beside him, his tongue hanging out as he panted. The dog looked at his master, and, when Rowe motioned, lay at his feet.

The afternoon sun slanted across the dusty porch. From Rowe's vantage point, he had a view of the still-empty road and the stone building. In the few minutes before a battle the senses are always keener Rowe mused. He heard the wind in the pines and smelled the freshness of the high, cool air. He remembered the pungent smell of cedar, the deep red glow of campfires he had fed with mesquite and buffalo chips.

Nightrose. The name moved like a ghost across his memory. It had something to do with Katy. The sensation of timelessness returned with sudden intensity, and he was in another time, another place. This had happened before. Sometime, somewhere, he had waited, just like this, waited to protect what was his. He shook his head and the feeling was gone. But he continued to think about Katy.

She was tall for a woman, and he liked that. Her eyebrows and lashes were just a shade darker than her hair. The perfect oval of her face with its small, fine nose and full, soft lips were a perfect background for her eyes. They were blue-gray as he had known they would be; and when they met his, they had held a definite shimmer of defiance. It raised her hackles to be told what to do, he thought, with a quirk of his lips. During that first moment when he had looked at her, he wondered if the shock he had felt registered on his face. It was so strange, this feeling of knowing her, knowing how she would fit into his arms, how her mouth would feel beneath his, how her breast would fill his hand, and how passionate she was beneath that cool facade.

The sound of hoofbeats brought Rowe out of his reverie and into the realization that he was about to face three men who would kill him if he stood between them and what they wanted. And if they succeeded, it would be only a matter of time until the women in the stone building werc discovered. Katy would not be able to hold out long against them. All the men would have to do was build a fire in front of the heavy oak door and smoke them out.

The sudden knowledge that now he had more than just himself to live for made Rowe extremely cautious. He was a man who took his time to study things out, never one to come to quick decisions or solutions. That single trait in his character had already brought him through a goodly number of crises.

The riders coming up from the south were also cautious. They stopped their horses in the middle of the road and talked together while looking over the town. After a few minutes of discussion, one of the men went east and another west; the man leading the dead man's horse stayed in the middle of the road.

The damn cow! Rowe thought. They would know there were women in town because no miner or cowman would waste time and effort on a milch cow. After looking behind the buildings on both sides of the street, the other two came back, re-joining the third rider. The three proceeded up the street, walking their horses slowly. They stopped in front of the saloon. The open doors had provided the temptation to lure them to him, just as Rowe expected. After ordering Modo to stay, he stepped out onto the porch and faced them.

"Ride on. There's nothing for you here." Rowe's voice rang loud with authority.

"Who said so?"

"I did."

"We're a patrol out of Fort Kearny and in need of a drink of whiskey. Hell! We need a bottle each." The man who spoke had a wide face and a scar on his cheekbone.

"A patrol?" The sneer in Rowe's voice told that he knew of the lie. "You must be lost."

The man didn't bother to deny it. "Yeah, we're lost," he said and laughed. "Are you the marshal here? Haw! Haw! Haw!"

"You might say that. Ride on and avoid trouble."

"I don't see anybody backin' his hand, Arch. I'm thinkin' he's here all by his own self."

"He ain't by his own self. He's got a woman 'round here somewheres. That's a fresh cow out back. A fresh cow means women. I ain't had me no white woman in quite a spell 'n' I'm hankerin' to get me one."

"May be she ain't white."

"I ain't a carin'. Red, white, or blue, it's all the same once ya've got yore pecker up." The man called Arch made to step down from his horse.

The rifle in Rowe's hand came up. "Don't."

"You goin' to hold us all off?" Arch asked and settled back into the saddle.

Rowe didn't bother to answer. It would be anytime now. The one doing the talking wasn't the one to watch. He was the diversion for the other two. The man on the left was trying to ease his horse into position so when he drew his gun, he would have an easy target. The other slouched in the saddle, but had kicked his feet free of the stirrups.

One second the tired horse Arch was riding stood with his head down; the next second he had reared and plunged. It was a practiced tactic that they had probably used before. Rowe shot to kill the man on the left, but because of the moving horses, the bullet struck the rider on the hip, knocking him sideways out of the saddle. The two bullets shot at Rowe were equally off target. One grazed the side of his head and hit the doorjamb; the other ripped splinters from the porch at his feet. A third bullet tore into his thigh as he dived inside the building. As he went down, the rifle flew from his hand.

Rowe blinked rapidly against the pain, then pushed himself erect as he heard boot heels hit the porch of the saloon. With a weaving, drunken gait, he took the necessary steps, getting himself in position to meet the men who were bent on killing him as they charged through the doorway and dived to the floor, rolling toward the protection of the bar.

"Attack!" he yelled. Modo sprang on the man nearest the door.

Rowe opened up a blinding roar of gunfire with the Smith & Wesson. His bullets struck the man kneeling on the floor. The intruder reared back, then sprawled, arms outstretched. Surprised and off balance by the big dog's attack, Arch fanned his gun. The range was close, and Rowe felt the searing impact of the bullet that passed through his upper arm. The gun in his hand felt like a hundred-pound weight, but he lifted it and aimed point-blank at Arch's head. The shot entered above the ear and the man slumped to the floor.

"Modo," he called. The dog released his hold on the dead man's arm and padded obediently to his master.

Rowe's head felt as if it were a huge drum, and someone was pounding on it with a hammer. Half-blinded with pain and his own blood that dripped from his lacerated scalp, he leaned against the wall and thumbed shells into the Smith & Wesson. Two of the three men were accounted for. The one he had knocked from the saddle was outside. If he still lived, he would be like a wounded bear because he had nothing to lose. Rowe staggered to the door and peered out into the street. It was empty. Had the wounded man ridden out?

A bullet coming in through the doorway struck the glasses on the bar, sending shards of glass in every direction. It answered the question. Rowe cursed and fell back. He wiped the blood out of his eye with his shirt sleeve. He hadn't even seen where the bullet had come from. The man was in no better condition to run than he was. Maybe he would surrender.

"Hey, out there!" he called. "Your friends are dead. You've been hit. Give up and I'll let you ride out."

"You stupid son of a bitch! Ya're in worse shape than I am, if I know Arch 'n' Roberts. I aim to keep ya in there till ya bleed to death!"

Rowe wondered if he had the strength to climb the stairs to the second floor so he would have a better view of the street. Then he remembered the windows on the front were still boarded up. They wouldn't do him much good. The only place the man could be hiding was behind the stone wall built around the well in the middle of the street.

Blood from the wound in his thigh had run down into his boot, squishing when he walked. Blood from his arm dripped onto the floor. His head was beginning to feel light. He sat down in a chair and tried to tie his neckerchief about his thigh. The sun coming in the doorway told him it would be hours before dark. He leaned forward in the chair to prop himself against the table. The straight line of the bar tilted and then vanished into a wavering mist. It returned for a brief instant before darkness fell.

To Katy and Mary, it seemed an eternity since the first shots were fired. Defying Rowe's orders, Katie had watched from the slit in the wall as the men rode into town and stopped in front of the saloon. Standing on tiptoes, she had a clear view. They heard Garrick Rowe ask the men to leave and heard their taunting answers. The presence of the cow had told the men that there were women in the town.

The violence had come suddenly. Garrick Rowe was talking to the men, then the shooting began. Katy saw one man fall from the saddle and drag himself behind the stone wall surrounding the well across from the saloon. Her heart leapt to her throat when Rowe fell back out of the doorway. She knew he had been hit. Almost before she could catch her breath, the two men had jumped from the saddles and charged into the building. The frightened horses bolted down the street, their reins dragging. Six shots were fired inside the saloon in rapid succession. It was unbelievable that one of them hadn't killed Garrick Rowe.

With her eyes glued to the doorway, Katy waited for someone to appear. Then, for only a brief instant, she saw a tall, lean, buckskin-clad figure, his face blood-streaked. The man behind the stone well fired, and Rowe backed from the doorway. Katy slumped against the wall during the quiet that followed.

Theresa began to cry a whimpering sound, trying to obey her mother's request not to make any noise.

"Shhh . . . darling. Don't cry now. You've been a brave girl. We must be as quiet as we can."

Rowe's voice, yelling from inside the saloon, brought Katie up on her tiptoes so that she could see out again. The man behind the well had his gun pointed at the doorway of the saloon.

"I aim to keep ya there till ya bleed to death."

The words sank into Katy's mind. If Rowe was badly hurt, the man behind the well could do just as he said, keep him pinned in the saloon.

"We've got to do something." Katy turned to her sister sitting on the bunk. "Mr. Rowe can't come out the front or the side door without that man shooting him."

"What can we do?" Mary asked quietly.

"We can't help him from here, that's certain. I'd shoot the low-down bast—" She looked down at Theresa and cut off the word. "The angle isn't right."

"We can't get out the door without him seeing us."

"I don't think he'll shoot a woman. He needs help too."

"You mean to go out in plain sight. Mr. Rowe told us to stay in here regardless of what happens."

"He can't help us now. We've got to help our-

59

selves and him. This is what we can do if you're willing, Mary. You could go out and walk up the street toward the saloon. He'll not be expecting a woman to do that. While he's watching, I'll slip out the door, go around behind this building, and shoot him."

"Oh, Katy. Are you sure you can do that?"

"I've got to, Mary. If Mr. Rowe dies and that man lives, we'll have to kill him sooner or later."

"You're right. If you can do *that*, then I can walk down the street toward the saloon. I'll carry Theresa. If something happens and we don't come through this, I'd rather she die with us than die here all alone." Mary set the child astraddle her hip and went to the door.

Katy took the little pistol from her pocket and put it in Mary's. "It's loaded," she said softly and kissed her sister's cheek. "Walk just as if you didn't know he was there. He's not going to know what to make of it at first, and it'll give me a chance to get behind him."

"Be careful. I love you, Katy."

"I love you too, sister." Katy placed a kiss on Theresa's cheek and lifted the bar from across the door. She peered out, then opened it wide enough for Mary and Theresa to slip out. "I'll wait until you're across the street before I go out."

Mary shifted Theresa to the side away from the gunman and walked into the dusty, deserted street. Katy watched as seconds ticked away. Near-panic coiled in her stomach. There was silence until Mary reached the other side and started down the boardwalk. Then a shout.

"Hey! Woman! Where the hell ya goin'?"

Mary continued to walk.

"Come here. I won't hurt ya none."

She walked on and Katy slipped out the door and behind the building.

"I ain't wantin' ta shoot ya or the kid, but I will." The voice was hard and desperate. "Gawd-dammit, woman, take another step —"

A bullet kicked dirt only a few feet from Mary, but her steps did not falter.

"I ain't lettin' ya go in there. I'll shoot ya 'n' the kid too, by Gawd. Stop —"

Katy stepped out from behind the building. The gunman's back was to her. He had propped his six-shooter up on the stone wall and was aiming it at Mary and Theresa. Katy raised the rifle and sighted between the man's shoulder blades, her mind numb to what she was doing. She steadied herself and squeezed the trigger just as her brothers had taught her to do long ago in Alabama when they hunted wild turkey. The bullet struck, throwing the man against the stone wall. He threw up his hands and fell back. The bullet, passing through his body, ricocheted back from the wall and tore a gaping hole in his chest.

Katy stood as if in a trance, then lowered the gun barrel until the end pointed to the ground. At the sound of the shot, Mary had stopped walking. Katy went alongside the building toward the street. She continued putting one foot in front of the other automatically, her head whirling, her stomach churning. By the time she reached the front of the building she could no longer hold back the bile that filled her throat. She grabbed hold of the corner for support, bent over, and the contents of her stomach came spilling out. When it was over, she wiped her mouth on the hem of her dress and crossed the street to where her sister waited.

CHAPTER

Four

A menacing growl greeted Katy and Mary when they reached the doorway of the saloon. The big brown dog, his teeth bared and the hair standing up on his back, stood between them and Rowe, who was slumped over a table. After the first glance, the women kept their eyes averted from the bodies on the floor. When Katy took a single step into the room, the dog lunged forward and snapped his teeth. She retreated and backed off.

"Now listen here, dog," she said sternly. "We're here to help your master and we don't need any trouble from you."

"He'll not let us near him. What'll we do?" Mary was holding Theresa's face against her shoulder to keep her from seeing the carnage.

"I don't know, but I'll think of something."

"Is he dead?"

The voices drifted into Rowe's consciousness. The only words that were distinguishable were the last three.

"Hell no, I'm not dead," he muttered.

"He's not dead!" Katy's voice sounded far away.

"I'm not dead," he repeated stupidly.

"Then call off the damn dog so we can help you!"

"Katy? One . . . by the well —" Rowe opened his eyes and tried to focus on the two women silhouetted against the light. His head felt as if it were about to explode.

"Don't worry about him. Call off the dog."

"Modo, down." The dog obeyed instantly and crawled under the table to lie at Rowe's feet. "Did he ride out?"

"No. He's dead," Katy spoke as she came toward him. He didn't question, and she asked, "How bad are you hurt? Oh, my God! You're covered with blood!"

"Katy, Katy. Don't fret. It's not my time to die —"

"Can you stand up? We've got to get you out of here."

"Stand up? I can't even see straight."

"Mary, help me get him to his feet. We've got to get him over to the jail building before he passes out."

"Our place is nearer." Mary brought the whiskey bottle from the bar. "See if you can get him to drink some of this while I take Theresa outside. I'll be right back."

Later Katy was to wonder not only how Rowe got to his feet, but also how he was able to walk to the funerary. She and Mary had somehow managed to bear up under his weight. Theresa, frightened by the blood and not understanding what was taking place, cried as she followed along behind them.

Mary cut his soft doeskin shirt up the front and slipped it off, baring his upper body. Katy held a blanket in place to hide his nakedness, while Mary pulled off his blood-soaked britches.

Rowe drifted in and out of consciousness while the women washed him and disinfected his wounds first with vinegar, then with whiskey. He heard Katy say that he would have a permanent part in his hair, and that the bullet in his leg would have to come out. The pain was excruciating when they probed the wound; then, blessed darkness came.

Afternoon turned into evening. Before dark, Katy found the dead men's horses standing at the water tank. She stripped them of saddles and turned them into the enclosure with Rowe's horse and mules. She closed the doors of the saloon and covered the dead man at the well with a blanket from Rowe's bunk. It was all she could do. She and Mary would be forced to dig graves when morning came, but for now they had their hands full taking care of the man who had faced the three outlaws and had almost been killed by them.

They had cut the fine, curly hair from around his headwound and found it to be only a crease that would give him a terrific headache, but nothing more. The thigh wound was on the side and had left a gaping hole. Mary had cleaned it and bound it as tightly as she could. The bullet had passed through the fleshy part of his arm, and they were reasonably sure the muscles had not been damaged.

When they could rouse Rowe, they made him drink sweetened whiskey weakened with water. He was no longer the fierce warrior who had come striding into their home hours before, demanding that they go to the stone building. He seemed young and gentle, in spite of his large, muscular body and his dark, hawklike face.

He was not what Katy would call a handsome man, but he was attractive. Never had she seen eyelashes as thick or as black or as long as his. His thin-lipped mouth, when relaxed, was soft and sensitive. She had not thought much about the human body being beautiful, especially a male body, but Garrick Rowe's was beautiful. Mary had covered his privates with a sheet, but the rest of him lay naked to her eyes. His legs were long, his thighs rock hard, his shoulders and arms muscular. He had a patch of dark hair on his chest that arrowed down toward his flat belly. He was lean and tough, like a timber wolf.

Although she and Mary were dead tired, they took turns sitting beside him all through the night. After the events of the day, they felt more vulnerable than ever in the lonely town. They barred the doors, and took great pains to see that no light escaped through the windows. The dog took up a vigil on the porch, and it was a comfort to know that he was there.

Once during the night Rowe awakened. He squinted his eyes against the glare of a lamp and saw a woman sitting in a chair beside him.

"You're here."

Katy leaned forward. "Yes, I'm here."

"Remember when I won the footrace at the games in Athens? Afterward we walked along the shore of the Aegean Sea and you wore my laurel wreath on your head —"

The words were spoken in a language that Katy couldn't identify. But she touched his hand and nodded as if she understood, and his eyes drifted shut again.

When next he awakened, Mary was sitting beside him. She forced him to drink the watered whiskey and sugar before allowing him to go back to sleep.

Morning came, and when Katy opened the door to let in fresh mountain air, Modo entered and went directly to the bunk where Rowe lay. He sniffed at his face, lifted his majestic head and looked around, then lay down beneath the bed, his jowls resting on his paws.

"It looks like he's going to stay," Mary said worriedly.

"I'd hate to try and put him out if he doesn't want to go. Let's just ignore him. But watch Theresa. I'll go milk the cow."

Rowe smelled food when he awakened. His head hurt, his arm and leg throbbed, but his mind was clear enough to tell Mary there was a medical kit among his belongings. She promised to get it, but first he had to eat. She spread a flapjack with butter and sugar, rolled so he could handle it and took it to him. He ate what Mary brought, then swung his feet off the bunk, and sat up on the side. He held his throbbing head in his hands. The dog came out from under the bed and sat looking at him.

"You shouldn't sit up, Mr. Rowe."

"I can't lie here and get weaker, ma'am. Do you suppose I could have a cup of coffee?"

"Of course. My name is Mrs. Stanton, but call me Mary. Would you like cream and sugar?"

"Yes, please. Lordy. My head aches."

"And it will for a few days. Katy thinks you may have a slight concussion. She knows about such things. She's my sister. I hope you understand the reason why she was so mistrustful of you yesterday."

"It pays to be careful. How long have you ladies been here?"

"We came last fall. Everyone left about two months ago. We stayed to wait for my husband. He'll be coming back for us any day now," Mary felt obligated to say. "Living out here like this has been hard on Katy."

"Does she have a man coming back for her?"

"No. Katy has never married."

"What happened to the man at the well?"

"Katy shot him. She didn't want to, Mr. Rowe. But there wasn't anything else we could do."

"She's quite a woman. You both are. I appreciate what you've done for me."

"We appreciate what you did for us. I shudder to think of what would have happened if you

68

hadn't been here."

"I've got to do something about the bodies. I can't wait. In this heat —"

"Katy and I have talked it over. We'll take care of them."

"It's not a job for a gentle woman," he protested.

"Mr. Rowe, Katy and I have survived this long by doing what had to be done. We will manage. There's only one thing. I'd like for my daughter to stay here with you while we're gone. It isn't something I want her to see."

"My men are on the way. Wait until afternoon —"

"If they don't come, it will only make the job more difficult. While you drink your coffee, I'll get your medical kit. If you have laudanum it will ease the pain."

"I have, but two drops in a glass of water is all I will take."

"About your dog, Mr. Rowe. I'm afraid to let Theresa near him."

"Modo is as gentle as a lamb unless I tell him otherwise. He'll not hurt your little girl. I'd stake my life on it, and please, no more of that mister stuff. Just call me Rowe."

Rowe had slept off and on all day. Mary roused him to eat, and to check the bandages on his thigh and his arm. Katy, worn out from a sleepless night and the strenuous work, lay sleeping on a pallet with Theresa close beside her. It was the twilight time of day that Mary liked the best. She sat in the rocking chair and recorded the events of the last two days in her journal.

Trinity, June 8, 1874.

Yesterday, June 7, was a day I shall never forget. Three bad men rode into town, and if not for Mr. Rowe's protection, I'm sure that Katy and I would have met a fate worse than death. I shudder to think of it and of Theresa witnessing such a thing. Katy killed one of the men; Mr. Rowe the other two. It was a terrible thing for Katy to have to do. I keep wondering where her courage comes from. Mr. Rowe suffered three gunshot wounds, but he will be all right. It was a struggle to get him from the saloon to our place. He is a strong, brave man, and very well educated. At times during the night he spoke in a foreign language that Katy and I have not heard before.

Today Katy and I buried the three men. I hope that neither of us is forced to do anything so gruesome again. The awful part was emptying their pockets and taking off their gun belts, which we left in the saloon. At Mr. Rowe's suggestion, we saddled the gentlest of the horses, tied a rope about the feet of the dead men, with the other end wrapped about the saddle horn, and dragged the men, one at a time, to a deep gully at the far end of town where we shoveled dirt over them.

It was hot, and flies were already beginning to swarm. I thought the task would never end. Not for an instant did I let myself think about the families of these men, or if there were a mother somewhere who wondered what had happened to her boy. Katy and I said a prayer over them, although to tell the truth, our hearts were not in it.

On the bunk, Rowe stirred restlessly. Dreams of his childhood came to haunt him. He was in a tree, the limb extending over rushing water. Something was pulling on his feet. He looked down to see a boy with white-blond hair and a sneering face looking up at him.

"Dirty, black foreigner, dirty, black foreigner," the boy chanted. "You and your ma are black as niggers —"

"We ain't! We ain't neither black! Let go my feet," he yelled. "I can't swim!"

"I hope you drown, I want you dead!"

"I'll tell Pa —"

"Tattle is all you're good for! Pa hates you."

"Pa don't hate me. Let go —"

"He does too hate you. He said you look like a nigger."

"He didn't. You're lying —"

"You ain't no Rowe, you're Greek —"

"I am too a Rowe —"

Rowe awakened and looked blankly at the woman bending over him. "I am too a Rowe."

"Of course you are," Mary said. "Your name

71

is Garrick Rowe. Go back to sleep. I'll be right here beside you."

The detective studied the man behind the massive walnut desk. He was like a lion ready to spring. In fact, it could be said that he resembled one with that thick mane of blond hair and blond mustache that curved down each side of his hard mouth.

"And that's all he's been up to?" Justin Rowe demanded of the Pinkerton man.

"He hasn't committed a crime, Mr. Rowe, if that's what you mean."

"I'm paying a lot of money for this piddling information," Justin sneered.

He pushed the chair back with a force that sent it crashing into the wall behind, got up, and went to the window. He looked down at the carefully tended lawn that sloped to the Hudson River. His wife moved amid the rose bushes. Somehow, seeing the blond hair piled atop her small head kindled the memory of a dark head bending over it, and the dark, savage face of his half brother flashed before his eyes. Justin whirled, with the air of an angry king ready to slice the head from the one who had brought him bad news. The detective's calm, his utter lack of servility, further infuriated him.

"I want more! I want something that will completely discredit him!"

The Pinkerton man got to his feet. "The facts are in the report, Mr. Rowe. Your brother went to Paris, buried his mother, and —"

"My *half brother!*"

"And when he returned he bought out the Farworth Mining Company's holdings in southwest Montana Territory."

Justin returned to the desk, pulled the chair back in place and sat down again. He quickly thumbed through the neatly written pages of the report.

"What's the mine's prospects? Is gold there?"

"I'm not a miner, but what I understand from one who knows — not much."

Justin eyed him sharply. "Garrick is a lot of things, but he's not a fool where money is concerned. He must have found something there worth buying."

"There's the town of Trinity. I've heard it's being abandoned as the gold peters out. I understand it's not much of a town but for a few hastily constructed buildings and a hole in the mountain. You'll find everything detailed in the report. The agency's bill is attached. Now, if you'll excuse me, I have another appointment."

Justin stood and looked down at the shorter man, ignoring what he had said about leaving. "Women? Has there been one in particular?"

"None during the past year and a half. Oh, there were the usual, a woman here, a woman there, but he didn't see any one of them more than a half-dozen times."

"All blond, I suppose," Justin said, his thin lips twisted in a sneer.

"On the contrary. All had dark hair," the detective was pleased to say.

The Pinkerton man looked into the hard steel blue eyes of the financier and wondered what had caused this man to despise his brother so much that he would go to any means to discredit him. The small, balding detective had not liked this case from the beginning. He was a railroad detective. It went against his grain to investigate a man's mother to determine if there had been something in her past that would have made her marriage to Justin Rowe's father illegal and his half brother a bastard. Justin Rowe wished to challenge a will that divided the estate equally between the two men after provisions had been made for the widow. Half of Preston Rowe's fortune would be more, much more, than most men dreamed of having, yet it seemed this greedy bastard wanted it all.

"You may go." The words came abruptly. Justin didn't even look up at the man who stood before his desk.

At the rude dismissal, the detective's face reddened, and a fierce resentment boiled up within him. It would be worth a year's pay to take the paper from his inside pocket and slam it on the desk. But the time wasn't right. It contained information that had come to him during the course of the investigation — information Justin Rowe had not asked for, or paid for. The detective swallowed his pride; holding himself proudly erect, he crossed the Persian carpet to the door. The higher they fly the harder they fall, he thought, and let himself out.

A small but pleasantly rounded woman came into the foyer from a room in the back. She had a basket of flowers on her arm. Could this lady be the wife of that arrogant ass in the office? The Pinkerton man nodded his respects to the lady, plucked his hat from the hand of the servant beside the door, and left the mansion, glad to see the last of Justin Rowe.

The colored servant stood silently until the woman looked his way. He motioned toward the office door. She shook her head in silent answer to his equally silent query. The servant bowed and disappeared into another room. For a moment, the woman held her hand tightly against her breast as if to calm her heartbeat, then took a deep breath and opened the office door.

"Oh, Justin, look at the roses. Aren't they beautiful?" she asked cheerfully.

The man at the desk gave her a cold stare. "I'm busy, Helga, but you knew that, didn't you? You saw the detective leave and you're dying to know what I found out about Garrick."

"Is that who that was? Oh, my, I thought detectives were big, hard, dangerous-looking men. He looked as mild as a lamb." Her smile did not reach her eyes. She turned and placed the basket on the wide windowsill.

"You like big, hard, dangerous-looking men, don't you?" Justin lifted the lid of his cigar box, selected a cigar, and bit off the end. After he blew out the wooden match, he dropped it in the basket beside the desk.

Helga watched the action. She knew when the black mood was on her husband. During the five years of their marriage, she had catalogued in her mind every move he made leading up to an explosion of temper that he would eventually take out on her. First, his voice would soften, and then, always neat and orderly with himself and his belongings, he became even more so. He had dropped the matchstick carefully in the wastebasket instead of breaking it in half and leaving it in the ashtray. It was a sure sign that he wasn't pleased with what the detective had told him. Helga began to quake inside, but as usual she played the game for as long as she could.

"Of course, Justin. You're a big, dangerous-looking man, and I love you."

"You love what I give you, Helga. You would have married the devil in order to live in a place like this."

"Oh, Justin —"

"The Greek bitch is dead," he blurted. "Your precious Garrick not only has what my father left to him, but what he left to her. Now he's richer than I am. Don't you want to take the next train west? He's in the wilds of Montana Territory where even you might look good to him."

"Justin, why can't you forget Garrick? He's out of our lives. You'll never have to see him again."

"Out of my life? Dear Helga, he'll never be out of my life until he's dead. The day my father brought that Greek fortune-hunter into my mother's house, my life was changed forever. She bewitched him. When she gave him another son, one as dark as a mulatto, he acted as if she had given him everlasting life. From that day on I was shoved aside. The new son was even given a Teutonic name. Garrick, mighty warrior."

"I'm sure your father didn't mean to slight you."

"You know nothing about it, so shut your mouth!" he shouted and jumped to his feet. "The Rowes had been pure Nordic up to that time. Why do you suppose I married a stupid chit like you? You can thank your lucky stars that you're blond, blue-eyed, pure Caucasian. Our son is the same; his son will be the same, by God, or he'll not inherit a dime."

Helga stood with her hands clasped in front of her and looked her husband in the eye. One show of weakness and he would be on her like a hawk on a rabbit. It was always the same. First, he would slap her with the open palm of his hand. It was the only time he struck her in the face, and then he was careful not to leave a mark. Many times she'd had to greet guests when her back, buttocks, stomach and thighs were cut and bleeding from the strap. Worse than the beatings were the sexual assaults that followed. He needed to feel that he had totally conquered her, before he was able to reach completion, but she always kept a secret part of herself from him. It was the only way that she could keep her sanity.

Thank goodness their son was down by the

river with his nurse, for Justin was working himself into a rage, and she knew what was to come. Helga had learned that her cries excited him to further violence; and unless it was a terribly bad beating, she was able to take it in silence.

"Your lover is in Montana Territory," Justin continued with a sneer. It was a sure sign of his rage when he repeated himself. He went to the window and stood with his back to her. "Would you like to see him?"

"Garrick is not and never has been my lover." If only that were not true, Helga thought. If only he would welcome me if I went to him! But he had showed her nothing but respect. At times she had seen pity in his dark eyes.

"No?" He turned to look at her. "You still claim that little black-haired bastard you had last year was mine?"

"Yes, she was your daughter," she answered calmly. "Many new-born infants have dark hair. The second growth of hair would have been light. Even the doctors told you that."

"We'll never know, will we? Had it lived, it would not have been raised in this house!" His voice had risen to a roar.

It won't be long now, Helga thought. Justin's obsession with his Nordic heritage and with besting his half brother ruled his life. She had seen Garrick Rowe only a few times. A few months after she and Justin were married he came home for a few weeks to visit his mother. He came back when his father died. After the funeral and the

78

reading of the will, he and his mother left for Paris where Justin's father had met her. As long as Preston Rowe had lived, Justin had kept his hatred for his stepmother and her son bottled up inside. The moment Justin learned that his father had included Whitecliff in his inheritance, he made it clear that Garrick and his mother were no longer welcome.

"How would you like to take a trip out West?" To Helga's surprise, Justin sat down on the arm of a chair and folded his arms across his chest.

"Out West? I don't know if it would be a good idea to take Ian away at this time."

"We won't take Ian."

"Not take him? But, I can't go and leave him."

"I think you can . . . and will if I say so. It will only be for a few months."

"Months! No, Justin. I don't want to leave my child for a week, much less for months." Helga began to wring her hands and plead. "Please, Justin —"

"No?" he said softly. "You know better than to say no to me. You'll do as I tell you, won't you, Helga? I'm the head of this family. Say it."

"You're the head of the family. But I'm Ian's mother, and I don't want to leave him. Justin. For once, please be reasonable."

"For once? So I'm unreasonable other times? Look at me when I'm talking to you." He was on his feet in an instant. His hand flashed out and he slapped her so hard she stumbled and almost fell. "You're trying my patience, Helga. I've taken all the sass I'll take from you." He sank his fingers in the carefully arranged hair at the top of her head and pulled her head back so he could look into her face. "I've fed you, clothed you, taken you away from that piss-poor family of yours, and made you into someone whom people look up to. You haven't appreciated any of it." He shoved her from him. "Tell the servants to find something to do down at the summer house. Then get upstairs and take off your clothes."

Helga stumbled from the room. *God help me to endure this,* she prayed. If only there were someplace she and Ian could go where he couldn't find them. If only there were someone who would help her get Ian away from Justin and that nurse who was accountable only to him. She could leave, but he would find her and bring her back. Not that he wanted her, but it was a matter of pride. Then he would lock her away and she would never see her son again.

The servant came hurrying from the back of the house. She saw the fear on his face change to pity when she told him to take the others and go. Refusing to acknowledge by the slightest gesture what they both knew was going to happen, or to show her fear, she lifted her skirts with her two hands, and with her head high, went up the curved stairway as if she were going to take her afternoon rest.

CHAPTER
Five

"Why are you avoiding me, Katy? You haven't said three words to me in three days."

Looking at Rowe now, Katy found it hard to believe it had been only four days since he had been shot. He had insisted on getting out of bed for a while on the second day. Yesterday he had gone back to the jail building, and today he had walked up to the funerary for his meals, refusing Mary's offer to bring them to him. Now he sat in a straight cane-bottomed chair on the porch, gazing at her with narrowed, intent eyes, and Katy returned the stare.

His eyes were like a deep, dark well with little lights dancing on the water. His features were rough, making him look hard and perhaps a little cruel. The woman who belonged to him would feel either terribly safe or terribly intimidated by him. Katy remembered how vulnerable and young he had looked while he lay unconscious on her bed and how he had opened his eyes and said, "You're here," as if he hadn't wanted to be alone.

"Katy, Katy, don't run away. Sit down and talk to me." The soft-spoken request told her something else about him. He could be a charmer when he wanted to be.

"I have things to do." Katy found herself wondering how it would feel to belong to such a man. Even though he overwhelmed her with the intensity of his maleness, he aroused her curiosity. She eyed him warily for a moment. Should she go, or should she stay?

Theresa came to lean against his knee and looked earnestly into his face. "I'll talk to you, Mr. Rowe."

Rowe's face softened as he looked at the child. He ran his palm down the long length of her hair that had just been washed and brushed.

"I've not had a better offer, Miss Sugarplum."

This was another thing that puzzled Katy about Rowe. Theresa had taken to him and he to her. He seemed to be genuinely fond of the child. Theresa was enthralled by him and his dog. She and Mary had held their breaths when Theresa, with squeals of childish laughter, had thrown her arms around the dog's shaggy neck. "He'll not hurt her," Rowe assured them.

"Theresa!" Mary called from inside the funerary. "Come let me braid your hair."

"Oh, shoot!" Theresa rested her small fists on her hips, a gesture she had picked up from her Aunt Katy.

A deep chuckle rumbled up out of Rowe's chest, and the dark eyes that sought Katy's gleamed with amusement. Her own spontaneous laughter rang out and Rowe sobered quickly as he watched her. He was a little stunned by the intensity of his feelings. She was a creature made for laughter, sunshine, and love. She made his heart jump at the sight of her as no other woman had ever done. He pulled his eyes away from her and brought them back to the child.

"You'd better go, Sugarplum, before your mamma comes with a willow switch."

"She never hits me with it," Theresa said confidentially, glancing toward the door. "She only acts like she will."

"There's always the first time," he whispered.

"Oh, all right." She started for the door, then turned back. Her small, pixie face was serious; her eyes large and round. "I love you more than Papa," she blurted, and then, as if embarrassed by what she had said, she ran across the porch and through the doorway.

For the second time in the last few minutes Rowe was overcome by emotion. He couldn't remember a time in his life when a female had said, "I love you," and he had believed her. His mother had loved him, but she wasn't the demonstrative type. Whores had said it, and a few of the women in his life had professed love for him. He had never taken the words seriously before.

"She means it." Katy stared at him, trying to read his thoughts. "Don't get too close to her. We'll be leaving here soon and I don't want her hurt."

"Why would she be hurt?"

"She adored her father, but he had little time for her. She's looking for a substitute."

"He must be a real bastard."

"He's just like all the other get-rich-quick gold-seekers. We're leaving here as soon as we can. Theresa needs to go to school with other children."

"Mary said she was going to wait for her husband."

"We're not going to wait for that fly-by-night to come back. We could be old, gray, and toothless by the time that happens," she flared. Katy's temper had never been easily harnessed and now she became flushed with anger.

"Where will you go?"

"Laramie. We have friends there. I can get a job." Her shoulders lifted in an imperial shrug.

"What kind of job?"

"Teaching. Our friends have an orphanage on their ranch. Mary and I can work there."

"You know the Gallaghers?"

Katy lifted her eyebrows. "Do you?"

"I know of Pack Gallagher. He was a bare-knuckle fighter. Now he raises longhorn cattle. I heard that he and his wife had built an orphanage on their land."

"If we don't go there, we'll go back to Montgomery where people are civilized."

"I intend to make Trinity a civilized town."

"Ha!" She raked her hair over her ear with her fingertip and shot him a contemptuous glance. "Another cow in the tree."

"What do you mean by that?" he said, thinking that she was wonderful to look at. *Blue is the color she should be wearing instead of that dreary brown. The color of her dress is all wrong, but it fits. Good Lord, how it fits her slim waist and soft breasts!*

"It means you have as much chance making this a civilized town as you have of finding a cow in a tree."

He grinned. She had a quick mind. Life with her would not be dull. "Stay and help me."

"No. After we leave this town, I never want to see another miner or another mine."

"Do you prefer a man with soft hands, a white shirt, and shiny black shoes? Do you have one waiting for you?"

"Goodness, no!" She said the words with such speed and force that he had to smile at her quick answer to the unexpected question. She stood still under the steady gaze of his black eyes. The frown of disapproval she shot at him did nothing but intensify his stare.

"That's one hurdle we'll not have to cross, not that I think it would complicate matters. Do you know what reincarnation means?"

Katy had turned away to look at the mountains. On hearing the question, her head swiveled around, and she looked at him to see if he were serious.

"Of course. I'm not stupid. I've known men who were snakes in their former lives and some who were buzzards."

He threw his head back and laughed. With her wit, her laughter so effortless, and her slow, liquid drawl, she was enchanting. He had been waiting for her all his life. They could no more halt the tide of coming events than they could stop the sun coming up in the morning. Triumph moved through him. *She was his.* With his triumph came the need to hold her, love her, soothe and protect her. Love in the romantic sense wasn't something he was familiar with, and it wasn't something he had sought. Until he had met Katy, it hadn't occurred to him that he would love a woman with all his heart and soul. He was dangerously close to doing that now.

"What would you say if I told you that I'm sure you and I have met in former lives?" He made the question a challenge, and his eyes gleamed with amusement as her mouth fell open and remained agape.

"I'd say that bullet that creased your scalp did more damage than I thought."

"It's very possible that we have been mates several times down through the centuries."

"That's certainly a farfetched but interesting assumption." Her lips began to twitch, and then her musical laughter came suddenly as she began to see the humor in the situation. "I can see you as Claudius, Emperor of Rome, or Henry the Eighth, lopping off the heads of your wives." Katy made some slashing movements as if she had a sword in her hand. "On the other hand, you may have been Genghis Khan, Captain Cook, or Pontiac, chief of the Ottawa Indians." She stopped play-acting and stared into his dark eyes that had suddenly gone serious.

"You may have been Helen of Troy, Cleopatra or Lady Godiva. All were very beautiful."

"Not my style. I'm not foolish enough to let a snake bite me, or to ride naked through the streets of Coventry. I'm more the Lucrezia Borgia type."

"You'll not poison me, Katy. Does the name *Nightrose* mean anything to you?"

"Nightrose? Oh, sure. It tells me that you've been in these mountains too long," she snorted and turned away.

"Don't go! I'm not up to chasing after you just yet." The commanding tone in his voice cracked across her pride like a whip.

"Don't order me around, *King Richard*. This isn't the Middle Ages." She whirled to face him, flung the thick rope of hair over her shoulder and rested her fists on her hips. "Women are no longer chattels," she spat at him. "We even vote now!" Her eyes burned at him resentfully, and her voice rose in spite of her wish to stay calm.

He looked searchingly into her eyes, and, ignoring her anger, spoke calmly.

"Katy, haven't you ever felt for an instant that you've done something before?"

"Of course, hasn't everyone? It's a phenomenon. To attach any significance to it is just ridiculous!"

"I don't think it is. I think that feeling opens a window into our past and offers a glimpse into our future. You and I will be continuing our relationship in this life, and we should start off on the right foot."

"What relationship, Mr. Rowe? We'll have no relationship because I'll not be here, and that's my final word on it." She felt shaken and a little out of breath. She wrapped her arm about the porch post and leaned against it.

"Katy, I hadn't planned to have this conversation with you just yet, but I think it best that I lay my cards on the table so that you'll know where I stand. I don't want you to leave Trinity, therefore you will stay until I've completed my business here. Then I will take you to where we will establish a home." His face had a harshness that made her shiver. His voice was so even that it took her a moment to hear the positive note in it.

"You're crazy!"

"Omnis amans amens," he said with a shake of his head.

"What gibberish is that?" she demanded.

"Latin. Every lover is demented."

As Katy's startled eyes met his, an icy hand squeezed her heart. "We're leaving as soon as we can, and you'll have nothing to say about it."

"But I will, Katy. You'll stay and help me build a town," he said confidently.

"And you'll fly to the moon on a broomstick!"

"You and your sister will not be alone again," he said, ignoring her outburst. "I'll provide for you and protect you while we get to know each other better."

It was the wrong thing to say, and Rowe realized it the instant Katy's face turned a dull red, her eyes blazing angrily. He had trampled upon

88

that damnable Southern pride that Southern ladies carried like a shield.

"You'll provide for us! And what do *you* expect in return? We're not beggars! We've not asked you for a damn thing. You volunteered your protection when the outlaws rode in. You demanded that we accept it. We don't want your charity, and as far as getting to know you — bullfoot! I know you as well right now as I ever will."

"You're wrong, but I realize I can't convince you of that just yet. I didn't mean to offend you. I admire your pride and your independence." He smiled at her, and that smile was a threat. It held admiration and such implacable determination that she shivered even though she was sweating with anger.

"You're not planning my life, Mary's life, or Theresa's life," she sputtered. "So back off!"

"I can't do that, Katy. You're the woman who will share my life. Sooner or later you'll realize that fate brought us together."

He spoke calmly again, as if he believed the ridiculous things he was saying. He's out of his head, she thought wildly.

"What you're saying is so farfetched it's not even worth discussing!" Katy crossed her arms in front of her and gripped her elbows with her hands. "If I thought I'd spend my life in a mining town like this one, I'd . . . I'd jump off the highest mountain."

"We'll not be in a mining town forever. I have some land picked out for a ranch."

"Sheep ranch or cattle ranch? Bullfoot! You're making me sorry I shot that man before he could shoot you," she blurted, knowing it was a childish thing to say. She wanted to say something that would really cut him down, but she realized she had failed when she looked into his dark laughing eyes. The humor of the situation hit her suddenly and the laughter that could come from her so unexpectedly rang out. "You're as crazy as a bedbug," she commented with a shake of her head and stalked off.

Behind the building and out of his sight, Katy stopped. The quiet hung heavily on the town, but Rowe's word's roared loudly in her head. *You're the woman who will share my life. You'll not leave until I do.* He was teasing her. Wasn't he?

Katy had felt strangely alive when she was with him, but she had put it down to the fact that she hadn't conversed with an interesting man in months. Suddenly she was jolted by an instant flash of memory: *This was not new to her! It had happened before!* The next thought that came to her was that she was losing her mind. Rowe had planted the seed in her mind that they had known each other in another life. The idea was interesting but not practical, her common sense told her, and the sooner she got it out of her head the better off she'd be.

Rowe watched her leave. He wanted to call her back, but knew that she wouldn't come. He wasn't sure why he had said all those things to her. Hell! He wasn't even sure that he really believed it all himself. It was interesting to think he had known her in another life. Her image had haunted his dreams as he lay in her bed. He had imagined long winter nights, holding her in his arms, loving her. She would be a passionate lover. Later, he would watch her stomach swell with his child. It wasn't that he just needed a woman. He was a man who believed in quality rather than quantity and had gone for long stretches of time without the relief other men sought from the bangtails who followed the miners.

Abruptly, he felt bitter resentment rising in him. He didn't like this compulsive need to look at her, to know where she was and what she was doing. He didn't like the power she had over him. He liked being in control. Katy was delicate and elusive, yet strong, a woman with a mind of her own, who would buck him every step of the way. He was certain, however, of two things: he wanted her, and she wasn't leaving Trinity until he did.

Mary was the first to see the train of wagons coming around the curve and down the road into town. She had been to the garden to check the potato vines for potato bugs. Since the shooting, she and Katy had moved about without fear, reassured by Rowe's presence.

"Rowe! Wagons are coming."

Rowe, making a reed whistle for Theresa, looked up, folded his jackknife, and slipped it into his pocket. Holding onto the porch post, he stepped down with a slight grunt. The wound in his thigh was healing, but he was stiff from inactivity. He squinted his eyes toward the huge lumbering wagons being pulled by four mules and six mule-hitches, with the riders coming ahead of the wagons.

"It's about time," he grumbled.

Mary stepped up onto the porch and took her daughter's hand. After more than two months of being here alone, it was exciting to see people coming into town.

"Is Papa coming?" Theresa asked.

"No, honey. I don't see Papa's horse."

"Where's Katy?" Rowe was suddenly anxious that she be with him when the men arrived. He would make it plain to them that she was his and that Mary was to be treated respectfully, or they would answer to him.

"She was with the horses. She'll come when she hears the wagons."

"I'm here," Katy said and stepped up onto the porch behind her sister.

"You've nothing to fear from my men. I'll see to that." Rowe saw the look of distaste on Katy's face as she watched the caravan approach.

"I know what kind of men they are. I'm prepared to take care of myself . . . and Mary." She drew the small pistol from her pocket. "It's small but very effective at close range."

"My God!" Rowe exclaimed. "Have you been carrying that Derringer around with you all this time?"

"I have, and I know how to use it." She cocked the gun. "It's loaded, and it has come in handy more than once. You'd be surprised at how a small gun can discourage a big man."

"That damn thing's got a hair trigger. You'll shoot your leg off. Give it to me." As he made a move toward her, Katy stepped back, easing the hammer down and slipping the pistol back into her apron pocket. The commanding tone in his voice set her teeth on edge.

"If you try to take it, Genghis Khan, I'll shoot you in your other leg."

"Katy! For goodness' sake!" Mary was shocked by Katy's words and the bitterness in her voice.

Because Katy's eyes were locked with Rowe's, she didn't see the horrified expression on her sister's face. He was obviously angry, and Katy felt a brief spurt of satisfaction. He raked his fingers roughly through his tight dark curls as his eyes narrowed to piercing black slits.

"I'll deal with you later," he threatened, his lips scarcely moving.

"You just plain scare me to death," Katy drawled.

The surge of anger was so strong that Rowe ground his teeth to keep from saying something he would regret later. Her face was calm, but her blue eyes sparkled angrily. She had an explosive temper, he realized, a temper that was usually hidden behind her smiles and spontaneous laughter. Rowe knew when to advance and when to retreat. He turned his back and walked down the boardwalk toward the saloon. Savoring her small victory, Katy went inside the funerary.

"Laws, Katy. What gets into you at times? What was that all about?" Mary asked.

"Nothing important. That man is so arrogant that he gets my back up. We're going to be in the first wagon that leaves this place. Sooner or later they'll have to go to Bannack for supplies. Let's hope it's sooner."

"I don't know, Katy. What if Roy should come back and we're not here?"

"Bushy-face can tell him where we are."

"He ain't bushy no more, Aunt Katy," Theresa said.

"He's got a mustache, ladybug. That's bush."

"But where will we go?" Mary had a worried look on her face.

"To Laramie. Mara Shannon told us to come back if things didn't work out. Both of us can work at the orphanage, and Theresa can go to school with the other children."

"But what if we can't? We'll be safe here as long as Rowe's here. And we should wait a little longer for Roy."

"I feel about as safe with that dark devil as I would be if I were tied to a keg of gunpowder." Katy's blue eyes flashed angrily.

"Why don't you like him?"

"I like him," Theresa chimed in, but her mother and her aunt were too engrossed to pay attention, so she went to the porch.

"Bullfoot!" Katy snorted. "He's a throwback

to the Dark Ages. He's a domineering male who thinks women were put on earth for the sole purpose of being subservient to him."

"He doesn't strike me like that at all. You must be mistaken about him. He's been very appreciative of everything we've done for him."

"Mary, for heaven's sake! You're too good for your own good. You only see what you want to see. He puts on a good face to you, but believe me, he's deep, dark, and devious. If he keeps us here, it'll be for some benefit to him, not out of the goodness of his heart."

"Mamma! Aunt Katy! Come look."

"Stay on the porch, Theresa," Mary called anxiously and went to the window. "My goodness! Six wagons and," she paused to count, "ten men on horseback. There's twenty-five or thirty men. Oh, my! He said some men were coming, but I didn't expect this many."

"I'm thinking that Mr. Rowe never does things on a small scale," Katy said looking over Mary's shoulder at the line of men and wagons going by. The men, dusty and whiskered, all looked toward the funerary; a few of them waved at Theresa and ogled the women staring out the window. "Just look at them," Katy said disgustedly. "They all look alike. All cut from the same dirty cloth."

"Of course they're dirty. They've been traveling for days. What did you expect?"

"Exactly what I'm seeing," Katy said tiredly and went to sit in the rocker. "At least they'll have their own cook, and we'll not have to bother feeding *Genghis Khan* anymore."

"Katy! I've never known you to take such a dislike to anyone. Why do you call him that? Who is Genghis Khan?"

"He was the cruel, sadistic warrior-ruler of Mongolia during the thirteenth century. More than likely he was one of Rowe's ancestors."

"Oh, no! Rowe isn't Asian. He told me his mother was from Greece, his father was Scandinavian. He's very interesting to talk to."

"Oh, he's quite the world traveler. He speaks Latin and Greek and heaven only knows what else."

"I'll miss him."

"So will I," Katy said with a deep sigh of relief. "But it'll be nice."

Katy leaned her head back and rocked gently. The wagons and the horsemen had passed, but the dust still hung over the road. She felt edgy. She was silly to let that man work her into a state of nerves with all that talk about former lives, not allowing them to leave Trinity, and spending her life with him. Nonsense, all of it.

Thank goodness he would be busy and easier to avoid in the future. He was maddeningly arrogant, and she sensed that he was attracted to her sharp wit and equally sharp tongue. He was probably surprised to find a woman out here in the wilds who knew how to do something more than clean fish and chew hides. A smile tilted her lips when that thought crossed her mind. It had been a mistake to exchange barbs with him, yet it had been enjoyable until he began to talk as if he owned her. To be in his company was to invite trouble, something she would avoid in the future.

"Are we going to wait for Mr. Rowe, Mamma?"

"No, love. I'm sure he'll eat with the men who came today." Mary lifted Theresa up onto the stool and pushed it close to the table.

"I wish he'd eat with us."

"He's busy, ladybug. You're going to have to settle for your mamma and your Aunt Katy," Katy said, taking her place at the table.

"Mr. Rowe likes me."

"Of course, he likes you. You're the prettiest little girl in Trinity."

"Papa didn't."

"Yes he did," Mary said staunchly. "He just didn't say so."

"He didn't let me sit on his lap or tell me stories."

"Maybe he thought you didn't like stories," Mary said lamely. "Now, clean your plate so you can have some gooseberry pie."

"Mr. Rowe likes gooseberry pie."

"We'll save a piece for him. How's that?"

"He was going to make me a swing." Theresa's lips began to quiver. "But now, he won't."

"Of course he will. The men being here won't change that, honey. Would you like some butter and sugar on your rice?" Mary asked.

"He won't come back. Aunt Katy hates him." Theresa burst into tears.

"Ah . . . ladybug." Katy looked helplessly at the small tearstained face. "Is that what gives you the mulligrubs? Honey, grown-ups can have a difference of opinion, but that doesn't mean they *hate* each other."

"You . . . said he was a . . . dark devil, and that's bad —"

"She didn't mean anything bad, honey. Your Aunt Katy's mouth is like a runaway horse sometimes. She says things she doesn't mean, just like when she's play-acting. Isn't that right?" Mary asked Katy.

"Sure. Now if I'd said he was as ugly as a horny toad, or he was an old flibbertigibbet, or smelled like a billy goat, you'd have laughed. Come on, ladybug, dry up and give me a big smile so I can eat. My belly button is sticking to my backbone."

"You'll not call him . . . bad things?"

"I promise."

Theresa smiled through her tears. "I love you, Aunt Katy."

"I love you too, honey."

The resentment Katy felt toward Rowe knotted her stomach and made it almost impossible for her to finish the meal. He had not only won her sister over but little Theresa as well. Damn him! When she found a way to leave this blasted town, Mary and Theresa would go with her, and she would like to see Mr. Garrick Rowe try to stop her.

CHAPTER
Six

The town had come alive.

Before, there had been only the sound of the wind whipping around the vacant buildings, rattling the loose windows, rippling over tin roofs. Now, coarse masculine laughter, boot heels on the boardwalks, hammer against steel, and the sound of an axe striking wood drifted up to the funerary. Within a few hours, the men had built a stockade for the animals and made a cookshack out of the building next to the long bunkhouse. Supper smoke was in the air.

As the sun vanished, darkness came quickly to the town in the valley. Lights shone from the windows of the saloon, the bunkhouse, and the stone building where Rowe had made his headquarters. In the funerary, after more than two months of loneliness, Theresa was excited about the sudden population and asked endless questions.

"Will they stay, Mamma? Do you think they've seen Papa? What did they bring in the big wagons? Will more wagons come and . . . bring little girls?" She stood on a stool while her mother washed her face, hands, and feet, then slipped her nightdress over her head.

Listening to Theresa's chatter, Katy put the last of the just washed supper dishes on the shelf and flipped a clean cloth over the necessaries left on the table. An unexpected rap on the door caused three heads to turn toward that solid slab of wood and the bar that lay across it. Katy picked up the rifle, checked the load, and went to the door.

"Who is it?" she called.

"Rowe." There was no mistaking the voice, or Theresa's squeal of joy on hearing it.

Katy lifted the bar. The door swung back and Rowe's big body filled the doorway.

"Good evening," he said, ignoring the rifle pointed at his midsection. "May we come in?" His eyes, with a faint glint of amusement, held Katy's.

She nodded and lowered the rifle.

"Mr. Rowe!" Theresa squealed. "Did ya come to make my swing?"

"Not tonight, Sugarplum. Maybe tomorrow."

"Maybe never," Katy murmured softly, but it brought his dark eyes back to her. He gave her an amused grin before he stepped over the threshold and entered the room.

Katy returned his grin with a haughty stare, then looked past him to the faces of the two men who had removed their hats and come in to stand beside him.

"Ladies, I'd like you to meet Anton Hooker." He indicated a tall, bookish-looking man with thin blond hair and wire-rimmed spectacles.

"Good evening," Hooker said politely.

"And Hank Weston, the foreman." The big red-haired man shifted uneasily from one foot to the other, plainly uncomfortable. "The ladies are Miss Katy Burns and her sister, Mrs. Stanton. The young lady is Theresa."

"It's a pleasure to meet you." Mary lifted Theresa down from the stool and came forward with her hand extended, giving their guests a generous and cordial reception. Katy stood where she was and nodded her acknowledgment to the introduction, very much aware that Rowe's dark eyes were on her again. "Won't you sit down?" Mary was saying.

"Thank you." The men stood hesitantly after Mary was seated, waiting for Katy to sit down, but she shook her head and leaned against the front wall of the building. They each took a chair. Theresa ran across the room and climbed upon Rowe's lap as soon as he was seated.

"Theresa, you shouldn't," Mary admonished.

"It's all right, Mary," Rowe said, settling the child on the side away from his injured thigh. "I like to hold pretty girls." He looked at Katy over Theresa's head. She stood stock-still, head tilted back, arms folded. The lamplight made a halo of the shiny blond hair that had come loose from the pins and hung in disarray around her face. Blue-gray eyes stared back at him with a mixture of suspicion and exasperation in their depths. Puzzled by her hostility, he raised his brows in silent question.

101

"We got gooseberry pie." Theresa placed her small hand on Rowe's cheek to turn his face toward her.

"I suppose you ate it all." His fingers gripped her small midsection and she giggled happily.

"We saved a piece for you — a big piece cause Mamma said you was big. But Aunt Katy said you —"

"Theresa remembered your saying you liked gooseberries," Mary said quickly.

Smile lines bracketed Rowe's wide mouth. He glanced at Katy's expressionless face, then smiled into the trusting face of the child. Theresa snuggled against him, her head on his shoulder, her thumb in her mouth. He didn't appear to be uncomfortable cuddling the little girl in his arms in the presence of his friends. In fact, he seemed to be rather pleased that she had run to him and climbed onto his lap. It was another strange thing about Garrick Rowe for Katy to note and file away in the back of her mind, to ponder over later when she had the time.

"Come sit down, Katy. Hank and I have a business deal to put to you and Mary."

Out of consideration for the guests, Katy refused to show that she was irritated at Rowe for inviting her to sit down in her own home. She pulled the stool out from the table and moved it so that he had to turn his head to look at her. She sat down and folded her hands in her lap.

"I never imagined a funerary could be made to look so homey." Anton Hooker spoke with a clipped Northern accent that brought back memories of the war to Mary and Katy.

"Necessity," Mary said. "When we were left here alone we explored all the buildings we could get into without breaking a window and discovered this one was the best suited for our purpose. Of course, if the owner should come back, we'll vacate."

Hooker looked at Rowe as if he expected him to say something, and when he didn't, Hooker said, "Rowe explained your reason for being here. You're mighty lucky. This area is full of outlaws, not to mention Cheyenne and Sioux who are mad enough at George Custer to take hair wherever they can get it."

"Oh, dear! An Indian uprising? It seems there's no end to the violence out here."

"I've not heard of any sizable raids this far west," Anton Hooker said. "It would take a considerable force to come up against the number of men we have here."

Anton Hooker was talking, but Katy watched the foreman, Hank Weston. He had dark red shaggy hair, a clean-shaven face, shoulders and biceps that bulged with muscles, and large freckled hands. He had planted his heavy boots wide apart, rested his forearms on his thighs, and twirled his hat between his spread knees. His light blue eyes were focused on Mary. Katy had always thought that Mary was extremely pretty. She was soft and sweet and biddable and undemanding; the type of woman a man wanted. Uneasiness coiled in her stomach as she felt a sudden premonition that Hank Weston might be thinking that she and her sister were women of loose morals. He hadn't said a word beyond his first greeting, but his eyes had been busy, first roaming over their home, and then over Mary's generous curves and soft brown hair. Damn him!

Anton Hooker was too much of a gentleman to stare. He was more Mary's type, Katy found herself thinking. He looked as if he had some refinement and would understand the predicament of two lone women in such a place as this. She decided to appeal to him.

"Mr. Hooker, my sister and I have been stranded here for more than two months. We want to go back to Laramie as soon as possible. We'd be grateful if you would arrange for an escort to take us to Bannack or to Virginia City where we could take the stage."

All eyes turned to Katy. She could feel the heat of Rowe's gaze, feel him willing her to look at him. Her eyes were on Anton Hooker. He glanced at Rowe then at Hank Weston before bringing his eyes back to her.

"That isn't a decision I can make, miss. You'll have to speak to Rowe about that."

Katy refused to look at Rowe. "Surely you can't refuse to let us ride out in one of the freight wagons when it goes out for supplies."

Anton stirred nervously. "We brought supplies for several weeks, miss. At any rate, it wouldn't be a safe trip. You're safe here —"

"Being safe is not the issue, Mr. Hooker," Katy said firmly. "There's nothing for us here. We want to go back to Laramie."

"Don't badger Anton, Katy." Rowe shifted the now-sleeping child in his arms and moved his chair back so that he could look at her. "I'm the one you'll have to deal with."

Katy's blue eyes swept over Rowe in a manner that could only be contemptuous. "Ah, yes." Coolly uplifted brows asked his intentions.

"For the time being, you'll have to stay here in Trinity."

Outraged astonishment was plain on Katy's face. Her eyes spit blue flame. "Genghis Khan has spoken," she said calmly, choking back her temper.

"Perhaps he has." Rowe grinned wickedly.

For a moment her eyes, like daggers, looked into the predatory gaze of eyes as black as a bottomless pit, then she lowered her lids as alarm tingled through her. He was as hard as stone. None of the men would help them unless they had his permission. How on earth were they going to get out of this godforsaken place?

"It's useless to pout, Katy." Rowe's deep, smooth voice broke into her thoughts. "You and Mary and Theresa are as safe here as you'd be in a church in Denver. You're free to move around the town. Hank and I will see to it that the men treat you respectfully."

She lifted her lashes and glared at him. A black brow over glittering black devil-eyes quirked upward. The spawn of Satan obviously thought he had all the cards stacked in his favor, and he was enjoying his control over her.

"What's the price for all of this *protection* you and Mr. Weston are providing? The . . . ah . . . er . . . usual?" She spoke coolly, refusing to look away as his dark eyes raked her face and heard her sister gasp at the blunt words.

His lips quirked in a semblance of a smile in spite of the savage anger that tore through him. He wanted to shake her. Yet, he told himself, he had never liked a mountain that was too easy to climb, a tame horse, or a dog who followed anyone who had a home. Life with this little hellion would be interesting.

"Few things in life are free."

"What price?"

"Regardless of whether or not you and Mary agree to our . . . ah, request, you'll be safe here."

"What price?" Her tone of voice stated plainly that her patience was wearing thin.

"First, I want to know if you, Mary, and Theresa have had measles."

"Why?"

"Damn it, Katy! Can't you answer a simple question?"

"We had them at Myrtle Gulch." Mary quickly interceded. "Theresa was not yet two at the time. I didn't have them as bad as Katy. She was awfully sick."

Katy shot her sister a frowning look of disapproval for giving out the information, then forced herself to look back at Rowe and speak matter of factly.

"Now I understand why you need us to stay here. You have an outbreak of measles and you want us to tend the sick. Let me warn you, Mr. *Blackbeard* Teach, that I could not have possibly been Florence Nightingale in my former life because, as far as I know, she is still living. Nor could I have been Clara Barton, for the same reason."

Rowe threw back his head and laughed.

At this moment Katy thoroughly hated him. More than anything she wanted to slam her knotted fist into his eye with every ounce of her strength. The thought sobered her. What was this man doing to her? She couldn't remember ever wanting to strike anyone before. When she was with Garrick Rowe, it was as if there were another person inside her clamoring to get out.

"What in the world are you talking about?" Mary asked, looking first at Rowe's smiling face then at her sister's angry one. Katy's lips were pressed in a downward arc, and her brows were beetled. "How many men are sick, Rowe?"

"Two, so far. Hank isolated them in one wagon. He says measles broke out in Bannack while they were there, so we expect more men to come down with them."

"Poor things. Sage tea will break the fever and baking-soda paste will help the itch —"

"They're a miserable lot with fever runnin' high," Hank said, and his Irish brogue reminded

Katy of Pack Gallagher, Mara Shannon's husband.

"Of course, we'll do what we can for them," Mary said firmly. "Are they still in the wagons?"

"We moved them to the house back of the livery."

"Is someone looking after them?"

"I've been doin' what I can."

"Then you've had measles."

"Not that I know of, but —"

"Laws! You'll be coming down with them next." Mary got to her feet and went to the cupboard. "We've got sage for tea but not much soda."

"There's plenty in the cookhouse," Hank said.

Katy watched Mary. She was in her glory when she was nursing the sick. Damn Garrick Rowe! He *was* playing all the right cards. Mary wouldn't even think of leaving Trinity as long as there was someone here who needed her.

"I'll go see what I can do, Katy. Men die of measles if they're not given enough water, if fever burns them up, or if they scratch and get infection."

"I figured you would," Katy said dryly.

"You needn't worry, miss," Hank said. "I'll see that no harm comes to her."

Katy looked at him, then at Rowe. Rowe was aggravating, but she was reasonably sure he wouldn't force himself on her or her sister. Hank Weston was another matter. He seemed nice enough, but so did the preacher who had met her

108

outside the house one night in Bonanza City and tried to throw her to the ground. She held him off with the little Derringer, and the next Sunday he was in the pulpit preaching hellfire and brimstone and looking as pious as ever.

"She'll be all right. Hank will stay close to her," Rowe said, seeing the doubt on her face.

"That's what I'm afraid of," Katy said bluntly.

"Katy!" Mary's cheeks turned red with mortification. "Please excuse us. I want to speak to my sister in private." Mary went to the back of the building and into the shadows. The men sat in embarrassed silence as Katy, with head high, followed her sister. "What in the world has gotten into you?" Mary demanded in an angry whisper.

"Why? Because I don't like the idea of you going out in the dark with that . . . big Irish rowdy?"

"How do you know he's a rowdy?" She held her hand up when Katy opened her mouth to speak. "Rowe risked his life for us. To my way of thinking, he's been a real gentleman. I'm certain that he'd not recommend Mr. Weston if he were not a gentleman also."

"Gentleman! Good Lord, Mary! Miners who live from hand-to-mouth, from one hole in the ground to another, are not gentlemen. There's *thirty* of them, and *two* of us. I don't trust any of them as far as I could throw a cow by the tail. That includes Mr. Garrick Rowe, for all his heroics."

"Why? Just tell me why you've become so cynical all of a sudden, and what Rowe has done to deserve the cutting edge of your tongue every time the two of you are together?"

"It isn't all of a sudden, and there's something about the man that gets my back up."

"You're bitter, Katy. I can't tell you how sorry I am to see that happen."

"Call me bitter, cynical, or whatever. If you go down to that sickhouse, we'll all go."

"I'll not take Theresa to a sickhouse," Mary said stubbornly.

"Why not? She's had measles."

"I may be there for hours. It's no place for a little girl. Please, Katy. The men here will be more inclined to help us if we show a little trust in them." Mary started to leave, then turned back. "I think you like Rowe and you don't want to admit it. That's why you're like a prickly pear every time you're near him."

"And I think you're out of your mind if you think I like that pigheaded son of Satan!" Katy hissed angrily.

Mary plucked her shawl from the peg on the wall and flung it about her shoulders. "Let me use my own judgment in this. I wouldn't do anything that I thought would put us in danger. Heavens! I've got a child to raise, and for some time now, I've thought I'll be doing it without any help from Roy."

"That's why we must be careful."

"I know," Mary said softly. "Don't worry. I'm ready, Mr. Weston," she called and hurried toward the front of the building.

"Mary, wait." Katy picked up the Derringer lying on the shelf over her bed and hurried after her sister. "Take this."

"I won't need it. I'm sure Mr. Weston or Mr. Hooker are equipped to shoot anyone who needs shooting."

"Oh, Lord! That damn Derringer again. Put it away." This came from Rowe who had moved to the rocking chair and was holding Theresa cradled in his arms.

The command fanned Katy's temper. She slipped the pistol into her pocket. "You can put Theresa in her bed and go with Mary."

"Hank and Anton will go with Mary. I'm staying here to . . . protect you." He tilted his head back and looked up at her with a lascivious look in his eyes.

Before she could retort, Anton said, "It was a pleasure meeting you, Miss Burns."

"It was nice meeting you too," Katy murmured. Then she turned to Mary, "Are you sure you don't want me to come with you?"

"I'm sure. After Rowe puts Theresa in her bed, dish up the gooseberry pie. I'm sorry I didn't make more." She smiled up into the face of the Irishman. "I'll make another pie for you and Mr. Hooker tomorrow."

Katy went to the door and watched her sister walk out into the darkness between two tall men. She turned to see Rowe getting out of the rocker.

"If anything happens to Mary, I'll . . . shoot

you!" The words exploded from her tense lips and her eyes burned up at him resentfully.

"I accept that. I'll stand perfectly still so that you won't miss." Amusement glinted in his dark eyes. Suddenly, he laughed.

"I'm glad you're amused," she snapped. "Put Theresa in her bed and get out of here."

"Yes, ma'am," he said with mock politeness.

Katy stood with her back to the room and looked out the door seeing nothing but the ray of light that made a path on the porch. The only sounds she heard were the creaking of the floorboards when Rowe went to the back of the room to place Theresa in her bed. Seconds passed while Katy drew a shallow breath, followed by deeper ones, as she waited for him to return and leave. She heard him coming and moved aside so that he could go out the doorway. He walked purposefully up behind her and stopped.

"You have magnificent hair, Nightrose. I can't wait to see it loose and hanging down your back . . . again."

She turned to look at him. She could see his eyes were full of laughter and her thoughts whirled.

"Don't be giving me any more of that gibberish about knowing me in another life. I'm not a complete fool even if I did let myself get stranded here." She moved farther back from the door. "Good night," she said pointedly.

He reached for her hand. "Come out on the porch. I want to show you something."

"What?" she said, even as she let him draw her through the doorway and into the darkness.

"It's a hurdle we have to cross." He turned her toward him.

"A hurdle? I don't —"

He settled his lips against her mouth and breathed. "This hurdle." She was pressed against his long length. His fingers slid into the hair at the back of her head to hold her mouth to his. The lips that touched hers were warm and gentle as they tingled across her mouth with fleeting kisses. The arms holding her gradually tightened as his feet moved apart to widen his stance. She felt herself being drawn against, then between, hard, muscular thighs that held hers.

Katy came to her senses and struggled against him, but he refused to loosen his hold. His strength won and she ceased her efforts to escape. Soon she was incapable of movement or thinking and surrendered herself to the delicious floating feeling as his kiss became more possessive and deepened. Her lips parted, his tongue flirted with the inside of her lower lip, and his hand left her head to stroke gently down the curve of her back. She was breathless when he pulled his mouth from hers and raised his head only a fraction.

"You see how it is, Nightrose?" His whisper was deep and husky. "The face of the earth may change, but that is all. You and I are together again in this place. We will love here, grow old here, die here. In time we'll come back to another part of this earth and meet again. You are my mate, my love —"

"You . . . are crazy —"

"Put your arms around my neck and try not to resent me for springing this on you so suddenly. I've been looking for you a long, long time."

"No! Let me go." She was breathless.

He placed a gentle kiss on her forehead. "Don't fight it, sweetheart." His hand moved up and down her back in a soothing motion. "Be still for just a little while and you'll see how right it is." The last words were spoken on her lips before his moved away to nuzzle into the hair at her temple.

Gradually the stiffness went out of her body and she found herself leaning against him. She was tired. It had been so long since there had been anyone to lean on. How wonderful it would be to have a strong man to take over the burden of taking care of her and Mary and Theresa. She closed her eyes, telling herself that she didn't have a chance against his strength, that she would rest for a moment.

Katy could feel the strong thud of his heartbeat, smell the tangy smoke on his soft cotton shirt, feel his breath on her forehead. His hands stroked her from the nape of her neck down her spinal column to the curve of her hips. Strong fingers massaged every vertebra on the way. It was comforting, she admitted begrudgingly, to be sheltered in this man's arms here in the darkness.

Oh! For Christ's sake! What was the matter

with her. She didn't behave this way . . . like a loose, fallen woman. She scarcely knew this man who was pressing her so intimately against him. She stiffened. Rowe sensed it immediately and loosened his hold, but not enough so that she could step away from him.

"You're worn out, Katy. There'll be no more chopping wood for you, or carrying water to the cow. I'll see that these things are done —"

"In exchange for . . . what?" She didn't know why she said it. She wanted to make him angry. It was her defense against him.

"For a kiss every night for the rest of our lives."

"Can't you get it through your head that I don't even . . . like you?"

"Shhh . . . hh. Shhh . . . Don't lie, my Nightrose." He bent closer. Under slanting black brows his eyes were clear and searching. His lips moved against her cheek while she struggled desperately to keep her wits about her. "I'm afraid I overwhelmed you. I know I'm going too fast, but I don't play games, Katy. When I find something I want, I go after it."

The arrogance of his words sent a thrill of excitement through her even while her independent spirit rebelled against them. She made an attempt to get control of her mind, only to find it an impossible task as his lips traveled over her forehead to her eyelids and then down her cheek to her mouth.

"Kiss me. Kiss me like I know you can." He pressed his mouth softly to hers, nibbled, caressed, and possessed. He raised his head and looked searchingly into her eyes. "I won't rush you into anything, but I intend to have you — make no mistake about it. Now kiss me, so I can go see how Mary is making out."

Confusion darkened Katy's eyes. She felt as if she had been run over by a lumber wagon. Her lips formed the word no, but it didn't come out of her mouth. She found herself giving quick answer to the gentle, tender kisses his lips pressed upon hers. A warm tide of contentment came over her as she realized there was no threat to his kiss. Her mouth trembled under his.

"Good night, love," he breathed against her lips.

The eyes that looked into hers glowed, sending her senses reeling. She wondered what strange madness possessed her to allow him to kiss her and for her to kiss him back. It was even more frightening to realize that it had been a most delightful interlude. But now it was over. His hands were on her shoulders, yet he was so close she could feel his breath on her wet lips.

"What are you thinking, Nightrose?" he whispered, his eyes searching hers. "Tell me before I go."

"I . . . was just wondering if you've . . . had measles."

He laughed and hugged her so tightly she could scarcely breathe.

"Are you worried about me?"

"No!"

"Don't worry, sweetheart. I've had measles."
He kissed her hard on the lips and stepped off
the porch. "See you in the morning," he called
from the darkness.

CHAPTER
Seven

It was middle of the afternoon. Mary was sitting at the table with her journal open to the first blank page. She could hear Theresa's happy laughter and Katy's voice coming from beneath the big elm tree where Rowe had attached the rope for the swing.

"Hold on, ladybug, you're going up to the sky."

Hearing the laughter in her sister's voice, Mary breathed a sigh of relief. The two people she loved the most were safe and happy . . . for the moment. Lately, Katy had been either strangely quiet or unusually waspish. She was still determined to leave Trinity at the first opportunity. Mary dreaded leaving, not only because Roy would be angry if he came back and she and Theresa were not here, but because it was comforting to know that they were under the protection of Rowe and Mr. Weston.

Mary didn't know what had taken place between her sister and Rowe on the night the wagons arrived, but since that time Katy had avoided him as if he had the plague. When Mary talked about how Rowe was bringing the town to life again, Katy remained tight-lipped and silent, refusing to acknowledge that Rowe had unusual organizational abilities, or that he was a man who was firmly in control.

Mary sighed again. Katy was fighting her attraction to the big dark man, and there was nothing she could do to help her. She moistened the lead in the pencil with her tongue and began to write in the journal.

Trinity, June 22, 1874.

The past two weeks have brought many changes to Trinity. The more than thirty miners who have come here are rough and lonely men. Most of them have families in Bannack or Virginia City and will bring them here if the work lasts. Mr. Weston, the foreman, said there is a chance the stage will be rerouted to come through Trinity. Rowe wants to make Trinity into a supply and banking center for the ranchers that he is sure will come after the mines play out.

The outbreak of measles has not been as bad as Rowe and Mr. Weston had feared. Only seven men have come down so far. Mr. Weston is one of them. He was awfully sick last night. I stayed with him until Rowe came at midnight to walk me home. This morning he was better. His fever broke and he wanted something to eat.

The blacksmith, John Beecher, is back and has set up shop. He was surprised that we were still here. He said that most of the miners that left here have gone on west. He has not heard anything of Roy.

Two Chinese men are doing laundry. The cook is a colored man. The men call him Belly Robber. The saloon is open in the evenings. The only rowdiness has been a few fistfights. Rowe and Mr. Weston have been able to keep order so far.

A freighter named Ashland came in yesterday with six wagons and a string of mules. He'll haul the ore to the smelter at Bay Horse. Right away one of his men got into a fight with a miner.

Rowe sees to it that we have wood for our cookstove and that the two water barrels just outside the side door are kept full in case of fire. We also use the barrel water for washing, but carry fresh drinking water from the well. Every few days the camp cook brings us fresh meat, either elk or deer.

Rowe comes by each evening. Theresa is terribly fond of him. Maybe too fond. She has stopped asking about Roy.

Katy is my worry. She's resentful of the things Rowe does for us and at times is extremely rude to him, which is so unlike her. It doesn't seem to bother Rowe as much as it does me. I don't have Katy's desire to go back to Laramie to work in the orphanage. I feel safe with Mr. Weston and Rowe. I could make a living here for me and Theresa by selling baked goods. If the town prospers,

Katy could open a school. But I'll not stay here if Katy is set against it.

I'm ashamed to say that I seldom think of my husband anymore. Roy has been gone for almost three months. I hope he is all right, but, God forgive me, I no longer care if he comes back or not.

Katy stopped the swing and Theresa slid off the plank seat and lifted her dress.

"I got to pee-pee, Aunt Katy."

"Not here! Go inside and use the chamber pot."

"You used to let me pee-pee out here," Theresa said and pulled her dress higher.

"That was before men came to town, ladybug," Katy said firmly. "Put your dress down and go in the house."

"It ain't a house. It's a *store!*" Theresa said, determined to have the last word. "I want to pee-pee right here."

Katy shrugged. "If you want to show your behind to the men, go ahead."

"They're not looking. So there!"

"How do you know?" Katy sat down in the swing. "There's one over there under the wagon. And the one fixing the roof of the store was looking this way. Go ahead, ladybug, it's your hinder they'll see, not mine."

"Oh, all right." Theresa dropped her skirt, put her small fists on her hips and stomped off toward the funerary.

A low laugh bubbled out of Katy. She gripped the ropes and pushed with her feet until she was swinging back and forth. She thought with a sudden pang of the times the child had tried to get Roy's attention and failed. She didn't lack for attention now. She had become the darling of the town. The men doted on her. Rowe built the swing; Hank Weston brought her a small hoop and showed her how to roll it. Anton Hooker made her a beanbag out of a mink pelt and came by at least once a day to toss it to her. She made a daily trip to the cookhouse for a treat, usually a handful of raisins.

The swing carried Katy higher and higher. The breeze lifted her skirts to her knees, cooled her face, and tugged at her hair. The swing made her a little homesick for the plantation down on the Tallapoosa River in Alabama. She closed her eyes and thought about magnolia trees, green grass, and tall glasses of lemonade.

Suddenly, an arm as strong as a steel band was flung around her waist and she was held against a hard chest with her feet dangling a foot from the ground. The only sound she made was a grunt when the air left her lungs. A quick turn of her head brought her cheek up against Rowe's chin.

"What the hell are you doing? Put me down!"

"Tut, tut. Don't swear, my love. I've been trying to catch you alone for days."

"I'm not alone. Rowe . . . put me down."

"Not until you say you'll come with me. I want to show you something."

"I've things to do."

"Something more important than being with me?"

His lips were actually nuzzling the nape of her neck. She leaned as far to the side as was possible, but they followed, and nipped her ear lobe.

"Stop that!"

He laughed. She could feel the vibration from his chest on her back and the warm puffs of breath on her ear.

"Katy, Katy. Why didn't I find you sooner? How old are you? I'd have married you at twelve. We could have had six children by now."

"Bullfoot! Let me go, or . . . I'll shoot you."

"No you won't." His cheek was against hers.

"I will! Dammit, I will!"

"You don't have the Derringer. I was watching while you were swinging Theresa and your skirt didn't sag."

"You were spying! You're a . . . sneak."

"Yeah, I am. I know when you blow out the lamp and go to bed. I know when you go to the privy and how long you stay there."

"That's . . . that's awful!" Katy was getting short of breath. Her heart was pounding so hard that she was sure he could feel it against his chest.

"Are you going with me, Nightrose?"

"It seems I have no choice, and . . . stop calling me that silly name."

"It isn't silly. It's beautiful . . . as you are." He walked forward until her feet touched the ground. "I hate giving up this advantage. I warn you, I'm going to watch and catch you in the swing again."

As soon as Katy's hand left the rope Rowe caught it in his as if he feared she would escape.

"As the owner of this great metropolis, you must be needed somewhere. The man by the wagon's looking this way. He wants to talk to you."

Rowe followed her gaze. "That's the freighter, Ashland. He's looking at you. Stay clear of him."

"Why? He doesn't look any worse than the rest of your employees — Hank Weston included. Anton looks a little more respectable."

Rowe's sable eyes hardened, and when he spoke, it was in a tone that revealed his irritation at the comparison.

"Hank is ten times the man that one is, and the best there is when it comes to using blasting powder. Art Ashland is a hard-living, self-centered man who'll fight at the drop of a hat. What's more, he has the reputation of being less than kind to women."

"Then why did you hire him?"

"Because he's the best freighter I know. He'll take a load where nine out of ten would fail. What he does outside his job is his business unless it concerns something of mine." His tone gave her no doubt that he considered *her* one of his possessions. "Stay away from Ashland. If he bothers you or Mary, let me know."

"I can take care of myself," she said with a toss of her head. Then added, "Mary and Theresa too."

"You stubborn little mule. Can't you get it into your pretty little head that you wouldn't stand a chance against a man like him? You don't have to take care of yourself now. I said I will do it and I will."

"And who will protect me from you, O mighty warrior?"

The hard-edged line of his jaw and the sudden narrowing of his eyes warned her that the question had made him angry. It stopped her from saying anything more. She turned her head, tilted her chin, and gave him a view of her profile.

"Keep it up, Katy. I'm already tempted to spank your bottom." She heard his breath hiss through his teeth. "You've been on your own for so long that you think it's a weakness to depend on me. In fact, it's the natural and right thing for you to do, whether you admit it or not."

His voice was dangerously soft, his smoldering look was pinning her to the ground. Katy couldn't stop the wave of apprehension that caused a shiver to travel the length of her spine. It was strange, she thought, how the same voice could be so full of laughter one moment, and so grating in its harshness the next. But that didn't keep the retort that formed in her mind from coming out her mouth.

"So you're less than kind to women too. I'm not surprised."

"My woman will love me enough to respect my wishes. I won't have to beat her."

"I pity her."

"Then you pity yourself."

"It seems that you've made up your mind about me," she said, after an intense silence. "And as far as you're concerned, I have nothing to say about it. Is that right?"

"I've made up my mind that I want you, but you'll have plenty to say about it . . . no doubt." He added the last dryly. "I have pride too, Katy. I'll not force myself on you if you find me repulsive."

The look he gave her was far from gentle. The teasing light was gone from his dark eyes; his mouth beneath the raven black mustache was grim. Suddenly Katy regretted her unguarded words and wanted desperately to see him smile again.

"You can get me madder than a wet hen quicker than anyone I've ever known." The edges of her lips curled upward.

The harshness started to leave his face. His eyes crinkled at the corners and some of the stiffness went from his body.

"At least you're not indifferent to me. I'd rather you be angry at me than to ignore me," he teased.

"If it's true that we lived another life before this one, you must have been a dog and I a cat."

His grin broadened to a full smile. "If you were a cat, I was a cat, and we did our part to see that the species survived." The glitter in his eyes made her feel as if she were riding high in the swing. At first she didn't get the meaning of his words, and then, instead of being offended, she burst out laughing.

It was a reaction he hadn't anticipated. He watched in fascination. The sound of her spontaneous laughter was as clear and as true as a bell. He loved to hear her laugh. He liked the way she held her head, the way her hair shone in the sun, but most of all he liked the way she laughed and the way her eyes reflected all her emotions. They sparkled now like moonlight on clear, still water.

"You are exasperating, my Nightrose. No . . . don't argue," he said when she opened her mouth to protest the name. "Let's go before we start fighting again."

"I'll tell Mary."

"I already did. Do you feel up to walking more than a mile?"

She grinned up at him. "If you can, I can."

His smile spread that horrible charm over his face again. They walked to the creek and then along the stony bank. Smiling still, he pulled her along beside him, walking between her and the dense woods, keeping firm hold of her hand. They shared a companionable silence. The sun fell warm and golden on their faces and uncovered heads. His hair shone blue-black like the wing of a raven, hers like fine silk threads of gold. He adjusted his longer steps to Katy's free-swinging stride. It was the first time they had walked together since that awful day she and Mary had helped him from the saloon to the funerary after he had been shot. Modo came out from under the bushes and trailed behind them.

Katy glanced up at Rowe. No longer smiling, he was as watchful as a stallion protecting his herd. His eyes searched each side of the path without moving his head. His hand held hers gently, but she felt alertness in him. He moved as warily as a wolf, studying the landscape ahead from all angles.

Farther along the creek the trees grew close to the bank, shutting out the breeze, and a film of perspiration dotted Katy's forehead and upper lip. When they came to where the creek bed narrowed and flowed over a bed of solid rock, Rowe swung Katy up in his arms and waded across. She accepted the action without protest. He grinned at her as he set her down on the other side, but said nothing. He took her hand again and they walked into the woods. Without hesitation the brown dog followed.

The quiet of the forest was awe-inspiring. In such a place the mind becomes a vast reservoir of impressions — shadows, sun-patterns, ferns, and the scent of damp leaves. The call of a whippoorwill broke the silence. Then she heard the whispers of squirrels scampering in the dry leaves and the scolding of bluejays in the upper branches of the trees. Surrounding Katy was an aura of timelessness. It was almost as if she were walking through the years to reach the present time. She wiggled her hand until her fingers could interlace with Rowe's, and their palms come together. A warmth and sense of connection pulsed between them. *This had happened before!* The instant flash of memory did not jolt her as it had that time before. She accepted it and wrapped her thumb more firmly around his.

He did not look down; she did not look up. They walked on.

Rowe stopped and put his lips close to Katy's ear. "We must be very quiet from here on," he whispered and motioned for Modo to stay.

"Why?" She mouthed the word.

"You'll see."

Rowe moved ahead of her, parting the foliage that grew profusely along the bank of a small lake. He got down on his knees and pulled her down beside him.

"Lie down and look under these bushes."

Without question, Katy stretched out beside him and looked out onto water, so clear and still that the trees above them were reflected there.

"Oh," she breathed. "Oh, how beautiful! We had swans back home."

"They're not swans. They're geese."

She turned her head to look at him and found her face close to his. "Geese?"

"Wild honkers. Their necks are not as long as the swan's. He's the gander. He stands watch while his mate hatches the eggs. Here she comes with their little goslings."

A large white goose, followed by six small, fluffy goslings, came out of the grasses that grew in the shallow water. The gander arched his neck and swam toward her. She went to him. They touched beaks, then he uttered a triumphant note that was echoed by his mate.

"They mate for life," Rowe whispered. "For some reason, one of them could go no farther north to the nesting ground, and they stopped here. By the time the summer is over, the young ones will be strong enough to fly south."

"Do you think one of them can't fly?"

"It's possible that one of them had an injured wing. If so, it's healed now. I was here yesterday and saw both of them fly a short distance. They could leave now but for the goslings."

"I heard the honkers flying over this spring," Katy whispered. They were lying close, shoulders touching. "How did you find them?"

"I was along the creek when I heard the babbling cry of the gander warning his mate of danger. I knew there was a small lake here. It's marked on my map. I blundered onto it and scared them. I didn't want to make that mistake today. I wanted you to see them."

"Someone from town will find them and shoot them."

"Not from our camp. I've already told the man who hunts meat for the cook that he can come here to fish, but that's all."

She turned back to watch the little family. The gander was feeding on the grasses while keeping a watchful eye on the goslings. Katy lay still, suddenly terribly conscious of the long, lean body lying next to hers.

"You're full of surprises," she whispered, not

looking at him although she knew his eyes were on her profile.

"Why do you say that?"

"I didn't think you were the type to get pleasure out of something as simple as a pair of lost honkers."

"There's a lot about me that would surprise you."

She turned her head slowly. Her round blue eyes looked into eyes so dark that she could see her reflection there.

"For instance?"

"It might surprise you to know that I'm using every bit of my self-control to keep from kissing you. And that I want you for my mate. I will stay with you, and protect you, as the gander stayed with his mate."

"Maybe he was the one who couldn't fly, and she stayed with him." It wasn't exactly what she had intended to say.

"Like you did when I was hurt and couldn't help myself."

"My helping you? Is that what's given you all of these . . . crazy notions?"

"They're not crazy and you know it. But no. I had these thoughts since I first saw you. One night I was bathing in the creek, and you brought the cow down for water. When you returned with the buckets, I followed you back up the path to be sure you were all right. I knew then that you and I were destined to belong to each other."

Katy made a move to get up. His arms went

around her but held her gently so that she could slip away if she wanted to. She sank back down, panic fading from her eyes. He lifted the heavy rope of blond hair from her back and looped it over her shoulder.

"Don't be afraid of me, Katy. I'll never force you —"

"I'm not afraid." Her voice was not quite steady.

He turned on his side facing her and pillowed his head on his bent arm.

"Lie beside me and tell me what you're thinking about when you look off toward the mountains with such yearning in your pretty eyes." Wisps of inky black hair lay on his forehead, matching heavy, straight eyebrows and a neatly trimmed mustache.

Without quite realizing it, she turned, leaned on her elbows, and looked down at him.

"I'm thinking about a place where I can walk through a crowd without a hand reaching out to grab my arm, pinch my backside, or whisper a lurid suggestion. I'm thinking that it would be nice to wear a soft gown again without a pocket for the Derringer. I'm hoping that when Roy Stanton comes back he'll not drag Mary and Theresa deeper into the wilds. And I dream of having a permanent home where I can lay out my ivory hairbrush and trinket box on the dresser scarves my mother embroidered —"

His hand moved up and down her braid while she was talking, and he brushed his face with the end that was tied with a thin faded ribbon when he said, "What else, Katy?"

"I want Theresa to grow up in a place where there is more than mud and rock and useless dreams of glitter." Her voice trailed and she looked over his head.

Something was happening to her. She begrudgingly admitted that she enjoyed being here, but this other thing . . . this feeling of being totally alive when she was with him, this seeing his face behind her closed eyelids disturbed her. And why in the world was she babbling on like a fool?

Rowe sensed the change immediately. "Tell me about your home. I've been in Alabama."

"During the war?"

"Yes."

"Then you know it was laid to waste by the Union soldiers."

"Yes." There was no use in denying it. "A terrible waste. I was a blockade runner. I brought supplies to the Union Army through the port at Mobile."

She was quiet for a long while, then breathed deeply. "It was a terrible war . . . for both sides."

"War has been hell down through the ages."

The geese on the lake began to babble, and Kate checked to see what was disturbing them. The parents were herding the goslings out of the water.

"They're going," she said absently, then looked at him. "We'd better go too."

"Yes," he said but made no move to get up.

133

"It's so peaceful here. Like we were in another world."

"But we're not. Mary will be worrying about me."

"She knows you're with me. Katy, kiss me before we go."

She shook her head slowly.

"Kiss me or I'll have to kiss you. Hadn't you rather be in control?" His eyes on hers moved to her mouth. "I'll not hold you." He picked up her hand and began kissing her fingertips one at a time. Her eyes were peeking at him through that golden frame of lashes. "Kiss me, love. Don't you want to?"

"You're a very persistent man," she whispered. "Kissing is . . . an expression of deep feelings."

"I know."

Katy lowered her head. Her lips touched his only fleetingly. "There," she breathed.

"Do you call that a kiss?" His eyes were teasing her. "Can't you do better than that?"

"I've not had much practice."

"Thank God! Practice on me. We could become expert kissers in only a lesson or two." He pulled her over so she was lying on his chest. "Someday we're going to lie like this in a soft bed. Your hair will be loose —" His palm caressed the back of her head. "There'll be nothing between us. We'll be so close that you'll not be able to tell where you leave off and I begin." His voice was husky; his breath was coming faster. She could feel the heavy beat of his heart against her soft breast.

As if detached from the physical world, she fitted her mouth to his again and turned her head so that her nose lay alongside his. The silky hair above his upper lip tickled her nose. She grinned against his mouth, then raised her head to look down at him with merry devilment in her eyes.

"Your mustache tickles."

"I'll shave it off."

"Don't." Her voice was a caress and she stroked the dark hair with the tip of her finger.

"Katy, get on with it. You're driving me insane!" He felt her stiffen when his arms tightened, and loosened them to hold her lightly. "Kiss me, sweetheart. Kiss me as if I were your lover returned from the war."

Katy placed her closed mouth against his again, not quite believing that she was doing such a thing. His lips were softer than she remembered. The silky hair of his mustache teased her face. She moved her head, sliding her lips over his. His parted; hers followed. Instinctively, she deepened the kiss and explored his mouth without haste. The tip of her tongue stroked his lips, sweetly, hesitantly, but did not enter his mouth. Never had she kissed with this freedom before. Her mind fed on the new sensations created by his scent and the taste of his mouth.

Her hand moved up to cup his cheek as if it were the most natural thing in the world for her to be lying across his chest, her mouth against his, her breasts flattened against his chest. Suddenly she realized that she was spinning off into a world she'd never even glimpsed before. She felt as if she had become an extension of him and a wild yearning possessed her. A need to fill her lungs caused her to lift her head. Her eyes lost themselves in the dark, smoldering depths of his.

"Katy! Katy, my love. I knew it would be like this —" His voice came softly through the roar in her ears.

She stared at him in almost total panic, then pushed herself away from him and got to her feet.

"I've got to go."

Rowe stood. "All right, sweetheart. We'll go if you want to."

He spoke to her back. Katy had already started back through the woods.

CHAPTER
Eight

Rowe held Katy's hand and they walked back through the forest without speaking. They both knew that something irreversible had happened. Rowe had expected passion to flare between them, but even he was shocked by its power. Katy was surprised by the attraction she felt for this strange dark man, and her common sense fought against it.

When they came to the creek, he lifted her in his arms, held her against his chest, and waded across to the other side. She slid slowly down his body when he removed his arm from beneath her bent knees. He held her against him for a long moment, his arms wrapped around her, his cheek pressed to hers, then he turned his head and kissed her. She did not protest the kiss — in fact she welcomed it. She wanted to fill her arms with him, to nuzzle the soft, silky mustache, to feel the flat rough planes of his cheeks that needed shaving twice a day.

His lips caressed and clung with a leisurely sweetness that held her enthralled. Half-shut eyes looked into hers when he lifted his head. The pit of her stomach quivered with restlessness as her gaze wavered beneath his direct stare. Small puffs of air wafted from her wet and parted lips as she tried to regulate her breathing.

"You feel it too?"

"Yes." The whispered word was an admission she hadn't even made to herself.

"It's something we have no control over, my Nightrose." His lips touched her nose with a butterfly kiss. "Don't say anything," he cautioned, took her hand and walked on.

He didn't speak again until they were going up the path from the creek to the town.

"I've another surprise."

Katy looked up and let her breath out in a shaky laugh. "Another surprise?"

"Before we left, one of my men rode in to tell me a train of five wagons was headed this way and would be here by sundown. It's about that time."

"More miners?"

"No. Settlers. I had a sign put up on the Oregon Trail saying that settlers were welcome in Trinity."

"What will they do here?"

"I won't know till they arrive. Trinity needs all the people it can get if it's going to survive after the mine plays out."

"You think it will?"

"Eventually."

"Then you'll leave."

"I'll not be going far. I like this part of the country."

Katy and Rowe came out onto the road where a group of people had gathered to meet the wagons that were approaching. Katy tried to slip her hand from Rowe's, but he gripped it tighter, refusing to let it go.

Theresa jerked loose from Mary and ran to Rowe. "Mr. Rowe! Where did you and Aunt Katy go? Do you see the wagons comin'? Will they have a little girl for me to play with?"

Rowe was forced to release Katy's hand when Theresa wrapped her arms about his knees.

"I don't know, honey. But we'll soon find out."

"I'll even play with a *boy* if there ain't no girls!"

Rowe laughed. "When you get older you'll like boys."

"I will not! Do you like girls?"

Rowe looked over Theresa's head. His laughing eyes snared Katy's. "You bet!"

Katy's face turned crimson, and Rowe laughed aloud, gripping her shoulder with his free hand. When she became conscious of the speculative looks she was receiving from the small crowd of men, she was acutely aware of the fact that Rowe's proprietary attitude toward her was creating the impression that she belonged to him.

"Come on, ladybug." Katy grabbed Theresa's hand. "Let's get over there by your mother and out of the way."

They crossed the road and stepped up onto the porch of the funerary where Mary waited. The wagons, pulled by tired teams, came slowly into town. Dust stirred up by the iron-rimmed wheels drifted in the light breeze.

The lead wagon, pulled by oxen, was a clumsy affair with a tattered canvas top. A plain-faced woman was driving. On the seat beside her sat a young girl and a boy of ten or twelve years. A man in a fancy suit rode beside the wagon on a long-legged, fine-blooded horse. He tipped his hat to Mary and Katy as he passed, his eyes lingering on the face of each of the women.

"There's a dandy for you. I've seen his type before," Katy murmured dryly.

The next two wagons were also driven by women. A large man-sized woman with a wide-brimmed straw hat on her head drove one. Her knees were spread and a booted foot rested against the headboard. A young woman sat on the seat beside her and another stood in the wagon behind them. She smiled and waved as they passed.

The other wagon was the finest Katy and Mary had seen in a long while. The large dray horses pulling it were driven by a rather frail-looking woman who held the reins limply, allowing the animals to merely follow the wagon ahead. A tiny girl with her finger in her mouth snuggled against her side.

The fourth wagon, pulled by a span of mules, was almost as long and as heavy as a freight wagon. A dark, slender man in a black suit sat on the wagon seat. His hair and his beard were black and neatly trimmed.

The lead wagon stopped. The man on the horse

rode ahead to where Rowe waited in front of the saloon.

Squeals of female laughter came from the last wagon in line. The back canvas was pulled aside, the tailgate dropped, and three gaudily dressed women jumped down. They completely ignored Mary and Katy on the porch of the funerary and hurried along the road to where the men had gathered to watch the wagons arrive.

Mary dug her elbow into Katy's ribs when she saw that their dresses were sleeveless and their legs were bare from the knees down.

"Well, I never! They're nothing but . . . hussies!"

"The whores are back. There'll be rejoicing in Trinity tonight," Katy replied dryly.

"Ruby! Goldie! Come back here!" The commanding voice came from a woman with flaming red hair who climbed backward out of the wagon. She wore a bustle on the back of her skirt, and her waist was tightly cinched with a corset. "Pearl!"

"Fiddle, Lizzibeth. There's men here!" The "girls" headed for the group in front of the saloon, paying no mind to the woman trying to catch up with them.

"Girls!" Then, "Gawddammit!" The red-headed woman tripped on a rut in the road and saved herself from falling by grabbing hold of a wagon wheel. She was more modestly dressed than the "girls." Her legs were covered, but a large expanse of her bosom was exposed. Holding up the skirt of her dark blue satin dress she went to the front of the wagon. "Stay here," she barked when the young girl driving the wagon protested that she wanted to go with the others; then she marched on down the line of wagons.

"Ruby, Goldie, and Pearl couldn't be their real names," Mary said.

Katy scarcely heard her sister's comment. She was watching the women walk brazenly up to Rowe and the miners. One man, on coming out of the saloon, and seeing the women, headed straight for the horse tank to duck his head. He slicked his hair down with both hands, and grinning like a tomcat, grabbed one of the unresisting women about the waist and swung her around. She shrieked and slapped at him playfully.

"This one's mine!" one of the women yelled and threw herself in Rowe's arms.

To Katy's irritation, he merely laughed. After a few comments to the woman, he gently peeled her away from him.

More men had joined the group by the time the older redhead in the blue satin dress reached them. She seemed to know that Rowe was the man in charge. They moved slightly apart from the others and she talked earnestly to him. Katy saw him pointing to the long building at the end of town that was known as the "girlie house." The red-headed woman waved at her driver. The wagon pulled out of line and on down the road.

"A new business has come to town," Katy commented, as if talking to herself.

"It was bound to happen," Mary said.

Rowe walked down the line of wagons, talking to each of the drivers for a few minutes and directing them to a place where they could camp temporarily. As he came nearer the funerary, Katy slipped inside and Mary followed.

"Don't you want to meet the people, Katy? It's been a long time since we've had a chance to talk to another woman."

"What would we talk about? How much do you charge for an hour in bed, Ruby? Well, blast my hide, Goldie, your knees are sunburned! Pearl, may I borrow your rouge pot?" Katy recited the words in her play-acting voice, still seeing in her mind's eye the bare-legged woman clinging to Rowe and stung by his reaction to her.

"The other women seemed decent."

"You go meet them."

"I want to go too," Theresa wailed.

"You can come with me. I've got to see about Mr. Weston."

Theresa stomped her foot. "I don't want to go to that old sickhouse. I saw a little girl. I want to ask her to swing in my swing."

"Don't stomp your foot at me, young lady," Mary said sternly. "You're getting a little too big for your britches lately."

The child's face puckered. "I want to play —"

"I know you do, but that's no excuse to be sassy. You'll get to play with the little girl. After she and her mother are settled for the night, you and I will go over to meet them. How's that?"

143

Katy sat down in the rocker after Mary and Theresa left. Her mind was a buzzing hive of confusion. Out of the chaotic thoughts came the realization that she had to be careful of Garrick Rowe. Why was it that she could see him so much more clearly when she was away from him? It was plain to her now that all of his talk about "Night-rose" and knowing her in another life was bunkum he'd dreamed up to get what he wanted — a few hours of diversion in this dull place. He'd not need her now. Ruby, Goldie, or Pearl would be happy to entertain him. Katy closed her eyes against the thought of his saying, "Kiss me, Goldie." *Of course he wouldn't have to ask!*

Her cheeks burned with embarrassment when she thought of how easily she had succumbed to his charm, how he had lain on his back in the grass and she had bent over him, kissing him, all of her own free will merely because he had asked her. She uttered a small groan of humiliation as she thought of what she had done.

The sound of Modo's toenails on the plank porch reached her. The dog passed the open door and lay down next to the building. A close relationship existed between the man and the dog although Rowe seldom spoke to him. Most of the commands were given by hand signals. Mary had asked Rowe about the dog's name. He had said it was short for Quasimodo, the hunchback in Victor Hugo's novel. He had gone on to tell her that the author was a friend of his mother's. Mary was impressed, mostly because she loved the writ-

144

ten word and because she greatly admired the author of a book, any book.

Katy's thoughts drifted back to the wagon train that came in today. Only one mounted man was riding with it. Did that mean the scare-talk about Indians and outlaws was only that — scare-talk to keep her, Mary, and Theresa here as a lure to bring other women to town? No doubt the small, slim, dark man could handle a gun, and the big woman in the straw hat looked as if she could lick a bear with a willow switch. But at that, three guns against outlaws or Indians wouldn't amount to much.

It would be interesting to know why these people had split from the wagon train to come to a desolate place like Trinity.

A sudden desire to see the last of Garrick Rowe caused Katy to remember the four horses that had belonged to the men she and Mary had buried. She might be able to hitch two of them to their wagon. The measles outbreak was about over. If only she could hear from that worthless Roy Stanton, Mary might be willing to leave.

Feeling lonely and miserable, Katy sat in the rocker and waited for her sister to return.

Mary and Theresa walked down the street past the men talking to the bare-legged women. The men tipped their hats respectfully to Mary, but the women ignored her. The wagons were moving to the flat area next to the stone building, and some of the miners were helping the women unhitch the teams. The dark, slim man had gone back to help the woman in the fancy wagon before he unhitched his own team. She stood by, clutching the hand of the little girl who hid her face in her mother's skirt each time someone looked at her.

Mary, like Katy back at the funerary, wondered what had happened to bring this mixture of people to Trinity.

At the livery Mary and Theresa turned up a path that had been hollowed out by water washing down the mountainside. The small cabin that housed the three men who were still infectious with measles nestled back on the hillside amid the trees. It was windowless, much like the one the Stantons and Katy had lived in the winter before. The front and back doors stood open to allow the breeze to circulate. The former owner had thrown out bits of broken crockery, and Theresa had entertained herself by digging up pieces of colored glass.

"Find some more pieces of that pretty blue glass, honey, and we'll hang them on a string in the window."

"When can we go see the little girl?"

"We'll stop by on our way back," Mary promised. She left Theresa playing in the dirt and went to within a few feet of the cabin door. "Hello," she called. "Is it all right for me to come in?"

Hank came to the door and leaned weakly against the frame for a moment before stepping out into the yard.

"The others are sleeping. They seem to be all right." He sat down on a stump that had been used for cutting wood.

"You should be in bed, Mr. Weston." Mary noted that his face was freshly shaven and that the telltale measle eruptions were fading from his skin.

"If I lie in there any longer, I'll scratch myself to death, ma'am."

"Would you like for me to put more soda water on your back?"

"I'd be obliged. I was goin' to ask Rowe to do it, but I take it he'll be busy."

"You saw the wagons come into town?" Mary asked after she had brought the wash dish and the bag of soda from the cabin.

"I was sittin' out here on the stump gettin' some air." Hank removed his shirt. "I heard women squealin' and carryin' on. I knew it wasn't you or Miss Katy."

"No, it wasn't me or Katy —"

Mary's voice disappeared into silence as she moved around behind him and began to dab at his shoulders and back with the paste she had made with the soda. Hank was not a young man. Mary judged him to be past thirty. Damp, dark red hair curled across his forehead and down on the nape of his neck. The skin that stretched across his muscled shoulders and back was bronzed like the skin on his face and arms. His chest was broad and hard and roped with muscles. Tightly curled dark hair spread across it and vee'd down to a flat and hard abdomen. He was a man of tremendous strength. Roy's body was almost feminine compared to this man's.

"Most of the new people are women. I saw only two men," Mary said, feeling like she had to say something.

"Probably widows from a train going west. Most women can't handle the trip alone." He held his arm away from his body so that she could reach the eruptions on his side. Mary smoothed the paste over them and moved around in front of him to dab at his chest. "I can do that, ma'am. It's the places I can't reach that drive me crazy." She surrendered the cloth and held the basin while he sloppily covered his chest with the soda water. "That feels good —"

"You should lie down and rest, Mr. Weston. I'm worried that you'll have a back-set."

When he laughed, Mary wondered why she had never noticed his white, even teeth and the creases that fanned out from eyes the color of a cloudless sky, when he smiled.

"My ma used to say, 'Now, Hank, you'll get a back-set.' I've not heard that or had anyone worry about me for a long time, ma'am."

"Worrying is what Katy says I do best."

"I don't know as I agree with that." Hank slipped his shirt over his head. "Feels good to have clean duds again."

"Did you tell the laundryman to boil the clothes apart from the others?" Mary reached around and pulled the shirt down over his wet back.

"Yes, ma'am. How long will I have to stay up here? I'm getting sick of this place."

"Another day or two and you'll be fit to come back to town." Mary threw the water from the basin out on the ground and set the pan on the step beside the door. "I'd better be going. I promised Theresa we'd not stay long."

Hank looked over his shoulder to see Theresa squatting down digging in the dirt. "The little one don't seem to be in no hurry. Talk to me a while, Mrs. Stanton." He pulled a flat gold watch from his pocket and looked at the time. "It'll be an hour yet before our suppertime."

After Hank pulled the watch from his pocket, Mary didn't hear another word he said. Words locked in her throat by a strong welling of fear. Only when Hank moved to return the watch to his pocket was she jarred from her shock. She grabbed at his wrist, her face tight with shock.

"Ma'am . . . Mary —"

"Where did you get . . . that watch?" Mary heard her voice come out thick and unsteady.

"Why? Have you seen it before?"

Mary nodded, feeling rather sick, nerves dancing like demons in her stomach. "I think so. Open the back . . . please —"

Hank took out his pocketknife and with the tip opened the back of the watch and placed it in her hands. She read the inscription: To Roy from Mamma and Papa — 1862.

Mary drew a long, shuddering breath. "It's my husband's watch. Where did you get it?"

Hank stood up and gently pressed her down on the stump where he had been sitting.

"Ach, lass. I be hurtin' to tell you —"

"Roy is dead, isn't he?" Mary said with her head bent over the watch. "He'd not part with this. He'd have let me and Theresa starve before he'd sell it."

"Yes, lass," he said simply. He knelt down beside her and held the hand that held the watch.

"Did you kill him?"

"No. I swear. Anton and I found him. We rode out from Bay Horse a couple of months back headed for Bannack. We found him along the trail, shot in the back. His pockets had been stripped and there were no papers to let us know who he was. We dug a grave and when we moved him to put him in it, I saw the watch under him. The killers had missed it or he had hid it from them. I'm plumb sorry, Mary."

"Did he have light-colored hair and a small goatee? Was he wearing a fancy vest with white braid stitched in a scroll pattern?"

"Yes, ma'am, he was. And I remember that he was a right handsome feller who took pride in looking good. I figured he was a gambler after I looked at his hands. They'd not done much hard work."

Mary sucked air into her lungs with jerky little gasps. She looked past the man kneeling beside her to where Theresa played in the dirt. Roy's death would be no big loss to their daughter. She would not grieve for him because she scarcely

150

knew him. Mary turned her head and focused wide, tearless eyes on Hank's face.

"Thank you for . . . burying him."

"I can take you there . . . someday."

"No," she said quickly. "I'd rather remember him as he was before we came to the gold camps, not buried in a lonely grave beside a trail."

Hank knew the woman was hurting, but she was holding it inside her. Had she loved that dressed-up dandy who had left her and her daughter to fend for themselves while he chased a rainbow? Anton had figured the gambler had run into someone slightly less clever with cards than he was, and that someone had followed him out of Bay Horse and killed him to get back his money. Of course, Hank couldn't tell Mary he thought she was better off without him.

"Roy was not a bad man. He wanted so much to go back home with gold in his pockets and take up life as it used to be. That way of life was over a long time ago, but Roy refused to believe it. And now he's gone —" she murmured. She looked into Hank's anxious face, wiggled her hand out of his, and held out the watch. "You should have it for burying him."

"Lord, no! Keep it, lass," he said fervently, folding her finger around the watch. He stood, drew Mary to her feet, and watched her slip the timepiece in her pocket.

"Thank you for what you did. I know it was unpleasant." She placed her hand on his arm. "Go lie down. I'll be back tomorrow."

"Mary . . . I wish I could walk with you —"

"You can't. Your fever just broke this morning. I'll be all right. For some time now I have suspected that something had happened to him. It was just a feeling I had. I'm kind of numb from the suddenness of finding out, but I think it's a relief to finally know one way or the other. Now Katy and I can make plans."

"You'll not leave?" he asked anxiously.

"I don't know. I'll have to consider what Katy wants to do. She's given up so much for me and Theresa."

"Don't decide anything right away. You know what you have here. Rowe and I owe you for . . . helping with the sick. We'll see to it that you have food for the table and wood for the stove this winter —" he finished lamely, looking down on soft brown hair at the nape of her neck. A spasm of apprehension tightened his chest. She couldn't leave! She couldn't . . . until his work here was done.

"I'll be back tomorrow. Come, Theresa —"

"I didn't find no blue glass yet, Mamma."

"Maybe tomorrow —"

CHAPTER
Nine

Somewhere, the sun was shining, but it certainly wasn't in Trinity. Katy sat in the rocking chair and listened to the rain, driven by gusty blasts of wind, lash the window of the funerary and pound on the tin roof. After three days of unceasing rain, the creek was out of its banks, and the road was a quagmire of mud.

Mary went to check the dishpan she had placed beneath the steady drip that came from the ceiling. She moved it a few inches as the slow stream now traveled down the beam before dropping off into the pan. She checked to make sure the roof wasn't leaking over the beds. When she went back to the window, she saw that riders were coming into town.

"Two horsemen coming in. They look wet and miserable," she said as she watched the horses slogging through the mud.

"Probably are," Katy replied listlessly.

Mary turned and looked at her sister with an inexpressible sadness. During the past week Katy had sunk even deeper into depression. A week ago she and Katy had had their first serious argument. Katy had waited until the morning after

Mary had been told that Roy was dead to speak to her about leaving Trinity.

"There's no reason to stay now," Katy had argued.

"I think there is. Be reasonable, Katy. We can't leave here by ourselves. It wouldn't be wise for two women and a child to be on the trail alone."

"Who said we'd be alone? I've a little money left. We'll hire a couple of men to go with us."

"Why are you so determined to leave here? Is it Rowe you're running away from?"

"Bullfoot! He's a two-bit miner in a two-bit town! Don't you want something better for Theresa than *this?*" Katy had demanded angrily and spread her arms to include the whole town.

"Trinity is only a raw mining town now, Katy, but Rowe has plans —"

"Rowe has plans! Good lord! You *are* gullible if you believe everything that fly-by-night tells you!"

"Thank you, sister, for your confidence in my judgment."

"How are we going to make a living, Mary? Tell me that. It's too late to open the 'girlie house.' Lizzibeth and her girls have already moved in," Katy had said caustically and then muttered, "I'm sure they had a very profitable night."

"I'm sure," Mary had retorted, tight-lipped. After a lengthy silence Mary spoke again. "We could bake pies and bearclaws and sell them to the men."

"Do you know how many pies we'd have to sell to pay for this building we're living in?"

"We can stay here as long as we want. Rowe said so."

"Rowe said so!" Katy's voice had raised until it filled every corner of the room and spilled out into the vacant street. "I'll not be obligated to that man! The Burns family, of which you are one, has always paid their own way. *I'll* not be the one to break the tradition by taking charity from a know-it-all, smooth-talking —"

"All right!" Mary's shout had taken Katy completely by surprise. "We'll move back into that little shack we moved out of if you're so dead-set against accepting a little help. I would like to remind you that Garrick Rowe saved our lives — at considerable risk to his own." Angrily, Mary had snatched clothes from the wall and threw them into her trunk. Suddenly she stopped and broke into a storm of weeping.

"Oh, gosh! I'm sorry, Mary." Katy had put her arms about her sister. "Don't cry. I shouldn't have jumped on you about this when you're all torn up over Roy. We've been here this long, so I guess there's no harm staying a little longer. I'm so mean I don't even know myself anymore."

A week had passed and Katy had not mentioned leaving Trinity again. In fact, Katy had not mentioned much at all. She had gone with Mary to call on Mrs. Hillard and her daughter, Julia, but had not gone out of her way to get to know any of the other women. Her time was spent in

155

the garden or tending the cow or cutting kindling. The floor of the funerary was spotless, or it had been before the rain.

Mary turned from the window. It was quiet in the funerary. The creak of the rockers on the uneven floor was the only sound to break the silence. Katy sat with her head resting against the back, her eyes closed. When Rowe had come to carry Theresa to Mrs. Hillard's so that she could play with Julia, Katy had gone behind the curtain and sat down on her bed until he had gone.

Her sister was hurting, and Mary didn't know what to do about it. Katy, who had always been so full of life, had been moping about since that first night when Hank and Anton came to call. It was so unlike Katy to be silent.

Wanting to do something to take her mind off the problems that bothered her, Mary lit a candle to dispel the gloom, sat down at the table with her journal, and began to write.

Trinity, June 30, 1874.

A week has passed since I learned of Roy's death. I recorded it in the Bible along with the date given me by Hank Weston and Anton Hooker. There is no one but distant relatives to notify back home. I will send letters to them at the first opportunity.

The people who came to Trinity from the Oregon-bound train all have interesting stories. Mr. Longstreet, the man who led the wagons to Trinity, reminds me so much of

Roy. He claims to be from an aristocratic family and is related to General James Longstreet. He acts as if he considers himself superior to his wife. They have a daughter, who is about thirteen, and a boy slightly younger, who is lame. Mrs. Chandler said they were asked to leave the train because their wagon was in such poor condition. Rowe hired him to run the hotel. His wife and children are busy cleaning. I've not seen Mr. Longstreet doing any of the work. Katy and I don't like him.

Mrs. Chandler and her daughters, Flossie and Myrtle, have set up business in the eatery. She was frank about their reason for leaving the train. One of her daughters was caught under the blanket with a married man. He was given ten lashes for adultery by the leaders. Mrs. Chandler switched her daughter, even though she thought they had made a lot of to-do about nothing. The women on the train had forced them to leave.

Lizzibeth and her girls were run out of a mining town southeast of here. They trailed behind the wagon train for protection. They have settled into the "girlie house." They seem a happy lot, but it's beyond me how a woman can do what they do.

Mrs. Hillard seems to be well off. Her husband drowned when they crossed the Bighorn River. Without a man to drive her wagon, keep it in repair, and care for the stock, she was slowing the others down. The leader asked her to leave or take one of the single men for a husband. How mean and cold-hearted some men are. She is a well-educated but timid person. I saw her cross the street so she wouldn't have to pass Mr. Longstreet who was sitting on the hotel porch. Rowe didn't want her in one of the houses on the hill, so for now she lives in the newspaper building.

Mr. Glossberg is a scholarly Jew. He had planned to open a store in Oregon with his wagon load of goods. He left the train when the people had become increasingly hostile to him because he didn't attend their church services. He moved his goods into the mercantile building after he and Rowe came to an agreement on the rent he would pay. I bought a spool of sewing thread the first day he was open for business.

Trinity is on its way to becoming a real town again. If Katy were happy here, I would be content to stay so long as we could find a means of making a living. The Chandlers are baking, so that possibility is out. The measles outbreak is over, and I'm not needed to nurse the sick. Hank keeps telling me that something will turn up. I sure hope so.

A brisk wind came up in the late afternoon and blew the rain clouds away. The sun came out and with it the people of the town. Katy stepped out into the cool, fresh air at the same time Rowe stepped up onto the porch with Theresa in his arms. It was too late for Katy to turn back. Her pride made it impossible for her to be so obvious that she was avoiding him. Her eyes passed over him as she spoke to Theresa.

"Hello, ladybug. Did you decide to come home?"

"Uncle Rowe said I had to."

"Uncle Rowe?" Katy repeated before she could stop herself.

Rowe took an overlong time setting the child on her feet. He gave her a gentle push toward the door.

"Run tell your mama you're back. I want to talk to your Aunt Katy."

"Why?" Theresa inquired from the doorway. "I don't think Aunt Katy likes you. But me and Mamma do."

"I'm glad of that."

Theresa grinned an impish grin that showed the gap in her front teeth. "Can you stay for supper, Uncle Rowe?"

"Not tonight, honey." After Theresa skipped into the house, he turned to Katy and lifted a questioning brow. "You're not going to second the invitation?" Her eyes met his with a small tightening of her mouth which prompted him to ask, "Have you still got the sulks?"

"Yes, I've got the sulks and the mulligrubs." Her voice was thick with exasperation. "I'm damn sick of this place!"

"That's what I want to talk to you about. You need a change."

"I sure do! A permanent one."

He watched her struggle to maintain her bored expression and her indifference to him. She was far more vulnerable than she imagined. It had been so sweet that day at the lake to see her off guard.

"Katy, my sweet one, pull in your claws for just a minute. Anton and I are going to Virginia City tomorrow. I want you to go with us."

Utterly taken back, Katy looked at him with eyes round with surprise. "You'll take me and Mary to Virginia City to catch the stage?"

"No. Just you, and not to catch the stage. We'll have to go on horseback through the mountains. I've already explained it to Mary. She thinks it would do you good to get away for a while."

"You and Mary are making plans for me behind my back. Well, well, that's nice."

"Cut the sarcasm, Katy. Mary is worried about you. It'll take two days to get to Virginia City if we cut through the mountains. I plan to stay three or four days. We'll be gone a week at the most. If we take a wagon and go by road it will take a lot longer."

"Two days and one night. Don't forget the night."

"I haven't. We'll spend it with some friends of mine who have a homestead a little more than halfway. In Virginia City we'll stay in the hotel — separate rooms, of course."

"No."

"No separate rooms?"

"No. I'm not going. Take Ruby, Pearl, or Goldie, then you'll not have to pay for separate rooms."

"Christamighty! Anton will be with us. Are you afraid the trip will be too rough for you?" He quirked an eyebrow with his question, a grin dancing around his mouth.

She resolutely kept her eyes on his face and something in the way she looked at him killed his grin.

"I'm not stupid enough to bite on a challenge to my stamina, Mr. Rowe. What has prompted this generous offer?" she asked softly, then added, "Not that I'm going."

"I do have an ulterior motive," he confessed.

"I thought you would."

"I'm trying to make arrangements for the stage that goes to Bannack to swing down here before it returns to Virginia City. I want you to go to see how the stage office is run so that we can set up one here."

"I'm not a permanent resident of Trinity. I've told you that."

"You will be for a while. Until then you can manage the office. There's more —"

"I'm not surprised," Katy said dryly and eyed him with heavy suspicion.

Rowe continued as if she hadn't spoken. "I bank in Virginia City. Eventually I hope to have a bank here, but, in the meanwhile, I need a bookkeeper here in Trinity to pay the men and keep records."

"No."

A perplexed look crossed Rowe's face. "I thought you could cipher."

"I can cipher as good as any man or woman in the Territory."

"What's eight times nine?"

"I'll not spar with you or be tested for the job."

"You're the only one here qualified for the job of running a stage office. If you don't do it, I'll have to give up on having the stage come to Trinity until I can find someone else."

"Mr. Glossberg could do it." Her voice was prickly.

"I asked him," Rowe turned his eyes away, lest she see the lie in them. "He wants to run his store and perhaps get some women to sew clothes for him. He's a very good businessman."

"How about the dandy running the hotel?"

"Longstreet? I wouldn't trust him as far as I could throw a mule by the tail. I don't look for him to last long out here. He'll smart off to the wrong man and get a bullet in the head. Besides that, I've got no use for a man who is unkind to his family."

"There's Mrs. Hillard."

"She's been so sheltered that if anyone said 'boo' to her, she'd swoon. It'll take a woman with guts to handle this job."

Katy's mind had already grasped what it would mean to her if the stage came to town on a regular

162

basis. She and Mary would be free to pay their fare and leave whenever they wanted to. Mary would realize, once she got over the shock of Roy's death, that there was no future here for her and Theresa.

It came into Katy's mind with the force of a thunderbolt that she couldn't afford *not* to go to Virginia City with Rowe and Anton.

Rowe watched the expressions flit across her face as she mulled over the situation. First came a puzzled scowl that gradually faded. After a long moment of silence, her eyes brightened, and she caught her upper lip firmly between her teeth as she tried to hide a smile of satisfaction.

She was the most exciting woman he'd ever known. He was still mystified by his attraction to her and his driving need to have her for his own. He was like a moth and she a flame. She was like a cool, clear stream and he a man dying of thirst. Since the day at the lake he had been peculiarly reluctant to rush things, and somehow, he had managed to stay away from her. His mouth went completely dry when he thought of her bending over him, kissing him. She had been indescribably lovely as she was now.

Katy had made up her mind what she was going to do, but her problem was how to tell him without letting him think he had talked her into it.

"Do they have a telegraph in Virginia City?"

"Of course. Virginia City is the Territorial Capital."

"How often does the mail go out?"

"Twice a day. The Overland Mail carries it to Bozeman, another stage takes it south to Salt Lake."

"Humm . . ." She looked off into the distance.

"Make up your mind," Rowe said irritably.

"I'll go with you. When are you leaving?"

"At dawn."

"I'll be ready."

Rowe walked back down the muddy street with thoughts that were unsettling. It irked him that she was going with him merely to send a wire or a letter. The message was evidently too personal to give to him to send. Pangs of jealousy gnawed at him. He pushed them aside and began to plan. He had a week to bind her to him for a lifetime.

Dressed in a tight-waisted, dark gray riding skirt and a striped shirt, Katy paced the porch of the funerary as night wore away toward dawn. Mary had prepared a food packet and had filled a canteen with fresh water while Katy ate breakfast.

"Are you sure that is all you'll need?" Mary asked, pointing to the small canvas valise that Katy had packed to tie behind her saddle.

"An extra shirt, dress, underwear, toilet articles and a nightdress. What else do I need? Thanks for packing the food."

"I'm sure Rowe will have packed provisions."

"I'd rather have my own." Katy settled the flat-crowned, brimmed hat on her head and tied the strings beneath her chin. She pulled soft leather gloves from her belt and slid them onto

not quite steady hands, evidence of the nervous-
ness she was trying to hide from her sister.

"Make the most of the trip, Katy, and enjoy
yourself. You've had to work so hard —"

"I don't like going off and leaving you and
Theresa here alone."

"Heavens! We're not *alone*. Theresa and I will
spend some time with Laura Hillard and Julia.
Did I tell you that Laura and I are thinking of
making some shirts for Mr. Glossberg to sell in
his store?"

"You told me. If anything happens and you
need any help, go to Mrs. Chandler. She strikes
me as a woman who can handle most any situation."

"Don't worry, nothing will happen. Hank will
be here if it does."

"Ah, yes. Hank. He shows up here pretty often.
Is he courting you?"

"Katherine Louise Burns! What a thing to say!"

The conversation was cut short when Rowe,
riding his big black Arabian horse and leading a
slender blazed-face mare, came suddenly out of
the mist-shrouded morning.

"I take it you ride astride," he said when he
reached the funerary and dismounted.

"I learned to ride astride when it was considered vulgar to do so," Katy replied and handed
him the valise when he reached for it. He tied it
behind a small high-backed saddle, amazingly like
the one she had used back home in Alabama.

"I got the saddle from Mr. Glossberg," he said

165

as if reading her thoughts. "He said he had taken it in trade."

"I hope he'll take it back when I'm through with it," Katy said. She kissed Mary good-bye and whispered to her that she was teasing about Hank courting her. Then she hung her food packet and canteen over the saddlehorn. "Give Theresa a kiss for me when she wakes up."

"I will. Take care and come back safely," Mary said with a note of worry in her voice.

Katy swung into the saddle before Rowe could come around to assist her. While he adjusted the stirrups, she asked, "What's the mare's name?"

"I don't know. You'll have to name her. The man that you . . . the man at the well was leading her when he rode into town with those other two brainless fools. I suspect she belonged to the man they killed out on the trail. There's no brand on her so I guess she's yours." Rowe turned to Mary. "Don't worry about Katy, Mary. I'll take care of her."

"I know you will. Take care of yourself, too." Mary looked eastward to where the sun was lighting the horizon. "It's going to be a hot, humid day."

"It'll be cooler in the mountains. We'll be back in about a week. Meanwhile, Hank is in charge. Go to him if you need anything or if anyone bothers you."

The big brown dog stood patiently beside the porch, his eyes on Rowe. Rowe squatted down and fondled the dog's ears.

"This trip would be too hard on you, old man. A few years ago you could have made it easily, but not now. You'll have to stay here with Mary and Theresa. Get up there on the porch and stay there until I come back." Rowe got to his feet and the dog obediently climbed up onto the porch, settling himself beside the door. "Don't feed Modo, Mary. He finds his own food. I told the cook not to feed him or he'd get lazy. Now I suspect he leaves food for him to find."

"Theresa and I will be glad for Modo's company. Bye, Rowe. Bye, Katy. You two be careful and have a good time."

Mary's words echoed in Katy's mind as she reined the roan around and followed the big black horse up the muddy street. *Have a good time, my foot!* She'd have to be on her guard every minute or this international, smooth-talking Casanova would have her eating out of his hand.

Anton Hooker was waiting at the end of town. After a brief greeting, he fell in line behind Katy. For the next half hour, while the sun was struggling to shine through the gray mist, they left the rain-soaked valley and rode toward the mountains.

Taught by her brothers, Katy had learned to ride at an early age. They had ridden away, each on a thoroughbred horse, at the start of the war, sure that it would be over in a month or two. It had been up to Katy to care for the horses left in the stable that was known as one of the finest in Alabama. The big stallion, Rufus, had been the first to go; confiscated by a Confederate captain whose mount had been killed out from under him. The other stallions and the mares had been taken one by one until only a young filly, Katy's favorite, was left. One night she was stolen by deserters. It was only the beginning of Katy's grief. Next came the news that her brothers had died at Gettysburg. Then the plantation was ransacked by Union soldiers while the family hid in the cellar. A month later her father died.

The mare Katy was riding was young but well trained like the filly she used to ride. She was sure-footed and alert. Her ears peaked and twitched when she heard the crackling noise of a deer scrambling through the underbrush. The mare was also dainty, and after considering several names, Katy decided that Juliet would be a fitting name. Of all the Shakespeare plays she had read, her favorite was the tragedy, *Romeo and Juliet.*

Katy had just begun to relax and enjoy herself when the trail dipped into a ravine and sloshed through a pool of stagnant water. A swarm of mosquitoes rose up to attack them. Katy swatted at the big hungry insects with her gloved hand as they settled on her arms and face.

"Let's get out of here," Rowe shouted. He put his heels to the big black and the horse took off up the slope on the run.

Katy gigged the mare. Juliet scrambled up out of the ravine and ran easily along the upward trail. Rowe stopped on a high flat plateau where a breeze was blowing. He quickly dismounted and ran his gloved hands over the shoulders, flanks, and beneath the belly of his mount to wipe away the mosquitoes who were stuck there by their blood-sucking beaks. He came back to do the same for Katy's mare.

"Are you all right?" he asked as he wiped the face of the mare.

"I'm fine," she said evenly, although she was itching in a dozen different places. She rubbed along her jawline with a square of cloth she pulled from her pocket and then wiped the nape of her neck beneath the thick braid of hair that hung down her back.

"Did they chew on you?" he asked as he ran his hands over her back and shoulders.

"Some."

"I'll get the water and you can wet your handkerchief."

"I have some right here." She patted the canteen that hung from her saddlehorn.

Anton stood by his horse. He took off his glasses and wiped his face with a bandanna. "Jesus! The bastards would eat a man alive."

"Do you want to rest a while, Katy?" Rowe asked.

"Not unless you do."

"All right, but sing out if you want to stop. You're not used to long hours in the saddle and might stiffen up."

"I'll not slow you down, Mr. Rowe. Lead on."

His slow smile altered the stern cast of his face. For a moment he stood gravely studying her, then finally nodded.

"All right." He went to his horse and swung up into the saddle. "Let's go," he said aloud, but to himself he muttered, "The stubborn, ornery little cuss would die before she'd admit she was tired."

CHAPTER

Ten

Katy gave the mare her head as they climbed into the higher hills in leisurely stages. She was awed by the beauty of the mountains. From the towering peaks, a silent, brooding quality emanated, flowing down over the treetops, sloping meadows, and fast-running streams with an almost tangible force. She was acutely conscious of the overpowering solitude of her surroundings.

The silence absorbed her completely.

Juliet followed the stallion as Rowe led them through the timbered terrain, across canyons, and down long slopes that fell into hidden meadows and draws. They rode along upthrust ridges, criss-crossing fast-moving mountain streams, and into a forest of long-sighing pines.

When they emerged from the pines, they rode along a narrow shelf, and Katy looked out over a widely sprawling landscape. She gazed with open-mouthed admiration and wished that she were an artist so that she could paint every detail, and could view this lovely scene again and again. In this broken, high country the air was cooler, sharper, sweeter, as she drew it into her nostrils and down into her lungs.

She was smiling but was unaware of it.

As they passed beneath a tall topless pine, the victim of a mountain storm, an outburst of furious scolding came from a bluejay, followed by a concerted chorus of profanity from a dozen others. Several minutes later, a doe with a fawn close to her flank ran out of the forest and on down the trail ahead of them, disappearing into the shelter of a thicket. When all was quiet again, the song of a mountain thrush came from far away. After that there was only the *tunk, tunk* of hoofs on the deep-cushioned humus.

The sun shone bright in the overhead greenness when they came through a thick grove. Rowe stopped. The mare moved up beside him. A steady, muted roar assailed Katy's ears before she caught the gleam of sunlight on water falling over sheer rock down into a wide pool. Rowe laughed aloud at the look of pure pleasure reflected on her face.

"It's beautiful!" she exclaimed.

"Yes," he agreed still looking at her. "I thought you'd like it. We'll noon here." He dismounted and came to help her dismount.

"I can do it." She swung her leg over the rump of the mare. When her foot hit the ground, the leg folded. She held to the pommel for long moments until the feeling came back to her limbs. Sensing her chagrin, Rowe turned away to speak to Anton, then lifted the saddle from his horse, tossed it to the ground and spread the sweat-soaked saddle-blanket in the sun.

Katy's legs stiffened, but were still unsteady from the long ride. She loosened the cinch and was lifting the saddle when Rowe took it from her hands.

"We've got a long ride this afternoon. We'll rest the horses for an hour. Care for a swim?"

"I don't swim."

"I'll teach you someday," he said and led the two horses down to the pool to drink.

Katy walked back and forth to strengthen her legs, then went into the thick foliage that surrounded the clearing. When she was sure that she was out of sight, she emptied her aching bladder, leisurely straightened her clothing, and walked back toward the waterfall. She entered the clearing to see Rowe running up from the pool. He stopped short when he saw her.

"Don't wander off like that! You scared the hell out of me."

A look of irritation settled on her face. "You scare easily. I've got my pistol in case an Indian grabs me."

"That damn pistol wouldn't do you much good if you ran into a grizzly."

"In that case, I'll yell and you can come running to save me." She refused to let him see the fear that knifed through her at the mention of a grizzly bear. She had seen the remains of a big, burly miner who had been surprised by one.

"You shouldn't be shy about having to relieve yourself. We all do it. The next time you feel the need for privacy let me know and I'll take a look around before you go behind the bushes."

A flush of color came to her cheeks and the light of battle came into her eyes, but she refused to argue with him. She tossed her hat on the ground beside her canteen and food pack, sat down, leaned against the trunk of a tall spruce and worked her fingers into the hair at her temples. She was terribly conscious of him standing there looking down at her, but she ignored him and took out a slice of buttered bread and a piece of venison.

"I'm going to take a quick swim." He stood his rifle against the tree beside her. "Do you know how to use a .44 Henry?"

"I think I can figure it out." Her tone was indifferent. She began to eat.

Struggling for patience, Rowe flipped off his hat, whipped his shirt up over his head, and threw them down on the ground beside her. Her lashes swept up; beneath them, her eyes burned bright with resentment. Suddenly, desperately, he wanted to see them shine with pleasure as they had done when she first saw the waterfall. Her face, paler than when he had first met her, showed signs of fatigue. Her eyes seemed larger, bluer, more mysterious with the dark bruises beneath.

Why couldn't they exchange a dozen words without locking horns? Damn her! He couldn't keep himself from staring at her. If anyone had told him that a light-haired, blue-eyed woman could tie his stomach in knots, dry up his throat and mouth, cause him sleepless nights and worthless days unless he was with her, he would have called him a liar. Yet it was true . . . and more. A grinding need to be with her was with him constantly.

A slip of a woman called Katy had led him to the border between heaven and hell.

"Rest, Katy," he murmured and fought the urge to say anything else by walking away.

The regret in his eyes, the kindness in his voice, forced Katy to swallow several times before the bread in her mouth would go down her throat. She watched him stride toward the far end of the pool. His dark hair glistened in the sunlight. The satin-smooth skin that stretched over his broad shoulders and back was as dark as the skin on his face. To her shame, she wanted to kiss him again as she had done before. It's only the mating urge, she told herself sternly, and it has nothing to do with love. When she chose a husband, it would be a man with whom she had a lot in common; a man who wanted roots, not a fly-by-night miner with his sights set on the pot at the end of the rainbow.

Rowe sat down on the bank and removed his boots. When he stood, Katy saw a flash of his naked body before he dived into the cold mountain pool. In growing disbelief she watched his dark head surface. He was naked! Knowing that he was in plain sight of her, he had stripped off his clothing. No one had seen *her* completely naked since she was old enough to bathe herself.

Katy stared at him with the dull, fixed expression of the hypnotized before she shifted her eyes toward the waterfall. Anton was there, climbing on the rocks. He, at least, had kept on his britches. Her eyes went back to Rowe circling the pool with long even strokes. What had he said? "I'll teach you someday." How wonderful it would be to be so uninhibited that you could bare your body and frolic in a mountain pool.

A stifling heat and a tangible palpitation centered in her groin, steadily mounting, causing her to clamp her thighs tightly together. The hand holding the meat and bread rested in her lap. The vision of Rowe's turgid maleness impaling her and setting up its own tempo of invasion and withdrawal caused her face to burn with shame. Quickly she got to her feet, walked a short distance, and stood with her back to the pool until the unnerving, alien thing inside her subsided.

The nooning past, they wasted no time saddling the horses and moving out. This time it was Anton who led, with Rowe falling back behind Katy. At first, the fact that his eyes were on her exerted a constant tension in her, and then the beauty of her surroundings assumed dominance over her mind.

For several miles they rode across barren places of exposed rock that in places were made wet by a mountain spring. Then they dipped down into thick forest, along a frequently used trail that followed the natural contour of the wooded mountainside. Once, they passed beneath an overhang where one corner was blackened by campfires made by travelers who had spent the night there.

The sun had gone behind the mountain and the air was decidedly cooler when Anton stopped and held up his hand.

"Someone coming up the trail," he said quietly over his shoulder.

"In here." Rowe rode around Katy and led the way into trees so thick that after twenty feet they were invisible from the trail. "Get down, Katy. Throw a rein around the mare's mouth and keep her quiet."

Katy did as she was told. The mare's ears were peaked and she tossed her head. Katy stroked her nose, but held tightly to the strap that kept her from nickering a greeting to the horses approaching.

Anton held the other two horses as Rowe, with rifle in hand, moved silently back through the trees toward the trail.

"Who is it?" Katy whispered.

"Don't know. Could be friendly, could be robbers, could be Indians. It's best to be sure."

The sound of male voices reached them, growing stronger as the riders neared the place where they had gone into the woods. The gruff laughter was an unnatural sound in this dim, cool place. Birds flew silently away; a rabbit bounded out of the brush and raced through the trees. Then it was so quiet she could almost hear her own heartbeat.

Katy glanced at Anton. She had no time to wonder why he was frowning. A voice came from directly behind them.

"Ya did jist what I 'spected ya'd do if ya heard us coming. Step out from behind that horse, mister."

Katy whirled around. The man who spoke was tall and gaunt. He wore filthy buckskins, a small leather hat, and his face was covered with a stubble of black beard. He held what looked like an ancient shotgun in the crook of his arm, the muzzle-end pointed at her.

Anton moved around, his eyes never leaving the stranger.

"What do you want?" Katy demanded.

"Wal, now. I was jist wantin' the horses, but seein' how ya're young 'n' ain't all used up yet, I just might take ya along too."

"You lay a hand on me and I'll blow a hole in you so wide that —"

"Katy." Anton's voice held a warning.

"He's not taking my horse . . . or me!" she flared.

"Whopzee-do! She be one of them what gets her dander up. I ain't had me no fightin' woman in a spell." He swung the gun toward Anton. "Stand clear a that horse."

Anton stood his ground. "If you shoot that gun, you'll hit both the horses and you'll still be afoot."

The gun swung back toward Katy.

"Not if I shoot her. Move, or I'll cut 'er in two with a blast from this buffalo gun."

Anton stepped back from the horses but held the reins in his hand.

It rankled Katy that Anton was so ready to do what this dirty, seedy character told him.

"You're a two-bit excuse for a man," she snarled recklessly. "You're no better than a belly-crawling snake!"

"Right sassy, ain't ya? I can fix that. A week on yore back, naked as a young jaybird, would take some of the sass outta ya. After that ya'd be lickin' my hand."

"I'd die first!" Katy's eyes darted toward the trees where Rowe had disappeared.

"That 'en ridin' that black ain't goin' ta help ya. Zoot and Willy'll take care of him. We seen ya from the bluff when ya come out on the rocks. Our horses is 'bout played out. Figured we'd take yores." The rebounding crack of a rifle punctuated his words. "See thar what I mean?" Two more shots were fired and the man began to laugh. "Haw, haw, haw."

The bone-chilling fear that pierced Katy was as sharp as a knife. Concern for Rowe took hold of her and shook her. A startled scream died in her throat as illogical rage took possession of her reason. *Rowe! Rowe!* As she turned, her hand delved into her pocket seeking the Derringer. Without removing it, she pointed it toward the hated laughing face and pulled the trigger. To her utter amazement the bullet missed and the tree behind him spat bark. The man's face stiffened with anger.

"Gawddamn! Ya'd shoot me when I was meanin' ta take ya with me? Ya gawddamn slut! I'll kill ya —"

"Drop the gun! I'll not miss from this range." Rowe, holding his rifle at waist height, stepped out from behind the shelter of the trees directly behind the attacker.

"Don't move, woman," the man warned, when Katy dropped the reins to run to Rowe.

"Mister, if you don't want my bullet to take away the base of your spine, and rip out the front of your belly, drop your gun." Rowe spoke calmly. The skin at the corners of his eyes tightened ever so slightly, narrowing his gaze.

Katy couldn't take her eyes off of Rowe. Relief made her weak.

"Ya'll shoot me anyways."

"Maybe. Maybe not."

"I can get the woman first."

"Then you'll die slow, strung up to a tree for the buzzards to pick at and the wolves to gnaw on."

To Katy, the entire scene seemed to play out with agonizing slowness. The air of nonchalance around Rowe was unrealistic. His eyes were devoid of expression, his features as blank and cold as marble.

"I ain't here all by my own self."

"Your friends were stupid, like you. Loud talk and looking this way told me right where to find you." Rowe spoke calmly, as if he were speaking of the weather. "One horse carried double by the looks of the sweat on his rump. I figured that man was in the woods. I gave them one shot, then I rushed matters a little to get back here."

"Ya kilt Zoot 'n' Willy?"

"Deader than hell."

"Wal, I guess I know when I'm licked."

Katy opened her mouth to shout a warning. The man's face was like that of a cornered wolf. His lips curled back in a snarl. He lowered the end of the gun, then, as he turned, he jerked it up.

"Don't!" Rowe said and fired.

The bullet crashed through the man's chest, out his back, and across the mare's rump. The snarl was still on the man's face as he was thrown back. He was dead before his body hit the ground. The frightened mare, stung by the bullet, charged into Katy, knocking her off her feet, then bolted through the trees.

"Katy!" She heard Rowe's voice through the pounding in her head. The breath had been knocked out of her when she hit the ground. She felt herself being lifted into a sitting position. Rowe brushed the wet leaves from her face. "Are you hurt?"

"No. I don't think so. Rowe, is he . . . ?"

"He's dead," he said bluntly, and then added when he felt her shudder, "I had to shoot."

"I know." She looked into his face as she lifted her palm to his cheek. "I thought they'd killed you."

On his knees beside her, he put his arms around

her and she put her arms around him. They held each other tightly.

"Rowe." The gold-tipped lashes lifted, and eyes, blue, deep, and filled with concern, searched his. "He wasn't a dozen feet from me and I . . . missed him."

"It's a good thing you did, honey. If you hadn't killed him outright, he'd have killed you with that buffalo gun. It's a wonder he didn't shoot." The arms encircling her tightened, making her feel the fear that trembled in his big frame.

"I shot a hole in my skirt," she whispered against his neck.

He chuckled nervously, and held her away from him so he could look into her face. "I'll buy you another when we get to Virginia City." He stood, pulled her to her feet, and turned her away from the gruesome sight of the dead man. "Anton went after the mare." He gathered up the reins of the two remaining horses and urged her out of the clearing.

"Are you going to just leave . . . him?"

"There's nothing we can do now. We're only an hour away from my friend's ranch. In the morning Sam and I will come back and bury them."

"I hate this country!" she blurted. "Death and violence is everywhere. I want to go home where I can sit on my porch and drink lemonade without being insulted. I want to walk along a path without having to look over my shoulder and carry a pistol in my pocket. I'm sick of the West. Sick!"

Rowe didn't answer. He knew by the trembling in her body that reaction to what had just occurred had set in. They came out of the woods to find Anton and the mare waiting.

The bullet had passed across the mare's rump, leaving a deep gash. Rowe found a place where water had seeped out of the rocks and onto the ground. He smeared mud on the cut to stop the bleeding and to protect it from flies.

"The movement of the saddle will keep that cut open. Katy will have to ride double with me until we get to Sam's." Rowe handed Anton Juliet's reins. "I hate leaving two saddled horses to fend for themselves. Maybe they'll follow us down to Sam's."

Anton nodded. He mounted his own horse and, leading the mare, proceeded up the trail.

"He doesn't talk much," Katy said.

"I hadn't noticed." Rowe stepped into the saddle and held his hand out to her. "Step on my foot," he instructed.

Katy obeyed. She swung her leg over the horse's neck so that she sat astride in front of him. Her buttocks were pressed firmly against his crotch, but she kept her back stiff and away from his chest. She took off her hat and held it in her hands, when she felt the brim bumping his chin.

Apollo settled into a pace behind the mare. After a while, Rowe looked over his shoulder and said, "The horses are following. The poor things look beat."

Katy looked down at the hand holding the

reins. Rowe's fingers were long, the nails short and clean. A sprinkling of fine black hair covered the back of his hand. His other hand rested on a long, hard thigh that lay alongside hers. Despite the cool mountain air she felt hot, alive, and . . . strange.

"You're going to be sore tomorrow." His hand moved the few inches from his thigh to Katy's.

"I'm aware of that." The warmth and the strength of his hand on her thigh caused her mind to go blank. In seconds, reason returned. She lifted his hand and moved it back to his own leg.

"You have beautiful hair, Nightrose." His lips were close to her ear. He blew into it, gently sending her mind spinning again.

"Many women have the same color."

"Do you ever let it hang?"

"What do you think I am? A hussy? Only a loose woman lets her hair hang down her back in public."

"Someday, I'm going to undo that braid and spread this glorious hair out over a pillow."

"I think not! And I thank you to keep such thoughts to yourself," she said tightly. For some crazy reason she was having difficulty breathing.

"Women back East are cutting their hair," he said, not at all put down by her sharp remark.

"Cutting it?" She looked at him over her shoulder. "How in the world do they do it up?"

"They don't. They cut it to about here." He ran his finger along the nape of her neck. "It works best on women who have curly hair."

"And that's socially accepted?"

"In some circles."

"How nice not to have to go to all that bother of brushing out the tangles. I think I'd like that new style."

"I don't. If you cut your hair, I'll beat your butt."

"It's none of your business what I do with my hair, Mr. Rowe."

"Yes, it is. Now, hush up. I don't want to spoil this sweet time with you by arguing." He felt her stiffen even more. He grinned and rubbed his chin against her head. "You're stiff as a poker. Loosen up, Nightrose. Lean back against me and we'll both be more comfortable. It feels right and natural for you to be riding in front of me with my arms around you. It's like we've done it a hundred times before. Don't you agree?"

He didn't expect an answer and he didn't get one. He didn't figure that she'd relax against him, and she didn't — until later. Gradually, fatigue overpowered her pride. Her shoulders slumped and her backbone curved as she sagged against him. Rowe made no comment. His arms enveloped her, shielding her from the brisk evening breeze that blew down from the snow-covered mountain peaks.

"Nights are cool up here in the high country," he murmured, pulling her even closer.

"I've got a shawl in my valise."

"I'll keep you warm. We'll be at Sam's in a little while. We're on his land now. You'll like

Emily. She speaks with a Southern drawl, but it's not as pronounced as yours." Rowe's lips were close to her ear. "I've known them for several years. Emily is almost blind without her glasses. Sam is crazy about her. They don't seem to need anyone but each other."

"Do they have children?"

"Their first baby was stillborn and now they're expecting another."

"I'd think she'd be lonesome way out here."

"They're only an hour from Virginia City."

"You said your friends lived halfway."

"I said they were more than halfway." He chuckled and she could feel the rumble against her back. "You're a surprising woman, Nightrose, and foolish. I'm going to take that Derringer away from you. Good Lord!" he exclaimed as he thought of her facing a man with a buffalo gun and shooting the measly pistol from her pocket.

"No you're not!"

"I died a thousand times when I saw that man holding his gun on you. Dammit, Katy, a man like that is like a timber wolf. He thinks no more of killing than he does of taking a drink of water."

"He was a horrible man! I wasn't going to give up without a fight."

"Spunky and foolish and . . . sweet." He breathed against her cheek. His warm lips nibbled at her ear, his tongue stroking the rim.

"Don't —" She wiggled trying to move her head away.

"Why not? I like tasting your ear."

"I don't want you to —" He caught the lobe lightly with his teeth and Katy lost track of her own words.

"Don't is such an ugly word."

"Rowe, I can't . . . think when you do that."

"Good. I'll keep it in mind."

"And . . . your mustache tickles." In spite of herself, she giggled as she placed her hand on his thigh and leaned to the side.

"Be still, sweet one!" he cautioned, and he sounded as if he were in pain. His arms lifted her and moved her bottom away from the part of him that was throbbing and painfully aware of what was pressed against it. "Be still or I'll embarrass the hell out of myself when I get off this horse," he whispered.

"Oh!" she murmured and let out a long shuddering breath.

"Yeah, oh!" he mocked and pressed his cheek against hers. "My natural male mating-instincts are causing me pain."

"Glory be! It's not my fault that you're as randy as a billy goat," she blurted.

Rowe burst out laughing. Katy had no control over the sudden laughter that joined his, or the words that came mixed with the laughter.

"It would serve you right to be embarrassed. Don't expect any sympathy from me. I didn't ask to ride with you."

The arm across her middle tightened, locking her to him. "You're right where you belong, Nightrose." He lowered his voice and whispered in her ear. "And I'm going to keep you with me forever."

"What are you using for brains, Mr. Rowe? You've no claim on me. I go where I please." She slammed her elbow into his ribs to emphasize the point and was pleased to hear a grunt of surprise.

"We'll see about that, little she-cat!" he gritted fiercely, but he was smiling as he buried his lips in her hair.

CHAPTER
Eleven

Rowe was right about Katy liking Emily Sparks. After thirty minutes in Emily's home, Katy felt as if she had known her for years. The tall woman, who, Katy suspected, was nearer to Mary's age than her own, was in the last stage of pregnancy. She wore moccasins on her swollen feet and a granny dress that hung loosely from her shoulders. Round, wire spectacles with thick lenses magnified her blue eyes. She smiled easily and seemed to be sincerely fond of Rowe.

It had been past supper time when they arrived. For her guests Emily had set a loaf of fresh bread on the table along with slices of cold meat and dried peach pie. The meat was delicious. Katy hadn't eaten beef for months and didn't realize how much she had missed it. Sam, Emily's husband, a tall, quiet man with a head of thick, dark hair, helped his wife lay out the meal.

Katy had expected to find the Sparks living in a crude log house. To her surprise, the house was built with sawed lumber and consisted of one large room with two smaller rooms to either side. Narrow-cut vertical boards ran partway up the walls; above them the walls were covered with wallpaper. Leading to the loft was an open stairway with a handrailing attached to the inside wall. Comfortable chairs sat on either side of a cobblestoned fireplace, and an oval-braided rug covered a large portion of the plank floor. A bookcase holding more books than Katy had seen at one time since she left Alabama was built into one wall.

Water was piped into the kitchen; a rare convenience even in a town. A black iron handpump sat on one end of a tin-lined sink. The shiny iron cookstove, big enough to help heat the house in the winter, looked as if it had just been scrubbed and greased. It had two warming ovens at the top and a large hot-water reservoir on the side.

Sam left his seat beside the table to take the teakettle from his wife's hands as she lifted it from the stove top. He carried it to the sink and worked the pump handle until the water flowed and filled the pot.

"I can do that, Sam," Emily whispered.

"You can do it when I'm not here, love." He set the teakettle on the stove; then he checked the firebox, added a few sticks of wood, and returned to his chair. "Three fellows came through about noon today. They wanted to trade three worn-out horses for three of mine with nothing to boot. I had the feeling they would have tried to take them when I refused to trade if it hadn't been for my crew in the corral breaking mustangs. Guess they're the ones you ran into up on Hogback Mountain."

"They may have run one of the horses to death," Rowe mused. "One horse was carrying double. Lend me a couple of men and digging tools, and I'll ride out in the morning to bury them. Sorry as they were, they were human, and I can't leave them for varmints to gnaw on."

"I'd go with you, but I don't want to leave Emily for more than an hour or two, now that her time is near."

Rowe's eyes were bright with affection as they settled on Emily. "You make the best pie I ever ate. Will you teach Katy how?"

"I'll be glad to. But there isn't anything special about it. I get a lot of practice. My husband has a sweet tooth."

Katy looked at Rowe as if she'd like to hit him with the plate she was drying.

"I pity the man who has to eat my cooking," Katy said, placing the plate on the shelf. "My sister, Mary, is a far better cook than I am. We're going back to Alabama soon where we can pick peaches right off the trees."

"Oh, my," Emily exclaimed. "It's been years since I've had a fresh peach. I'd almost forgotten that those dried up little chips were once a whole fresh peach."

Her hand unconsciously wandered to the small of her back as she spoke. Sam got up immediately and went to take her elbow.

"You've been on your feet long enough, Emily Rose." He steered her to a chair and eased her into it. "Sit down. I'll get the tea." Before he straightened, he placed a light kiss on her temple.

It would be wonderful to be loved like that, Katy thought, as she watched Emily reach for her husband's hand, then release it reluctantly when he moved away to get the tea. Emily was so lucky! Rowe said that they didn't seem to need anyone but each other, and for once Katy believed him.

"He spoils me," Emily was saying with a small smile on her lips.

"You deserve to be spoiled. You're giving your man a son to carry life into another generation." Rowe spoke gently, but his eyes had narrowed and his mouth tightened, as they always did when he was agitated.

"How's your brother, Mrs. Sparks?" Anton asked smoothly, seeing the need to steer the conversation into a less personal channel.

"Charlie is fine. He helped to build the Federal Penitentiary at Laramie and then went back to his homestead when Sam and I came out here. Charlie decided that he prefers the ranch to working with prisoners." Emily's eyes sought Sam's. "Sam and I wouldn't be surprised if he got married. He's been calling on a lady who works at the orphanage. We're waiting for Mara Shannon and Pack to get here and tell us the news."

"Do you know the Gallaghers?" Katy asked.

"We certainly do! Heavens to Betsy! Mara Shannon and Pack are our dearest friends."

"Well, it certainly is a small world," Katy exclaimed. "I worked for them a while. I'm hoping to go back to the orphanage and work again for a few months before my sister and I go home."

"The Gallaghers are due out here anytime now. Pack went back east and bought two Hereford bulls: one for him and one for Sam. They have hopes of improving their herds. Pack and his young brothers are bringing Sam's bull out. Mara Shannon and Brita are coming partway on the train and the rest of the way by stage. They're going to stay with us for awhile."

"What about the children's home?"

"Mara Shannon wouldn't leave it unless it was in good hands. In her last letter she said they have eighteen children there now. She and Pack are devoted to that farm for homeless children." She smiled mischievously at her husband. "Sam and I think they left it in Charlie's hands so he'd have to spend more time with the new teacher."

The new teacher. Katy felt as if she'd had a rug pulled out from under her. She didn't have enough money to see her and Mary and Theresa back to Alabama, and she had counted on teaching at the orphanage. One thing she was sure of as she glanced at Rowe and at what she considered his self-satisfied look: *he* would never know that she didn't have sufficient funds to leave Trinity. She turned a bright smile to Emily.

"Have you seen Mara Shannon's little girl?"

"Oh, yes. Brita is three. They named her after Pack's mother. She's a darling. Her hair is black like Pack's and her eyes are blue like Mara's. Mara wrote that Pack dotes on her and has already taught her an Irish jig."

"She was only a tiny baby when I saw her last."

"Does Mara Shannon know you want to go back to work at the orphanage?"

"No. I've been in Trinity for the past ten months and couldn't get a letter out. Heavens! It seems more like ten years. I can hardly wait to get to civilization." Katy was careful not to look in Rowe's direction. She heard the chair squeak as he moved restlessly; she decided to add a little more fat to the fire. "Mr. Rowe was kind enough to escort me to Virginia City where I can send a wire to ah . . . friends back home. I also intend to look for work while I'm there."

"You shouldn't have any trouble. A lot of women live in Virginia City, but a very few of them are qualified to teach school." Emily's laughing eyes sought her husband's again, and they smiled at each other.

It came to Katy's mind that Emily and her husband were so close that they even shared the same thoughts. She felt a pang of envy, then a pang of guilt for being jealous of this sweet, gracious woman who was so nearsighted that she couldn't see without thick glasses.

Trying to choke down his anger, Rowe leaned back in the chair and listened to the conversation. His dark eyes were rooted to Katy's face. *The ornery, single-minded little devil.* He wanted to shake her until the freckles on her nose rattled. This prattle about going back to Alabama was just that, prattle. Mary had told him that they

194

only had distant cousins there. Katy had better get it into her pretty head that she wasn't going anywhere without him. They were meant for each other. He knew it as sure as he knew his own name, and he thought he had made it clear to her. Hell! She knew it, but she wouldn't admit it. But by damn, she would! She would be his, legally, before they left Virginia City. He hadn't wanted to do it that way, but if that was what it took to keep her near him so that he'd have time to win her love, that was what he'd do.

Sam poured the tea, and when he came back to the table, Emily got up, giving him her chair. He pulled her down on his lap, and she leaned wearily against him. His hand moved caressingly over her swollen abdomen.

"Does your back hurt, honey?" Sam's eyes moved over Emily's face with so much love reflected in them that it almost brought tears to Katy's.

"No more than usual."

Unconsciously, Katy's eyes went to Rowe. His lids were lowered, and through the tangle of black lashes, she could see the gleam of his dark eyes. She pulled her lower lip in and held it with her teeth while she struggled with the yearning to be held and loved as Sam was holding and loving Emily. Rowe's slitted eyes held hers until a flush came to her cheeks; then he opened them wider and smiled.

Damn him! Can he read my mind? Katy tossed her head and turned her smile on Emily.

"Would you mind if I wash up before I go to bed?"

"Of course not. How remiss of me." Emily sat up on her husband's knees. "Sam will bring a pail of warm water to your room." She indicated the doorway beneath the stairs. "A washbowl, soap, and towels are already there." Emily made a move to get up from her husband's lap.

"Sit still, Emily," Rowe said, rising. "I'll take care of it."

"Thanks, Rowe," Sam said. "I think I'll take my wife and son to bed."

"It may be a girl, Sam," Emily chided gently and flashed him a tired smile before she spoke to Rowe. "If it is, we're going to call her Rose, after Sam's sister who was killed while he was away fighting during the war."

"And if it's a boy?"

"We've decided on Gavin McCourtney Sparks, after my father who came to this country from Scotland when he was nine years old and became an orphan before his feet touched the soil. He made his own way after that and captured the heart of my mother, a beautiful Southern belle, who loved him to distraction until the day he died. Sam and I are hoping our son will have the courage and convictions of the first Gavin McCourtney."

"And why wouldn't he, with two such parents to love and guide him?" Rowe asked.

Katy thought she heard a note of wistfulness in his voice and was surprised by it. Abruptly, he turned to the stove, lifted the lid on the reservoir, and dipped the warm water into a pail.

Katy pushed herself away from the table and carried the teacups to the tin sink. She was so stiff and sore she could scarcely feel her feet on the plank floor, but she kept her back straight and gritted her teeth to keep from groaning.

"Anton, your bed's in the loft, same as before," Sam said. "I'm going to make this woman of mine get off her feet." He put his arm around his wife and urged her toward the bedroom door.

"Good night," Anton said. "I think I'll sit on the porch for a while and smoke."

"Make yourselves at home," Emily called. "Good night, everyone."

"I'll blow out the lamp after I light the one in Katy's room," Rowe said. "Good night."

Left alone with Rowe, Katy did her best to ignore him. She picked up her valise and headed for the adjoining room. Rowe came behind her carrying the lamp and the bucket of water. She moved aside for him to enter, then followed him into the room.

The room was small and neat. A black iron bedstead with shiny brass knobs on the corner posts took up one-half of the room. The bed was covered with a pieced quilt of bright colors; on the floor was a braided rag rug. A washstand and a low chest completed the furnishings except for a wooden cradle that stood beneath the only window. Waiting for Rowe to light the lamp and leave, Katy rocked the cradle gently and wondered if it had been made for the child who was stillborn.

"Take off your shoes and lie down on the bed, Katy. I'll rub the soreness out of your legs."

Katy's head jerked around as if it were pulled by invisible strings. "What?"

Rowe blew out the lamp he had brought from the kitchen. "Are you deaf as well as so stiff and sore you can hardly walk? I can rub some of that soreness out of your legs."

"I *thought* that was what you said. You'll do no such thing! I'll thank you to leave," she said haughtily.

Rowe stood with his hands resting on his hips, his head jutted forward, his eyes so narrow that she couldn't see them.

"Get on that bed face down, or I'll put you there."

"You touch me and you'll have a fight on your hands." She faced him with tight lips, the light of battle in her eyes.

He took a step toward her. "It's no more than I expected."

"I'll scream," she threatened. "Then what will you tell the Sparks who think you're so *wonderful?*"

"Go ahead. Scream, if that's what you want to do. I'll wait."

"I'm not . . . bluffing —"

"I think you are, but if you're not, I'll tell them we've been sleeping together and that we're going to be married when we get to Virginia City. I'll

198

tell them we've had a lover's quarrel and that I'm trying to make up with you."

"They wouldn't believe that! I told them I'm going home!" Anger raised her voice.

"Be quiet unless you want them to hear you," he whispered. "Get on the bed, Katy. If you don't, I'll spend the night in here with you, and I guarantee you'll not get much sleep."

"You . . . wouldn't dare!"

"I'd dare anything where you're concerned. But rest assured, sweetheart, I've no intentions of taking your virginity tonight. I'm going to wait until we are completely alone and I have plenty of time to enjoy it. Then, my girl, you're going to know what it's like to be thoroughly and completely loved by a man, and, I might add, you'll think you're in heaven!"

"You're disgusting! Don't you dare talk to me like *that*. You're the most egotistical, despicable creature I've ever met. I was right about you, Garrick Rowe. You're mean, and the blood of every blackguard for centuries must run in your veins."

"So you do believe in reincarnation."

"I do not. Get out of this room."

"Not until you let me rub the kinks out of your legs and back. On second thought, lie down on the rug. The bed's too soft and it'll squeak."

"You're . . . you're another Bluebeard!"

"Ah . . . so you read the Classics too. We'll discuss them some long winter night as we sit before our fire with our little ones at our knees."

"What?"

"Katy, arguing with you makes me . . . randy as a billy goat."

"What?"

"You said that, sweetheart. Do you want me to shout it?" He raised his voice. "Arguing with you makes me —"

"Hush up!" she hissed. "Oh, all right." She got down on her knees, then stretched out on her stomach. "I can't believe I'm doing this."

"You'll be glad you did, sweetheart. Trust me." Smothering his chuckle, he sat down on the floor beside her, lifted her foot, and began to unlace her shoes.

"I'd sooner trust a hungry wolf!"

Rowe removed her shoes. When he reached up inside the leg of the riding skirt to unfasten the knot in her stocking just below her knee and pull it off, Katy drew in a gasping breath and tried to roll away from him. Her head and shoulders came up off the floor.

"Stop it! That's indecent!"

Rowe laughed softly. With his hand in the small of her back he pushed her back down on the floor while his other hand traveled up her leg to work on the knot in the other stocking.

"There's nothing indecent about what I'm doing. Be still, sweet one." Oh, God! Did he have the strength to do no more than this? He longed to caress her bare legs, her smooth, tight buttocks, to hold her soft breasts in the palms of his hands. He wanted to feel the full length of her naked body against him and bury the rigidly erect staff of his maleness in her so that the fruit of his love would grow in her body. But he must take one step at a time, he cautioned himself. "Turn your cheek to the floor, and bring your arms down to your sides." He spoke in a conversational tone meant to calm her.

His hand cradled her bare foot while his fingers worked the joints of her ankle and toes. He worked on first one foot and then the other before his strong hands moved up to knead the muscles in the calves of her legs. At first she let out little gasps of pain which Rowe ignored. He worked the backs of her thighs with thumbs and fingers and then rubbed them vigorously with the palms of his hands. Even through the heavy material of her riding skirt, he could feel the muscles relax.

Katy felt in no way threatened by the hands that worked her stiff muscles, and she was almost asleep by the time he finished with her legs and thighs. On his knees beside her, he lifted the thick rope of hair off her back before his large, strong hands massaged the muscles between her shoulder blades. His fingers traveled down her spine, exerting pressure on each vertebra. Her eyes were closed and small moans of pleasure came from her parted lips.

Rowe thought she was the most beautiful, exciting woman he had ever known. Her hair, the color of pure honey, was fine and warm, her body was straight and strong, yet incredibly soft. She was a full, mature woman, fiery in character, bright in mind, and high in spirit.

He loved her!

Just how much he loved her struck him suddenly, with all the power and force of a bullet. He stopped rubbing her back, rested his clenched fists on his thighs and stared down at her. It came to him that his entire way of looking at himself and the world had changed since he had met her. He had not believed himself capable of such love. Small, petty things no longer mattered. The hatred his half brother Justin bore him was a fact he'd had to contend with all his life. It was no longer important. The emotions he felt for Katherine Burns were awesome, exhilarating, frightening, and far stronger than any feeling he'd had for mother, country, or sense of justice. This mouthy little imp-eyed, headstrong woman was in his heart. He would hold her there until the end of time.

Rowe came out of his near-trance and made circles beneath her shoulder blades with his fingers. Katy sighed with pleasure, turned her head, and looked at him with dreamy eyes. A warm, lopsided smile curved her lips.

"That feels wonderful, Rowe. Thank you," she murmured and closed her eyes.

She was tired. Rowe felt his heart expand in his chest. She would love him, he vowed, and they would spend all their days together. He continued to lightly stroke her back; soon, she was sleeping soundly. Rowe sat on the floor beside her, gazing upon her. Slowly he reached out and picked up the end of her braid, untied the thin leather string, and began to loosen the strands that slid through his fingers like silk threads. When he finished he spread her hair over her back and ran his palm down the length of it to her hips.

Katy, Katy, you belong to me so stop trying to run away. I could no more let you go than I could voluntarily stop breathing.

Rowe heard Anton moving around in the loft. He got to his feet and turned back the bed covers. Katy had been too tired to wash. He carefully picked her up and stood beside the bed for a long moment looking at the woman in his arms. Her head had fallen to his shoulder, her hair flowed down over his arm. He wanted to kiss her but refused to take advantage. She didn't awaken when he placed her on the bed, or when he unbuttoned her shirt, or when he carefully slipped the riding skirt down over her hips.

He smiled when he saw the blue stain on the leg of her drawers. This was the pair he had seen drying by the creek; the pair the bluejay had left his calling card on when he failed to pluck the shiny button from the waistband. Katy rolled onto her side and tucked a palm beneath her cheek.

Rowe stooped and placed a light kiss on the soft swell of her breast, which was covered by only the thin camisole. He moved so the light of the lamp shone on her face. She was his Nightrose. Fate had brought them together, and they would be together always. He looked at her for long, endless minutes before he drew the covers up around her, blew out the lamp, and quietly left the room.

He would be gone by the time she awakened in the morning and discovered he had opened her shirt and removed her skirt. He grinned in the dark as he made his way up the stairs to the loft. She would be madder than a wet hen, but she'd have a few hours to cool down before he returned from Hogback Mountain.

CHAPTER
Twelve

Allowing Theresa to skip along in front of her, Mary walked down the street toward the mercantile. After so many days of rain, it was good to feel the sun on her face. A group of off-duty miners were waiting to go into Mrs. Chandler's eatery as soon as she announced the meal was ready. A few of them were so bashful that they turned their heads away from the small, well-rounded woman with her tiny waist and generous curves. All of them feasted their eyes on Theresa. Most of the men were married and lonesome for their families. They doted on the only two children in town, Theresa and little Julia Hillard.

Mary went up the steps and onto the clean porch of Mr. Glossberg's store. She stood just inside the door, her eyes sweeping the room. It had already taken on the scent of new goods, spices, and saddle leather. Elias Glossberg had sold out almost completely the goods he had brought to Trinity ten days before. He came from behind the counter to greet her.

"Good day to you, Mrs. Stanton. And to you too, young miss," he said to Theresa.

Elias Glossberg was younger than Mary had at

first believed him to be. It was the expression he wore on his face that was old. He was well educated, tended to the business of his store, and never intruded on anyone. He had come to the new country from Romania; and in the ten years he had been here, he had learned that people were the same the world over. The men on the wagon train considered him an outsider because he didn't attend their church services on Sunday. Here in Trinity he was also an outsider because he didn't speak the rough language of the miners.

Elias, however, was a realist. He'd not had grand illusions when he had come to America. He had expected to work hard and live hard. He had traveled extensively, and at age thirty he wanted to settle down where there were people to buy his goods. He would have gone on with the wagon train to Oregon if they had allowed it. Now he was glad he had been forced to stop at Trinity. He found no pleasure in being among people who hold a man at arm's length. Garrick Rowe, however, had not appeared to think him different. He had accepted him for what he was — a merchant with goods to sell.

"Mr. Glossberg, I can't believe you've sold so much goods. I was hoping you'd have a bit of white cloth left. I have need of a yard or two."

"I have a small length of white. I'll measure it to see if it's what you need." Elias took a paper-wrapped bundle from the shelf and laid the white material out on a spotlessly clean counter. Mary watched his long slender fingers carefully unroll the cloth and measure it against the notches he had made in the countertop. "Two- and one-fourth yards, Mrs. Stanton. If you can use it, take it for the price of two yards."

"And what is that, Mr. Glossberg?"

"Twenty-five cents. Would you like for me to make a bill of it?"

"No, thank you. I have the coin." Mary dug into the purse that hung on her arm and produced the money.

"I'll have more goods as soon as the freight wagons come in. I sent a list to be filled with Mr. Ashland's man." Elias folded the cloth and wrapped it in the paper.

"And when will that be?"

"Tomorrow or the next day, little lady. The wagons'll be here before the fourth." The voice had came from behind Mary. She turned to see that Art Ashland, the freighter, had entered the store with the assurance of a man who believed he was welcome wherever he went.

"How are you this fine day, ma'am?" He ignored Elias, leaned on the counter with his back to him, and looked boldly at Mary.

"Fine," Mary said abruptly. She smiled at Elias when he handed her the package. "Thank you, Mr. Glossberg."

"Ain't you wantin' to know what's comin' in on my freight wagons?" Art asked when Mary turned to leave.

"Not particularly."

"Par-tic-u-lee? What does that mean? You want

to know only part of what the Jew's havin' brought in?"

"You figure it out, Mr. Ashland." Mary took Theresa's hand and started for the door.

"Hold on, Mrs. Stanton. What'er ya leavin' for? Ya was talkin' up a storm to the Jew man. Ain't I good enough to talk to?" He moved around to stand in front of her.

"I was making a purchase."

"Has he showed ya that little round cap he wears when he talks that mumble jumble to his-self?"

"Move out of my way." Mary tried to step around him. He moved sideways, blocking her way to the door.

" 'Pears to me like he give ya a real bargain on that cloth, Mrs. Stanton. Ever' man's got a different way of gettin' around a woman. This'n's a new wrinkle on me."

"I don't know what you're talking about, but if it's meant to be insulting to me or to Mr. Glossberg, I don't appreciate it. Move out of my way."

"Gawdamighty! Do ya like talkin' to that Jew?" Ashland asked with a puzzled frown on his bloated face. His eyes were red and watery, and his breath smelled as if he had recently lost what he had overindulged in the night before.

"Yes, I like talking to Mr. Glossberg. *He* is a gentleman."

"And I ain't?" When Mary snapped her mouth shut and glared at him, Ashland began to laugh.

"Now if this ain't the damnedest thin' I ever heard of. Who'n hell wants to be a gentleman? Why is a pretty hunk of wench like you cozzin' up to a Jew? Hell! This whole town is plumbful a folks not worth a buffalo's droppin's. A Jew, a dandy still fightin' the war, old lady Chandler and her gals — one's a whore, the other'n pure as snow, so she says. And Lizzibeth who guards her whores like they was jewels. This is a hell of a place!"

"Then why don't you leave?"

"Then why don't ya leave?" he mimicked. "I'll tell ya why I don't leave. 'Cause I get paid good wages to haul that damn ore to the smelters. I hear your sister's gone off with Rowe. How 'bout me comin' by and pleasurin' you like he's a doin' her?"

Mary gasped with angry indignation, "If you come near my place, I'll fill you full of buckshot!"

Ashland roared with laughter. While still laughing, he reached out in a lightning-fast, unexpected move and pinched her nipple with his thumb and forefinger. Then he stepped around her and walked away.

Mary was numb with shock.

"I don't like him!" Theresa jerked on Mary's hand to get her attention. "Why'd he pinch you?"

"Shhh . . . shhh . . . It's all right."

Mary stood for a moment longer with her back to Elias, hoping he had not seen Art Ashland pinch her breast. When she turned, her cheeks were burning with embarrassment. She looked directly into his dark eyes. Feeling her humiliation, he winced.

"Mr. Glossberg, I'm so . . . ashamed —"

"Oh, don't be sorry on my account!" Elias came quickly from behind the counter. "It's all right. There are good people and bad people wherever you go. Mr. Ashland is a hard, narrow-minded man, a product of his environment. Had he not been the way he is, perhaps he would not have survived."

"You're very generous. I don't believe I could be so forgiving."

"Believe me, Mrs. Stanton, the opinion of a man like Mr. Ashland is not important. I'll use his services to bring goods to my store. It's business. But . . . the things he said to you were . . . shameful!"

"He's a crude man."

"And ruthless. You should speak to Mr. Weston about him."

"Oh, no. I think the less made of it the better."

"Mamma! Here's Julia!" Theresa jerked free of Mary's hand and ran to her new friend who was coming in with her mother.

"Hello, Mary. I thought I saw you and Theresa come in here. Hello, Elias."

"Theresa and I were planning to stop by on our way home. Theresa, stay on the porch," she called as the two little girls, hand in hand, happily headed for the door.

Julia Hillard was a year younger than Theresa and they spent several hours a day together. It made life considerably easier for both of their mothers.

Mary liked Laura Hillard very much. Small and delicate to look at, Laura had more strength than appeared on the surface or she would not have been able to endure the long trek from New York and the loss of her husband.

"My, you're almost sold out, Elias." Laura turned completely around, surveying the room. "Business must be good."

Elias held out his hands. "I don't have any competition."

When the women laughed, his dark eyes brightened.

"I'm so glad you came here," Mary exclaimed, looking from one to the other. "Both of you."

"I'm glad too, now," Laura said. "But at first I thought it was the end of the world."

"So did I. Then, somehow during the months Katy, Theresa, and I were here alone, I became fond of it."

"I would have been scared to death."

"I was," Mary admitted, then added, "But only part of the time. Laura, do you realize that it is the second of July, and Independence Day is almost here? What would you two think about having a celebration here in Trinity?"

"A celebration?"

"A day celebration. Surely the mine will shut down for the day."

"I think it's a splendid idea." Laura turned to Elias, her eyes bright with excitement. "What do you think, Elias?"

"Well, I think it would be . . . fine. Do you think the others will want to participate?"

"We can ask them."

"It would take planning. Why don't you two come to supper tonight?" Mary said impulsively. "I'll ask Mr. Weston to come and we'll talk it over."

Elias looked at Laura and saw that she was smiling in agreement. "I accept with pleasure, that is, if . . . you ladies and the children will have dinner with me today at Mrs. Chandler's."

Laura and Mary looked at each other, before turning pleased smiles on Elias. "That would be lovely, Elias." Laura accepted for both of them. "Thank you."

"I suggest we wait until after the noon rush is over." His slim, dark face was alight with pleasure. "It'll be less noisy."

Dressed in a white shirt, black suit, and a carefully brushed beaver hat, Elias escorted Mary, Laura, and the girls into the restaurant at half past twelve.

The Chandlers had made the most of what they had to work with, which was a squat, square building with a door in front, another in back, and one window on the side. Every inch of the small building had been scrubbed with lye soap and white-washed. Mrs. Chandler was a big, rough-looking woman, but she was clean, her girls were clean, and her restaurant was clean. The pleasant aroma coming from the stew pots and the strong smell of coffee boiling on the range greeted the diners.

"Glory be! We got ladies today. Come in, come in." Mrs. Chandler's voice boomed from the back of the room where a counter holding a pan for the soiled dishes served as a barrier between the kitchen and two long tables where the diners were served. Her face was red from the heat of the stove. She lifted the end of her apron and wiped the sweat off her brow. "Flossy! Clear off that table so the folks can sit. Hurry it up!"

"I'm hurryin', Maw."

Flossie's plain, broad face wore a perpetual smile, making it rather pleasant to look at. She hurried to the table, her wide hips swinging, her apron sash tied so tightly about her waist that it emphasized her generous breasts. She stacked the tin plates in her one hand, grabbed three granite cups by their handles with the other, and dumped them carelessly into the dishpan, splashing water on her sister.

"Are them china plates clean, Myrtle?" Mrs. Chandler's voice boomed in the small building, and Mary wondered if she ever talked softly.

"Yes, Maw."

"Get 'em out for me to dish up for the ladies and Mr. Glossberg. Sit, folks. We got hoppin' jack stew 'n' buttermilk biscuits. Floss, see if them benches is clean before the ladies sit." Mrs. Chandler issued orders like a drill sergeant and the girls jumped to obey.

Myrtle was the shy one, the exact opposite of

213

Flossie. She was younger, prettier, and more slightly built than her sister. Her hair was light and curly while Flossie's was dark and straight. Myrtle seldom raised her eyelids, but when she did, her eyes were cornflower blue. Mary judged her to be about fourteen. She stayed near her mother. Flossie, on the other hand, could be seen on the street or on the steps of the restaurant in the evenings, flirting, laughing, and talking with anyone who happened by. It was easy to tell which of the Chandler girls had been caught in the indiscretion that forced the family to leave the wagon train.

Mrs. Chandler had wanted to buy the cow the Flannerys had abandoned when they left town to hurry to the next gold strike, but Mary couldn't bring herself to sell something that wasn't hers. So they struck up a deal. The Chandlers took over the care of the cow, and each day, after the morning milking, Flossie brought a small pail of milk to the funerary. When they churned, she brought butter. The arrangement had worked out very well.

Elias removed his hat and hung it on one of a dozen nails Mrs. Chandler had pounded into the wall. She had made it known from the beginning that no man would eat at her table with a hat on his head. Now, after a little more than a week, a man seldom had to be reminded. Elias seated the women with as much courtesy as if they were dining at a fancy New York restaurant.

Flossie brought the plates to the table after her

mother had filled them in the kitchen. The stew was hot, the biscuits light and golden brown. A crock of butter and a pitcher of sorghum were brought to the table. After she poured coffee for the adults, she brought each of the girls a cup of cold buttermilk.

"It's a treat to eat something I haven't cooked myself." Mary made the confession while she smeared butter on a biscuit for her daughter.

"Mrs. Chandler was kind enough to allow me to sample her cooking while we were with the wagon train," Elias said. "I knew she could run a successful restaurant."

Although Elias had spoken softly, Mrs. Chandler's sharp ears picked up his words.

"And Mr. Glossberg was kind enough to give me supplies when I didn't have a dime in my pocket." Her voice boomed. "Business is good. Them miners get tired of eatin' a man's cookin'. They can eat a dishpan full of bearclaws at the drop of a hat." She laughed heartily. "Another week or two and I can pay you off, Elias."

Before Elias could reply, Lee Longstreet came into the restaurant. He paused in the doorway, his eyes sweeping the room, before he removed his hat and slicked the sides of his hair back with his palms. He nodded and spoke to Mary and Laura, ignored Elias, and sat down at the end of the only other table in the room.

"Howdy," Mrs. Chandler called, but to Mary the greeting seemed to lack enthusiasm. "Myrtle, take Mr. Longstreet some coffee while I dish up."

As Myrtle reached the table where Mr. Longstreet was sitting, Mary turned to tell Theresa to stop giggling and eat her dinner. Myrtle had placed the cup of hot coffee on the table and was turning away when the man reached out and ran his hand down the inside of her leg. Myrtle was so startled that she jumped and jarred the table. Coffee spilled and puddled around the cup.

"Can't you do anything right, Myrt?" Flossie spoke sharply to her sister and grabbed up a cloth to mop up the spill.

Myrtle hung her head, hurried behind the counter, and plunged her hands into the dishwater.

"It's all right, Miss Flossie," Mr. Longstreet said smoothly. "Your sister is just a little nervous."

He looked over at Mary. His eyes locked with her accusing ones. A slight smile twisted his thin lips, and he lifted his brows slightly in question. The lecher! Myrtle was a child no older than his own daughter! The man looked steadily back at Mary, daring her with his eyes to voice what she had witnessed. His gaze shifted to Laura, then to Elias, and back to Laura before settling on Mary's breasts. He had the coldest eyes Mary had ever seen. She decided then and there that she detested him even more than she detested Art Ashland.

His presence had put a chilling effect on everyone in the restaurant with the exception of the children. They giggled and whispered and

216

nudged each other. The adults ate in almost total silence. Flossie brought Mr. Longstreet a plate of food and went back to the kitchen.

Lee Longstreet was a short, thin man, about forty, who had always schemed big and functioned small. He refused to think of himself as other than the elegant son of a large plantation owner in Mississippi. One of his greatest pleasures was counting the number of slave families his father had owned, the number of wenches he and his father had ridden, and the number of mulattos they had produced.

Before the war, due to mismanagement, the family fortune had begun to dwindle and his father had taken to drink. In order to keep the creditors at bay, Lee had been forced to wed the homely daughter of a merchant to whom the family owed a great sum of money. The marriage had not changed his lifestyle. He used the woman occasionally and begat two children to whom he paid no more attention than if they had been borne by one of his slaves.

During the war the slaves deserted the plantation. One morning Lee had returned home after a night of debauchery to find that his father, unable to face a new way of life, had killed himself. Had his father lived, they might have had a chance to preserve their way of life to a certain degree; without him, there was no chance at all. The banks foreclosed, taking everything. Since that time, Lee had gone from town to town, working his small swindles, selling bad stock, and dreaming the big dream. His family had tagged along because they had nowhere else to go. He felt nothing but contempt for his wife, Vera, his daughter, Agnes, and his lame son, Taylor. They were a humiliation that he suffered each day.

Lee Longstreet had a score to settle with Mrs. Chandler. To him it was simple. A man who had pride settled his accounts. He bristled when he thought of the humiliation he had faced when she had berated him in front of the men of the wagon train because his wife and children were unloading the wagon so that a wheel could be replaced. It had not occurred to him to dismount and help them when the rear wheel on the wagon splintered and the wagon dropped to the side and back. The wagons behind, including the Chandler wagon, had stopped. He bought an extra wheel from the blacksmith and put his family to unloading the wagon. Mrs. Chandler had been very vocal with her criticism that hot day. She had drawn attention to their poverty, an insult he could not allow to go unavenged.

"You're a poor excuse for a man, Lee Longstreet, lettin' your woman and kids do the work," she had bellowed. "It ain't no wonder to me you got such a piss-poor, make-do rig. If'n I was Vera, I'd tie a can to your tail, that's what I'd do. Her and them younguns'd be better off with you gone."

"But you're not Vera, Mrs. Chandler, and I'll thank you to tend to your own affairs."

Mrs. Chandler had made a few more vulgar

remarks, then said, "Come on, girls, let's give Mrs. Longstreet a hand. Looks like Mr. Longstreet ain't goin' to get his boots dusty. He's goin' to sit on that horse like he was overseein' his slaves."

The men had turned their backs on him after that. He was no longer accepted or welcomed at their campfires. A day before they came to the forks in the road, the wagon master had told him that he would have to leave the train with the others. They feared his rig wouldn't make it over the mountains. Misfits, the wagon master had called them. Misfits who would hold the rest of them back.

Since that time the need for revenge had eaten at Lee. He had been humbled by a woman of inferior class and it was not to be tolerated. Days ago he had figured out what path his revenge would take. He felt good just thinking about it. What he had in mind would be as pleasurable as it was simple.

Lee ate quickly so that he could leave. It galled him that Laura Hillard, a lady of quality, had so venomously rebuffed his attentions and had taken up with the Jew. The woman had money or access to it by the looks of her outfit. She spurned every attempt he had made to be friendly with her. Hell! He could wait. His time would come. If there was one thing Lee knew about, it was women. Laura Hillard had been without a man for months and soon she would be wanting one. He would make sure it was he that was available when that time came, and not the Jew.

As soon as Lee placed a coin beside his plate and left, the mood inside the restaurant changed. Flossie, who had not had much to say while he was there, began to chatter as she scraped what he had left on his plate in the slop bucket.

"I don't think the *elegant* Mr. Longstreet liked your stew, Maw."

"I ain't a carin' if he liked it or not. He wasn't here by my invite. Vera and them two kids is probably eatin' biscuits and milk. Floss takes them a pail a milk once in a while," she said to the others as she came from the kitchen, wiping her hands on her apron.

"I liked the stew." Theresa tilted her head and grinned with her mouth full at the big woman who sank down on the bench beside her.

"Well, now. Ain't you a little charmer!" Lottie Chandler fanned her face with the end of her apron. "I'm gettin' low on sugar, flour, coffee beans, and snuff, Elias. I got to have my snuff to keep me goin'."

"Mr. Ashland said the wagons will be here before the Fourth, so that leaves today or tomorrow."

"Fiddle!" she snorted. "I'm thinkin' all the brains he's got is right a'tween his legs."

Mary looked quickly at Theresa and Julia and was relieved to see they were whispering to each other and not listening to the conversation.

"You may not like him," Elias said with a smile. "But he's a good teamster. I have every confidence his wagons will be here if he says they will. I'd hate to be one of his drivers. He's a hard taskmaster."

"In more ways than one, from what I hear."

"Mrs. Chandler, what do you and your girls think about having a day celebration on the Fourth?" Mary said trying to steer the conversation into a safer channel.

"What kind a celebration?"

"We don't know exactly until we talk to Mr. Weston and find out if he's going to close down the mine for the day. One year Katy and I were in Laramie on the Fourth. They had footraces, horse races, a dance in the street —"

"That darky at the cookshack plays the banjo," Flossie said brightly, coming to the table with a dishcloth in her hand.

"How'd you know that?" her mother demanded.

"I heard talk about it, Maw. I ain't deaf." Flossie tossed her head defiantly and flounced back to the dishpan.

"It'd be a good day for business," Mrs. Chandler admitted. "If the supplies come, me'n the girls could make pies and bearclaws —"

"I feel that I should mention something," Elias said with some hesitation. "There may be some ah . . . unpleasantness if the ladies at the Bee Hive are not included."

"I don't see how we could exclude them. Do you, Laura?" Mary asked.

"I guess not, if they behave themselves."

"Lizzibeth runs a good house and keeps her girls in line. She'll not let them shame the town," Mrs. Chandler put in. "I got to say one thing for Lizzibeth; she ain't strippin' the men's pockets like some do. Laws, we been in some towns where the whores'd take the nickels off a dead man's eyes."

"Did you see the sign she put up?" Flossie was back at the table, her dishcloth flung over her shoulder. "It's got a painted picture of a beehive on it with bees buzzin' all around." Flossie began to recite in a singsong voice:

"Within this hive, we're all alive,
    We're waitin' and we're horny,
Don't be shy, come in and try,
    The flavor of our honey."

"Flossie, for Gawd's sake! Watch your mouth." Her mother glared at her and jerked her head toward the children.

"Pshaw, Maw! Them younguns don't even know what I'm talking about. That sign's cute, is what it is."

"I don't know what I'm goin' to do with you, Floss." Mrs. Chandler wiped her face with her apron and shook her head. "Get your work done up. We got washin' to do."

The conversation dwindled after that. Mary looked at Laura's red face and remembered having the same reaction when she and Roy first came West. There wasn't a town west of the

Mississippi that didn't have one or more brothels. Mary had heard of a town on the Colorado-Kansas border called Trail City. It boasted of having twenty-seven saloons with cribs upstairs, nine hotels with a woman for each room and eleven brothels. In this incredible town all were after business, and naked women stood on porches to entice the men into their establishments. One man had told Roy that he actually got tired of looking at naked women.

Mary was sure that Hank and Rowe would never let something like that happen in Trinity. As trollops go, Mary thought, the ones at the Bee Hive were fairly decent.

Elias got up to pay for the meals.

"Take it off what I owe you, Elias."

"All right. If that's what you want."

As soon as they left the restaurant, Mary said, "I'll have to get word to Mr. Weston to come to supper tonight."

"I understand from Theresa that he comes almost every evening. Now why would this evening be any exception?" Laura asked teasingly. She looked from Mary's suddenly flushed face to Elias's as if they shared a secret.

"Would you like for me to see that he gets the message?" Elias asked.

"If it wouldn't be too much trouble. He doesn't come to supper every evening, Laura. Mr. Weston comes by because he . . . because he's grateful for the nursing care I gave the men during the outbreak of measles."

Laura laughed. "That's a perfectly good reason."

"Oh, you're as bad as Katy when it comes to teasing. Let Julia come home with Theresa for the afternoon. Thank you for the dinner, Mr. Glossberg. I'll see you two at suppertime."

CHAPTER
Thirteen

"Why'd they go? I want to play with Julia," Theresa whined, and clung to Mary's hand as they stood beside Hank on the porch of the funerary after saying goodnight to Laura and Elias.

"You're too tired to play. You can hardly hold your eyes open and Julia was already asleep. Mr. Glossberg had to carry her home."

"I want Uncle Hank to carry me."

"You're not going anywhere tonight, honey. It's past your bedtime."

Theresa whimpered and pushed her face into Mary's skirt.

"Come here, puddin'." Hank knelt down beside her. "We'll go out to the swing and back. How's that?" Theresa went to him eagerly, wrapping her arms around his neck. He lifted her up, and she snuggled her head against his shoulder.

"You're spoiling her," Mary felt compelled to murmur, when their eyes met over the child's head.

"Aye. Lassies need spoilin', to my way of thinkin'," he answered gruffly and stepped off the porch.

Mary leaned against the post and watched Hank walk into the darkness with her daughter in his arms. She felt a pang of regret that Theresa had not known the joy of having a father who wanted to hold her. It never ceased to amaze Mary that a big rough man like Hank Weston could be so gentle with a child. It was no wonder that Theresa adored him. He had given her more attention during the few weeks they had known him than her father had given her during her lifetime.

Rowe's dog came up onto the porch and lay down in his usual place against the wall. He rested his jowls on his paws and looked at Mary. She never touched the big animal, but sometimes she talked to him. He always looked as if he understood every word she said. But of course that was ridiculous.

"Do you miss Rowe, Modo?" Mary whispered softly. "I bet you do because I miss Katy. I hope she'll have a good time in Virginia City. Rowe will take care of her. He's in love with her. I can tell by the way he acts when he's around her. He watches every move she makes. It's almost as if his eyes are feasting on her. She's attracted to him too, but she won't admit it. She's afraid that she'll make the mistake I made and be stuck with a way of life she detests."

The dog heaved a big groaning sigh as if the problem was too much for him. Mary turned back to scan the night sky. She found the Big Dipper, the Little Dipper; and as a star streaked across the sky, she made a wish.

"I wish happiness for Katy and Theresa."

Minutes later Hank came quietly out of the darkness. Despite his large size, he was a graceful person though he didn't have the antelope agility of Rowe. Nor was he as educated as Rowe, but he was just as sure of himself. Although the two men came from different backgrounds, they were alike in many ways. It was understandable to Mary that they were loyal friends, as well as employee and employer.

Hank stopped at the edge of the porch. His face, suddenly dear and familiar, was on a level with Mary's. He didn't say anything, just looked at her. A gust of cool night wind coming off the snow-peaked mountains caused her to shiver. Mary had a sudden yearning to be in Hank's arms, cuddled against the warmth of his chest, his hand stroking her hair as it was stroking the hair of her child.

Hank saw the pensive look on her face and wondered what put it there.

"Is she asleep?"

"Aye." His big hand continued to stroke Theresa's hair while his eyes remained on Mary's face.

"I'll take her to bed."

"She's too heavy for you to be carryin', Mary."

Hank stepped up onto the porch and waited for Mary to lead the way into the funerary to the big bed at the end of the building. Theresa had been sleeping with her mother since she became aware that the crate she had been using for a bed was a burial box. Mary turned down the covers and Hank placed the child gently on the bed. He unlaced her shoes and pulled them off while Mary unbuttoned her dress.

There was silence as they worked over the small life between them. A wrenching, lonely ache pressing against the wall of her heart prevented Mary from being aware of the intimacy of the task they performed as if they were husband and wife and the child between them theirs. But she would think about it later when she lay in her bed listening to the wind ripple the tin roof overhead. Now, she pulled the covers over Theresa, tucking them in. When she looked up, Hank was still standing at the end of the bed.

"Thank you." Her calm voice and placid expression masked the ache of loneliness.

He shook his head slowly and continued to gaze at her. "I don't want you thankin' me, Mary, for doing what 'twas my pleasure to be doin'."

"Oh, well —" Mary picked up the lamp, not knowing what else to say. She carried it to the front of the long, narrow room and placed it on the eating table.

"Will you sit on the porch with me for a bit, Mary?"

She nodded, her mind responding to the persuasion of his voice. "I'll turn off the lamp. No use wasting the oil."

Hank's fingers curled around her forearm to guide her to the door. His nearness in the dark was something she hadn't anticipated as being so disturbing. Her silly heart was pounding like that of a scared rabbit. Every nerve in her body seemed to respond and reach out to the touch of his warm fingers.

Mary plunged into talk of the coming celebration as soon as they sat down on the edge of the porch.

"I realize we can't do much on such a short notice. The contests will be all the more exciting because of the prizes to the winners. Elias is going to donate a shaving mug and brush as well as a couple of shirts. Lottie Chandler will give tickets to a free meal. I'm going to bake pies to use in a pie-eating contest." She laughed and added, "We're going to see who can eat the fastest, not the most pies. Laura wants to donate a wool blanket and two pairs of leather gloves her husband hadn't worn."

"Don't be worryin'. It'll be a fine day. Big John's been itchin' to have a game of baseball. He played it durin' the war 'n' fancies himself quite a player. The company can afford to give a silver dollar to each of the players on the winning team."

"That's wonderful! I've seen the game played. Does John have the ball and bat?"

"Aye. He made the bat himself out of good stout hickory."

Hank pulled his pipe from his pocket and stuffed the bowl with tobacco. He lit it with a sulfur match, drew deeply, and the sweet smell of tobacco smoke that hung on the air reminded

229

Mary of the warm summer nights back home when her mother and father, with his pipe smoking, sat on the veranda.

"Are you going to play on one of the teams?"

"Will you come watch me if I play?"

"Of course."

"Then I'll be tempted to give it a try; but without a lawman here in town, it'll be my job to keep the peace that day."

Hank began to chuckle and Mary glanced up to see him smiling broadly around the stem of the pipe he held in his teeth.

"What's funny?"

"I'm thinkin' that you and Mrs. Hillard are forgettin' to ask Lizzibeth down at the Bee Hive what she'd be willin' to give for prizes."

"We haven't forgotten at all! We'll not be asking *her* for a donation, but she and her *girls* are part of the town and have as much right to come to the celebration as any of us."

Mary's voice was icy with disapproval. When she saw the grin on Hank's face, she clamped her mouth shut, tilted her chin and refused to look away from him. She was not sure if he was teasing her or not, but the thought of him in that *place* unnerved and angered her. Surely he didn't go *there*. That place was for other men, not for *him*.

Over the loud laughter drifting up from the saloon, Mary heard the questioning call of an owl in a far-off place and tried to concentrate her attention on the hundreds of fireflies flickering their brief lives away in the area between them and the timber. She turned her gaze toward Hank once again, miserably conscious of his eyes on her. She didn't know when it began, but suddenly she realized his fingers were lightly stroking her arm. It seemed to her that the fine hairs on her skin rose to meet his rough touch, and she wanted to lean against his hand.

"Were you happy with him?"

Mary was shocked by the intensity of his words, as well as by his tone, but she knew to whom he was referring.

"I suppose so."

"That's no answer to what I want to know. Were you happy with him?"

"He didn't beat me, if that's what you mean."

"Did you love the man?" His words were husky and hurried.

Mary pondered a way to evade his question. Finally she said, "We were not really suited to one another. He wanted one thing out of life and I wanted another."

"What did you want, Mary?" His fingers curled around her arm. She felt the same connecting warmth she had felt before when he held her arm. The emotional bruising of the past years seemed to melt and flow away through his fingertips.

"What did I want?" She repeated Hank's question, sighed deeply, and let several minutes go by before she answered. "I guess I wanted what most women want — to be . . . happy."

"What would it be takin' to do that?"

"Oh, I don't know. A home and security for

my child. And I want Katy to be happy. She's spent some of the best years of her life helping me." She couldn't go on. His hand on her arm was making coherent thought impossible.

Mary's brain pounded with a million vague thoughts she couldn't voice. She had always had the craving for the kind of love and companionship shared by her parents. It was the reason, she thought now, that she had been so susceptible to Roy. She had allowed him to charm her with promises and bits of flattery, all meaningless. But at the time she had believed the affection she felt for him would grow into an enduring love. She had been wrong. Roy had been like a small boy, refusing to grow up and take the responsibility for a family.

"You've never talked about yourself, Hank. Have you a family somewhere?"

"That I do. Two sisters back east. Both tryin' to fill the state with Kellys and O'Connells. Last count was thirteen. Could be more by now." He chuckled again.

"No brothers?"

"Two killed in the war."

"We lost our brothers in the war too."

"After my brothers were lost, I signed onboard a ship set to run the blockade. Rowe was the captain and he went where no other dared to go."

"That's where you met him?"

"Aye. You get to know a man when you face death together time and again."

His hand moved to her back and made soothing

circles between her shoulder blades. A small sigh of pleasure bubbled from her lips.

"Do you like that?"

"Oh, yes!" Mary felt the tightness of her muscles relax and the strain of the day fade into nothingness. This is dangerous, she told herself. Later she'd be embarrassed that she'd permitted such a thing to happen. She shoved the warning voice to the back of her mind and gave herself up to the intoxicating sensation of his strong fingers massaging her muscles. Suddenly his fingers stilled and spread until his palm lay flat on her back.

"I want to kiss you, Mary. You're so sweet and all —" His husky voice came to her through the cloud of unreality. She turned her head to look into his face. "Don't be scared. If you don't want it, say so."

Mary couldn't have said no if her life had depended on that one short word. His face was so close to hers that they were almost breathing the same air, so close she couldn't look into his eyes. Her hand moved up to his cheek, scraped across the day's growth of whiskers and into thick unruly hair. She closed her eyes, closed her fingers and pulled, offering her lips in a way she had never offered them to another man. Her parted lips eased up to his. The feel of his lips was hotly exciting, unfamiliarly hard, yet gentle. The hand on her back pressed her closer to him until she could feel the strong vibrations of his powerful heart. The strong pull of the attraction between them goaded her to kiss him with a fiery hunger. Without conscious thought, her arm moved to encircle his neck. He gently urged her mouth open and the tip of his tongue moved slowly along the inside of her lip. A fierce sensual need swept through her and she rode the crest of wild, sweet abandonment.

"Gawdamighty! You're a sweet woman," he breathed in her ear when finally their lips parted.

"Hank —" Mary took a deep, trembling breath. Suddenly dumbfounded by what she had done and what she had permitted him to do, she tried to pull away.

"Don't be sorry —" he said hearing the agony in her voice. "You're a warm-blooded woman. I'm a warm-blooded man. We harmed no one by kissin' each other."

He smoothed the hair back from her cheeks and tilted her chin so she had to look at him. She tried to turn her face aside, but his hand cupped her chin and held it so she had to look at him. The loving, caring expression on his rough, craggy features reached deep inside her and shook her into an awareness that Hank Weston was the type of man she had dreamed about.

"But I'm not . . . I'm not a loose woman."

"I know you're not a bold woman, Mary Stanton," he said gruffly. "I knew it the minute I laid eyes on you standin' with your hands folded in your apron, your cheeks rosy from the stove, your eyes lookin' at me like I was some strange creature that had just come out of a cave."

"I didn't! Hank, I didn't look at you like that."

"Aye, you did. And I was wantin' to kiss you then, too. Of late, I've been wanting it so bad, I was willin' to give a year of my life for one small kiss given to me without havin' to ask for it. Let me hold you for just a minute." He drew her head to his shoulder, his arms held her gently to him. "Don't be 'fraid. You feel good in my arms . . . all soft and sweet smellin' like a woman should." He buried his face in her hair.

"We shouldn't . . ." Mary said from somewhere beneath his chin.

"Is it so wrong that we take this short minute of pleasure together? Humm? Look at me, Mary." He raised her face with a finger beneath her chin. "I swear before God I'll never force myself on you."

"I know that, Hank. Heavens! You're the last man in town I'd be afraid of. But I feel sort of . . . guilty. I've not been a . . . widow for very long."

"The man's been dead for more than two months. He gave you a sweet little girl. For that you should remember him kindly, despite the fact the bas— despite the fact he went off and left you here unprotected. You're a woman, Mary, with a need to be loved and with a woman's love to give a man."

"I don't know, Hank." She moved her head back, trying to see his face in the dim light.

"I think you know, sweetheart."

His mouth touched hers softly, gently, and moved against it. She could have backed away and he would have let her go. A sigh trembled through her. *Sweetheart!* Did that mean he cared for her? She had to know, so she pulled back and put her hand to his cheek.

"Don't play with me, Hank. I can't afford a . . . dalliance."

"Dalliance? You think I want to dally with you when I'm carryin' such a strong feelin' for you and your child?"

"I don't know what to think."

"Then don't. Just let me hold you for a while. Later, you'll know if it's right or not." He whispered the words while looking earnestly into her eyes. His fingers moved into her hair. His lips were a mere breath away. "This is strange to me too. I've never wanted just to hold a woman before." He held her snugly against him, his arms shielding her from the cool night breeze. "I'll take care of you and Theresa forever if you'll let me. I ask for nothin' more," he whispered urgently.

His breath was warm and smelled of tobacco. His cheeks were pleasantly rough against her face, his body hard and warm against hers. It was heaven to feel so safe, so protected. He cradled her to him with a tenderness that she had not known since she was a child. The tension eased out of her as his fingers stroked the hair back from her ear and his warm lips stroked her brow.

I ask for nothing more.

A sudden flood of tenderness for this rugged man came over her as she mused over his words. She lay relaxed against him. His arms were like a safe haven in a violent storm. Feeling wonderfully happy, she closed her eyes. For the first time in her life she knew the meaning of the word *cherished*. This moment was hers, and nothing could take it away from her.

Katy and Rowe arrived in Virginia City in the middle of the afternoon. For the most part, it had been a silent ride on a well-packed road. Riding a gentle mare borrowed from the Sparkses' ranch, Katy rode beside Rowe, with Anton a short way behind.

When Katy had awakened that morning to discover that Rowe had removed her skirt and had unbuttoned her shirt, she had been so angry that for a while, a short while, she had thought of taking the mare and heading back over the mountains to Trinity, or riding on into Virginia City without him. But after careful consideration, she decided if she did the former, she would be defeating her purpose for coming; and if she did the latter, she would appear to be a fool in Emily Sparks's eyes. Before she left the bedroom, Katy decided for the time being to ignore the dastardly act and seek vengeance later.

Rowe and the burial party had returned to the ranch shortly before the noon meal. After that they had taken their leave, promising to stop on their way back to Trinity.

Virginia City, the capital of Wyoming Territory, was much more of a town than Katy had expected. The town had been founded more than ten years before, when gold was discovered in Alder Gulch. It was here that the vigilantes had exterminated the notorious Plummer outlaw gang.

A continuous row of buildings lined each side of the main street, which was clogged with horsemen and conveyances of every description. High-wheeled freight wagons pulled by six-mule hitches passed surreys with shiny black canopy tops and brass lamps attached to the sides. There was even a *volante,* a two-passenger carriage with two wheels and an open, hooded body. The body was set in front of the wheels and attached to the long shafts. The carriage was pulled by one horse that was ridden by a coachman. Katy hadn't seen a *volante* since she had left Alabama.

Women and children in calico dresses and bonnets waited on the seats of heavy wagons and watched ladies with painted faces walking by in silks and satins and wearing hats decorated with ostrich plumes perched atop high-piled, carefully arranged hair.

The Overland Stage came careening into town, the driver shouting obscenities to the tired team, urging them into a run suitable for a noticeable entrance. The distraction kept Katy from thinking about how shabby she looked in her wrinkled clothes, her hair hanging down her back in a long, unkempt braid, the sweat trickling down her dust-covered face.

The main street of town was decorated for the Fourth of July celebration. Banners and trailing streamers hung from upstairs windows and porch railings. Placards telling of the events of the day were nailed to the walls of the shops.

At a side street they paused to allow a funeral procession to pass. The enclosed, glass-windowed hearse was pulled by a black team whose harnesses were wrapped in black; black plumes attached to their bridles bobbed between their ears. The driver in a black serge suit and high-topped hat even wore black gloves. Following the hearse to the burial grounds were a half-dozen buggies filled with fashionably dressed ladies.

"Must of been somebody important," Anton said and moved up beside Rowe and Katy.

"Yer gawddammed right 'twas somebody important." The whiskered man who spoke sat on his horse a few feet away, his hat in his hand out of respect for the dead. " 'Twas Jodee Miller, is who it was. Take yore hat off, mister."

"Sorry." Anton removed his hat and glanced at Rowe. His leather hat was tucked in his belt.

"Feller what did 'er in was gunned down on the spot. Jodee was a good whore, give a man his money's worth and deserves a good send-off."

"Rowe! Rowe!" A black-haired woman leaned from the last buggy in the procession and waved a black handkerchief. "Rowe, darlin'. Yoo-hoo! It's me, Nan. I missed ya like hell, ya handsome devil! Come see me tonight at the Opera House."

Rowe waved, then turned to see Katy regarding him with disgust. He lifted his shoulders and grinned sheepishly.

"Nan Neal. She sings and dances at the Opera House."

"The same Nan Neal who had the tonsorial parlor in Laramie? How did she get way up here?"

"Who knows? Maybe she came because I'm here."

"Just your type."

"Jealous because she likes me?" he teased.

"Bullfoot!" Katy gigged her horse and moved ahead. "She likes anything with britches on."

They moved on down the street, turned a corner, and stopped at the livery. A boy sat on a stump in front of a folded back door. He jumped to his feet when Rowe slid from the saddle.

"Ya want me ta give 'em a rub, mister?"

"Sure. And some extra grain."

"Gonna be here long?"

"Several days. Tell your pa to put the bill on a tab for Garrick Rowe. I'll be at the Crescent Hotel. Can you remember that?"

"Sure, Mr. Rowe."

Katy stepped from the saddle before Rowe could reach her to help her down. She untied her valise from the back of the saddle and stood waiting. Anton turned his horse over to the boy, shouldered his pack, and took off down the street after speaking a few words to Rowe and tipping his hat to Katy.

After taking the valise from Katy's hand, Rowe took her arm and they walked back to the main street of town without speaking. When they started down the boardwalk, he held her close to

240

his side and steered her around the men loitering in front of the Pony Saloon, down the steps to cross another street, and up onto another boardwalk that fronted a series of shops. Katy noticed the women on the walk had eyes only for Rowe and that they scarcely glanced at her at all.

When they passed the office of the *Post*, Montana's first newspaper, Katy saw their reflection in the glass of the window. Rowe *was* an attractive man, but she looked as if she had come from a soddy somewhere out on the prairie. Katy lifted her chin a little higher. She had been educated in all the social graces and was confident that she could dress and hold her own in any level of society. But she wasn't here to charm anyone. She would learn to run the stage office, and one day in the near future, she and Mary and Theresa would be on a stage heading for the railroad that would take them home.

CHAPTER
Fourteen

Katy had time for no more than a glance at the lobby of the Crescent Hotel, where deep leather chairs sat on polished floors and a crystal chandelier hung from the ceiling. Rowe steered her to the desk where he was greeted with a welcoming smile and a handshake by a potbellied man in a white vest with a gold watch chain stretched across the front of it.

"Mr. Rowe! It's a pleasure to have you back again."

"Thank you. I need a room for the lady."

The smile left the man's face. "I'm sorry, Mr. Rowe. We're full up. There's not a room left. People have flocked in for the celebration."

"Did you let out my room?" Rowe asked sharply.

"No! Of course not! You're paid up for six months. It's just as you left it."

"Then the lady can have my room. I'll find something else." Rowe picked up Katy's valise and urged her toward the stairway.

"I'm sorry about not having a room for your . . . for your . . . ah . . . lady."

Katy spun around, her eyes as cold as a frozen

pond. "Miss Burns. Miss Katherine Burns. And I'm not his *lady*."

"Oh, I didn't mean —" His eyes darted to Rowe to see if he had also taken offense. Rowe lifted his brows and shrugged.

"You're sure you don't have a spare bed somewhere?"

"Not even a bedroll, sir. I had to hire a new man and he has things in a terrible mess. A man came in yesterday, and because his name was Rowe, the desk clerk gave him the key to your room, assuming it was you. I had the unpleasant task of having to tell the man and his wife to leave. Needless to say, he was very angry."

With one foot on the stairs, Rowe turned abruptly. "The man's name was Rowe? Where was he from?"

"Back East. He said he had come out to hunt buffalo. Funny, though! Men from the East don't usually bring their wives when they come to hunt. Ah . . . you know what I mean," he stammered. "I put your mail in your room myself, Mr. Rowe."

"Thank you. Send up a bath for Miss Burns."

"The bath at the end of the hall —"

"Send up a bath, Wilson." The tone of Rowe's voice left no room for argument.

"Yes, sir."

When they reached the second floor, they walked down a long, narrow hallway to the corner room. Rowe produced a key and unlocked the door. The room was dim, hot, and airless. He pushed back heavy draperies and opened the windows. Katy stood just inside the door and surveyed the room. The four-poster bed had a deep mattress. A mirror framed in oak hung over a bureau of polished wood. The other furnishings were a commode, a washstand with real linen towels hanging from the towel bar, and an armoire standing against the inside wall. She took the two steps necessary to reach the armoire and opened one of the doors. Clothes, men's clothes, hung neatly from wire hangers. Now she understood why Rowe had brought such a small pack from Trinity. Everything he needed was here.

"Where will you go?"

"Are you worried I'll have to sleep in the livery with the horses?"

"Why do you always answer my questions with a question? It's irritating."

The grin appeared and spread charmingly on his face, rearranging his dark features until he was breathtakingly handsome in a roguish way.

"I'd far rather irritate you than make no impression on you at all." He picked up several letters lying on the bureau, thumbed through them, then opened a drawer and shoved them inside. "I'll go down to the barbershop and take a bath while you're taking one here. Then I'll come back and change clothes. You can stand in the corner with your face to the wall." His eyes laughed at the frosty look that swept over her face.

A sharp rap on the door caused Katy to bite back a retort. Rowe opened it to admit a large, dark-skinned colored woman in a starched white apron. She came in carrying a highbacked tin bathing tub.

"Howdy, Mistah Rowe."

"Howdy, Beulah. How's things with you?"

"Things is fine. This yore lady?"

"I'm a business associate," Katy said before Rowe could answer.

"Buzzness? Hummm —" The woman's large expressive eyes went first to Rowe, then back to Katy. She smiled broadly. "Buzzness. Well, Lordy me."

"Yeah, Beulah. Business, pure and simple."

"Well — I never knowed 'bout no *pure* buzzness, Mr. Rowe. Matter a fact, ain't never knowed no simple buzzness either." The chuckle was deep and rich.

"Beulah sings like an angel, Katy. Maybe she'll sing for us sometime."

"Get on with yo, Mistah Rowe," Beulah snorted, but she was beaming with pleasure. "Singin' don't put no grub on the table; makin' beds and emptyin' slop jars does. Get yore lazy selfs on in here," she said to the two lanky youths who appeared at the door with a bucket of steaming water in each hand. "Don't yawl spill a drop on the floor or I'll nail yore hides to the barn door." Beulah placed a stack of fluffy towels on the chair, watched the boys carefully pour the water in the tub, then went to the door.

"Yawl need somethin', holler down that tube."

As soon as they were alone, Katy turned on

Rowe like a spitting cat.

"She thinks . . . she thinks that I'm your . . . your paramour!"

"What's so bad about that?"

"There you go again! Dammit to hell, Rowe!"

"Don't swear, love. I don't like to hear swear-words coming from your pretty mouth. I'll go so you can take your bath and maybe you'll be in a more pleasant frame of mind by the time I get back."

"What tube was Beulah talking about?"

Rowe moved a metal plate on an inner wall. "When you're through with the tub, call down and Beulah will send the boys to get it."

"Well for goodness' sake!"

"All the modern conveniences, sweetheart," he said on his way to the door.

Suddenly his arm snaked out and pulled her to him. Before she could utter a word of protest, he closed her mouth with his and kissed her, deeply, thoroughly. His mouth, warm, possessive, and flavored with the musky sweetness of the cigar he had smoked on the way into town, forced her lips apart in an intimacy greater than any of the other kisses they had shared. His breath was hot and fierce, his tongue bold, sensuous, and demanding, robbing her of the ability to think, breathe, or even begin to test her strength against the arms holding her. When he reluctantly released her mouth, he let out a rasping breath that blew warm on her wet lips. The eyes that looked into hers were dark mirrors that reflected her image. The exasperated look in her eyes had been replaced by an emotion of a different kind.

"Make yourself pretty for me," he said in a husky whisper, pinching her chin with his thumb and forefinger. "I want to show you off at supper tonight."

He left the door open when he went out. More angry at herself than him, Katy slammed it shut and twisted the key in the lock. She raised her hand and pressed her fingertips to her lips. They were warm and wet. Her whole body felt strangely hot as her mind roiled in a confused array of emotions. She had felt something totally unexpected just now when he held her in his arms and kissed her. He had felt it too, because in spite of his nonchalant manner, his heart had been pounding like a sledge hammer against her breasts.

The night before she had been completely at ease with him when he massaged her tired muscles. There had been no mistaking the gentleness of his touch or the compassion he had displayed for her discomfort. She was not at ease now. Her heart was racing like that of a runaway horse, and in the core of her femininity was a gnawing ache.

On one hand, she thought as she began to remove her clothing, she was beginning more and more to rely on Rowe. On the other hand, she had come to realize how dangerous and unpredictable he was. He was certainly capable of taking another human life. He had killed five men during the short time she had known him. Of course, she reasoned, the five men were trying to kill him. There was more to Garrick Rowe than met the eye. He was well-known here in Virginia City. But that wasn't saying anything in his favor. In a town such as this, money spoke with a loud voice, but even if he had none, his looks would have made him attractive to women. The thought that he might have brought Nan Neal, the woman who waved at him from the funeral procession, to this room crossed her mind and troubled it.

Katy pulled the draperies over the windows before she shed her last garment, climbed into the tub, and sank down in the warm, soothing water. It was heavenly! She leaned her head against the high back of the tub and scooted down until only the pink nipples of her breasts were above the water. She willed the warm water to soak away the aches and pains, the weariness, the anxieties.

With her eyes closed, she tried to picture how Mary would look when she told her the way was clear for them to leave Trinity, but a dark face with straight black brows and eyes as dark as the bottom of a well kept getting in the way. The firm, hard lips opened, smiled, and whispered, "Nightrose."

Katy's eyes flew open. "Nightrose!" She said the word aloud with a snort of disgust. The sound of her own voice had a strange sound in this strange room. "Damn you, Garrick Rowe, get out of my mind!" she snarled, cupped her hands, and splashed water up onto her face.

She would have lingered in the tub, but the thought of Rowe returning and pounding on the door caused her to rush the bath. After she dried herself, she was tempted to wash her stockings, her drawers, and her shirt in the water, but then she reasoned that they would have to hang in the room to dry, exposed to Rowe's eyes, and thought better of it. Later, she promised herself, she would ask Beulah for directions to the laundry.

Now, dressed in the wrinkled dress that had been folded for two days in her valise, she brushed her hair, rebraided it, and pinned the braid to the back of her head.

Make yourself pretty.

She recalled Rowe's words as she looked at herself critically in the mirror. The light blue dress had a white lace collar decorating the scooped neckline and three-inch lace on the cuffs. The dress was neat and in good taste, but far from fashionable. She'd look like a rag doll compared to some of the women she'd seen on the street today. The thought of appearing shabby and out of place made her cringe. Then pride came forward and restored her confidence. She hadn't asked Rowe to take her to supper. As a matter of fact, there was no reason at all why she had to eat with him. She had two perfectly good legs and money in her pocket. There were other places in this town to eat besides the dining room of the Crescent Hotel.

After she put all her things back in the valise, she stood by the window and looked down on the street. It was dusk and the traffic was not as heavy as when they had first arrived. Katy saw Rowe cross the street. She recognized the way he walked. Even without a hat, he was a half-head taller than any man on the street.

A strange feeling centered in the region of Katy's heart. She didn't know if it was because he was the only person in sight who was familiar to her or anticipation of being with him in this small room. She watched him until he stepped under the canopy covering the porch of the hotel, then listened for his footsteps coming down the hall.

Down the street at the Anaconda Hotel, Justin Rowe stood in the large oriel window built out from the wall and nesting on a bracket. From this point he could see up and down the main street of Virginia City. His pale blue eyes were drawn to Rowe's tall, lanky frame for he was a man who stood out in a crowd. As Justin watched, Rowe paused to let a carriage pass, then quickly crossed the street.

"Helga," Justin said sharply. "Come here." The woman jumped off the chair and hurried to the window. "Isn't that Garrick?"

"Where?"

"There! Going up the steps to the walk in front of the newspaper."

"Why, yes, I believe it is. Although I've never seen him in clothes like that."

"What did you expect, a cutaway coat and

striped trousers?" he sneered.

Helga backed away from the window and took her place once again on the straight-backed chair. Justin had been in a strange mood for the past day and a half. It had something to do with the letter he had taken from Garrick's bureau during the brief few minutes they had been in his room. They had no more than set their bags on the floor and removed their hats when the manager had knocked on the door and ordered them out. The room, he had said, was rented by the month to a Mr. Garrick Rowe. He was sorry for the inconvenience, but the new clerk had made a mistake because of the name.

Justin had already seen the mail on the bureau addressed to Garrick and had slipped a letter into his pocket before he opened the door to admit the manager. He had put up a fuss, but in the end they had gone across to the Anaconda Hotel and were given one of the last rooms available.

Last evening and today he had stood or sat by the window looking down on the street. He didn't talk or complain about the shabbiness of the room. He didn't even berate her when it took so long for her to bring him a tray of food. Helga didn't know what to make of it. She had thought she knew all of her husband's moods. Justin acted almost as if his self-confidence had been wiped out of him. Impossible, she reasoned. Justin Rowe was the most arrogant, confident person she had ever known. But something had given him a jolt.

251

Helga had no hope that he would share it with her. He never did.

Helga took advantage of the quiet time to think about her son at home. She missed him so desperately and was so fearful of the training he was receiving at the hands of the nurse Justin had hired. He was being taught that he was so superior to the children of the servants he played with that if he wanted them to lie down and be walked on, they should do so.

To leave Ian had been one of the hardest things Helga had ever had to do. She hoped and prayed that Justin would hurry and do whatever it was he had come here for so they could go home.

The sight of his half brother had set the demons of hatred working again in Justin. The black bastard! Even in buckskin pants and rough shirt, he walked with his head high as if he were a king instead of the half-caste son of a bitch that he was. Papa, he asked silently as he had done a million or more times, how could you have married that near-black woman from a foreign shore?

Justin thought about the contents of the letter in his pocket. The gods had been on his side, letting the fool clerk give them the key to Garrick's room, letting the letter lie there in plain sight, and giving him time to slip it into his pocket before the manager arrived. No one would ever know the contents of that letter except himself and the man who wrote it. He would settle with that Pinkerton detective after he had dealt with Garrick. As far as Justin knew, his half brother had never married. If Garrick died, he would be the next of kin and would inherit the fortune that was rightfully his but for the dark, Greek bitch Preston Rowe had married on that fateful trip to Paris. He would have to be very careful. There must be no connection between him and Garrick's demise; and *that* would take some planning.

Justin looked across the room at his wife sitting so placidly in the chair, her hands folded in her lap. She was the picture of womanhood with her blond hair, blue eyes, and milk white skin. They had produced a son of their superior race. A blond, blue-eyed boy to carry their bloodline into the next generation. What further need did he have of Helga now, except to bury himself between her soft thighs when he had excited himself to the degree that his manhood demanded release. It was getting harder and harder for him to reach that point. The last time he had whipped her bare white ass until it bled, and he hadn't even experienced a weak erection.

His thoughts switched to his mother. The goddamn stupid bitch! If he could get his hands on her at this moment, he was quite certain that he would wring her neck. His hand sought the envelope in his pocket, reassuring himself that it was still there.

"We're leaving tomorrow or the next day," Justin said suddenly.

"Oh, Justin. I'm so glad." Helga lifted her bowed head and smiled. "I'm so anxious to get home and see Ian."

"Goddammit, Helga. You're as dumb as a gourd. I didn't say we were going home. We're not going home until I've done what I came out here to do. See if you can get that into that stupid head of yours." He turned back to the window. "Get downstairs and get me something to eat. I'm going out after a while, but you're not to stir from this room. Understand?"

Katy unlocked the door and opened it when Rowe knocked. She had a small pouch purse looped over her arm. He stood in the doorway for a moment and looked at her, then came inside, closed the door, and leaned his back against it. He had been shaved. His hair, free of trail dust, was as black and shiny as a crow's wing.

"Pretty." As he spoke she heard the key turn in the lock. "And all set to run out on me."

"There's nothing in our agreement that says I must take my meals with you. Open the door and let me out."

"Not on your sweet life. There are more drunks down on the street than you've seen in a lifetime. You're not leaving here without me." Holding the door key between his teeth, he went to the armoire and took out a pair of dark cord britches and a soft white shirt.

"I'm not staying in here while you . . . strip!"

"How are you going to get out? Through the window? You'll need a ladder." He yanked his shirt out of his britches, pulled it off over his head, and tossed it onto the floor beside the bathtub.

"Did you have a good bath? I'd rather have taken mine here with you, but the woman at the barbershop did a good job scrubbing my back." He whipped the belt from the waist of his trousers and began to unbutton his fly.

Katy spun around and went to the window, her face flaming. "Don't you have any refinement? You're the crudest man I ever met."

"Then you've not met many men. That suits me just fine. Greek men are possessive of their women."

"I'm not your *woman!* I'm not a horse or a dog to be *owned* by a man," she said heatedly.

"No, honey, you are certainly not a horse or a dog. You're a soft, pretty, sweet woman and I'm mighty glad of it. I don't know why you're so embarrassed about being in the same room with me when I take off my clothes. There's a beautiful race of people in the South Sea Islands who don't bother with clothes at all."

"Savages!"

"We'll soon know everything there is to know about each other, Nightrose." His britches flew across the room and landed on the floor at her feet. "I'll know how deep your belly hole is, and you'll discover I've got a brown birthmark on the inside of my thigh right up close to my —"

"Shut up!"

Katy's hands gripped the thick, velvet draperies. She stood there, stiff with indignation, and listened to him whistle a tune through his teeth as he dressed. Finally, he moved up behind her and placed his hands over hers.

"I can't resist teasing you, Katy. You're as pretty as a speckled pup when you get your dander up." With his hands on her shoulders, he turned her around so he could see her face. "Cheer up, honey. We'll have a good supper, then we'll walk up and down the street and see the sights."

"And that's supposed to thrill me to death?"

He ignored her sarcasm. "Tomorrow is a big day. There's going to be a boxing match and your friend's husband, Pack Gallagher, will referee it. Did you know that he was the bare-knuckle champion of a few years back? I don't know him, but I've seen him fight. He's trying to promote fighting with padded gloves. He says there are less injuries to the fighters."

"It's barbaric for two men to stand toe-to-toe and strike each other!"

"This is an exhibition match. The fighters will wear gloves and I'll just bet there'll be ladies present."

"Well, I won't be there. And I doubt that Mara Shannon will either, if she's here."

"There'll be footraces," he said in his low persuasive voice, "and sack races, and contests to catch a greased pig and climb a greased flagpole. Wouldn't you like to see the mud fight between the girls from the Bucket of Blood Saloon? The winner will receive ten silver dollars, and she'll be allowed to keep all her take of the upstairs money for a week."

"Why, that's disgraceful!" she said staunchly,

256

but there was a twinkle in her eyes. "Ever since women earned the right to vote they've been trying to do everything men do. Voting and using your brain is one thing; making a spectacle of yourself is another."

"I agree. Perfect."

"Perfect?"

"You."

"Now cut that out! I came here to learn something about how to run the stage office."

"Tomorrow we'll celebrate, the next day we'll work. And tonight I'm going to show you the sights."

CHAPTER
Fifteen

From the doorway of the dining room, Katy's eyes swept over the elegantly dressed diners and almost groaned. In her wrinkled cotton dress she felt terribly shabby and out of place. She glanced up to see Rowe smiling down at her, a challenge in his dark eyes as if he were waiting to see if she was going to turn and run. Pride stiffened her backbone, lifted her chin, and gave her courage a needed boost. The calm, placid expression on her face masked her wrenching embarrassment as she walked into the room as if she were the best-dressed woman there.

"Nightrose, darling, you're priceless. There isn't a woman in this town half as beautiful as you," Rowe murmured as he seated her at a small table beside a round column painted with a climbing vine.

"Flowery words don't change a thing," she replied when he was seated opposite her. "I'm aware, as you are, that everyone is gawking at us because I look as if I had slept in my clothes for a week."

"At least they know we were not sleeping together," he said softly. "For you would have been sleeping in nothing at all." His eyes laughed at her.

Katy's face reddened and she tried to be angry. The words coming from another man would have been insulting, but her lips twitched and she had to hold back a bubble of laughter. A small flutter of gratitude jerked at her heart as she suddenly realized he was a very considerate man. Rowe was the only man in the dining room without a coat. He had dressed in keeping with the dress she wore.

A woman in a dark dress, white starched apron and cap came to the table. She had a large, sturdy frame, rosy cheeks, and eyes only for Rowe.

"Oh, Mr. Rowe, you've come back."

"Ah, yes." He rubbed his chin and grinned at her.

"You cut off your beard!"

"My . . . ah . . . lady friend likes to see my face."

"So do I."

Rowe watched Katy as she rolled her eyes toward the ceiling with a bored expression on her face.

"According to the posted bill of fare they're serving river trout or roast beef and creamed potatoes. Which do you want, sweetheart?"

Katy could feel the woman's eyes, curious yet resentful, glaring down on her, but she refused to look up. Instead she gave Rowe one of her warmest smiles.

"The roast beef, *darlin'*."

"Two roast beef plates, and afterward we'll each have a dish of ice cream."

"Are you trying to break the poor girl's heart?" Katy asked as soon as the serving woman hurried away.

"Why do you say that?"

"She looked at you as if she could eat you."

"She's friendly, that's all. I was here for a month before I came to Trinity."

"And apparently became well acquainted with the hotel staff."

"I learned a long time ago that being pleasant instead of unkind to those who serve me will get me a lot better service."

"Being pleasant to this employee need not include paying for her supper. I pay my own way. I want to make myself clear on that point."

"And I'll make this clear. You're not my employee . . . yet. Tonight and tomorrow you're my guest. Don't mention it again or I'll be forced to take drastic action."

"Being pleasant does not extend to . . . guests?"

"Where you're concerned, Nightrose, I make and break the rules as the occasion demands." He raked his scorching eyes over each feature of her face, then laughed, a deep, masculine laugh. "Give up, sweetheart. You won't be able to hold out against me. I'm determined to make you mine."

"You're setting yourself up for a disappointment, Mr. Rowe."

"I think not, Miss Burns."

"You make me so . . . damn mad!" she whispered. "You know I'll not make a scene here!"

"I know no such thing. That's what makes being with you so exciting. You're my soul mate, Nightrose. A hundred years from now we'll meet again. We'll fight, make up, love each other to distraction, and fight again."

The twinkle in his eyes both infuriated and frightened her. Her heart gave a sickening leap. The big jackass knew that she was attracted to him! She felt as if the licorice black eyes beneath the thick, straight brows were reading her innermost thoughts, attacking the barrier she had erected to protect herself against his magnetism.

"I don't believe in your stupid theory of reincarnation."

"Shhh . . . here comes our meal. You can fuss at me later."

The meal was delicious. Despite Katy's unease when they first entered the dining room, despite Rowe's teasing words, she relaxed and enjoyed it. While they were eating, he told her about his plans for Trinity.

"I want to make Trinity a real town with a bank, stores, a church, and a school. I want decent houses for the workers. The mine will play out eventually and that's the reason I'll not build a smelter plant. It will last long enough for me to keep the men busy while my other plan formulates."

"If the mine plays out, the workers will leave, and your town will go the way of hundreds of other mining towns."

"The country is opening up, Nightrose. Cattle and lumber will be the thing. People will need lumber to build homes. North and west of Trinity is the finest stand of timber I've seen. I have a man working on getting us the cutting rights. I have every hope that before we leave Virginia City we'll be in the lumber business."

"You'll build a saw mill at Trinity?"

"With a little dredging of the creek and the pond where we saw the honkers it will be ideal. We can freight our lumber south to Salt Lake, or north to Helena. I think our biggest market will be right here in Montana. Cattlemen are coming in and they'll need building supplies."

"I heard that the government has set aside a large parcel of land for a National Park."

"That was a couple of years ago. The area is east of here and called the Yellowstone, after the river. A very smart move by the government. It's a land with geysers, waterfalls, hot sulfur springs, and bubbling mud pots. One of the geysers comes up out of the ground about every half hour and shoots a hundred feet in the air. Someday I'll take you there."

"It sounds scary."

"It is, at first. I'm fascinated with this country. It's wild, beautiful, tough, and at times brutal."

"I know. Mary, Theresa, and I almost froze to death last winter."

A dark scowl covered Rowe's face. "You'll never again suffer from neglect. I promise you."

"I'm not your responsibility, Rowe. I've told you that. And while I'm about it, I want to repeat once again I'm not turning my life over to you."

"Sweetheart, you won't have a thing to say about it."

The scowl disappeared from his face, and a soft, loving light shone from his dark eyes. His words and the sound of his deep voice touched something in Katy's memory, making her heart jump out of rhythm.

The serving woman returned with the ice cream. Katy savored each bite while wishing fervently that Mary and Theresa were here to enjoy the treat. Aware that Rowe watched her and was enjoying her obvious delight in the creamy, bitingly cold dessert, she smiled at him with more happiness in her eyes than he had ever seen before.

When they finished, Rowe escorted her from the room with his hand cupped about her elbow, holding her possessively to his side. Katy was conscious of the stares, but failed to see the envious glances of the women they passed while threading their way among the tables.

As soon as they entered the almost empty lobby, Katy's eyes were drawn to the stairway by a child's joyous laughter. A man and a woman were holding onto the hands of a small girl. Two steps from the bottom, the girl paused and they swung her the rest of the way down. Her childish laughter rang out. Her small arms circled the man's leg.

"Hold me, Papa."

The big dark-haired man scooped the child up in his arms. She wrapped her arms about his neck and placed wet kisses on his cheek. He grinned at the disapproving look on his wife's face.

"I'll swear, Pack. You'll be carrying that child when she's twenty years old."

"I hope so, love."

"It's the Gallaghers from Laramie," Katy said and hurried across the lobby to speak to them before they went into the dining room. "Mara Shannon —"

The auburn-haired woman with skin that was like fine white china turned when she heard her name. She was beautifully dressed in a tight-waisted green taffeta dress with large mutton sleeves. The bodice was buttoned to her chin. She was not a beautiful woman, but she was attractive in a soft, womanly way.

"Katy? Oh, Pack, it's Katy Burns. Katy, imagine seeing you way up here!"

"I knew you were coming to town and I was hoping to see you. Mr. and Mrs. Gallagher and Brita, I'd like you to meet Mr. Garrick Rowe. I'm going to be working for him for a while."

"For a good long while if I have anything to say about it," Rowe said, extending his hand to Mara Shannon, then to Pack Gallagher. "It's a pleasure to meet you. I saw you fight Kilkenny a few years ago in Laramie and decided that if I ever met you, I'd do my best to stay on your good side."

Pack laughed and glanced down at his wife. "That was my last fight. If I get into the ring for any reason other than to referee, my wife will clean my clock when I get home. Her temper is something to behold."

"You can bet your buttons I would, Pack Gallagher," Mara Shannon retorted quickly. She looked up at her husband, her eyes shining with love. "Pack raises money to support the orphanage by promoting boxing exhibitions," she explained, beaming with pride.

"It took a long time, but my wife has finally come to appreciate the sport," Pack said.

"Only with gloves."

"Yes, love. Only with gloves."

"How are things at the orphanage?" Katy asked.

"Fine. Just fine. We have twenty-one children there now. After you left, we advertised for a teacher and hired a woman from Nebraska. She's working out just fine. Are Mary and Theresa with you?"

"No. They're back in Trinity. On our way here we spent the night with Sam and Emily Sparks. Emily told me you were coming to stay with her for a while."

"I wondered how you knew. How is Emily? As soon as Pack is finished tomorrow, we're going out to the ranch until after the baby arrives."

"I bet Sam's watching over Emily like a mother hen," Pack said with a deep chuckle.

"I can't say that I blame him a bit. I'd be doing

the same if my wife was giving me a child." Rowe's arm went about Katy's waist and drew her close against his side. "We'd better let these people go in and eat, sweetheart."

Mara Shannon's expressive eyes went from Katy to Rowe. "I'll see you tomorrow, Katy. Are you staying here?"

"In Room 204," Rowe said before Katy could answer. "It was a pleasure meeting you, Mrs. Gallagher." He offered his hand to Pack. "You're a lucky man."

"I be knowin' it. So are you." Pack grinned at Katy.

"Katy and I are going for a walk about town," Rowe said before she could retort. "We'll see you tomorrow."

On the boardwalk in front of the hotel, Katy turned to face Rowe. "You deliberately let them think that you and I . . . that we . . . that we are —"

"A couple? We are, sweetheart. Will you be cold without a shawl?"

"No! And don't change the subject."

"What's wrong with letting them know we're mates?"

"Mates? We're not *mates!*"

"We will be . . . soon. Come on." He took her elbow and urged her down the walk away from the hotel. "Don't get in a huff over minor details."

Rowe held her close to his side as he steered her past the loafers leaning against the buildings lining the street. Light streamed out of the windows and doors of the shops and saloons they passed. The town was alive with drovers, drifters, gamblers, miners, and soldiers who had come to town to celebrate the Fourth of July.

They passed a saloon where someone was playing on an off-key piano. Loud male voices, the scraping of boot heels on the plank floor, and the clinking of glasses came from another wide entranceway with twin swinging doors. Further down the street, a woman was singing "Believe Me If All Those Endearing Young Charms." The voice was surprisingly good, and the audience was quiet while she sang, but when she finished, a roar of shouting, stomping on the floor, and the pounding of whiskey bottles on the tables proclaimed their approval of the popular song's rendition.

Rowe moved Katy quickly against the wall and stood protectively in front of her when a man with a white apron wrapped about his waist suddenly burst from the dark interior of a saloon and propelled a bearded drunk from his establishment. With a loud string of obscenities the burly bartender threw the man into the street. Stunned, he lay there. A horseman coming down the street jumped his horse over the inert body, and a carriage with iron-rimmed wheels passed, barely missing him.

"He'll get run over," Katy exclaimed. Even as she spoke the drunk was rolling toward the side of the street and came up against the edge of the walk.

"He'll be all right. This is the rough part of town. We'll cross here and go back on the other side," Rowe said as they stepped down from the walk into the street.

Katy was cold. No matter how hot the days, the nights were cool in the mountains. Her teeth almost chattered when she asked, "Where's the Opera House?"

"At the other end of town. Do you want to see the show?"

"No. I thought you might want to see it. You were invited, you know."

"I know. Nan Neal is quite a woman. She can kick higher than a man's head."

"What a glorious accomplishment!"

A satisfied smile settled on Rowe's face. If he read the tone right, Katy was jealous. A good sign.

"The stage office is down this side street and on the corner is the bank where I do business. This is the Territorial Government Building," he explained and paused in front of a two-storied brick building.

"Clearly the most impressive building in town," Katy murmured. "Are there any churches?"

"Three. The churches and the school are behind this side of the main part of town up there on the hill. The cemetery is on the hill beyond the other side of the street. Here's E. Olinghouse & Co. They have one of the best lines of merchandise in town. Is there something you want?"

Katy read the sign posted at the side of the

door. GOOD NEWS! JUST ARRIVED VIA THE MISSOURI RIVER AND FORT BEN-TON: A LARGE STOCK OF FANCY AND STAPLE GOODS. The variety of the items listed below the large block letters ranged from sugar to hay forks and everything in between. The open door of the store looked inviting, and Katy wished that she had the money to buy something pretty for Mary and Theresa. Not for anything did she want Rowe to know she had only a small amount of money left. Even while she was thinking these thoughts, Rowe was leading her into the store.

"I don't need anything."

"Look around, honey. I want to get some cigars."

It was warmer inside. The scent of spices mixed with leather goods, wool, new wood, and cured meat was a pleasant smell that at one time had been familiar, but one she hadn't experienced for more than a year. An array of tools, rope, and all manner of supplies essential to life in a mining town and its surrounding area filled the store. One had to maneuver around barrels, chairs, wagon seats, plows, shovels and nails. Crocks and wooden churns lined the aisles, as did huge iron kettles and washboards.

Katy paused at a long table where ribbons in all the colors of the rainbow were wound neatly on spools. She fingered the satin cloth and once again wished she had money to buy a length for Mary and for Theresa. She moved on to gaze at the bolts of material, the boxes of buttons, the lace trimmings, and a spool cabinet of thread. There were ostrich feathers for hats and whalebones for corsets.

At a table piled high with men's hats, both wide-brimmed and bowler, she came face-to-face with a man who was moving toward the door. He stopped, and the way he looked at her was so intense that she couldn't look away from his piercing blue eyes. Katy's fleeting impression was that his hair beneath the gray bowler hat was very light, as were his brows, lashes, and mustache. It seemed that he towered over her ready to spring, reminding her strongly of the cougar that stalked her from the ledge behind the funerary in Trinity. She knew instinctively that this was a dangerous man.

Justin stared at the woman. He had seen his half brother come into the store with her and had heard the endearment. A wave of almost uncontrollable anger flowed over him. The horny black devil had latched onto this beautiful blond, blue-eyed woman! Damn his rotten soul to hell! He was set to mix his dark blood with that of a pure Caucasian. He hadn't married her. If he had, the marriage hadn't been recorded. Justin had checked into that as soon as he'd come to town.

For all the woman's beauty, she was dirt or she'd not have taken up with a foreigner who was as dark as a mulatto. Feeling the veins in his neck begin to swell as anger and hatred consumed him, Justin quickly sidestepped around the woman and walked quickly out the door. He had to get away, to think and plan. He headed down the street toward the saloons where the whiskey was watered down and the tarnished angels who served it wore faded satin and had holes in their stockings. Justin was certain that before the night was over, he would find someone willing to do what had to be done.

Katy had faced the man for no more than ten seconds, yet she felt as if she would remember his face always. He looked nothing like anyone she had ever seen before. So why had he glared as if he despised her? A good bit of the excitement of being in the store left her, and she wandered on back to the counter where the clerk was handing Rowe a box of cigars.

"Did you see something you want?" Rowe asked.

"No."

Rowe picked up a bundle from the counter and tucked it under his arm. They walked back through the store, and when they reached the doorway, Rowe unfurled a blue shawl and flipped it around her shoulders.

"I can't have my Nightrose getting cold," he whispered softly against her ear.

"No! I have a shawl back at the hotel." Katy reached to jerk it off, but Rowe's hands closed over hers.

"Now you have two."

"No, Rowe. I'll not accept gifts from you. I'm not your poor relation."

"Thank God for that! Wear the shawl, or I'm

going to grab you up and kiss you right here."

"You wouldn't!" she sputtered, but she knew by the look in his eyes that he would.

"If you don't like the wrap after you see it in the light of day, give it to Beulah. I hope you'll keep it. It matches your eyes perfectly and it's my first gift to you."

"I want to go back to the room. You can go on to see your friend at the Opera House."

Rowe ignored the suggestion. "Are you warm?"

"Yes. It feels wonderful. I didn't realize I was so cold until we went into the store."

As they walked past the Chicago Hotel, the Occidental Billiard Hall, the assay office and on past the store with a swinging sign that read Mechanical Bakery, Katy kept thinking about the man in the store who had stared at her. She considered mentioning it to Rowe, but what could she say? A man had looked at her, and a cold chill had run down her spine?

They crossed the street to the building that housed the printing press, stopping at the window for a moment to watch the printer roll the ink roller over the page of set type locked into the press, and then deftly place the paper over the print.

"Have you ever watched them set the type?" Rowe asked. "It's amazing how fast they can go."

"I've watched a printer's helper break down the page. Each letter goes into its proper slot so when the typesetter reaches for a letter he'll know what he is getting."

There were a number of rowdies and drunks on the street, and Katy was thankful to have Rowe beside her. One look at his large, muscular frame and dark, scowling face caused more than one man to make sure he didn't come within touching distance of her, and usually the groups that congregated in front of the saloons quieted down as the couple passed by.

The hotel lobby was almost empty when they reached it. They went up the stairs and down the hall to the room. Rowe unlocked the door, went inside, and lit the lamp. Katy stood just inside the room. The bathtub had been taken away and the room tidied. Rowe placed the door key on the table beside the bed.

"Come on in and shut the door."

"It's not proper. What if Mara Shannon should come by?"

"She'd think we were sleeping together." His voice was slightly husky. He drew her into the room and closed the door. "I only wish it were true." His eyes looked into hers for a long, delicious moment, and tides of warmth washed over her. His hands gripped the shawl and pulled her to him. "Come hell, high water, *or* the Gallaghers, I'm going to kiss you before I leave this room." The words came out on a soft breath.

"Nooo—"

"Yesss — every time we kiss something wonderful happens and I just want it to go on and on." His eyes held hers, his hands slid down her

273

arms to grasp her hands and bring them up, around his neck. "Sometime soon I'm going to hold you all night long and love you in all the ways a man loves his mate —" His strange, thickened voice broke off.

His mouth pressed against her cheek, then slid to close over her mouth. He kissed her gently, sweetly, and she thought only vaguely of resisting. Her mouth trembled beneath the searching movement of his, and a whisper-soft sigh escaped her. He sighed, "Nightrose," when he came up for breath, but in the next instant he was back, renewing the kiss, sipping, coaxing, and stirring her until she slowly began to respond.

She didn't want to give in to the pleasure of his lips, the warm hardness of his body, the protective strength of his arms. She wanted to remain stiff and unfeeling, but his lips were loving hers and hers had no choice but to love him back. Feeling her melt against him, Rowe took possession of her mouth in a wild, sweet, wonderful way. His tongue began a sensuous exploration of the inside of her lower lip, his hands slid up her sides. The soft globes of her breasts against his chest were too great a temptation. His fingers stroked the sides, then moved around until the warm swells filled his hands.

The feel of Rowe's long body against hers was wreaking havoc with Katy's logic. She had to think, sort out her emotions, untangle the confused motivations, and decide if this was right. His hands cupped her breasts, and a slow, dangerous fire began to seep upward from her toes until it reached the top of her head. The arms about his neck tightened and she strained closer and closer, needing to fit her body tightly to his.

Rowe lifted his mouth from hers. His eyes, soft with love, drank in her face. Her hands slid down over his shoulders, her palms lay flat against his chest, but she didn't push herself away from him. His heart was pounding and that surprised her because the rest of him was so still.

"Right now —" he began with difficulty, "I'm wondering how I survived my empty life before I found you."

"Rowe . . . please. I think you'd better go. I can't think clearly when . . . we're like this." She raised her head, her eyes beseeching and wide.

Rowe moaned and held her tightly to him. "You liked it, didn't you? Say it. You like kissing me."

"Yes," she admitted. "But that only means that I'm attracted to you." She buried her face against his chest and let him hold her.

"It means more than that, sweetheart. But I'll not press the point."

He wanted her to know that she was the dearest thing in his life, that she was his love until the end of time. With gentle fingers beneath her chin, he lifted her face, kissing her eyes, her nose.

"When I hold you I feel as if I have been lost and have returned home. Oh, Nightrose, we could have gone on for years and not found each other." He rocked her in his arms. "Deep down in your heart you know we were meant to be together. Hurry, my love, sort it all out in your mind and admit it."

She lowered her eyes to the throbbing pulse in his throat, incapable of but one thought. Oh, Lord! He'd seeped into her heart and there hadn't been a thing she could do about it.

"It's all right, sweetheart. Don't pull a long face. We've all the time in the world." He tilted her face up to him and gently pressed his lips to hers. "You'll be safe here. I'll lock the door when I leave."

"Good night. Thank you for the supper."

Katy stood with her head down and heard Rowe let himself out of the room, then came the rasp of the key as it turned in the lock.

CHAPTER
Sixteen

"I was beginning to wonder if you were coming down," Anton said drily as he placed the newspaper on the chair beside him and rose to his feet.

"What does that mean?"

"The clerk said you took the lady to her room a half hour ago. He's been watching to see if you came down. If not, he'd have a tale to tell tomorrow." Anton's usually unsmiling face broke into a grin.

Rowe didn't smile in return. He cast a threatening glance at the clerk watching them from behind the counter.

"If I hear one word said about the lady in my room, someone will come up missing a few teeth tomorrow." He directed his words toward the slick-haired young man who suddenly became very busy with the pigeonholes behind him.

Anton chuckled. "There's a spare bed over at the boardinghouse if you need it."

"I've got something lined up for the night. What did you find out at the courthouse?" Rowe led the way to the far corner of the lobby and Anton followed.

"Our petition was granted to cut timber on

4,000 acres. It's a small grant, but enough to get our saw mill into operation. Later, we can buy and process from independent loggers. The Rowe-Hooker Lumber Company is in business."

Rowe nodded as if he had expected to hear this. He took a cigar from his breast pocket, lit it, and spoke while holding the cigar between his teeth.

"Justin is in town."

Anton's head jerked around. "Your brother?"

"My *half* brother."

"What's he doin' out here?"

"That's what I've got to find out. I'm sure he didn't make the trip out of brotherly love."

Rowe had discussed his and Justin's relationship with Anton and Hank one night when he was feeling rather lonely. Now he told Anton about the clerk giving his room key to a man named Rowe from back East and about getting a brief glimpse of his half brother in the mercantile.

"If I hadn't had a suspicion it was Justin whom the manager referred to, I might not have noticed him scurrying to get out of sight when Katy and I went into the store. I saw him from the back, but it was Justin. He always wears some shade of gray and his gray bowler sat square on his head."

"He could have heard about our petition to the Territorial governor to cut timber on public land. If that's what he came for, it's too late for him to do anything about it."

"He'll think of something. He's obsessed with making my life difficult."

"Maybe he's backing another company." Anton's fingers went to the wire rim on the bridge of his nose, as they usually did when he was agitated. "What the hell does he know about the lumber business?"

"About as much as I did when I bought in with you in Minnesota."

"You learned fast. From what I've heard about your brother, he's not a man to start up from the bottom."

"Justin has hated me ever since I can remember. After our father died, his hatred for me and my mother intensified until he wouldn't stay in the same room with us. I think he may be a little mad. He's had Pinkerton's on me for the past year and a half."

"How'd you find out about that?"

"There are ways." Rowe grinned. "When I discovered it, I had a detective follow the detective. The Pinkerton was just doing a job. He must have reported to Justin that I had bought the mine and the town of Trinity. Maybe Justin came out to see what I was up to."

"And maybe he came out to ruin you if he can."

Rowe snorted. "There's no maybe about that."

"What do you think we should do about it?"

"Nothing but keep our eyes open. Has there been any news from the teamsters bringing the equipment?"

"The bookkeeper over at the bank got a wire last week. The freighter expects to have six wagon-loads in Trinity by the end of the month.

Six more a month later."

Rowe stood and grinned down at the shorter man.

"That's good news. Now aren't you glad we went ahead and took the chance we'd get the cutting rights?"

"I figured if we didn't get them, you'd think of something. You always do."

"When I get back to Trinity, I'll give the men time off to fix up cabins so they can bring in their families. We have good people and we want to keep them."

"What we're getting out of that mine is barely enough to pay the cost of taking it out."

"It served its purpose."

"I've been meaning to ask you something," Anton said, pushing the wire-frame glasses up on his nose again. "Why did we ride over the mountain when we could have intercepted the stage from Salt Lake City, ridden it to Bannack, and taken the Overland to Virginia City?"

"It was faster coming by horseback, and I wanted Katy to meet Sam and Emily Sparks."

"It was a mighty uncomfortable trip for the lady."

"Katy handled it all right. I'm going to marry her before we leave here."

"You're going to *what?*"

"Marry her."

"I knew you were attracted to her, but you've . . . had other women. I didn't realize marriage was on your mind."

"I thought you liked Katy," Rowe said walking beside him toward the door.

"I do. But she's made it plain that she hates this country. If you're going to stay out here, there could be problems ahead."

"I'm not worried about that. She doesn't realize it, but she loves this country and would miss it if she left."

"But are you giving her enough time to make up her own mind? You can be pretty overpowering where women are concerned."

"I'll not force her to do anything against her will. I want her to want and need me every bit as much as I want and need her," he said, fixing Anton with his piercing stare.

Anton shook his head. "She's not a weak-kneed woman. She's got enough grit for a dozen women. Seeing her face up to that outlaw up on the mountain convinced me of that. I'm thinking you'll have your hands full if you push her."

"I'll have to push her. She's taken a stand and she doesn't know how to back down and save her face. She's stubborn and has far too much pride for her own good. I've got to work around it."

Anton nodded. He had no argument against that.

"One thing worries me," Rowe continued as they paused on the hotel porch. He swung around to look into his friend's face.

"One thing? Hellfire! If I were tying myself to a woman for life, there'd be a million things worrying me."

281

"It's Justin. I've thought for sometime that he'd kill me if he got the chance. If that should happen, I want you to see that Katy and her sister are taken care of."

"I don't think you need to worry about her sister. Hank's so besotted with her and the little girl he can't see straight. He'd make sure that she was taken care of even if she won't have him for her man."

"I thought that was the way the wind blew. As soon as the Fourth is over, I'll get a letter off to my solicitor stating that I want Katy to have everything I own except the lumber business. I want you and Hank to divide my half between you. I don't want anything of mine, or what my mother left me, to go to Justin. If something should happen to me before I marry Katy and before my letter reaches my solicitor, Justin, as my next of kin, will step in and try to take over."

"Is that why you're marrying Katy in such a hurry?"

"One of the reasons. The other and most important one is that I love her."

Anton realized that the admission was made openly and honestly. It came from the strength of the man's character, not from any weakness. He had heard men say that they wanted a woman or needed a woman, but seldom did a man say to another man that he was going to marry a woman because he loved her.

"Where are you going?" Anton asked when

Rowe went to the steps leading down into the street.

"I thought I'd check with the hotels and see where Justin is staying."

"The smart thing for you to do is stay out of sight. I'll check the hotels. Your brother might not have used his real name. Give me a description."

"I don't like piling my trouble on you."

"I'll have more troubles if he puts a hole in you." Irritation deepened Anton's voice.

Rowe clapped his friend on the shoulder. "Justin's about my size, only heavier. His hair and brows are very light, and like I said before, he always wears gray. The woman with him may be his wife. Helga is a pretty, soft, sweet woman with blond hair and blue eyes. She was always very formal with me when Justin was near; but the few times I was able to speak to her alone, I could see a look in her eyes that bordered on desperation. I'd not be surprised if Justin abuses her. I think she's scared to death of him, but she never as much as hinted that she wanted to leave him."

"He sounds like a low-down bastard."

"They have a son, but the hotel man said nothing about a child being with them."

"Where do you think I should start?"

"Justin is used to the best, so try the best hotels first."

"Watch your back," Anton cautioned.

"I intend to. See you in the morning."

After Justin had left her, Helga moved into the chair that he had occupied for most of the day and looked down at the activity on the street below. People strolled along the boardwalks. Carriages passed beneath her window, taking stylishly dressed couples to the Opera House. Helga's mind was so full of her own problems that she was scarcely aware that Virginia City was celebrating a holiday.

Grateful for the opportunity to allow her shoulders to slump and to allow her usually carefully composed features to reflect her misery, Helga leaned back against the chair and wondered if she would ever get used to the strain of being Justin Rowe's wife. Only the thought of leaving her son completely helpless in the hands of his father kept her from walking out the door, out of town, and into the vast wilderness that lay beyond, walking on until she found a place where she could lie down and die peacefully. But she had to stay alive to seize the moment if someday she could get Ian out from under Justin's control. It was what she lived for.

Hours later, Helga heard the key turn in the lock. She lay perfectly still in the bed where she had cried herself to sleep a few hours before. In the chicken yards, roosters had come out to prance, preen, and announce the coming of dawn. A long night was almost over; another uncertain day was beginning.

Justin came into the room, closed the door and

locked it. Helga peeked at him while feigning sleep. He placed his hat on a hook at the end of the wardrobe, struck a match, and lit the lamp. After he hung up his coat, he sat down on the edge of the bed to take off his shoes.

"You're awake, Helga, so open your eyes and listen. I've had a very interesting night." With the end of the bed cover, he carefully wiped the dust from his shoes before setting them side by side on the floor of the wardrobe. "Don't you want to know what I've been doing?"

His voice was slurred as if he had drunk too much. But, Helga thought, Justin never drinks too much. She watched him fumble with the buttons on his shirt.

"If you want me to know, tell me."

"I want to tell you, or I wouldn't have asked." He tossed his shirt on the bed. The soft cloth floated down and covered Helga's face. "Smell that perfume, Helga. That's not the cheap stuff whores wear. Who would have thought that in this backwoods place there'd be a woman who wore perfume like that?"

Helga uncovered her face. This was something she had not expected. Justin had left the hotel in a strange, dejected mood and had returned calm, a placid smile on his face.

"Don't you have anything to say to that?" he asked, going to the mirror above the commode and looking at himself.

"I don't recognize the scent."

"Of course you don't. It's straight from Paris."

He laughed and she couldn't believe her ears. Justin didn't laugh often. "It's always the darkest before the dawn, Helga." He continued, still gazing at his reflection in the mirror. "When I left here last night I wasn't sure I could live. I've been dealt a blow, Helga. A cruel one. But now I know what I'm going to do. Do you want to know why I'm so damn certain I can bring that Greek bastard to his knees?"

"Yes, of course, I do," she murmured, doubting that he even heard her reply.

"I had the most amazing streak of luck tonight. I met a bank employee, and after plying him with more than one round of drinks, he spilled his guts. My dear half brother is going into the lumber business. He's acquired cutting rights to a vast number of acres and has equipment on the way to set up a mill in the town of Trinity. What do you think of that?"

"Well . . . I —"

"Buying the mine was a cover. It was the only way to get the town. The son of a bitch wanted the location."

"Did the man from the bank tell you this?" Helga knew from past experience she had to express an interest during the rare times Justin imparted information to her.

"That and more. My new acquaintance does not like the high-handed way Garrick does business. Once, he made a minor error in Garrick's accounts, and Garrick went to the president of the bank and demanded that another clerk handle his accounts or he'd take his business elsewhere. That put the man in a bad light, and he's a man who does not forgive his enemies."

Helga listened. She did not dare voice her opinion, that Garrick had a right to ask for another clerk.

"Between the two of us, we've concocted a plan." Justin laughed nastily. "There are men in this town who would kill their own mothers for a price."

"Justin! You wouldn't do such a thing!"

"You think not, Helga? You don't know me very well if you think I'll stand by and allow that bastard to enjoy Preston Rowe's money. But don't fret about it. I'll try other tactics first. Wagons break down, rivers freeze over, dams break, fires start, and oh, how these forests can burn." He recited the words in a singsong voice. "Small things lumped together make big things."

Helga went pale. Was Justin planning to kill his half brother? What she saw in her husband's face was so chilling she had trouble bringing her chaotic thoughts back to what he was saying.

"I've met a man just waiting to be used. But my ah . . . associate has a flaw that may or may not be a problem for me."

Justin took off his pants and folded them neatly, smoothing the creases in front that sitting for hours in the dimly lit saloon had left.

"He's besotted by a twitchy twat who sings and dances at the Opera House. A pecker with a full load would split the skinny little bitch wide open.

Her name's Nan and she cavorts on the stage like a filly in heat. She can kick higher than her head, giving the audience a tantalizing glimpse of her twat." His lips twitched in a half smile and a trickle of spit ran from the corner. "The bastard watches her and plays with himself."

His brow furrowed. Had the creases been in his trousers when he went to the Opera House and later to that magical place on the hill?

"I want these pants pressed today, Helga. I don't want to see a single wrinkle, understand?"

"All right. Do you want the shirt washed?"

"Are you wanting to get rid of that delightful fragrance? I've been with another woman. How do you feel about that?" Naked, Justin walked to the end of the bed and placed his hands on the ornate foot of the iron bedstead. While he sucked in his stomach and puffed out his chest, he looked down at his sex hanging between his thighs. "Answer me, Helga," he said in a softly menacing tone.

"I don't like for you to go to other women." She made an effort to inject a suggestion of tears in her voice to please him.

"I met a woman tonight that made this stand so high it reached my belly hole. It stood at attention three times, and I didn't have to beat her ass to do it," he said proudly. "Shall I tell you how she did it?"

"No. I don't want to hear." Helga knew the role she had to play. She thanked God for the unknown woman who had drained her husband

and saved her from an unpleasant ordeal this morning.

"You're going to hear whether you like it or not. Take your hands away from your ears," he commanded. "The man I met tonight took me up on the hill to a place called the Doll House. He was as stiff as a poker after watching the twit prance around on the stage, and I offered to foot the bill. The Doll House was expensive, but well worth every dollar. I've never felt so calm, so peaceful, as I do at this moment.

"As soon as we entered the house, he went one way and I another. The room where I was taken had walls hung with silk. I sat down on a lounge piled with silk-covered pillows. There was incense burning in an iron pot. I waited just a couple of minutes, and then the lady of the house came in. She wore some kind of a dress made of the thinnest material. It was more exciting than seeing her completely naked. Her tits were covered with something sticky and a powder sprinkled on them. They poked through slits in her dress."

"Please don't —" Helga was appalled. He'd never been so explicit before.

"Shut up and listen! The woman was small, doll-like, and extremely beautiful. At first I was repulsed because she was an Oriental. I've never laid on a black-haired woman and had sworn not to, but I had paid the money and decided to stay and see what she could do. Good God! I'm glad I did. Guess what she did first, Helga?"

"She . . . took off your clothes?"

"She served tea. I don't know what was in that tea, but after drinking two small cups and wondering what she had on her nipples, I began to swell. I asked her if the price included switching her bottom. She said the price included anything I wanted to do, but switching was rather an old-fashioned way of achieving what I wanted. She said that I was about to have an experience beyond my wildest dreams.

"Later, she took me to another room, undressed me, and pushed me down on a low couch. She liked what she saw, Helga. She ran her hands over me and little moans came from her small, red mouth. She nipped me with her teeth and filled her two small hands with my sex, pulling and squeezing until I got hard as I used to when I was sixteen."

He paused to see how his story was affecting Helga.

"Justin, it isn't necessary to tell me this —"

"I want you to hear it! You can learn something if you pay attention. I licked her titties clean. I don't know what was on them. It was both sour and sweet. Almost right away, I felt as if I were floating off the couch. I was big and hard, but she shook her head when I tried to pull her down on top of me. I didn't see how I could possibly get any bigger, but I did.

"She brought a basin of reddish brown liquid and rubbed it on my balls and pecker." He grinned at the horrified expression on his wife's face. "In a minute or two they began to feel warm, then hot. A while later I was up and prancing around the room like a horny stallion in a pen with a dozen mares in heat."

Helga tried to block her mind to keep from hearing the description of the orgy that followed. She knew with a certainty that Justin was deranged or he'd not be telling her, his wife, about the unspeakable acts he and the woman had performed. She looked unseeingly into his eyes while he gloated. He had never felt so good in his entire life, he said, and speculated that he just might take the woman with him when he went back East.

"No. I'll not stand for it!" Helga protested because she knew it was expected. Her eyes flicked to the flesh between his legs, and she was thankful to see that he was not sexually aroused. His lids drooped over his eyes and his mouth sagged. He looked old and tired.

"You're getting brave, Helga," he said, but the words didn't have the cutting edge they usually did. "I'll take the little doll with me if I want to, and you'll not say a word. Now, get up. I need some sleep. I'm going back there tonight. Godamighty! I hate to think of what I've been missing out on all these years." Helga got out of bed and went to the far side of the room to dress. "Don't leave this room, Helga," he said as he settled himself on the bed.

"I'll have to go downstairs to get your trousers pressed. And I've got to eat."

"Very well, but stay in the hotel." He yawned,

spread his legs, and scratched his crotch. "I think I'll get a house here in Virginia City for the rest of the summer and let that little doll move in with me."

Helga brushed her hair and piled it atop her head. She cast furtive glances at the man on the bed and breathed a sigh of relief when he began to snore. She waited until she was sure he was sleeping soundly before she picked up the trousers and quietly left the room.

CHAPTER
Seventeen

On her side with the covers drawn up to her ears, Katy stared into the darkness, unmindful of the noise drifting up from the street below, or the muffled voices and footsteps of hotel guests going to their rooms.

Time and again she asked herself the same question. How could she have fallen in love with a man like Garrick Rowe? He was an overbearing manipulator; yet her body had responded to his when he held her. She had wanted his mouth on hers; and when he kissed her, she felt as if she had taken leave of her body and was soaring above the clouds on a wave of sheer delight. Every nerve within her had vibrated with the pleasure that had flowed between them. She would never forget the feeling of acute abandonment when he left her.

The fairy tale Rowe had told her about their knowing each other in another life was beginning to make sense, Katy thought, realizing that she might be thinking with her heart rather than her head. She had gone willingly into his arms as if she had done it a thousand times. It had felt right and . . . wonderful. Could it be true that when a person died, the soul entered another body? And did souls such as hers and Rowe's meet and meet again down through time that had no beginning or end?

Puzzling through that thought, Katy began to analyze her attraction to the big dark man. Aside from being good to look at, he had a quick mind, was gentle, yet extremely violent when threatened. Rowe was a man who had traveled the world, yet he took pleasure in simple things such as watching the honkers on the lake and showing her the beautiful waterfall. His body strength was massive, protective. When she was with him, she felt as if nothing in the world could harm her. She questioned herself as to why she felt cherished instead of irritated by his possessiveness, but could not come up with an answer.

Katy felt sure that Rowe would never leave this hard, cruel land for a long period of time. He was fascinated by the challenge of it. For the past several years she had thought of nothing but going back home to the warm South. She remembered the desperation of the past winter, the anxiety of having to find fuel to heat the cabin to keep them from freezing, and how hard it had been to stretch their food supplies to keep from starving to death. She wanted to spend the rest of her life in a real *town*, not some wide spot in the road like Trinity.

Or did she?

Just the thought of not seeing Rowe again, or knowing the excitement he brought into her life, sent a chill of loneliness through her. Katy Burns, she told herself sternly, you can have one or the other, but it was a certainty that she couldn't have both.

She drifted to sleep thinking that maybe when morning came, she might see Garrick Rowe in an entirely different light, and his fascination for her would be gone.

Pressure from a full bladder awoke Katy. Dawn lit the room. All was quiet except for the sounds made by the iron-rimmed wagon wheels and the clip-clop of the horses' hooves on the street below. Katy lay quietly, dreading getting up, but knowing she'd not be able to go back to sleep if she didn't relieve herself; the luxury of another hour's sleep was too tempting.

Her warm feet hit the cold floor. She winced and groped beneath the bed for the chamber pot. In her haste to pull it out, the lid slipped from her fingers and made a loud clanking sound as it hit the bare floor. She winced again as she hoisted up her long gown and bunched it around her waist. The glass rim of the pot was cold, but a sigh of pure pleasure escaped her as water flowed. When she finished, she replaced the lid and carefully slid the half-filled chamber beneath the bed.

The crack of a whip, a muffled curse, and the slamming of a door below told Katy the town was awakening. She went to the window to peer out. She saw nothing, and went back to the bed, eager to sink down in the soft warmth.

When she saw the long shadowy shape stretched out on a bedroll against the door, she blinked rapidly to bring it into focus. Too startled to be frightened, she opened her eyes wide and jutted her chin forward in order to see better: A pair of boots sat against the wall a few feet from a head of coal black hair. Relief that it was Rowe who lay there came over her, but an instant later it was swept away by anger and mortification.

The buzzard! The unspeakable rotter! He had waited until she was asleep and then had come sneaking back into the room. The sound of the lid hitting the floor would have awakened the dead, she thought bitterly. Her face burned and her heart hammered as humiliation consumed her. He had seen her pull up her gown and heard her use the chamber pot! And he had just lain there like a big . . . lump of lard, not having the decency to let her know he was there or to leave the room so she could have some privacy. Damn him!

Katy eased away from the bed and backed the few feet necessary to reach the water pitcher that sat in the bowl on the washstand. She lifted it with her two hands, watching to see if the dark head moved He was feigning sleep now, but not for long, she thought with a vicious spurt of pleasure. She moved silently to the end of the bed, then made two long, heavy steps, lifted the pitcher, and threw every last drop of the water at his head.

Rowe came up out of the bedroll as if he had been propelled by a slingshot.

"Goddammit! What the hell?" He wiped the

water from his face with his hands and glared up at her. "What's the matter with you, for Christ's sake?"

In a long white gown, with the empty pitcher swinging from one hand, her hair hanging down about her shoulders, Katy stood over him like an avenging angel.

"You deserved it, you sneaky, slimy toad! You . . . you addle-brained bunghead. You've got about as much honor as a suck-egged mule! You sneaked in here like a belly crawling snake after I went to sleep."

"Keep your voice down. Do you want everyone in the hotel to hear?"

She raised her voice deliberately. "I want everyone in this town to know what a low-down polecat you are!"

"Thanks to you," he shouted, forgetting his warning to her, "I'm a low-down *wet* polecat."

"Damn you to hell, Garrick Rowe!"

"Hush swearing."

"It's all right for you, but not for me."

"Ladies don't swear. Men do."

"You're a *man?*"

"You little shrew. I should teach you a lesson."

"And I should have dumped the chamber pot on you. Golly damn and holy hell!" she yelled defiantly. "It's not too late!"

"Katy! For God's sake, calm down!" Before she could move her feet, his hands snaked out and grasped her ankles. She tumbled facedown onto the bed. The pitcher flew from her hand and crashed against the wardrobe. "Well, that does it!" Rowe swore viciously. "Everyone will think I'm beating you."

"Don't tell me to calm down, you . . . you Benedict Arnold!"

"Why the hell are you so riled up?" He sounded honestly confused.

"Because you make me so damn mad I could bite a nail in half!" she yelled. "Let go of me or I'll scream *fire* and empty every room in this hotel!"

"Dammit, Katy, I'm wet and my bed's wet. I could beat your rear! And if you don't stop yelling, I'll go out in the hall and shout that you're having a temper fit because you didn't think I'd paid you enough for your services."

"You'd do what?" She was as still as a rock for a moment, then kicked out viciously, catching him off guard. "You're lower than I thought!"

"Stop kicking me or — dammit, you kicked me in the mouth!"

"Serves you right. Let go of me or I'll kick your teeth down your throat!"

"Kick me again and you'll be rubbing your sweet little rear for the rest of the day," he snarled.

She kicked at him again, stubbornly, defiantly, and missed her mark. Abruptly she stopped thrashing about, and a second later sudden laughter bubbled from her lips. It filled every corner of the room. The sound was like pure, sweet music. With her hands clasped over her head, she turned her face and peeked at him through the tangle of hair that covered her back and shoulders.

Rowe was on his knees beside the bed, his hands still tightly around her ankles. His hair was wet and plastered to his head. Water ran down his cheeks and dripped from his jaw to his bare shoulders and chest already wet from the soaking.

"Ohhh . . . ohhh —" It was all Katy was able to say between spasms of uncontrollable giggles. "Oh, I wish I'd thought of the . . . chamber pot —"

"It's a damn good thing you didn't!"

"You can bet your sweet patoody I'd have doused you, you . . . snooper. You're the bottom of the barrel, Garrick Rowe. The absolute bottom!"

"If I'm the bottom, you're not far from it. You're acting like a shrew."

"What about yourself? You've got the guts of a mule coming in here and spying on me."

"Hell! It's my room."

"You insisted that I take it."

"Because I'm a gentleman."

"Gentleman! Ha! A gentleman wouldn't have sneaked back in like a . . . like a thief."

"I wasn't going to sleep in the hall and I sure as hell wasn't going to sit up all night," he growled.

Katy turned her face into the bedclothes to stifle her laughter. Rowe let go of her ankles and sat on the edge of the bed. He threw his leg over hers to hold them there while he wiped his head and face with the shirt he picked up off the floor.

"Get off me, you . . . bounder!"

"Be still!" He continued to run the shirt over his chest and arms that were covered with goose-flesh and quivering with cold.

"I said get off me."

"And I said be still."

"Get off me or I'll scream that you're murdering me."

"If you do, I might do just that."

Rowe reached over and swatted her on the rear. The sound made by the palm of his hand against the solid flesh of her buttocks with only the thin layer of cloth to shield them was like the crack of a whip.

"Ouch!" Katy reared up in surprise.

Rowe realized instantly that what he had intended to be a light tap had been a heavy blow.

"Oh, God, honey, I'm sorry." He lifted his heavy thigh from hers and he began to rub vigorously at the stinging area where his hand had landed. "Did I hurt you? I didn't mean to swat you so hard. I'm sorry, honey."

His deep voice and the warm hand caressing her released tumultuous waves of feeling in Katy. The stinging slap on her buttocks combined with the strain of the last several days brought her to the breaking point. She felt as if a knife had severed the cord that held her control in check. She felt as if she were suddenly caught in a whirlwind and was being tossed about like a leaf in a mighty gale. It was impossible to hold back the tears. She buried her face in her arms as agonizing sobs tore from her throat.

"Oh, my God! Nightrose?" Rowe's voice was choked. He rolled down onto the bed beside her, grabbed her into his embrace, pulling her head to his shoulder. "I wouldn't have hurt you for the world, sweetheart." He kissed her forehead with wild roughness. "I'm sorry . . . I'm sorry." He wrapped her limp body in his arms, pressing it tightly, protectively against his own. He stroked her hair back from her face and whispered to her in a shaky, anxious voice. "I didn't mean to hurt you. I'm so crazy about you, my sweet, that I'd kill any man who laid a hand on you."

Real pain shone in his eyes. Katy didn't see it, but she heard his voice and wanted to tell him that it wasn't the pain of the blow that made her cry, but a combination of disappointments that spanned the past few years. As emotion and reason seesawed for dominance, she was unable to speak. She clasped her arms around him and held on as if he were the only solid thing in a tilting world. Katy burrowed her face into his broad shoulder. It felt so good to be cosseted and comforted that she melted against his chest, not knowing or caring that only the thin material of her nightdress was between them, or that it was not at all proper that she should be lying on the bed clasped in the arms of a man who was not her husband.

Her tears sent tremors of remorse through Rowe.

"Shhhh . . . don't cry. Hush, dear heart. It tears me up to hear you cry." Sensitive fingers played lightly with the strands of hair sticking to her cheeks, then moved beneath the heavy masses to the nape of her neck. "I'd give ten years of my life to undo what I just did, my love, my Nightrose." The words were murmured against her ear in such an inexpressibly moving voice, so filled with pain that she cried all the more.

"It's not . . . that —" She sobbed against a chest now wet with her tears.

"Then what is it, love?" His voice, kind and comforting, was close to her ear. She was penned against the length of his long, hard body and her head was caught in the crook of his arm.

"I don't know what to do about . . . you. You . . . sweep me along and I end up doing what you want me to do just as if I didn't have a mind of my own."

"Has that made you so unhappy?" he asked with a soft voice full of tenderness.

"Not . . . yet, but it will. I know it will."

"I was afraid to leave you in here alone tonight, love. The town is full of drunken rowdies. I noticed a number of them eyeing you when we were down on the street. I had no choice but to sleep on this side of the door or on the other side, and I didn't figure I'd get much sleep with people stepping over me in the hall," he whispered against the curve of her ear, her cheek.

Rowe was savoring the moment. His love was in his arms. The two of them were in a world where time was suspended. Her firm, round buttocks were a pleasure in his hand, her thigh resting naturally between his.

"I didn't know you were here and I —"

"It was too late for me to leave, love, when I heard you get up to use the chamber. I lay there hoping you'd go back to sleep and I could sneak out again. I'm sorry you're embarrassed." He lifted her face so his lips could sip her tears.

"I'm mortified," she corrected.

"It isn't important," he whispered, trailing kisses from her eyes along her cheek and slowly over to the corner of her mouth.

"It is to me."

"It would have been all right if we were married."

"Nooo—"

"A husband and wife know everything about each other."

"But we're not married."

"We can be. Today. Marry me, Katy. Marry me so I can take care of you. I promise that you'll be a full partner and share in each and every decision that affects our lives."

Dazed, she leaned away from him and looked into his beseeching ebony eyes. "You don't love me," she protested.

"Don't love you? I'm crazy about you."

Katy closed her eyelids, but the stroking of his fingers from the nape of her neck to her spine, learning the smoothness of her back and haunches, pressing her to his body could not be shut out. Her body throbbed with an almost painful burning, a joyful and alien longing, a new and unknown sensation that lapped at her senses causing her to forget everything except the wild pleasure of being in his arms.

"I think I'm a little loony," she whispered. "The thought of not being with you leaves me dreadfully lonely, but I don't know if it's love. I don't know if it'll last."

"It's got to be love, sweetheart. And, of course, it'll last. You like being close to me like this, don't you?" He held her tightly. His body, lean and powerful, was trembling like a great oak in a gale.

Her palm moved across the thickly matted hair on his chest to his back and shoulders and slid over muscle and tight flesh. What would it be like to lie in bed with him without anything between them and have him come inside her? The thought sent erotic signals through her body. Her palm moved searchingly over his quivering flesh.

"You're cold," she whispered.

Rowe's chuckle was hoarse and strained. She filled his senses to the brim. How could he tell her that he was using every ounce of his control to keep from pressing his hard erection against her soft, flat belly? He held her to his chest as tightly as he dared and kissed her temple, the curve and hollow of her cheek, and settled his mouth gently for a moment beneath one ear.

"Sweet little innocent love. I'm not cold. I'm shaking because I want you so much." A groan ripped from him. "You're a fire in my body, in my heart, in my soul."

Katy knew that his mouth was moving toward hers and she tilted her face to meet it. His lips took hers gently, then took slow, but firm, possession. She felt the drag of his new beard on her cheek, his pounding heart against her breasts. She felt boneless and deliciously comfortable, yet restless too. For a long time they lay entwined, kissing; and Katy knew for the first time the beauty of simply holding and being held in return. She didn't question why she was doing these intimate things with him. Completely guiltless, she gave herself up to the enjoyment of his gentle possession.

He was a careful lover and held her as if she were a prize beyond value. Kissing her hungrily, but choosing not to be too intimate, his hand moved down over her hips and up her side to the fullness of her breast and back again in a slow caress. His lips eased the pressure to nibble at her lips and she nibbled his in turn. Her arms tightened. Her full breasts pressed to his chest, her nipples achingly peaked. Slowly, she twisted, rubbing her hard-tipped breasts against him. A sweet agony burned between her thighs. He trembled and helplessly moved his erection against her, increasing the marvelous contact.

The kisses changed, becoming more intense as his aching flesh pressed hungrily against the softness of hers. The lusciousness of her mouth drove him to taste her inner lips, his tongue moved restlessly along the sharp edge of her teeth while his hand caressed the soft, rounded flesh of her hips. Katy moved urgently against him, stirred by strange and wonderful feelings.

My God! This sweet, responsive woman was his! Rowe's love for her grew, blossomed, bloomed until it was all consuming. She was a treasure, a rare flower. She was his Nightrose, his soul mate. The precious bundle in his arms was the only thing in the world that mattered. Everything else faded into a void. How had he lived almost thirty years without her?

Her hips moved, pressing against his. Rowe's flesh quivered with the force of the desire that raced from his head to the soles of his feet. Reason returned. This wasn't the time to join his body to hers. He wouldn't take his pleasure of her now and give her cause for regrets later. When it happened, he was going to make it the most beautiful experience of her life.

"Sweetheart, I've got to stop while I can," he said, turning his lips away from her clinging ones. "I'm just a breath away from coming inside you to put out this fire that's about to consume me."

Katy opened her eyes to look at him. They were dreamy and trusting and innocent. The way she had melted into his kiss was achingly sweet. He found himself wanting to hold onto this tiny minuscule in time.

"Is that why you're shaking?" Her hand moved up and down, over the corded muscles of his arm and shoulder, pausing at the base of his neck.

"Yes, sweetheart, it is. I'm not made of stone."

He watched her face, her eyes. "I want to mate with you. God, I've never wanted anything as much in my life, but I can wait until after we're married. I want you to come to me freely, not because I've compromised you."

Katy cupped his cheek with her palm. "Oh, Rowe. I don't know if I can give my life over to you as completely as you want. I have dreams of my own and they don't include living a hand-to-mouth existence in a town like Trinity. If I marry you it will mean that I must go where you go and do what you want me to do. I've seen what that's done to my sister."

"We will go where *we* want to go and do what *we* want to do. It will be Katy and Rowe, Rowe and Katy. I want to spend the rest of my life with you, and your safety and happiness will be more important to me than my life. If you want to go back East, we'll talk about it and decide together. I'll tell you my dreams and you tell me yours. I love you, Katy. I've loved you since the beginning of time. I could bear losing you easier than I could stand by and see you unhappy."

Katy moved her arms around his neck and reverently kissed the corner of his mouth. The words he had whispered so urgently had a familiar ring to them. He was so dear and familiar. She placed her lips on his and kissed him gently. Her eyes, when they looked into his, were brilliant with laughter, holding his gaze with mischievous bondage.

"I'm stubborn and like to have my own way.

When I don't get it I throw a temper fit," she whispered.

"I'm pushy and I'll want to know where you are every minute of the day."

"If I ever find out you've been with another woman, I'll bash your head."

"I'm jealous of any man who looks at you. I want to punch him in the nose." His face was a mixture of astonishment and delight. He pinched her bottom.

"Yeooo . . ." she choked off a yelp and tickled his ribs. "I fly off the handle at the drop of a hat."

"I have a temper too. Ask Hank and Anton."

"We should have an exciting life together . . . if I don't knock you senseless before I get used to your overbearing ways." The laughter he loved bubbled up.

"We'll be happy together, but I may have to beat your behind regularly to keep you in line." The radiance of his smile touched her heart.

He kissed her nose. She kissed his lips. They lay quietly, looking at each other. Her mouth couldn't keep from smiling. His eyes shone into hers. It was magical to lie with their arms locked around each other, their minds attuned. She laughed with pure pleasure.

"I love to hear you laugh. Promise me you'll laugh every day for the next ten thousand years." He leaned over her to rest on his forearms and kiss her mouth again and again.

"Make it twenty thousand, and I'll consider it."

"Get out of bed, lazy woman. This is your

wedding day." He kissed her laughing mouth lingeringly and eased her out of his arms.

Katy watched him go to the wardrobe and take out a clean shirt.

"I wish Mary and Theresa were here."

"I know you do, sweetheart."

"Rowe! We can't get married today. I don't have anything to wear."

"What you wore last night looked mighty fine to me, but if there's anything in this town you want, you only have to point your finger at it."

"We're not married yet, Mr. Rowe. It's not decent for an unmarried woman to allow a man to buy clothes for her. I'll buy my own dress, thank you."

Rowe reached for his boots. "I can see that I'm going to have my hands full managing you. You're going to have to get it through your pretty head that what I have is yours and what you have is —"

His words were cut off by an urgent rap on the door.

CHAPTER
Eighteen

Katy slid quickly off the bed taking the cover with her. Her eyes met Rowe's as she wrapped the bedsheet around her. The rap came again.

"What'll we do?" she whispered urgently. "It could be Mara Shannon! What in the world will she think of me?"

"It may be Beulah."

"This early? It's barely daylight."

"I'll stand behind the door," he whispered, picking up his bedroll and stuffing it beneath the bed. "If it's Mrs. Gallagher, she'll not come in when she sees that you're not dressed."

The knock sounded for the third time. Katy pulled the sheet around her and went to the door, glancing once again at Rowe as she turned the key in the lock. Standing close to the door, her hand raised to knock again, was a pretty, stylishly dressed woman a few years older than Katy. Her hair was blond, her eyes blue, her face very pale. She opened her mouth and then closed it without having said anything.

"Yes?" Katy murmured with brows raised.

"I'm . . . sorry. I thought this was Garrick Rowe's room." The woman turned quickly and hurried back down the hallway.

A desperate unknown fear knifed through Katy and froze her vocal cords for several seconds. Anger thawed them. She was able to speak, barely.

"He's here," she called. "*Mister* Rowe is here if you wish to speak to him."

The woman turned and came slowly back toward the open doorway. She was very pretty, a soft, biddable-looking lady who looked as if she had never known hardship. The thought flashed through Katy's mind that Rowe's taste in women was not restricted to one type. Nan Neal was one type, this woman another, herself yet another.

Anger and jealousy flared. Katy flung the door back with a force that bounced it off the toes of Rowe's boots.

"You have company, Mr. Rowe," she said tightly. "If you will step out into the hall and give me privacy to dress, I'll give you privacy to entertain your guest."

Rowe stepped around from behind the door and stared at the woman who stared back at him.

"Helga?"

"Hello, Garrick. May I . . . speak to you for a moment?"

"Of course. Come in."

Helga hesitated. She looked at the stiff back of the woman who had answered the door. Resentment was in every line of her body. "I'm sorry if I came at an inopportune time."

"It's all right. Come in."

"I would . . . like to speak to you . . . in private."

"If you'll give me time to dress, I'll be more than happy to vacate the room and give you all the privacy you want." Katy turned and glared at Rowe.

He reached out a hand, drew Helga into the room, and closed the door. He turned to meet Katy's furious eyes. *The little wildcat was jealous!* The smile that lit his eyes threatened Katy's control and she wanted to hit him.

"Katy, I'd like for you to meet my sister-in-law, Helga Rowe. Helga, this is Katherine Burns, my fiancée. We're being married today. Katy is a very proper lady. She used my room last night, and now she's madder than a hornet because you caught me in it."

Katy's jaw went slack, and her eyes went from Rowe's sloe-eyed look of gleeful satisfaction to the woman's worried blue eyes. Katy felt both relief and embarrassment, if it were possible to feel both at once. Her shoulders slumped and a grin tilted the corners of her mouth.

"All I can say is that I'm very good at putting my foot in my mouth. I'm afraid I'm inclined to jump to conclusions where Rowe is concerned. You see we've only known each other for eighteen centuries." Katy stuck her hand out from under the sheet. "How do you do?"

"Ah . . . well . . . how do you do?" Helga said hesitantly. "Please don't be distressed on my account."

"Rowe couldn't find another room last night

and slept here on the floor —"

"Katy, love —" Rowe chastised gently. "You know we've been on the bed for the past hour."

"Dammit, Rowe. Will you kindly stop making things look worse than they are!" Her mouth tightened angrily, and she looked at the ceiling as if praying for deliverance.

Rowe's soft chuckle stopped abruptly when he glanced at Helga and saw her fingers gripping her purse so tightly that her knuckles were white; her lips quivered, and she looked as if she were about to cry.

"Sit down, Helga. I heard you and Justin were in town."

"We've only been here a few days."

"Is something wrong, Helga?" Rowe asked gently.

"Well . . . ah . . . I don't have much time."

"Does Justin know you're here?"

"No! Oh, heavens, no! He's asleep, or was when I left him." She glanced at Katy and then down at the floor.

"Helga, you needn't worry about Katy. From this day on, what I know, Katy will know," Rowe said gently. "Tell us what's troubling you. If I can help you, I will. You should know that."

Helga gripped Rowe's arm. "I think . . . Justin is planning to have you killed."

Rowe's eyes flicked to Katy when he heard her indrawn breath. He saw the fear in her eyes and silently cursed the fact that she had to hear this on her wedding day.

"Helga." Rowe placed his hand on her arm. "This is nothing new to me. I've known for some time Justin would kill me if he could. Is that why he came to Montana Territory?"

"He said that there were men in this town who would kill their own mothers for a price."

"He's right. But when he gets mixed up with that sort, he's in more danger than I am. Men like that will turn on him if he crosses them, and they will be vicious."

"I've never understood why he hates you so much. It's an obsession with him."

"We both know it's because of my mother. Preston Rowe dared to mix his pure Nordic blood with that of a Greek woman. I am the result."

"The only reason Justin married me is that my ancestors were pure Caucasian. He's told me that many times. He's proud of our son because he's so fair."

"Helga, I know Justin had the Pinkertons on me. Was killing me his only reason to come here, or does it have something to do with the mine at Trinity?"

"I don't know. Something is driving him. Yesterday he was in a mood I've never seen before. He had a letter, and he must have read it a dozen times. I don't know when he got it or what was in it, but it seemed to depress him terribly."

"Did you try to find it after he went out? I saw him in the mercantile."

"Was he the man in the gray hat?" Katy asked.

314

"Yes, sweetheart, he was. Justin always wears gray."

"He looked at me as if he hated me," Katy exclaimed. "I'll never forget the expression in his eyes."

"I didn't dare look for the letter, Garrick," Helga said, twisting the purse in her hands. "He has laid little traps for me before. A thread, a hair, a little dusting of powder. I don't dare prowl through his personal things."

"I understand. Helga, does Justin abuse you physically?"

"Of course not," she scoffed, desperately hoping she sounded convincing. "Garrick, he wants to ruin you. He's very upset that you've got your mother's share of Preston Rowe's money. He knows about the lumber mill and the permit to cut trees."

"How did he find out about that?"

"Someone from the bank. A man who dislikes you because you refuse to allow him to work on your accounts."

Rowe swore under his breath. "Oscar Gable. The son of a bitch!"

"Justin mentioned breakdowns and . . . fires. Be careful, Garrick."

"Helga, I've thought for a long time that my half brother is a little mad. Do you want to get away from him?"

"No. I couldn't. I can't leave my son."

"If I could manage to find a place where Justin couldn't find you, would you go?"

315

"He'd find me. Then he'd never let me see . . . Ian again. Besides, I have no way of supporting us."

"I can do that. Ian is my nephew."

"Thank you, Garrick, but not now. Perhaps later when we get back home and I know Ian is safe. The woman who takes care of him works only for Justin. I don't dare cross him." She turned to the door. The thought crossed her mind to tell him about her husband's visit to the house on the hill and his strange behavior afterward, but she didn't think she could bear the humiliation. "I must go. He told me not to leave the hotel."

"I appreciate the warning. Katy and I will go back to Trinity. I'd hate to have to kill my own brother, but I will if he attacks me or mine. Anton Hooker, my partner in the lumber business, will be here. He has a room at the National House on Jackson Street. If you need help, go to him. Remember the name, Helga: Anton Hooker. He knows about Justin."

"Justin said something about getting a house here for the summer. I hope and pray it was just something he said to worry me." Helga turned to Katy. "I'm sorry that I brought troubles to you and Garrick on your wedding day."

"I wish . . . I wish there was a way that we could be friends."

"My husband doesn't allow me to have friends," she whispered and tried desperately to blink away the tears that filled her eyes. "I wish you every happiness."

Rowe held open the door. As Helga passed him, he placed his hand on her shoulder and a kiss on her cheek. He watched as she hurried down the hall to the stairs, then he went to the window and watched her walk quickly down the street and into the Chinese laundry.

When Rowe turned from the window, his eyes met Katy's. She was standing at the end of the bed.

"I suppose you're wondering what this is all about?"

"I don't have to wonder about one thing. That poor woman is scared to death of your brother."

Rowe combed his hair with his fingers. He went to Katy and placed his hands on her shoulders, looking at her earnestly before he pulled her against him and wrapped his arms around her. She tilted her face. Her eyes were filled with love and trust. His eager kiss traveled over her face.

"I want to tell you about my mother, my father, and Justin."

"You don't have to tell me now. I don't care about them. Only you."

"I want to tell you." Rowe moved to the side of the bed taking her with him. He sat on its edge and pulled her down on his lap.

"I'm worried," Katy said, hiding her face in his shoulder. "How can you protect yourself from hired killers?"

"Find them before they find me. Justin hates me more than anything in the world. When he discovers that you're my wife, he'll hate you too, and he'll hurt you if he can. I want you to know about it before we say our vows."

"What did you ever do to him to make him hate you so?"

"I was born," he said simply. He leaned back against the head of the bed and cuddled her in his arms.

While Rowe talked, he stroked her hair. He told her about his father, Preston Rowe, a widower who went to Paris and met a Greek girl, fell in love, and married her.

"Justin was eight years old when I was born. At first, my parents thought his dislike of me was due to natural rivalry between brothers. Then several things happened and my mother became convinced they were not just accidents.

"When I was three or four, my bed caught fire from a candle when there had been no candles in the room. When I was five, Justin tried to drown me. Father came running to the river edge when he heard my screams. Justin pretended to be saving me, but Father dressed him down severely for letting me get close to the bank. Another time Justin grabbed my feet and pulled me out of a tree causing me to break my arm. If I had a kitten, a frog, a puppy, or any small pet, it would turn up dead. He was constantly calling me black boy and telling me I was as black as the slaves. I was terrified of him."

"Was your father aware of what Justin was doing?"

"Father never knew the extent of Justin's hatred

of me and my mother. I was eight when Justin went away to school. When he came home on vacations, Father was very busy. Mother managed to keep me out of Justin's way. As he got older, Justin became very sly and kept his hatred bottled up while in the presence of my father. As Father's health began to decline, he depended more and more on Justin. I went away to school, then to the war. I returned home to find Justin firmly entrenched in the business. It was all right with me. I wasn't interested in banking and finance. Then Father died five years ago. After the funeral I took Mother to Paris. The estate on the Hudson was no longer her home. She died last year."

"I find it hard to believe that your half brother would follow you all the way out here to do you harm." Katy raised her head so that she could look into Rowe's face. Her lashes lifted, revealing to him the worry in her eyes.

"You wouldn't find it hard to believe if you knew Justin, sweetheart. Long ago I stopped trying to figure him out. I just stay away from him." He dropped a kiss around the curving line of her mouth.

"What are you going to do?"

"I want more than anything in the world to marry you. I wanted us to have a beautiful wedding that you can look back on and tell our children and grandchildren about. Now, I'm afraid that Justin will figure a way to hurt me through you."

"I'm afraid for you! Oh, Rowe! Let's get out of this rotten town and go back to Trinity."

"First we're going to be married. Anton is probably downstairs waiting for me. I'll have him make arrangements. After we're married, we'll ride out." Rowe hugged her close and murmured, "It isn't the kind of wedding I wanted for you, my love —"

Rowe's face had a taut, almost agonized expression that pierced Katy's heart. Protectiveness came boiling up inside her. How dare that pissant of a half brother make his life miserable!

"Shhh . . . Do you think that I'm so frivolous that I have to have ribbons and lace to remember my wedding day? Darling, it'll be a wedding I'll be proud to tell our children about. For all I care, you can have the preacher come here, and I'll wear this bedsheet to give more spice to add to the story."

The intensity of his love for her shook him, and like the surging warmth of the sun, a radiant feeling of being at last complete through him. Dear God, how wonderful she was!

"I love you, my Nightrose," he said, his voice rough with the effort it took not to let her see the moisture in his eyes.

"I love you." The unfamiliar words sounded strange coming from her own lips. She tried them again. "I love you." It was easier the second time. She wrapped her arms about his neck. "I love you," she said with the tip of her nose pressed to his.

Rowe found Anton in the corner of the hotel lobby, his head tilted back against the wall, a newspaper over his face. Rowe jerked the paper aside and Anton was instantly awake.

"Holy hell, Rowe. I didn't get much sleep last night," Anton complained and stretched, then pushed his glasses up on his nose.

"What did you find out?"

"Plenty."

"Let's have it." Rowe glanced around the lobby to see if anyone was within hearing distance, then sat down.

"Justin and his wife are registered at the Anaconda. At least she's registered as his wife. I didn't have any trouble spotting him at the Occidental Billiard Hall. The way he looks and dresses, he stood out like a privy in the moonlight. He had already made the acquaintance of our friend from the bank, Oscar Gable. They attended the show at the Opera House and later went up the hill to the house of the woman they call 'the Doll.' "

"Good God! That place is an opium den. I thought Justin had more sense than that."

"I heard you can get any kind of dope you want there. Any kind of sex too. Maybe I ought to try it." Mischief lit Anton's eyes through the oval wires of his glasses.

"She sets a trap with sex and dope," Rowe growled.

"How do you know so much about it?"

"I've been to the Barbary Coast. Places such

as the Doll House are common there."

"Justin may have met his match with that woman."

"Time will tell. What else did you find out?"

"Gable is enamored of your little friend, Nan Neal. He never misses one of her shows. Afterwards, he usually heads for one of the cribs in the lower part of town, but last night he went up the hill because more likely your brother was paying."

"Paying for information. Justin does nothing out of the kindness of his heart."

"I hung around until about two o'clock, then went back to the boardinghouse to bed."

"That's the reason Justin is sleeping late this morning."

"What?"

Rowe told Anton in as few words as possible about Helga's visit, ending with, "It took an extraordinary amount of courage for her to come warn me. Justin would make her suffer if he knew. He's taken her son away from her and holds the threat over her head that she may never see him again. What a hell of a way to live."

"He and Gable were pretty thick last night. They had their heads together for several hours. Gable knows Justin has money and he'll play him for as much of it as he can get. He's not above setting up a murder."

"Katy and I will be married today. Then, we'll go back to Trinity. It goes against the grain to run from my own brother, but it would go harder if I had to kill him."

"Too bad he even found out you're here."

"Coincidences." Rowe grinned. "Two, in fact, provided by fate. One brought us here at this time; the other let us know Justin was here."

"You really believe in that malarkey?"

"Why not? It's better than not believing it." Rowe sobered. His dark brows drew together in a deep frown. "Find the preacher of that church with the cross on top and tell him we'll be there in, say" — he drew out his pocket watch and consulted it — "about two hours. Tell him that Katy has a jealous suitor who has threatened her, and that we want to be married quietly so we can get out of town."

"You expect me to lie to a preacher?"

"Sure. You've done it before. Remember the time in Minnesota when —"

"Never mind. Have you forgotten that Hank shot the top off that cross? The preacher was mad as hell."

"He got over it when we paid for it and bought him a glass window to boot."

"What are you going to do now?"

"Three things. The first is to write out a will and get it over to Wells Fargo to post. The second is to call on a friend of mine over on Idaho Street."

"You'd go see *her* when you're marrying Katy today?"

"We're friends, just friends."

"Bull hocky! What's the third?"

"Never mind. Be at the church with the preacher in two hours. And spruce yourself up a little for my wedding — huh?"

Rowe found Beulah, ordered a breakfast to be taken to Katy, then asked the desk clerk for paper, pen, and ink. He took it to a corner of the lobby and wrote busily for a quarter of an hour. When he finished, he carefully read what he had written before he put the paper in the envelope and addressed it to his attorney in New York City.

On the porch of the hotel he paused to look up and down the flag-draped street. Already, it was clogged with wagons of farm and ranch families, miners from the Alder Gulch area, and a large number of lonely drifters hungering for female company. It would be a big day for the hurdy-gurdy girls, the saloons, billiard parlors, and brothels. By afternoon, when the contests began, the street would be a sea of people, dancing, singing, and celebrating.

After Rowe posted his letter with the Overland Mail, he went to the livery to look in on his horse and the mare Katy had ridden. He was pleased to see the cut on the horse's rump was healing. He left the livery and walked along the back of the buildings until he reached the one that housed the hurdy-gurdy girls. The backs of the structures along this side of the street, having been undermined by water rushing down hill, were supported by ten-foot stilts. Rowe went quickly up the side stairs, down a dark hall to a room on the end, and rapped smartly on the door.

"Who is it?" The irritated voice came after Rowe had knocked repeatedly.

"Rowe." He spoke quietly and wasn't sure he had been heard until a key turned in the lock and a disheveled Nan Neal opened the door.

"Darlin'! This is a hell of a time to come callin'." Dark hair framed a pixie face with a wide generous mouth and slightly turned up nose. The wide neck of the garment she wore had slipped off her shoulder and hung beneath a small, firm, rosy-tipped breast. She made no attempt to cover it.

"Hello, sleepyhead. Were you going to sleep all day and miss the big doings?" Rowe gently pushed her back until he could come into the room and close the door. He reached for her, pulled the gown up over her breast, then held her shoulders to keep her from wrapping her arms about him.

"I want to talk to you, honey."

"Talk? You're enough to make a preacher cuss. You'd rather talk than go to bed?"

"I need your help. I'm getting married today."

"Married? Oh, poot!" She stomped her bare foot. "You know I don't diddle with married men. Why do all the good men get *married?* Mara Shannon snatched Pack right out from under my nose, and now you're gettin' yourself tied up. Who is she? I'll pull her hair out."

Rowe chuckled. He knew that Nan's talk was just that — talk. She loved her life of singing and dancing and turned down proposals of marriage on almost a weekly basis. She could have her choice of any number of men who had the means to take care of her in grand style, but she refused to give up her independence.

"You wantin' to get married, honey?" he teased.

"Hell, no!" she flared, then gave him a sideways flirtatious glance. "You askin'?"

"I'm taken, but I bet I could get Oscar Gable for you."

"That pissant! How did you know about him? I'm goin' to use his balls for target practice if he don't stop followin' me around with that big stick in his britches and the look of a dying cow on his face."

"Do you suppose you could get any information out of him?"

"Rowe, darlin' " — Nan's lips curled in a crooked, confident smile — "I can make him pee his pants by just lookin' at him. He'd babble like a brook if I worked on him just a little bitty bit. Tell me what you want to know."

"Nothing right now. Sit down, honey. I've something to tell you."

Rowe told Nan about Justin and his newly formed friendship with Oscar Gable.

"That big, light-haired man that was with Oscar last night is your half brother? Holy shit! His eyes were as cold as a bucket of ice."

Rowe explained that if his half brother hired someone to kill him or sabotage his lumber business, Gable would be in on it. He asked Nan to keep her ears open and get word to Anton if she heard anything.

"I will, darlin'. I sure as hell will. Now tell me about this woman who stole you away from me."

"She's about your size, only a little bigger up here," Rowe laughed and pulled on the rosette at the neck of her gown.

"Bigger ain't always better, you silly man!" Nan flashed him a grin. "I bet she can't kick the hat off your head."

"No. She can't do that. But I think you'd like her, Nan. She's proud, independent, and she's a warm, sweet woman like you."

Nan framed his face with her palms and kissed him on the lips. "I'm happy for you, darlin'. If you love her, she must be a hell of a woman — and a damn lucky one. I might of even married you myself — if you'd of asked me."

"Come to Trinity, Nan. Katy and I are going to make it a real town."

"Build me an Opera House and I will." She followed Rowe to the door. "Darlin', why don't you just kill that asshole brother of yours and get it over with?"

"I can't, honey, unless it comes down to his life or mine."

"If I hear anything, I'll get word to that old stick-in-the-mud Anton."

"I thought you liked Anton."

"I do. He's just not any fun."

"You and Anton are the only ones in town I can depend on. Thanks, honey. You know where to find me if ever you're in need."

"I know. Bye, darlin'. Be happy."

CHAPTER
Nineteen

On the way back to the hotel Rowe passed the dressmaker's shop and paused briefly. He thought of buying something pretty for Katy, but discarded the idea for fear of stepping on her pride. He continued on down the boardwalk to the goldsmith's shop and ten minutes later came out with a small gold ring in his pocket.

He stood with his back to the building and debated whether or not to go over to the Anaconda Hotel and confront his brother. What good would it do? he asked himself. The last three times they had come face-to-face, Justin had lost control and they had almost killed each other. What could Garrick say to him that would make a difference? There would be no reasoning with a man who had so many years of hate built up inside him. Justin was still competing with him, Rowe realized. Not for their father's love, as he had done when he was eight years old, but for things such as success and peace of mind. Rowe supposed it was Justin's warped view that if he made his brother's life miserable, he, himself, would be happier.

His face grave and quiet, Rowe once again

moved into the stream of traffic on the walk and headed back to the hotel and Katy. It had been over an hour since he left her, and he couldn't wait to see her again.

They had dressed carefully for the ceremony that would make them man and wife; Katy in her freshly ironed blue dress, and Rowe in a white shirt, black string tie and a coat that made his shoulders seem a yard wide.

At the door of the church Katy paused, removed her hand from his, lifted the blue shawl from her shoulders and folded it. Carefully she placed it on her head with the point at the top of her forehead and the soft folds falling along her shoulders. She stroked the softness of the shawl, took a steadying breath, and raised her eyes to the man watching her.

"I was right," he said softly. "That shawl is just the color of your eyes."

"It's beautiful. Thank you."

"You're the one that's beautiful." His dark eyes were soft with love.

She reached up and touched his face with her fingertips. In a short time this man would be her husband. The suddenness of her decision was shocking, yet she knew in her heart that she had lived all her life for this moment. They had been drawn to each other like steel to a magnet. The bond that held them together was exquisitely beautiful, but as strong as chains forged in iron.

"I love you." She raised her lips for his kiss.

"I love you. Will you be my wife?" he whispered.

"Forever and ever. Will you be my husband?" she asked with sweet solemnity.

"For as long as we live and throughout eternity," he vowed; he bent his head and took her lips softly, adoringly, lingeringly. It was a kiss of deep commitment. "When I first saw you on the path in the moonlight, I knew I had found what I had been looking for all my life. In my heart you're my wife, but we must go in and make our vows legal in the eyes of man."

Anton was waiting just inside the door with a bouquet of flowers that he thrust into Katy's arms. He then led the way to the front of the church.

The preacher stood stoop-shouldered and old in the stream of yellow light from the window. His voice, however, was strong.

"Mr. Garrick Rowe. Miss Katherine Burns. Please step forward. As you have no witnesses other than Mr. Hooker, and two signatures are required on the marriage paper, my wife will be pleased to act as the second witness." He nodded toward a woman with a sweet face and gray hair tightly coiled on the top of her head. After both Katy and Rowe nodded to the woman, he took up a large Bible, stepped out in front of the pulpit and said, "Stand before me."

Rowe and Katy moved to face him, holding tightly to each other's hands. Anton and the preacher's wife arranged themselves for the ceremony; Anton on Rowe's right, the woman on Katy's left.

The preacher opened the Book.

"Take her left hand."

Katy placed her hand in Rowe's and their fingers entwined in a knot of love. She watched the preacher's old, spotted hands turn the thin pages of the Bible and wished that Mary were standing here beside her as she took her vows. Today she was joining her life to that of a rugged, earthy man who would love, cherish, and protect her and their children. They would live out the days of their lives together, grow old together. Never again would she wake to a day of loneliness stretching out before her. Katy was realistic enough to know that, as she and Rowe traveled through life together, there would be rough spots, that she may not always feel this glow of happiness, but she was confident their love would be enduring.

The service began. The preacher's hushed, reverent tones brought her back to the present. Her eyes went quickly to Rowe's and found that he was gazing down at her.

"Do you, Garrick Rowe, take this woman, Katherine Burns, to be your lawful wedded wife? Do you promise, before God, to love her and cherish her in sickness and in health, for better or worse, until death do you part?"

While Rowe listened to the words, his eyes were on the face of the woman who had become dearer than life to him.

"I do promise."

"Do you, Katherine Burns, take this man, Garrick Rowe, to be your lawful wedded husband? Do you promise, before God, to love him and cherish him, to honor and obey him, in sickness and in health, for better or for worse, until death do you part?"

With her eyes locked with Rowe's, she whispered, "I do."

"The ring, please."

Rowe reached into his pocket for the gold band and placed it on Katy's finger. With his eyes holding hers, he lifted her hand to his lips and kissed the symbol of their union.

"By the right invested in me by the Church of our Lord and Savior, and by the law of Montana Territory in this year of our Lord, eighteen hundred and seventy-four, I declare you man and wife."

The ceremony that changed their lives forever was over quickly. Rowe and Katy turned to each other. He looked into her face, then slowly pulled her into his arms. His lips touched hers gently and reverently, then a smile stripped years from his face.

"Hello, wife," he whispered.

"Hello . . . husband," she answered.

For the longest time he simply held her against him, looking at her, unmindful of the others. In her eyes was such a look of adoration that he was suddenly fearful. Her love was so great a miracle that all he could think of was how well he would care for this magnificent woman who was the core of his life.

"Are you two going to look at each other all day?" Anton's bored voice finally broke the silence. "I want to kiss the bride."

Rowe released her reluctantly, stepped back, and bore nobly Anton's kissing his wife. Dear God, how had he lived until now without her sweet, joyous presence in his life?

The preacher stepped over to a table and indicated a document spread on it. "If you will both sign, the witnesses will affix their signatures."

He dipped the pen in the inkhorn and handed it to Katy. She set her name to the paper and passed the pen to Rowe. When he finished, first Anton, then the preacher's wife signed the marriage papers. The preacher waved the paper until he was sure the ink was dry, then he handed it to Katy.

She folded it carefully, said, "Thank you, sir." And to his wife, "Thank you too, ma'am."

"The marriage will be recorded at the courthouse the first thing in the morning." The preacher spoke while Rowe was pressing some bills in his hand.

"I wish you a long and happy life," his wife was saying to Katy.

"Thank you. And . . . good-bye."

They walked back down the aisle as man and wife. Anton trailed behind them. When they opened the doors to step out onto the porch, a volley of gunfire came from the heart of Virginia

City and a roar went up from the crowd that lined the streets.

The celebration had begun.

Katy smiled radiantly up at her husband. "You'll never have an excuse to forget our wedding anniversary." Mischief lit her eyes.

"That goes for you too."

"I'll never forget a minute of it. Rowe, I didn't expect a ring. When did you get it?" She held up her hand. The gold band gleamed in the sunlight.

"I wish it were a diamond as big as a hen's egg, but this was all they had at the goldsmith's."

"It's perfect. I'll never take it off."

Katy hugged his arm. She hadn't known there was this much happiness in the whole world. She knew she was loved and that she loved in return. Rowe knew it too. She could tell by the unfettered look of love in his eyes when he gazed at her as he was doing now. Home would be wherever he was, if it were on the top of a mountain, in a soddy on the prairie, or an igloo in Alaska. She looked up at him, and the laughter he loved came bubbling out of her.

"Why are you laughing?" Rowe couldn't stop looking at her. God, how could it be that she could make him feel like a king with just her smile?

"How are you at making an igloo?"

"An igloo?"

Aware that Anton was looking at her as if she had lost her mind, she whispered, "I'll tell you later."

"Har-u-m-ph!" Anton said, watching one and then the other as they continued to smile into each other's eyes. "Har-u-m-ph!" he said again.

Rowe reluctantly glanced away from his bride's radiant face and frowned impatiently at his friend. "Do you want something, Anton?"

"Well, yes," Anton said drily. "If it isn't too much trouble, I'd like to know your plans for the day. That is, if you've made any."

"We have. Tell him, sweetheart."

"We're going back to the hotel, change our clothes, pick up the wedding supper Beulah has packed for us, and head back to Trinity."

"Now? In case you haven't noticed, there's a celebration going on here. I thought you'd at least spend the night. I ordered a private table, champagne, and a cake —"

"Oh, Anton, I'm sorry. It's just that I'm not used to so many people around. There's so much noise!"

Rowe clapped him on the shoulder. "Cheer up, partner. It looks like you'll get to drink champagne and eat cake for a week."

As they walked on the downhill slant toward the main street, Anton muttered under his breath something that sounded like he'd be damned if he ever made such a fool of himself over a woman.

Wagons, buggies, and carts were parked in every available place along the streets. Tethered horses and mules munched on feed brought by the owners. Dogs barked, donkeys brayed, and children shrieked, adding to the noise made by the rhythmic beat of a drum leading the parade up from the lower part of town.

Katy put her hands over her ears. "A person can hardly think in this racket."

"Do you want to watch the parade?"

"No. Do you?"

"It's the last thing I want to do. But I thought you wanted to see the girls from the Bucket of Blood fight in the mud."

"It doesn't sound as exciting as it did yesterday. I wonder why?" Her eyes smiled up at him.

"Then we'll go into the hotel from the back and avoid the crowd. Anton, we'll meet you at the livery in half an hour."

"Are you sure?"

"Yes, we're sure." Katy placed her hand on his arm. "Thank you for making the arrangements for us, Anton. You're really a sweet man but you don't want anyone to know it."

They rode out of Virginia City, leaving the noisy celebration behind, and headed for the quiet serenity of the mountains. Rowe, riding his black Arabian and leading a packhorse, was first; Katy followed on the mare she had named Juliet.

While she was changing into her riding clothes and packing her valise, Rowe had gone to the mercantile and made a few purchases to add to the supplies Anton had bought earlier. When they were ready to leave, they went by the kitchen and picked up the food sack. As he put a five dollar gold piece in Beulah's hand, all she could say was, "Lawsy, lawsy, if you ain't the limit."

Rowe turned in the saddle and looked back often. He was taking extra precautions although he was reasonably sure that his brother had not had time to set up an ambush. But other dangers lurked along the trail. A lone man with a woman might seem like easy prey.

Each time Rowe looked back, his eyes swept the terrain before he allowed them to feast on the woman who rode behind him. His dark, intense gaze clung to her thick, wind-tousled hair, her passionate mouth, and tight, slim body. That he had found her and she loved him was a wonder of ever-expanding proportions. She was his mate for ever and always. He was not a religious man, and had seldom called on God for anything, but now, with only the sky above them, he thanked Him for bringing her into his life and asked His help to keep her safe and happy until the end of their days on earth.

When they reached the cooling shade of the pines, Rowe reined up so that Katy could come alongside him. He edged his horse closer to hers. He leaned toward her and found her soft, trembling mouth with his. When he released her from his arms, she laughed with girlish sweetness.

"I'm so happy! Oh, Rowe! I never thought I'd be happy again. I'll be a good wife. I'll help you build Trinity into a town, if that's what you want," she promised solemnly, then continued with a sparkle in her eyes. "Confusion over my feelings for you made me a real grouch these last few weeks. Mary could hardly stand me. She'll be surprised and pleased. I never dreamed that when I left Trinity that I'd return as a married woman. Oh, shoot!" She caught her lower lip between her teeth. "I didn't learn how to run the stage office or how to help you with the books. I clean forgot about it!" Words rushed out of Katy's mouth like water from a dam.

"Sweetheart, I was desperate to get you away and be alone with you. Would you be awfully angry if I told you that I made up the story about the stage coming to Trinity in order to get you to come to Virginia City with me so that I could marry you?"

"I would be furious!"

"Then I won't tell you."

"Rowe! That was dishonest."

"Yeah, it was. It took me three days to think of how I could lie convincingly enough for you to believe me." There was a look of unabashed pride on his face.

"The stage isn't coming to Trinity?"

"Ah . . . maybe someday."

"Garrick Rowe! You're not only a sneak, you're a liar too. What am I going to do with you?" she scolded, but her eyes were full of merriment.

"But I'm other things too, sweetheart." He teased her.

"For instance?"

"I'm sweet, kind, overly intelligent, patient, and sort of . . . handsome."

"All true, I'm sorry to say. But you forgot to add conceited, overbearing and arrogant. Well" — she said with mock sternness — "I know how to cure that."

"You've already paid me back for being sneaky. Tonight you can pay me back for lying. But I'll make damn sure that we don't camp near the water."

She laughed again, and his big, booming laugh joined hers. The smile on his face was the most beautiful one she'd ever seen. There was no past, no lonely future, only Rowe, her husband forever and always.

"I want to kiss you again. I've been thinking about it since we left town." His voice lowered huskily as his hand moved up from her shoulder to curl about her neck and pull her toward him.

"Then get on with it, Genghis Khan, or I'll shoot your toe off." Her eyes danced lovingly over his face.

He drew back and looked at her. "Dammit, Katy. Do you still have that Derringer in your pocket?"

"Uh-huh." She cocked her head to one side and wrinkled her nose at him. "It isn't loaded, but no one knows that but me and now you." Her laughter floated on the cool, crisp air.

He reached for her and pulled her over to sit on his thighs. Apollo protested the extra weight until Rowe spoke a sharp word to him.

"I've been waiting too," Katy said before she took his kiss thirstily. "I'm going to give you enough love to make up for your brother." Their kisses were long and deep and full of promised passion. His fingers moved up into her hair, their touch strong and possessive. His lips pulled away, but he kept her close.

"I love everything about you, Mrs. Rowe," he said quietly.

"I'm glad. I want to be with you forever."

"You shall be, my Nightrose. We'll know the perfect fusion of soul and spirit that comes only when two people are matched as we are matched and love as we love —"

"I don't know if I knew you in another life, my sweet love, but I'm sure glad I found you in this one."

He kissed her again. Her lips clung moistly to his. His hand slipped inside her shirt. His eyes held hers while his fingers cupped about the soft flesh of her breast and his forefinger teased a nipple that hardened instantly.

"These are mine now," he whispered huskily.

"Yes, yours —"

His lips fell hungrily to hers. They were demanding, yet tender. His tongue deeply invaded the mouth that parted so eagerly for him as Katy snuggled in his arms and tugged at the hair on the nape of his neck, innocently unaware of the arousal that was giving him pain.

"Sweetheart, we'd better stop this, or we'll be camping here tonight in plain view of Virginia City."

She laughed, pulled away from him, and slid

to the ground. When she was mounted again, she looked into his dark, craggy face and her eyes mirrored the love in her heart.

"You're also brave and dependable and I'm proud you'll be the father of my children," she said as if adding to their early conversation.

They headed south at a leisurely walk, staying among the trees and climbing. Rowe explained that the trail they followed crossed the corner of Sam Sparks' ranch, but was miles from the house. He promised that they would come back for a visit before the snow clogged the mountain trails.

In the late afternoon they entered an area where the quiet hung over the timbered mountainside. In the diffused sunlight and dense shade, birds flitted, squirrels scolded, and a deer with a fawn by her side stared at them, then bounded away. Katy watched, wondering how she could have ever hated this beautiful country. Nothing in Alabama could compare with the wild, raw beauty of these cool green mountains with their cold, fast-moving streams.

Katy was jarred from her reverie when Juliet stopped behind the packhorse Rowe was leading. He had turned in the saddle and was looking at her.

"Tired?"

"I haven't even thought about it."

"Come here, sweetheart. I want to show you something." Katy urged Juliet up beside the big black. Rowe reached for her hand. "See that cabin down there. It's abandoned. Anton and I have stayed there a couple of times. I had planned for us to spend our wedding night out under the stars, but it looks as if it will rain before long."

The small log structure seemed scarcely high enough for Rowe to stand upright within it. It sat beside a small stream and nestled against a bluff. To the front and one side was an open area of meadow grass on which a herd of elk were grazing.

"It's beautiful. Why would someone build such a place and then leave it?"

"Many reasons. Some people can't stand the loneliness."

"There's nothing as lonely as a town after all the people are gone," she said quietly.

Rowe looked at her and thought with a sinking feeling that she should have a wedding night in a soft, sweet-smelling bed, not in a cold, drafty mountain cabin with a dirt floor and a roof that probably leaked.

"Katy, darling, you can have any kind of house you want, anywhere you want it —"

She saw the distressed look on his face and was moved by it. "Do you think I regret leaving Virginia City and coming into the wilderness for our wedding night? It was my suggestion. Remember? Let's get on down to our home for the night before we get rained on."

The cabin, when they reached it, was far more dilapidated than it had looked to be from a distance. But it was shelter. A low rumble of thunder came from the southwest, dark clouds rolled overhead, and the wind turned cold. Katy unsaddled her mare and carried the saddle into the cabin. Rowe worked swiftly. He stashed the bundles from the packhorse inside; while he fastened the horses to a quickly rigged picket line, Katy gathered firewood and piled it beside the crude but adequate fireplace. Rowe came in with a load of wood in his arms just as the rain began to fall.

Katy shivered while Rowe built a fire that illuminated the small enclosure. The cabin was completely bare except for two empty tin cans, the tops partially opened and folded back. She was amazed at her own feelings. She had been appalled by some of the places she and Mary had been forced to live in these past years, but none of them were as crude as this one. Yet, because Rowe was with her, it seemed not to matter at all.

As soon as the fire was going, he stood and opened his arms. Katy went into them. He held her bruisingly close. The drabness of their surroundings was forgotten as his trembling hands traced the form of her softly rounded breasts, spanned her small waist, and stroked the curve of her hips while his mouth closed over hers.

CHAPTER

Twenty

A low growl of protest came from Rowe's throat. His arms tightened and the words he muttered were scattered from her ear along her jaw to her mouth.

"I didn't plan for us to spend our wedding night in a shack with a dirt floor."

"What did you plan?" she breathed, entranced, her fingers caressing his nape.

"I wanted us to be under a clear, star-filled sky, far away from everything and everyone."

"You've got half of it, love. We're far away from everyone." She drew back to look into his dark face. Her fingers moved to stroke the silky hair above his lips. "I can do without the clear, star-filled sky, if you can."

"Katy, Katy, Katy. You're wonderful."

"I'm no such thing!" She laughed happily. "I'm hungry. Let's eat our supper. I'm going to need my strength for the full night of loving ahead."

"You're right about that!" He kissed her thoroughly and deeply while his hands roved over her back and buttocks. Needing to feel more of her, he leaned into her and levered his upper body away, pushing his aching arousal against her soft body.

Katy's breath quickened at the touch. She melted into him, helpless to deny him anything. It felt so good, so right, leaning against his most intimate part. She moved her pelvis from side to side and watched his face light with pleasure as his breath quickened along with hers.

"Where did you learn to do that?" he demanded gruffly.

"From you. You taught me a thousand years ago."

"I'll thank God every day of my life for letting me meet you again!" He pressed his hardness against her softness for a delicious moment, then determinedly moved back. "You're perfect. Sweet and perfect" — he kissed her because he couldn't help himself and because he wanted her so much — "but we'd better stop, eat, and fix our bed."

"I know." The regret in her voice was obvious.

Carefully, gently, he put her from him while looking deeply into eyes that gazed adoringly back into his. God help me to go slowly, he prayed silently. Help me to make our coming together a sacred commitment and not purely an act of gratifying my lust. With all the restraint he could muster, he placed little pecking kisses on her nose, her forehead, and then turned to untie the pack beside the door.

While the rain beat at the walls and roof of the shack, Rowe spread a canvas on the floor in front of the fire, covered it with several blankets, and placed his saddle at one end for Katy to lean against. The sparks in his dark eyes danced like embers in the night as he bowed at the waist with Old World courtesy and invited her to sit down.

Sitting side by side they ate the feast of meat, buttered bread, boiled eggs, and honey cakes Beulah had prepared and drank the coffee Rowe made from the water in their canteens. They sat quietly, listening to the rain, content to be together, eyes catching, escaping, meeting again. There was no yesterday and no tomorrow, just the present; the two of them were alone in the world. They were eating because it was necessary, but to them, corn pone and sow belly would have served.

While Katy wrapped the remainder of the food in a cloth and put it back in the bag, Rowe wedged a stout pole against the door.

"I'm quite sure there's no one around, but just in case I'm wrong, we don't want a surprise visit." He squatted down, poked at the fire and added another piece of wood.

Katy came to stand beside him, gazing down on his dark head. When he looked up, the longing in his eyes stirred her. She'd seen this big hard man do what he had to do the day the outlaws came to Trinity and on the day they were attacked on the trail. Right now, he seemed like a small boy silently asking for her approval. He needed love as much as she did. She reached out and drew his head against her thigh and ran her fingers through his thick, wild hair.

"I'm going to give you enough love to make up for Justin," she promised softly. "I'm going to give you sunshine and peace and love every day of our lives," she vowed and commanded herself not to cry.

"I know I have that when I'm with you," he told her, his voice suddenly thick.

"I'm glad," she whispered. "I'm so glad."

Katy sat down on the blanket and removed her shoes. She pulled the thick braid of hair over her shoulder, untied the end and unraveled the braid. Kneeling beside her, Rowe took the long tresses from her hands, and with fingers both strong and gentle combed through her hair, spreading it about her shoulders. Then he tipped her face back so that she would have to meet his eyes.

"I love you. I have loved you always." His words were husky with emotion. He held her tightly, but Katy could not get close enough. She pressed herself to him, desiring to melt into his body. His kisses were fierce, his mouth moist and firm, forcing hers to open so that his tongue could wander over her soft inner lips before venturing deeper. Then he raised his head to look into her face, and she saw all he was feeling. "You're so beautiful, so sweet —"

There were no secrets. Right there in his eyes was all Katy ever wanted to know. When he sat and drew her across his lap, and his mouth found hers again, she yielded to him fully, responding naturally, ardently.

"If I kissed you ten million times, my Night-rose, it would not be enough," he breathed against her mouth. His lips moved across hers slowly, as if afraid he would miss a tiny part while his fingers worked at the buttons on her shirt. Finally her breast was bare, and, he drew in a deep trembling breath, his eyes filled with awe and pleasure.

Katy trembled with delight at each tantalizing caress of his fingers as he stroked her nipples. When his mouth replaced his fingers and his tongue continued the stroking, she sucked in her breath, so great was the pleasure.

"Feel good?"

"Oh, yes!"

"Do you want me to get your nightdress?"

"Do I need one?"

"I'd just take it off."

"Then don't bother, my love."

With trustful innocence, Katy moved out of his arms to take off her shirt and pull the short shift up over her head. She was bare to the waist. Rowe watched her, caressing her with his eyes.

"You're lovelier than I ever imagined."

She reached out to caress his face, to place her hand against his chest and whisper his name, and he trembled at the depth of his need to have her warm and naked in his arms.

"You're beautiful too."

"Turn around, sweetheart, while I take off my clothes. I don't want to scare you to death."

Rowe quickly shed his clothing and pulled one

of the blankets over him to cover his throbbing erection. Sitting on the edge of the blanket in her drawers, Katy folded her riding skirt and shivered in the cool, damp air.

Behind her, Rowe's fingers parted her hair and flung it over her shoulders. His arms, lightly sprinkled with soft black hair, came around her to cross in front beneath the rich fall of her tresses. His hands covered her breasts. With her back pressed tightly to his naked chest, he pressed his face into the curve of her neck.

"I just had to do this. I just had to," he murmured between biting kisses. "It feels so natural and good —" He spread his fingers, catching the dusky pink tips of her nipples between them, and squeezing gently.

He pulled her down on the make-shift bed, covered them with the blanket and helped her to wiggle out of her drawers. Then he drew her soft naked body against the swelling hardness of his manhood. For a long time he simply held her against him, letting his body tell her of itself while learning the shy secrets of her own.

Closing her eyes against the mist of tears that gathered, Katy buried her face in the warmth of his chest, tightened her arms around him, inhaling the rich masculine scent of him, and realizing that she had never known a more beautiful moment.

She sought his mouth with hers as he tantalized the tips of her breasts with nibbling fingers. The soft flesh filled his palm. He fondled it as carefully as if he were holding a precious life in his hands. He made love to her slowly, kissing her temples, the curve of her cheeks, the sides of her mouth. He closed her eyes with gentle kisses. His sex was large, firm, and throbbingly erect against the thigh pinned between his. It seemed enormous to Katy, yet she did not feel threatened by this giant of a man who trembled beneath her touch.

He turned her on her back, swinging his leg over hers, pressing her to the blanket. She wrapped her arms around his naked torso. Her ragged breath was trapped inside her mouth by his lips. He lifted his head and looked into her face, his hand gentle in her hair.

"You're very precious to me. I'll take care of you always," he whispered urgently.

"I know that."

He lowered his head and nuzzled her breast. His lips captured a nipple, and the rough drag of his tongue was so exquisitely painful that she drew a gasping breath. Her mind whirled, her flesh tingled. This was something she had dreamed about while she lay in her lonely bed, but the reality was far more wonderful than the dream.

"I wanted to do that from the very first," he whispered. "The day we went to see the honkers, I felt myself growing hard and I took a deep breath and said to myself, don't let this sweet woman think you're a rutting stag. I wanted to take off your clothes and taste every bit of you until you were hot and wet and wanting me. But more than that, I wanted you to trust me. I desperately wanted your love."

As he caressed her thighs, her hips, his touch was patient, yet sweetly demanding. Katy did not know what to expect, but the sensations he was building made her desperate for more and more. His hand moved over her body and suddenly it was there at the mysterious moistness between her thighs. She parted her legs voluntarily, aching for him to explore more deeply. When he slipped his fingers inside her, she tensed, wholly caught up in the feelings trembling from that secret place. At first she was tight with newness, but as his exploring fingers caressed her, she opened with a small, strangled cry and tremors shot through her in rocketing waves.

He did not have to urge her hand to the part of him that begged to be touched. Fingers that had lost their shyness closed around him. A low moan came from his lips as she teased his hardened flesh. He had not expected this sweet willingness, the astounding passion that lay slumbering beneath her innocence. She held nothing from him; he held nothing from her. The swift honesty with which she offered herself to him was a surprise and a delight.

"Sweetheart, I'll hurt you when I go inside you the first time." He leaned over her, supporting himself on his forearms, cupped her head in his hands and rained tender, soft kisses on her face. She clung to him, her hand stroking his shoulder and back. She was drowning in desire, swept by emotion, responding to each new sensation with growing urgency. She caressed his hard shaft and begged with motions for him to enter her.

"Rowe, Rowe," she cried, and wrapped her arms around him, spreading her legs so his thighs could sink between hers. Cradled together, his hardness cushioned against her soft mound, they rocked from side to side.

His kisses were hard and swift on her mouth, but kisses were not enough now. Only by joining their bodies would they begin to appease the hunger they had for each other. He lifted his hips, as her hand urgently moved between them to guide him into her.

He raised his head. "Look at me, sweetheart," he said urgently. "This is the most beautiful moment of my life." His body begged for release, but he held himself in check to savor the pleasure. He smiled down at her and leaned to kiss her hungry mouth.

Slowly, he began to penetrate her. She was wet and ready, but tight. Anticipation of her pain filled him with anxiety. He hated having to hurt her, but determinedly he drove himself deep inside her, met the final barrier of her innocence, and destroyed it. Her eyes went wide with surprise; she gasped at the sharp pain. He held himself still while her body adjusted itself to his presence. He withdrew, then eased forward. She gasped again, not from pain, but at the strangeness of his full length invading her. Then, the fire inside her body where he was began to build into an overwhelming need. The whole world was the man joined to her. His mouth and her mouth were one. He was at home in her, moving gently, caressingly, lovingly. She arched her hips wildly and he hungrily took what she offered.

The spasms of pleasure that followed danced gloriously throughout her body. The tip of him touched her very soul. She wanted the moment to go on forever — but she had no choice. She had to let go. The teasing tension that had built in their coupled bodies exploded into rapturous release. Katy wasn't really aware when it ended. When she returned to reality Rowe was leaning over her, his weight again on his forearms.

"Are you all right, love?"

The light touch of his lips at the corner of her mouth brought a small inarticulate sound from her. She tightened her arms around him, folded her legs over his to hold him inside her warmth. Her hands moved into his wild, thick hair and fondled his neck, then came up to stroke his cheeks and caress his ears.

"Are you all right?"

"Yes! Oh, yes. So this is what some women think is so dreadful." She laughed, caught his lower lip between her teeth and bit gently. She struggled for words to express her feelings. "Darling, we've done something wonderful together. And I'm . . . I'm so full of you," she exclaimed. Hearing and feeling the slow rumbling of his deep chuckle, she laughed, and her soft belly moved against his hard one.

"Yes, my rose of the night, we have done something special together." He stroked the hair from her flushed face. "I truly love you, Katherine Burns Rowe. So help me God, I do!"

Suddenly their passion swelled again. It rocked them, enveloped them in a swirling, translucent world where nothing existed but the two of them and the ecstasy they shared. He was still enclosed in the sweet softness, pillowed in a warm and silken place. Seeking more of the delicious feeling, she thrust upward to envelop his entire length, helpless to suppress the groan of pleasure that rose to her lips with every surge of his magnificent prodding flesh.

Rowe drowned his burning, bursting manhood in the writhing sweetness it had entered. The world waited while the irreversible tempo built toward consuming release. Then he was floating free above the earth with only the warm sheath holding him. The heated flow of his life-giving fluid spurted from his body in a great flood, filling her. His mind and his body separated and he was beyond himself.

Afterward, they lay side by side and held each other while their heartbeats slowed and the glorious throbbing of their bodies ceased. It had been so beautiful; tears slipped from Katy's eyes and wet the shoulder beneath her head.

"Sweetheart! Why are you crying? Did I hurt you? I tried to keep control, but it slipped away from me and I lost myself in you."

"You were sweet and gentle. I've thought about

bedding with the man I loved, but I never imagined it to be so wonderful. I love you so much, Rowe. Don't break my heart." Her breath caught and her voice ended in a sob.

A growl of protest came from his throat. He tilted her face up and kissed her deeply before he raised his head to look at her again.

"Heart of my heart, once, long ago, I loved you in another life and I shall love you in this one until time has no more meaning for us. You are mine and I am yours."

In the flickering firelight, his eyes possessed a mysterious magnetic force. She couldn't look away. She felt suddenly immersed in a sumptuously delicious joy. Love and tenderness welled within her, and a feeling of peace unfolded and traveled slowly throughout her body.

"Yes," she whispered. "I am yours and you are mine."

Once during the night Rowe got up to add more fuel to their fire. Katy lay with her head on her arm and watched him. His naked body was magnificent as he moved about without shame, unmindful of her eyes upon him. He was strong and lean, broad of chest, with long legs and flat abdomen. Katy had touched all of him, but his was the first completely naked male body she had seen. A triangle of curly black hair spread above his nipples to almost disappear just below his navel. Below that, springing out of a nest of thick black hair, was the male part of him that she had seen only in pictures of statues. They had not prepared her for the wonder of a man's body ready for love.

He slipped back into the warm nest of blankets, redolent with the musky scent of their love, and gathered her to him. Their bodies came together perfectly, and Katy felt the stirring of his maleness as she teased it with the soft down on her mound.

"How do people who love each other like we do manage to get any sleep?" Her face was damp and flushed and covered with a happy smile.

"There are no other people who love each other like we do," he contradicted softly and began to caress her mouth gently but firmly.

Her hand, pressed flat, slid over his shoulder, over his collarbone to his chest. She spread her fingers through his chest hair and straightened her legs so that she could move closer to the lower part of him that had begun to swell, to pillow it against her soft belly.

"I like to touch you." She turned her face and kissed the lean muscles that rippled beneath her lips.

"I like it too. Don't stop, sweetheart," he coaxed in a hoarse whisper. His need was a tumultuous pressure in his groin, a throbbing all-over ache. "I've had you twice already and I want you again."

"Then have me, darling. I'm yours."

Her words made his heart leap. "You'll have trouble walking tomorrow, much less riding."

"Remember when we were at Emily's?" She caught his hand and brought it down to press against the tight curls below her belly. "You rubbed the soreness out of me. You'll just have to do it again."

She could feel the thunderous pounding of his heart against her breast. "I'll never get enough of you!" His voice trembled with emotion.

"But you'll keep trying, won't you?"

They made love deep into the night until sheer exhaustion sent Katy into a deep sleep. Rowe's protective instincts kept him poised in the void between sleep and awareness. Katy lay molded to his naked body, her cheek nestled in the warm hollow of his shoulder. His fingers absently caressed the rounded flesh of her breasts, fondling the stiff peaks.

A whimpering sound came from her as her own hand came up to clasp his and press it tighter to her breast.

"Rowe . . ." His name came from her lips even as she was searching for his. "Kiss me, hold me —"

He kissed her soft, eager lips and murmured, "Go to sleep, love. You're worn out."

Morning came and with it sunshine. Katy awakened and opened one eye to see the bright pattern of light splashed across the floor. Seconds later it was gone as Rowe's body filled the open doorway.

"Morning, sleepyhead." He stepped into the shack and dropped an armload of wood beside the fireplace.

Katy stretched and opened her other eye to find

his face just inches from hers. She ran her fingers over his smooth cheeks and chin.

"You've shaved. How long have you been up?"

"A long time. I wanted to look at you. Coffee is ready and I've heated water for you to wash." He looked as happy as a small boy with a new slingshot.

"I'm sorry I didn't wake up. I was tired." Her fingers moved inside his shirt and combed the hair on his chest. "It was a long, delicious night," she whispered.

"For me too."

"No woman ever had a more wonderful wedding night!" Her words melted on her lips when she tried to speak and were swept away by his kisses.

"No man ever had a sweeter bride."

"I'm so hungry I could eat a horse."

"Your wish is my command, my lady. Shall it be Apollo or Juliet?" His face was soft with love, his eyes teasing.

"Hummm —" She appeared to be deliberating.

"You look very smug this morning, Mrs. Rowe. Are you pleased that you finally had your way with me?"

"Very pleased. I might even go into the business. Do you think Lizzibeth could use another girl at the Bee Hive?"

"I'll give you all the business you can handle, little tease," he said gruffly. "Now that I've had time to reconsider, I'm not sure that I'll share a can of peaches with you."

"Peaches? You've been holding out on me."

"Would you like to stay here today, sweetheart? We can go on to Trinity tomorrow."

Katy sat up, holding the blanket up over her breasts, and shivered as the cold air hit her back. A tangle of golden hair hung around her face and over her shoulders.

"Oh, Rowe. Let's stay. I don't even know where we'll live when we get to Trinity. Besides —" she gave him a sideways look — "I may be too sore to ride today."

He reached for the blanket and pulled it up to cover her back and shoulders. With a devilish grin he pulled down on the part that covered her breasts, then lowered his head and placed a kiss on each puckered peak.

"If we stay here today, it's *sure* you'll be too sore to ride tomorrow."

"Will you swear to that on your mother's Bible?" she asked solemnly with eyes wide and innocent.

He eased her back down onto the bed, covered her with the blanket, then kicked off his boots. Holding her with his eyes, he unbuckled his belt and pulled off his britches.

"I do solemnly swear that I'll do my very best to see that Katherine Burns Rowe will be very uncomfortable straddling a horse tomorrow, so uncomfortable, in fact, that she will insist upon sitting on her husband's lap all the way to Trinity." Laughter rippled in his voice at the last.

"Well, Mr. Billy Goat Rowe." Her eyes glinted up at him. "You've got your work cut out for you."

He pounced on her like a cat. They rolled on the blankets, arms and legs tangled, her hair covering the both of them. He captured her mouth, kissing, nibbling, growling, while laughter bubbled out of her.

"Rowe!" she gasped when she was able to free her mouth. "The door's open and we're naked —"

"There's no one to see us except the platoon of soldiers camped in front of the cabin."

"Noooo . . ." She reared up and grabbed for the covers. When she saw the delight on his face she paused, reached around him, and pinched his bottom. "Garrick Rowe! You've got to do something about your lying," she said with exaggerated sternness.

"What do you suggest?" He rolled her over him, kissed her face, and nibbled on her neck, biting softly and sucking gently.

"Prayer. Repentance. Self-flagellation. You great lout! You scared the fool out of me —"

"Mrs. Rowe," he said firmly, "stop your complaining. You've got better things to do . . ."

CHAPTER
Twenty-one

By two o'clock almost the entire population of
Trinity had gathered at the baseball field either
to play on one of the teams or to watch the game.
It was the last event of a full afternoon of celebrating. Most of the players had to be taught the
rudiments of the game, but once they got the
hang of it, they played as if life or death depended
on the outcome. John, the blacksmith, was the
captain of one team and Art Ashland, the
freighter, the captain of the other.

Elias had been recruited to act as umpire. He
was reluctant to accept the role, but when he was
finally persuaded to officiate, he did so fairly and
firmly. His first close decision had been met with
curses and threats from Art Ashland and his team.
Elias stood his ground and declared that as umpire his decisions were final, and if there were any
more threats of violence, the other team would
be declared the winner. Art scowled, backed
down, and snarled at his team to keep quiet.

Laura, sitting beside Mary, cheered in support
of Elias. Her shout was lost in the roar of approval
from John's team.

"That just tickles me to death, Mary. This is

one time that big hairy beast isn't going to push Elias around. Elias has more brains in his little finger than that arrogant man has in his entire unwashed body." She pushed strands of hair back into the knot pinned to the nape of her neck and eyed Mary accusingly.

"My goodness, Laura. I agree with you!" Mary looked at her friend's set features and tilted chin and added softly, "I declare if you don't sound like a woman in love."

"Where did you get that idea? What a thing to say! Just because I'm glad Elias is standing his ground doesn't mean . . . doesn't mean —" Laura sputtered, and her face turned a delightful pink.

"Of course, it doesn't," Mary said staunchly and giggled. "Elias Glossberg is a very nice man. He's good-looking, gentle, intelligent, and as dependable as the day is long. He likes children, is a hard worker, is interesting to talk to, likes to read and discuss various topics . . . Hummm . . . I just now realized all those nice things about Elias. I should set my cap for him."

Mary's words washed the pink from Laura's face, leaving it pale and her eyes bleak.

"But, Mary, I thought that you and Hank — you said that you thought Hank was . . . nice."

Mary placed her hand on Laura's arm when she saw the distress in her friend's face.

"I was teasing, Laura. Hank is nice and I think I'm in love with him. Elias is perfect for you. I've been hoping that things would work out for the two of you. I've seen him watching you and I'm sure he's smitten, but he's afraid to say any-thing."

"Afraid? Well, for goodness' sake. Why would he be afraid of me? I don't know what I would have done without him while we were on the trail. Every other man that offered to help me wanted something in return. Elias was there each time I needed someone and later he'd just dis-appear."

"He may be afraid of being rejected. You're friends now and he may not want to take a chance of losing your friendship."

"He wouldn't!"

"He doesn't know that. Elias is a gentleman. That's why it's hard for the men in this rough country to accept him. Not that Hank isn't a gentleman," she added quickly.

"It just makes my blood boil when these igno-rant louts refer to him as the Jew. They don't call other men 'the Irish' or 'the French' or 'the En-glish.' Elias is a man who happens to be Jewish. People with prejudices are small-minded."

"Speaking of small-minded, there's Mr. Long-street."

Mary and Laura watched the Southerner walk up to where his daughter, Agnes, sat on a make-shift bench with Myrtle Chandler. He stood sev-eral feet away from them for a moment, fingering the watch chain looped across the front of his vest and looking around. Presently he moved up be-hind Myrtle and rubbed himself against her back. The young girl inched forward, then stood, and moved away. Agnes would have followed, but her father pressed her down on the seat with a heavy hand on her shoulder.

"Did you see that?" Laura asked, shocked. "That lustful old lecher was pushing himself against Myrtle. One of us should tell Mrs. Chandler."

"We can't . . . now. The men are so worked up it could start a fight if she screamed loudly enough. Oh! That nasty man. Why doesn't he go after one of the girls from the Bee Hive? She'd know how to handle him."

"Poor Myrtle. She's going over to stand beside her mother."

Mrs. Chandler had brought a dishpanfull of bearclaws to the game and was busily handing them out and taking the coin.

"Look, Mary. Lizzibeth from the Bee Hive is glaring at Mr. Longstreet. She saw what he did and she doesn't like it —"

"Goddamn you, Jew! I'm not out!" The shout came from first base. A miner picked himself up out of the dirt and shook his fist at Elias.

"You're out! Get off the field."

"Make me, Jew —"

"It ain't Mr. Glossberg's job to make ya, Arnie," Hank yelled. "It's mine. Do what he says or you'll forfeit the game."

"Ya cause us to lose this here game, ya mule-headed jackass, and I'll stomp yore ass in the ground," Big John yelled.

"Awright! Goddammit, I warn't out."

"Ya was too out. Yore a sorehead, Arnie Dorenkamp," the player at first base called as the disgruntled miner walked back to his teammates, and the next batter stepped up to the gunnysack that served as the plate.

"Oh, dear," Laura said. "I hope Elias doesn't get in trouble."

"Don't worry. Hank has already told the players that if there's any trouble there'll not be another game. Some of the men have asked Elias to read to them from the rule book. I think you'll find after this the men will have more respect for Elias. It could be what Hank had in mind."

A low rumble of thunder came from the southwest where the sky had darkened, and wind was pushing rain clouds toward them.

"I hope the rain holds off until they finish the game. My goodness, Mary. Here come Julia and Theresa walking hand in hand with Pearl from the Bee Hive!"

Mary laughed. "Shocking, isn't it? We're in a different time and a different place, Laura. What used to be unheard of back home is normal here."

"Julia has a tummy ache," Pearl called as they approached. "Poor little darlin's had too many sweet tarts."

Later that night after Mary had put a tired Theresa to bed, she moved the lamp to the table and opened her journal. Hank had promised to come by after he made a tour of the town to see if everything was peaceful. In the meanwhile she would record her thoughts of the day.

Trinity, July 4, 1874.

It has been a grand day of celebration. Sack races were held before noon and two girls from the Bee Hive won. The wood-chopping, barrel-rolling and axe-throwing contests followed. Flossie Chandler won the footrace for the women and was given a length of dress goods donated by Elias. The miners' cook won the leather gloves. Everyone enjoyed the horse and mule races, but the baseball game was the highlight of the day. Art Ashland's team won. Each man was given a silver dollar by the mining company. All in all, it was a very nice day. Even the rain held off until the game was over. I wish Katy and Rowe had been here.

Today I discovered that Laura is in love with Elias Glossberg. I'm almost sure he has feelings for her. His dark eyes are so sad at times, but they brighten when Laura and Julia are around. The bad part of the day was the way Mr. Longstreet stood on the sidelines with a sneer on his face. There is something sinister and wicked about the man. His own children stay as far as possible from him.

Hank has kept peace but some of the miners are getting restless. I think they miss their families.

While Mary was putting her journal back in the trunk, a particularly loud crash of thunder caused her to wince and glance at the sleeping child on the bed. The wind whipped the side of the funerary with rain, and the tin roof rumbled. The sound of boot heels on the porch and the soft rap on the door brought a smile to her face as she hurried to open it. Hank stood outside with water dripping from the brim of his hat, his cotton shirt glued to his broad shoulders and chest.

"Hank! For goodness' sake! You're soaking wet." Mary reached for his hat when he stepped inside.

"I'll muddy up your floor, Mary."

"Oh, pooh! Come on in. Don't you have an oilskin? I declare, men are like children at times."

Hank grinned at her scolding. "I'd of been just this wet, lass, if I'd gone to the bunkhouse to get it."

"But you could have changed into a dry shirt and britches while you were there. Leave your boots by the door and come on over by the cookstove before you catch your death of cold."

Hank kicked off his boots and accepted the towel Mary offered. He wiped his face and rubbed his dark red hair while watching her stoke the fire in the cookstove and set the teakettle directly over the blaze.

"After Rowe was shot, I fixed him a drink with hot water, whiskey, and sugar. There's still some whiskey left in the bottle." She glanced over her shoulder. Hank was still standing beside the door. "Come on. Sit right here." She pulled a chair up beside the stove. "And take off that shirt so I can dry it."

"I've not been bossed so much since I was a tad," Hank grumbled, but there was a pleased smile on his face. He draped the towel on the back of the chair and removed his shirt.

Mary tried not to look at the curly hair on his broad, muscular chest, or at the hard, flat plain of his stomach as she took his shirt, squeezed the water from it, and hung it on a cord above the stove.

She moved behind him and dried the tight skin of his shoulders and back with the towel. A long red welt, the edges turning blue, ran diagonally from his shoulder blade down to the small of his back. Mary dabbed at it gently with the cloth.

"Hank? What's this mark on your back?"

"What mark?"

"You know what mark. It must have hurt when it happened." Mary leaned around so she could look into his face.

"It's nothin', lass. A bit of a scuffle at the saloon."

"You mean a fight." She ran the towel over his arms and chest. "Oh, Hank! There's so many of them and only one of you —" Fear for him put a worried tone in her voice and anguish in her face.

He searched her face for a long moment, then gently pulled her down onto his lap.

"You're not to worry, sweet lassie. Ashland'll keep his men in line or he'll be out of a job. And he wants this job."

"I'll be glad when Rowe gets back to help you."

Mary looped her arms about his neck. "Ashland is a mean man. Flossie Chandler said Lizzibeth won't let him in the Bee Hive anymore."

Hank grinned. "Lizzibeth is a woman to reckon with."

"Stop grinning, Hank Weston! Do you . . . go there?" she whispered with her cheek against his, not wanting him to see her face.

"Well —"

Mary gave a strangled cry. Her head jerked back from his and her arms slid from around his neck. She looked into blue eyes dancing with deviltry and a weathered face creased with smiles.

"Would ya care, Mary mine?"

"Care? I'd be mad enough to kick a stump if you did! Oh, Hank, you don't go there . . . do you?"

"Not for . . . *that.*"

"Then why?"

"A time or two someone was rough with the girls. Lizzibeth sent for me."

"Art Ashland again. I'm scared something will happen to you," she blurted.

"Ah . . . sweet lassie —" He held her close against him, feeling his heart pounding heavily against her breast. "Life is precious to me now 'cause of you and the babe. I be takin' care to see nothin' happens."

"I love you, Hank. I said that once to another man. It was a long time ago, but I had my head in the clouds then and didn't know the meaning of the word. I know there will be good times and bad times, but I'll be a good wife to you, if you still want me."

"Want you?" His voice was husky, tender. He was holding her fast and kissing her cheek. "I want you," he murmured again and again. "I love you, love you —" He held her away from him and looked into her eyes with great tenderness. "When Rowe gets back, we'll go to Bannack and be wed." His hand began stroking her forehead, pushing her hair back and smoothing it caressingly. "We'll make a home wherever you want."

"It isn't *where* we are that matters."

He kissed her gently, lovingly. Her soft mouth parted with yearning, and the kiss deepened, and went on and on. When she drew back, her eyes were like two bright pools, her lips wet with his kiss. She looked down at the hand caressing the soft curve of her breast, covered it with hers and pressed.

"Hank, I'm not young and innocent. You want to do more than just kiss me, don't you?"

"Mary . . . sweet lassie. I'd not be human if I didn't." His voice was a groan against her lips. He kissed her. The sweet burning pressure of his lips on hers fused them together, blotting out everything else. Finally he lifted his head. "I'm going to have to leave you, or I'll be doin' the *more* you spoke of."

"Don't go!" Mary whispered the words in his ear, and shivered with an excitement that was sheer heaven.

"You're sure?" Hank asked after a long hesitation.

"We've pledged our love," she said simply and slid off his lap. She moved the teakettle to the back of the stove, took his hand, and pulled him to his feet. When he was standing, she wrapped her arms about his waist, rested her chin on his chest, and looked up at him. "Are you shocked by my suggestion? It may be months before we can be wed." She ran her hands over the smooth skin of his back and felt him tremble beneath her touch.

"Not shocked, lass. Surprised. I be wonderin' why God let such a woman as ye be lovin' a rough, ignorant man like Hank Weston." Due to the emotions churning through him, Hank reverted back to the Irish brogue of his childhood.

"And why not, Hank Weston. You're a good, gentle man. I'll be *proud* to call you husband."

"I'll be lovin' you till my dyin' day," he croaked and swung her up in his arms.

"Hank! I've not been carried since I was a child."

"Then it's time, sweet woman," he whispered, his lips in her hair. He went to the end of the funerary and stood beside Katy's bed, holding Mary tightly to him. His hungry mouth searched, found hers, and held it with fierce possession before he placed her gently on the bed and breathed, "If you've changed your mind, I'll go. If not, I'll blow out the lamp."

"Blow out the lamp," she whispered.

Mary's heart beat like a wild thing as she slipped out of her clothes. Ingrained teachings of the proper behavior required of a Southern wife came forward to plague her. She had lain like a stone while Roy took his pleasure of her. It was what he expected. He would have been appalled had she attempted to touch him intimately. Only whores and wanton women were allowed that privilege. She would ask Hank his feelings on the matter, she decided as she lay down and pulled the blanket up over her trembling, naked body. If he was repelled by her boldness, it would be better to know before they were wed.

Hank's tall, shadowy figure came out of the darkness. She heard him remove his britches. Sweet warmth washed over her and she felt as if her heart would gallop right out of her breast. The bed sagged when he sat down on the edge. An instant later the covers lifted and she felt long, cool, hair-roughened legs against her and arms that seemed a yard long scoop under and around her. She was gathered tenderly to a naked chest. Never had she been held with such gentle strength.

"Your legs are cold," she whispered and threaded her legs between his to give him her warmth. Her hands moved caressingly up and down his side and over his hips to the small of his back. His sex was large and firm and throbbed against her belly. She gloried in the feel of him, knowing that soon he would fill that aching emptiness inside her.

His breath came in quick gasps. He turned her on her back so that he could hover over her. His kisses were hard and anxious on her mouth before he lowered his head to kiss her breast. His tongue flicked the bud, then grasped it gently with his teeth. His nuzzle of the soft mound was like a baby's seeking mouth. His big hands moved over her body, prowling ever closer to the mysterious moistness. She opened her legs for him.

"Wait — I've got to ask you something."

He lifted his head and attempted to pull his hand from between her legs. She grasped his wrist and held it there.

"I want . . . I don't know how to say it," she whispered urgently.

"Say what? What's troubling you, lass? You've only to say the word and I'll go."

"No! I want to love you, hold you, caress you the way you're caressing me. I was never allowed to . . . before —"

"You were never allowed — Jesus, my God! What kind of man was he?"

"It wasn't his fault. The women he knew were raised to do their duty to their husbands and he . . . went to a mistress or to a place like the Bee Hive for more."

"Sweet, little love!" he groaned against the side of her face. "As long as we live I'll never seek another. I swear to you —" He lifted his head, frantically seeking her lips.

"You'll not be angry or disgusted if I touch you?" she gasped when she could free her lips.

"No! God no! I want it, crave it — touch me," he coaxed in that same hoarse whisper. He placed her hand palm down on the cushion from which his male hardness sprang.

For Mary, it was a time of blissful discovery. She spread her fingers through springy hair and felt the movement of his extended sex quivering against the back of her hand. Tremors shot through her in waves when his own exploring fingers moved into the pulsing flesh of her womanhood. She arched frantically, seeking more of the wondrous feeling. Instinctively, she reached for the thick shaft to fill her. Her hand encircled him and pulled. He trembled violently as he slid between her spread thighs and held himself poised above her while she led him to the warm cavern he sought.

Hank supported himself on his forearms, tangled his hands in her hair, and rained feverish kisses on her face. He remained motionless, his lips searching her face, while she became accustomed to the feel of him inside her. Then, slowly, he moved, thrusting carefully. She could feel his muscles strain and stir beneath her palms. Naked hunger, sweet and violent, caught them both, and he plunged faster and faster. Hank quivered with the effort to love her tenderly. His heart thundered against her breast. She could feel it over the hammering of her own. Every part of him that touched her brought her nearer to the fiery unknown heights she had never before reached; frantically she moved her hips with the surging rhythm of his.

When the pain-pleasure became so intense that she thought she would explode, she cried out his name. Then the explosion came, lifting and spinning her into a blissful eddy of sensation. Almost simultaneously, Hank thrust into her for the last time. The tip of him poised against the mouth of her womb. He held it there for exhilarating seconds before he gripped her fiercely, and the life-giving fluid exploded from his body. Then, he was quiet.

Mary lay spent and still beneath him even though her heart beat like a hammer in her breast. Hank slid to the side and gathered her gently to him.

"My love. My sweet lass —" he muttered thickly. He dropped soft kisses on her forehead, her eyes, and smoothed the hair back from her damp face. His hand moved down her back to her bottom, then on to her thigh, pulling it up to rest across his, settling her more snugly against him.

"It's almost frightening to be so . . . lost." She spoke against his neck. "There was only you, Hank. Only you. We could have fallen off the world and I wouldn't have known it. I've never felt like that before."

"Never?"

"Never. Roy would have thought me shameless if . . . I'd moved or . . . acted like I enjoyed it."

"Sweet woman, there's no shame to you wantin' me to come inside you. The pleasure is one of God's greatest gifts. He wouldn't of given it to man alone."

"Oh, Hank! And you call yourself an ignorant Irishman. You're the sweetest, wisest man I've ever known. Theresa already loves you."

"And you, Mary mine? Tell me again. It's a hard thing for me to be believin'."

"Then, believe it, you thick-headed Irishman," she whispered laughingly. "I love you, love you, love you."

"And . . . is the marriage bed something you'll be likin', sweetheart?" he asked anxiously.

"Like it?" Mary cupped his rough cheeks between her palms and turned his face so she could kiss his lips. "You've made me feel so wonderful, so complete. You're a special man, my love." Emotion weakened her voice until it was a mere breath.

"I liked it too," he whispered unbelievingly, his voice almost as faint as hers.

CHAPTER
Twenty-two

In the saloon down the street from the funerary, Art Ashland sat with his back to the wall, his feet on a chair in front of him, a half-filled whiskey bottle on the table. Less than a dozen men were in the saloon. They all ignored him or appeared to. It was common knowledge among the men that when Art was drinking, he was meaner than a cornered rattlesnake. Tonight his attitude was, "Don't bother me, or you'll get your tail twisted."

Big John, on a high stool behind the bar, had the same scowl on his face that he'd worn since his team had lost the baseball game. Big John was a poor loser and was already looking forward to another game to avenge the loss. He kept an eye on Art, the four men who played cards at a scarred table, as well as the two, more than slightly drunk freighters, who lolled on a bench in the corner arguing about the charms of two of the girls at the Bee Hive.

"I say Pearl's the best gal-durned whore in the territory! Dammit it to hell, ya know it's so. Ruby don't hold no candle to Pearl!"

"She ain't no such thing. Holy shit! Her tits ain't no bigger'n a walnut, if'n they's that big," his companion protested, holding his thumb and forefinger together to make a small circle. "I like big-titted women. Ruby's tits is big as — let me see —" the drunk looked around the room for something to use for comparison.

"Shut up!" Ashland snarled quietly, but his voice carried to the two drunks. The men gave him a blurry stare, looked at each other knowingly, and snickered behind their hands, but they stopped talking and quickly emptied their glasses.

Lee Longstreet sat alone at a table and surveyed the scene with interest. He had learned to listen. He never knew when he would pick up news that would be to his advantage. He hated this place, hated the whole town, hated the necessity of kowtowing to men like Ashland and Weston. He considered himself more on a level with Garrick Rowe. Rowe had traveled in higher-class company than what was here in Trinity, and why he was associating with these ignorant louts was a mystery to Lee.

Lee looked with distaste at the muddy wet floor where the rain had blown in under the bat-winged doors and at the other set that led into the dimly lit hotel lobby. Good God! How had he arrived at such a low that he would even consider staying in this place and running a bug-infested hotel? Of course, he had not considered staying any longer than it would take to get enough money to leave. Since, fortunately for him, the miners he played cards with were unskilled and had little else to do with their time after working hours, Lee now had money in his pocket. When he shook the dust of Trinity off for the last time, he would be alone. He'd had a millstone about his neck long enough.

However, Lee had something important to do before he left Trinity. He might be slightly impoverished at the moment, he told himself, but he was a man of pride who settled his accounts. He bristled when he thought of the humiliation he had faced when forced to leave the wagon train. His ancestors had come from England to establish a class of distinction in America. All his life he had been contemptuous of the lower forms of humans who made up the world outside his own class. He had been set up to be ridiculed by a woman of dirt-farm mentality. The memory of that scene played in his mind and ate at him like an infected sore eating away at his flesh. He would have his revenge. It mattered little what people would think of him after he left town. What was important to him was that the Chandler woman would suffer.

The doors were flung back suddenly, and two wet, miserable-looking men stomped into the saloon. They paused and blinked against the light, then dropped their saddlebags beside the door and went to the bar.

"Howdy," Big John said. "Just ride in?"

"What the hell does it look like?" one of the men retorted as he flung his dripping hat down on the bar. "Do ya think we've jist been standing out there 'cause we needed a bath?"

"I wasn't thinkin' anythin'," John growled.

"What'a ya want?"

"Wal, we ain't wantin' tea."

The two drunks on the bench laughed uproariously and slapped their thighs with their hands. The stranger turned to look at them through close-set eyes, then turned back to John.

"Whiskey."

John set a half-filled bottle on the counter. "Two dollars."

"Two dollars? That's robbery!"

The other man threw a dollar on the bar and snatched the bottle just as John reached for it.

"Pay your dollar, Sporty, and bring the glasses," he said and headed for a table at the end of the room.

The man glared at John, sent a dollar spinning down the bar, pinched two glasses between his thumb and forefinger, and followed his friend.

"Goddammit, Cullen. That bottle ain't worth no two dollars," he said loudly enough for every man in the room to hear.

"We've paid five for less," his friend murmured and sank wearily down in a chair.

Each of the men downed two drinks in rapid succession before the one named Cullen wiped his mouth with the back of his hand and took off his rain-soaked hat. He was short, with a hard face and alert blue eyes. His friend was taller, slimmer, with the face of a fox. He had a gun tucked into his belt and a knife in a holster. Both men looked as if they hadn't seen soap or a razor for weeks.

"I ain't liking this place." Sporty Howard was a swaggering, two-bit gunman with more mouth than brains.

After riding with Sporty off and on for more than five years, the short hard-faced man knew that Sporty would rather gripe than eat. Cullen had often told Sporty that he'd complain if it was raining soup and biscuits were growing on trees.

"There ain't nothin' here," Sporty continued between gulps of whiskey. "I didn't even see no bank or stage station. And I'm hungry enough to eat the ass out of a skunk."

"What the hell place is this?" Cullen raised his voice and addressed the question to the room in general. "It's deader than a graveyard."

No one said anything for a minute, then Art said, "Who wants to know?"

The short man's eyes turned to the big man leaning against the wall. He had been in enough rough towns to know that this man was not to be fooled with even if you had him hog-tied. He was the kind of man who could explode and rain all over you, so Cullen answered him in a civil tone.

"Cullen McCall, late of Californey and Oregon Territory. Is there work around these parts?"

"What can you do?"

"Name it and I'll give it a try."

"Goddammit! A man that works for me gives it more than a *try*. He does the job or I break his damn neck."

"What's your business?"

"It ain't no business of yours what I do. But when I do it, I use real men, not two-bit drifters."

"Now you just hold on there!" Sporty rose up out of his chair.

"Sit, Sporty," Cullen said sharply. "The man meant no offense."

"The hell I didn't!" Art growled. "I meant just what I said."

Art had been in a fighting mood since Lizzibeth had turned him away from the Bee Hive. John knew this and stepped into the conversation before Art's fuse was ignited and chairs began to fly.

"This is Trinity, stranger. It'll be a real thrivin' town again before long."

"Looks like shit to me," Sporty growled and poured himself another drink. "Is there a hotel in this *thrivin'* town, or a place where a man can get a decent meal?"

"The man sitting right over there runs the hotel. You can ask him." John tilted his head toward Lee Longstreet, picked up a rag, and wiped the water from the bar where the stranger had flung his hat.

"Are you robbin' strangers too?" Shorty looked pointedly at John, then swiveled around to glare at Lee. "What'er you askin' for a room?"

"Step into the lobby when you've finished your drink and I'll tell you." Lee stood, pulled his watch out of his vest pocket, flipped open the case, and checked the time as if he had an important appointment. He smoothed his black hair carefully and walked through the bat-winged doors leading to the hotel lobby.

"Well, now, ain't he a highfalutin' cuss?" Shorty sneered.

Lee heard the remark. It pleased him. He was highborn, and glad that he was recognized as such. Whenever he lived among a group of people, he strove hard to set himself above them. Lee had lived in one of the finest plantation houses in the South, and he had been waited on hand and foot from the time he was born. Now, with a look of utter disdain on his face, he viewed the bare floors of the chairless lobby of the hotel. Lee believed firmly that the future would right itself, that this was merely a stop along the way.

He removed his hat and placed it on the shelf beneath the counter before he went down the narrow hallway to the two rooms that served as living quarters for Vera, Agnes, and Taylor. His room was upstairs at the front of the building.

His wife sat in a chair beside the cookstove. She looked up from her knitting the instant he appeared in the doorway. Vera was a tall, thin woman, and strong. She was in her midthirties, and every dream she had ever dreamed had been knocked out of her during the time she had been married to Lee. Now, the only thing she lived for were her children, Agnes and Taylor. Vera was tired most of the time and exceedingly weary of Lee and his demands. Not that he bothered her at night. That part of their marriage had ended when Taylor was born. He never spoke to her or the children unless it was to demand that they do something.

Lee had squandered her dowry the first year of their marriage. At his insistence, she had asked her father for more money and had been turned down. It was the last time she had seen any of her family. There was no question in Vera's mind that her husband was a scoundrel. Lee was able to justify every sin he committed by saying it was in defense of his honor. *Honor!* He didn't know the meaning of the word.

Vera was neither stupid nor dull as Lee would have liked everyone to believe. Being quiet and staying out of the way, she had found, made her life and the lives of her children much less difficult. She felt shame before the women of the town for the way her husband treated her, just as she had while on the wagon train, but she tried to keep her head high, nonetheless. She was sure, however, of one thing. When Lee left Trinity, he would go alone. She and the children were not going to leave the town. For the first time in her married life she had found a place where she could work and take care of her children. She had spoken to Mr. Rowe, and he had assured her Trinity would grow and the hotel would prosper so that they could earn a living. Until the time when paying guests arrived and the hotel was earning its way, he would pay Mr. Longstreet a wage. Although Vera and the children had done all the work, she had not seen a penny of the salary Mr. Rowe paid to her husband. Agnes and

Taylor were growing resentful, and Vera feared an open display of the children's hatred for their father would lead to trouble.

"Two men rode in. They'll be wanting a room," Lee told Vera.

"Mr. Ashland and his men are using the rooms."

"I know that. Put them in the room in back."

"That's where the children sleep."

"In the same bed, I suppose," Lee said sarcastically.

"Of course not!"

"It isn't fitting for them to be sleeping in the same room. How old is that boy? Eleven? Twelve? I'd plowed a half-hundred wenches by the time I was his age." Lee liked to tell Vera about his wenching days. She always snapped her mouth shut with such a look of indignation on her face. "He may be a scrawny little good-for-nothing, but he's got enough Longstreet in him to know what his pecker is used for."

"Don't talk like that about Taylor." She spoke sharply.

"I'll talk anyway I please and you'll listen. My papa used every buck he sired as a stud and raised the finest crop of niggers in Mississippi. That gimpy little bugger knows what he's got and by now he knows how to use it."

Lee hated Taylor because he was born with a twisted foot that caused him to limp slightly. The fact that the boy was exceedingly bright didn't matter in the least to his father. He saw the boy's deformity as a reflection on himself and regularly reminded Vera that it was her inferior blood that had caused it. He used the boy to get to Vera because it was one of the few things that riled her enough that she gave him cause to slap her.

With a great effort Vera controlled her anger and refused to comment. Instead she said, "Why don't you tell the men to go to the bunkhouse? I'm sure they'd not be turned away on a night like this."

"I don't think you heard me correctly. Wake up those damn kids and put them in here on a pallet. I want you to fix those men some supper. Fry the meat the hunter brought this morning."

"The meat was for us. Taylor worked for it." Vera got to her feet, flung open the firebox to the cook stove, and shoved in a chunk of wood.

"Haven't you learned not to argue with me? You know you'll do what I tell you to do. You've gotten lippy lately, Vera, and I don't like it. Now, are you going to get those kids out of there or am I going to have to do it?"

"I'll do it."

"I thought you would."

Lee went back down the narrow hallway to the dimly lit lobby and waited for the two strangers to come from the saloon. The price of the room for a night or two and the meals would add a little more money to his pocket when he left this place and took the stage to Salt Lake City.

Two quiet days passed. On the sixth of July,

late in the afternoon, Katy and Rowe returned to Trinity. Modo, Rowe's dog, met them at the far end of town as if he knew they were coming and had been waiting for them. Rowe dismounted, squatted down, and scratched the ears of his old friend.

"Miss me, boy?" The dog licked his hand, frolicked for a moment, then sedately led the way up the main street to the funerary where Mary and Theresa, attracted by Modo's welcoming bark, waited on the porch.

"Oh, Rowe!" Katy said regretfully as they approached. "I didn't get anything for Theresa."

"I did. I forgot to tell you about it. It's in my saddle bag."

"You're a constant surprise." Happiness spread warmly throughout her body when she looked at the man who would be her mate for life.

"And you're a constant delight." His dark eyes adored her.

"You'd better watch it. I'm going to be spoiled," she murmured and smiled into his eyes.

"It will be my pleasure to spoil you, Mrs. Rowe."

"Aunt Katy! I'm glad you're comed back!"

"I'm glad to be back," Katy called. "It seems as if we've been gone a month, and it hasn't even been a week." Katy stepped down from the saddle before Rowe could alight to help her. She hugged her sister, then bent down to hug her niece. "I've missed you both."

"You don't look at all unhappy . . ." Mary's

voice trailed when Rowe stepped up on the porch and put his arm across Katy's shoulder.

"I've never been so happy in all my life. Mary, meet your new brother-in-law."

Katy's laughter rang out when Mary drew in a gasping breath of surprise.

"You're married?"

"Yes." Katy raised her eyes to Rowe's smiling face. "I let him talk me into it."

Rowe's deep chuckle mingled with Katy's light laughter and his arm tightened, drawing her closer to him.

"That isn't the way it was, sweetheart, and you know it. Mary, she saw that all the women in Virginia City were after me and was afraid I'd get away, so she married me."

"Garrick Rowe! You're lying again!"

Mary looked from Rowe to Katy as if she could not believe what she was seeing and hearing. Katy was radiant with happiness, Rowe's face creased in smiles. Mary's heart was filled with thankfulness that her sister, who had given up so much for her and Theresa, had found happiness.

"You two have a lot of explaining to do." She tried to make her voice stern and failed.

"Mary, I've got so much to tell you."

"And I've got a lot to tell you."

"We had races and a ballgame." Theresa hung on Katy's hand. "We had Fourth of July, Aunt Katy. Uncle Hank stayed all night. He and Mamma slept —"

"Theresa!" Mary's hand flew up and covered

the child's mouth. "Oh, my God!" Mary's face turned first white and then red as a beet. "Oh, my God," she whispered brokenly. "I didn't know she knew —"

"Sweetheart," Rowe's voice broke into the silence that followed. "I've got to get up to the mine. I'll stop by the hotel and ask Mrs. Longstreet to fix up the upstairs front room for us to use for the time being."

"Can't we stay here with Mary? We'd have to eat all our meals at Mrs. Chandler's." Katy looked at Mary for approval, but Mary still had a stunned look on her face and tears had gathered at the corners of her eyes.

"If that's what you want to do and Mary doesn't mind, it's all right with me. You two figure it out." He bent his head and touched his lips lightly to hers. "I'll unpack the horse. I think I saw something in there for Miss Sugarplum."

"Something for me?" Theresa squealed.

"You're the only Miss Sugarplum I know. Stay here on the porch while I get the pack and we'll see what we can find."

Katy looped her arm in Mary's. "I've so much to tell you, you won't believe it all. You'll never guess who I saw in Virginia City. Mara Shannon, her husband, and their little girl."

Mary, mortified into silence, walked numbly into the house. When she turned to look at her sister, she burst into tears.

"Oh, Katy. I'm so ashamed. At the time . . . it seemed so natural and beautiful. I had no idea that Theresa knew. Hank left before daylight —"

Katy put her arms around her sister. "Don't take on, Mary. You love him, don't you? Rowe said he was sure Hank had fallen in love with you."

"I do love him and he loves me. But we're not . . . married, and Theresa may have told every-one —"

"Who would she have told beside Julia and Laura? I'm glad for you and Hank. He's a staying man, Mary. He'll not leave you and Theresa and go off looking for a rainbow."

"You . . . didn't like him. You said so before you left."

"I said a lot of stupid things because I was so mixed up and fighting my love for Rowe. He was so straightforward with his feelings that I got my defenses up and balked. That's the only way I can explain it. We're going to stay here and build Trinity into a regular town. You and Hank will be here too. Oh, Mary, things have turned out wonderfully for both of us."

CHAPTER
Twenty-three

Trinity, July 15, 1874.

So much has happened since my last entry in this journal. I am now Mrs. Hank Weston. Hank and I were married in Bannack on July 10, 1874. We were gone two days and two nights. It is wonderful knowing I have a strong man beside me. He is so good and so loving. He dotes on Theresa. I'm going to have to talk to him about spoiling her. He loves to hear her call him Papa. I am so happy that it scares me. While we were away, Rowe fixed up our old cabin for him and Katy to live in temporarily. The first night Hank and I were home we were shivareed by almost every one in town. Rowe made certain things didn't get out of hand. The noise didn't let up until Hank shoved some money out the door and sent them all up to the saloon.

The mine has been closed down. The men are using this time to get houses ready for their families. They are excited about being reunited with their loved ones and are working like beavers. Rowe expects the first train of wagons with materials for the mill to arrive in a few weeks. They want to get the building underway before winter.

There has been some trouble. Art Ashland got into a fight with one of his freighters and beat him senseless. Hank said that Art is smitten with one of the girls at the Bee Hive but she will have nothing to do with him because he was drunk and rough with her. After he went to sleep she hit him in the head with the heel of her shoe and kicked him out of the bed. He had a terrible headache. Hank and I had a laugh about that.

Mr. Longstreet has gotten awfully thick with two drifters who seem to me an unlikely pair for him to choose for friends. Rowe gave them jobs cutting timber along the creek where the mill will be located. They are quarrelsome and Hank would just as soon be rid of them, but right now they need every man.

We are going to have a church and a school. The minister who married Hank and me talked favorably about coming here to Trinity and building a church next spring. Katy has taken a count from the men who have families coming, and there will be sixteen children of school-age here this winter. Rowe is going to build a schoolhouse and Katy will teach them. She has already ordered slates and books. Rowe is so proud of her.

Katy told me about Rowe's half brother being in Virginia City and how he has always hated Rowe because his father married a foreign woman. Katy and Rowe are waiting to hear from Anton, hoping that Justin Rowe has left to go back home and will not try to cause trouble here.

In Virginia City Nan Neal walked down the boardwalk toward the bank about the time Oscar Gable would be leaving to go to dinner. The town was alive with rumors about Justin Rowe and his visits to the Doll House on the hill. Nan had decided to find out what Oscar knew about it in case there was something she should pass along to Rowe.

"Oscar! Oscar, honey!" she called when she saw the pouchy figure come from the bank. *You fat fart* — she murmured under her breath even as she smiled and waved — *I'd like to poke you in the gut with the end of my parasol.*

"Did you call me, Miss Neal?" Oscar thought surely he was dreaming. This lovely creature he'd yearned for so long had actually called him honey.

"Course, I did. I missed seeing you at the Opera House."

"You did? I only missed one performance, Miss Neal."

"I'm used to seeing you there and I don't like it one bit when you're not in the front row." Nan tucked her hand in the crook of his arm and smiled sweetly, all the time thinking what fun it would be to kick his dinger, that is, if she could find it beneath his doughy belly. "What's kept you away from me? Important business, no doubt," she said trying to stifle the giggles.

"Well, I guess you could call it that." Oscar beamed and patted the hand in the crook of his arm as he looked about to see if anyone noticed who was holding onto him.

"Was the business with that important-looking man I saw you with? He looked like an Easterner."

"He's a friend from back East. A financier. We may do some business together."

"How wonderful. Are you selling him something or is he selling you something?"

"No, nothing like that. I . . . may go back East with him."

"I don't want you to go!"

"Well, it won't be for a while." Oscar's chest swelled and his heart thumped so hard that he could hear it in his ears. Trying desperately to think of something that would keep her walking beside him, he said, "I'm a little worried about my friend. He's been going to the Doll House." He leaned his head toward hers and said the last in a low and confidential tone.

"The Doll House? Oh, Oscar dear, you should tell him to stay away from that place."

"I have, uh . . . Nan." Oscar was floating along the walk. He never dared hope he would be walking with her like this, much less hearing her call him *dear*. "I told him that woman was dangerous, but he keeps going back."

"It was sweet of you to warn him. It's a pity,

is what it is. You know all she's after is money."
Nan hung her parasol over her arm and clung to
his with both hands.

"I'm afraid so. He was in the bank this morning
and drew out a huge sum." He put his head close
to hers again and whispered. "We both know
what it was for, don't we?"

"Surely he wouldn't give it to *her* for *that!*"

"That's just what he's going to do. He's been
there every night for two weeks. She's got him so
befuddled, he'd give her ten years of his life for
. . . you know —"

"Yes, I know. Oh, what a pity!" Nan exclaimed
and pulled her hand from his arm. "I've got to
go, Oscar darlin'. Will you come to the Opera
House tonight?"

"Will you look for me?"

"I always do."

"I'll be there . . . sweetheart."

The adoring look on Oscar's face turned Nan's
stomach. *Oh, yes,* she murmured to herself as she
walked away. *You'll be there with your hands in
your britches as usual . . . you dirty old son of a
bitch!*

Nan waited in the millinery shop until Oscar
went into the eatery on the corner, then went out
a side door and walked quickly up the outside
stairs to Anton Hooker's office.

On the desk where Anton was working were
several neat stacks of papers. He was busy with
pen and ink and didn't hear Nan open the door
but he looked up when she closed it. She came

to the desk and peered over his shoulder.

"I always did want to do that." She laughed, and it was so infectious that Anton found himself smiling. "It looks like chicken scratchings. Can you read it?"

"My penmanship is not the best, but I can read it."

Nan shook her head in wonderment as she ran her fingers along the bindings of the books lining a shelf.

"Can you read all of these, Anton? Rowe can read French words on the bill of fare at the Star. He told me that I should learn to read." She sighed. "Someday I will — when I get time."

Anton took off his wire-framed spectacles, placed his pen in the coiled wire holder, and put the stopper in the ink bottle while he waited for Nan to tell him the reason for the visit. Anton liked Nan because she was what she was and made no pretense to be otherwise. For all her lack of education, she was said to have amassed a considerable amount of money and was careful with the management of it. Anton respected her for that too.

"Rowe said to come to you if I found out anythin' at all about that brother of his. The man's an asshole even a turd would despise."

Nan liked to shock a man as serious as Anton. Her eyes twinkled as she waited to see his face turn red. It didn't. Anton looked up and grinned. He had been around the world, and it took a lot to shock him, even words such as these coming from such a pretty mouth.

"My thoughts exactly, Nan. What's he up to now?" Anton wiped the lens of his glasses with a cloth and put them on again.

"He's been to the Doll House every night for two weeks. The Doll fed him one of her famous potions to make him horny as a two-peckered billy goat for a night or two to keep him coming back. Oscar Gable just told me Justin took a lot of money out of the bank this morning. If I read that right, the Doll now has him hooked on dope."

"It couldn't have happened to a more deserving soul. I don't care if he sinks in the privy hole up to his ears as long as he stays away from Rowe."

Nan shrugged.

"Maybe he'll get so crazy he'll blow his stupid brains out. The talk is that his wife spends her days and nights in that room at the Anaconda. People at the hotel say she's a nice lady and he treats her like dirt. They feel sorry for her."

"Rowe said the same. I'm thinking she could use a friend."

"Maybe so, but it won't be me, Anton. Women don't like me and I don't like them!" Nan bent over and peered into his face. "You're kind of handsome, Anton, even with glasses."

"Thanks," he said drily. "I wonder why the marshal doesn't do something about the Doll House. Everyone knows that it's more than just a whorehouse."

"There's no law against what she's doin'." Nan

lifted her shoulders again. "The men get what they want. The Doll gets what she wants. And maybe the marshal gets what he wants." She tapped Anton lightly on the nose with her fore-finger, then headed for the door.

"Thanks for the information, Nan. I'll pass it along to Rowe."

"Give him my love." She grinned impishly, tossing her head so that her midnight black curls danced around her face.

"I'll do no such thing. You get to messing around with Rowe, and Katy will wipe the floor up with you. She's not a weak-kneed woman and she'll not put up with much. I think you'd like her."

"I would not!" Nan denied staunchly. "I hate her because she got Rowe." She sniffed dramati-cally, jerked her chin up and grinned. "Bye, Anton. You're sweet, but at times you're as dull as shit!"

Anton chuckled. "Bye, Nan, if you had any heart left, I'd come courting."

After Nan left, Anton leaned on his elbows and thought about what she had told him. He already knew Justin spent his nights at the Doll House. Anton had seen him coming down the hill, scarcely able to climb the back stairway of the hotel. The Anaconda, like other buildings along that side of the street, had been undermined by floodwaters and was supported by stilts all along the rear.

What worried Anton was the fact that Justin's

actions were not predictable. He had expected him to hire thugs to stop the supply wagons from reaching Trinity, that is, if he knew about them, or set into motion a legal bid to deny them cutting rights on the land they had leased. Anton suspected that Justin might hire someone to waylay and ambush Rowe. Rowe thought so too, and that was why he had been so anxious to get Katy out of town.

As far as Anton knew, Justin spent his nights in a drug-induced stupor. From what Rowe had told him about the man, this was entirely out of character. One thing was sure: the Doll would bleed the sap for every dollar she could get out of him. That prospect didn't bother Anton in the least, but he did have a halfway guilty feeling about not offering his assistance to Justin's wife. Rowe had said she was a nice woman who had risked a lot to warn him of Justin's threat to kill him. Anton decided he owed her something for that.

That evening he stood in front of the newspaper office and waited for Justin Rowe to leave the hotel. A dollar here and there slipped into the hands of the underpaid hotel help that afternoon had bought quite a bit of information about the Easterner and his wife. Many rich and influential people had stayed at the Anaconda, but none had stirred as much curiosity as the Rowes. Justin's nightly trips to the Doll House were freely discussed and chuckled over. His arrogance had not endeared him to the people who served him. The hotel help felt sorry for his wife, but none respected her for staying with him and taking his abuse. Anton intended to offer her his help. If she turned it down, at least his conscience would be clear.

It was almost dark when Justin came out of the hotel and walked quickly up the street. Anton followed him and watched as he slipped into a dark passage between two buildings, cut across a weedy patch bordering the livery, and hurried up the road leading to the Doll House. Anton turned back, entered the Anaconda, and spoke to the clerk.

"I'm going up to speak with Mrs. Rowe. If Mr. Rowe should come back, delay him and send someone to warn me." He placed a silver dollar on the desk.

The grinning clerk picked up the dollar. "He won't be back until dawn. He'll have a grin on his face like the wave on a slop bucket, and he'll be so bleary-eyed he'll not be able to see straight."

"What room?"

"Front left."

A few minutes later Anton tapped softly on the door. "Mrs. Rowe," he called when she didn't answer after several raps.

"Who is it?"

"Anton Hooker. I'm Garrick Rowe's friend and partner."

"I . . . can't see you right now, Mr. Hooker. I'm indisposed."

"I'm sorry to hear that. Is there something I can do for you?"

"No. But thank . . . you." The voice that came through the door was hoarse and strained.

"Mrs. Rowe?"

Anton waited. When he heard no reply, he turned and headed back down the narrow hallway.

"Mr. Hooker —"

Anton turned. The door had opened a few inches. He retraced his steps and stood before the door, peering into the darkened room.

"Mrs. Rowe?"

"Come in, please. I'm . . . sorry —"

Anton stepped inside. "Do you mind if I close the door? I'm perfectly harmless." He tried to make his voice light. "Rowe, that is Garrick, said he mentioned me to you."

"Yes, he did." The woman stood at the far end of the room. He could see that she had something about her shoulders. "What do you want?"

"I came to see if there was something I could do for you."

"It's nice of you to inquire . . . and I appreciate it, but —"

"Have you had supper?"

"I usually have something here in the room."

"I'd be honored to take you over to the Star restaurant on Jackson Street. They have a broad selection on their bill of fare."

"No. No, thank you."

"Mrs. Rowe, I would like to talk to you, but

frankly I'm uncomfortable being in this dark room with you. Please go out to supper with me or allow me to light the lamp."

A long silence followed Anton's words. A small groan came from the woman, then whispered words.

"I'll . . . light the lamp."

Anton stood with his back to the door, his hat in his hand and waited. When the room was flooded with light, Helga Rowe moved quickly to the window and stood with her back to him. Anton looked about the room. It was tidy except for the bed. When he looked back, the woman was turning around.

"It's rude of me to stand with my back to you and I apologize, Mr. Hooker."

"My God!" Anton sailed his hat onto a chair and slowly came toward her. "Did that bastard do this to you?"

"Now you know why I didn't want to light the lamp. It's not a pretty sight —" Her swollen lips quivered.

Her face had obviously been pounded by heavy fists. Around her eyes were dark bruises. The skin over her cheekbone was cut and another cut crossed her eyebrow.

"Sit down, Mr. Hooker." Helga seated herself in a chair opposite him. She sat erect with her hands in her lap.

"Please let me help you!"

"There is nothing you can do. Nothing anyone can do."

"Was he drunk when he did this to you?"

She shook her head. "Justin never drinks much. Something else has a hold on him . . . now."

"Would it be easier if I told you what I know about your husband? And would it ease your mind to know that the clerk downstairs will delay him if he comes back so that I'll have time to leave?"

Tears that Helga could not control rolled from her eyes and down her cheeks.

"Thank you."

"Garrick told me about the trouble between him and Justin. He also told me to help you if you needed help. Mrs. Rowe, I know Justin has spent every night for two weeks at a place on the hill called the Doll House. The place is an opium den. Why do you stay and take his abuse? If you want to go back home, I'll make the arrangements."

"Oh, if I only could! I want so desperately to see my son. But I can't leave. If Justin came back to this room and I wasn't here, he'd send a wire immediately to the woman who cares for my son. She would take my boy away and I would never see him again." Helga buried her face in her hands. "He arranged it before we left New York. I can't leave him."

Bit by bit the story came out. After a while, it became easier for Helga to talk to the serious-faced young man with the wire-rimmed glasses and the lank blond hair. She told him everything, holding back nothing except the whippings on her bottom and what Justin told her he did when he went to the Doll House. She couldn't repeat that!

"His hatred for Garrick and his mother has eaten away at him until I think he is mad. He came here thinking he would do something to ruin his half brother, to even the score because he believes his father was partial to Garrick. He resents the money Garrick inherited from his mother. All the way out here he talked about the Rowes' pure Caucasian blood and how Garrick, being part Greek, was a disgrace to the name.

"Then suddenly Justin changed. It was after we got to this hotel. He sat in the chair beside the window and read a letter over and over. Hours went by and he never said a word. Then he saw Garrick on the street below. All the old hatred came bubbling up again. That night he went out and someone took him to . . . that place. He told me he had met a man who would do whatever he wanted him to do. That is why I went to warn Garrick. But now Justin seems to have forgotten Garrick. He hasn't mentioned him for days. He spends the day sleeping, wakes up toward evening and gets ready to go back to that place."

"Did he tell you what was in the letter?"

"Heavens, no! But I suspect it was something about Garrick. He locked it in his valise and I haven't seen it since."

"Mrs. Rowe, he may hurt you badly, even kill you if you stay —"

"I know that, but it would be a living death if he takes my son away from me."

Anton looked into Helga's eyes, saw the torment she was enduring, and desperately wanted to help her. His quick mind went over the story she had told him. He sorted out the pros and the cons of several plans until one that would work began to formulate. He started to see a way out for Helga. Anton was crafty at out-maneuvering the opposition. That talent had made him an exceptionally good businessman.

"I think I know a way for you to get your son *and* start a new life, if you're willing to take the risk."

"I've thought about it and thought about it, but there's no place I could go that Justin wouldn't find me."

"I think there is." Anton leaned forward, his forearms on his thighs. He was getting excited about the strategy developing in his mind. "Listen, Helga, we can outwit Justin. What if Justin should send a wire to your son's nurse telling her the plan has changed and she is to take the boy to George Hooker in Philadelphia? I'll send a wire to my brother explaining things. He'll handle matters on that end. I'll tell him to pay off the nurse and have him instruct her to go away for a while."

"Oh, but —"

"George will guard the boy with his life. He thinks a lot of Garrick. Your son will be safe, but you'll have to stay with Justin until we hear the child is with George. It should take only a few days."

"When he finds out . . . he'll kill me!"

"He won't find out for weeks unless someone from his home sends him a wire. By then, you'll be gone."

"But where will I go? I have no money of my own."

"Leave it to me, Helga. Do you think Justin will head back East if he hears the child is gone?"

"I don't know about that. I do know he'll blame Garrick, and there's no telling what he may try to do."

"I think it's about time the brothers had a showdown. Katy and Garrick were married before they went back to Trinity. I've never seen him happier, but he can't have peace of mind as long as he knows his brother is this near and wishes him dead."

"I'm glad for Garrick. The morning I went to see him I could tell that he adored Katy."

"Well, what do you think, Helga? Do I have your permission to send the wire to your son's nurse?" He took an envelope from his pocket. "I'll need her name and the address."

Ten minutes later Helga stood at the door beside Anton. Suddenly she took his hand and raised it to her lips.

"Thank you," she whispered on a sob.

"Ah . . . don't cry." Anton put his arm across her shoulders. "Be careful not to rile Justin. You'll have to stay here for only a few more days."

"Why are you doing this, Mr. Hooker?"

"Because I'm Garrick's friend and yours too . . . now. I'll stop by the dining room and tell them to send you up some supper. Bathe your face with a cold cloth and try to get a night's rest. I'll be back tomorrow night."

After the door closed behind Anton, Helga leaned her forehead against it, wincing when it touched a bruised spot.

"Thank you, God," she murmured. "Thank you for sending this kind man to help me. Keep my son safe. Guard Garrick's happiness and . . . please, God, help me to endure the next few days."

CHAPTER
Twenty-four

Katy and Rowe stood beside the big soft bed in the corner of their one-room cabin with their arms wrapped about each other. When he turned his face, she could feel the soft, silky brush of his mustache, then his mouth against her cheek. For Rowe it was heaven, pure heaven to feel and taste her, to know that she returned his love.

"Rowe, do you ever think about your brother and wonder if he is still in Virginia City?" Katy asked the question, her nose pressed tightly to his neck.

"I don't think of him at all." He raised his head. Katy burrowed her nose deeper into his neck.

"Don't lie to me, Garrick Rowe."

"Why would I think about him when I have all of this to think about?" His hands traveled down over her hips and up to cup her breasts beneath the thin nightdress.

"Stop trying to change the subject." She leaned back and gazed into his eyes, so astonishingly dark and luminous in the dim light.

"I want to love my wife, not talk about something as unpleasant as Justin."

"You've already loved me once today."

"That was early this morning. All day I've been thinking about loving you again."

"While you were marking trees to be cut, setting the corner post for the mill, blasting rock from the cliff, and shouting orders to the men, you were thinking of this?" She ran her palm down his chest, over his belly to the bulge in the front of his britches. She made a clicking noise with her tongue as her hand moved in a caressing motion. "Shame on you! You must have been a sight!"

"You little hellion!" He closed his eyes for an instant, savoring the pleasure she was giving him. Then with one of his sudden moves, he grasped her shoulders and shoved her backward onto the bed.

"Ohooo . . . !" she yelled as she landed on the soft, down-filled mattress. Amid peals of laughter she tried to scramble to the far end of the bed, but Rowe caught hold of one of her ankles.

"Just you wait!" He hopped on one foot in an attempt to get out of his britches. Needing both hands to pull his shirt off over his head, he captured her foot between his thighs and held it while she pushed at him with her other foot and yelled threats between giggles. When he was naked, he growled fiercely, pounced on her and held her captive with his arms and legs.

"Get off me, you big . . . horny ox!" she shouted, trying to buck him off.

He grinned with devilish sensuality. "No."

"You're not playing fair! You're taking advantage of your superior strength."

"Yeah." The sweet, hot excitement of playing with her like this was exhilarating. Rowe was at a loss to explain it, but each time he wanted to prolong it.

"You're dumb as a stump!" she gasped, panting with exertion.

"Yeah," he said again, laughed down at her and moved so his large, swollen member was against her belly.

"When you go to sleep, I'll . . . cut *it* off!" she threatened.

"No, you won't!" Uncontrollable laughter rumbled up out of his chest. He rolled over with her until she lay on top of him. Her nightdress was bunched at her waist. "You don't need this," he said and pulled it off over her head. "Katy, darling, you're more fun than a barrel of fish." He grasped her hips with his two hands and held her tightly to him.

"If I was charging you for this — I'd be rich!"

He laughed again, a full, satisfied laugh.

"You're wonderful, my Nightrose of a thousand years."

"I know," she said arrogantly, grinning down at him and rubbing the tip of her nose against his.

"Are you happy?" he asked softly, hopefully, his hands gently squeezing her buttocks and moving her up and down. He could feel himself thickening even more against that damp, warm part of her.

"Can't you tell?"

Her mouth hovered over his for a moment, teasing him, before her lips touched his, lightly at first, then with longer and more intense kisses, concentrating first on his mouth, then his cheeks, chin, eyes, and back to his mouth, nibbling, licking, and then kissing hotly.

She lay between his thighs, naked flesh on naked flesh. His hands sought the insides of her thighs, spreading her legs so that they lay outside of his and moving her until he was inside her just a little. Her hands clenched in his hair and she kissed him, hard, hungrily. Rowe's heart beat wildly and he fought against the pounding desire to hurry and bury himself inside her. He lay passively, determined to allow her to lead the way. Her hips edged down, pulling him into her slowly. It was the most exquisite agony for both of them.

"Do you like that?" she whispered on his mouth.

She moved pressing him deeper. His breath came in short, hot bursts. He lifted her hips, moving her faster, then giving in to his fierce urge, he flipped her on her back, impaling her with the full length of his flesh.

"My darling . . . Katy. My darling . . . Nightrose. I love you —" he whispered fiercely. He kissed every part of her face in a kind of frenzied joy.

"Love me, love me. Don't stop —"

It was boundless pleasure to Rowe to hear her

breathless plea. She writhed beneath him and met his thrusts, moaning in shameless abandon. Astounding, incredible feelings rolled like a tidal wave through him. When she made a soft little sound, the hot spiral of excitement coiled tighter and tighter. She was so slim, so soft, so precious to him. He was braced on his forearms to relieve her of his weight; and the muscles in his arms trembled with the strain of holding back, but he needed to see her face. Katy's soft little cries filled Rowe's heart to bursting. He knew the pleasure was not his alone —

"Look at me, darling!" he cried, feeling himself empty into her. "I love you. I love you." The words came again and again in English, in French, in Greek.

They lay side by side, feeling utterly drained, blissfully filled, and waited for their hearts to slow to normal rhythm. Katy sighed and pressed her mouth to his neck. Responsively, he tightened his hold on her and kissed her brow.

"Katy Rowe," he whispered, caressing her name. "Katy, Katy, Katy Rowe —"

His love for her was a fire smoldering deep inside him, needing only her touch to flare into flames. The wonder of it! The intense joy of being able to feel this deeply about a woman and have his love returned was a never-ending wonder that shook him anew each time they came together. What they shared was no ordinary thing.

"Do you want to get up before you go to sleep?" he asked against her ear.

"Uh-huh, but not now." She cuddled against him, sliding her leg between his. "Rowe?" She moved her hand up his ribs to his armpit, a favorite place, and he clamped his arm to hold it tightly.

"Something wrong, honey? If there is, I'll put it right if I can."

"I have a scary feeling that this is borrowed time for us, that I'm too happy and I don't deserve it. I'm afraid something will happen —"

"Nothing will happen, sweetheart. You're going to be too busy to have time for worry — you've got to help me lay out the town. We've got a schoolhouse to build, and a church. Next spring we'll start on our house. You've got to plan just what you want because we're going to live in it for a long time."

Katy was quiet for a long while, then she asked, "Do you think Justin will come here?"

"No," he said quickly. "I don't think Justin will come here." It would be Justin's way to send someone to do his dirty work, he thought, hating his brother for causing her worry. "Anton will get word to me if there is something he thinks I should know. Trust him, sweetheart. And trust me."

"I do trust you, but Mary and I were on our own for so long and we were so scared. It's hard to get used to not being afraid of the future."

"I'll take care of you, sweetheart. And Hank will take care of Mary and Theresa."

"Hank and Roy Stanton are as different as

daylight and dark. I'm glad Mary and Theresa have him."

"That big Irishman loves them. He thinks he's got the world by the tail going downhill backwards," he said lightly in an attempt to lighten her mood.

Katy moved her hand from his armpit and traced a path with her fingers up and down his spine. Then her hand flattened and she ran her palm over his tight buttocks. Her mouth nuzzled against his and she caught his lower lip between her teeth and gave it a lover's nip. His breath quickened, his heart picked up speed and his arms tightened around her.

"Nightrose," he whispered fiercely, "you're going to make a hobbling, mindless wreck out of me if you don't cut that out!"

Her laughter was like the soft tinkling of a bell on a frosty morning.

Shortly before dark a little more than a week later, Katy and Rowe walked along the path south of town inspecting the site where the mill would be built.

"The first logging camp will be a mile to the west of the mill." Rowe pointed toward the mountains that rimmed the town. "We'll build it into the side of a hill and make it large enough to accommodate thirty men. There'll be teamsters hired to haul the logs, choppers to fell the trees, sawyers to saw the trees into logs, and swampers to prepare the roads."

"I thought the men would all live in Trinity."

"The men who work at the mill will live in Trinity and some of the logging crew will too, if they bring their families. They'll come home on Sunday and at other times when the weather gets bad. But we'll have a number of woodsmen who make the lumber camps their home."

Rowe showed her the path being cut through the timber where the logs would be snaked down to the mill and where the cut would be made connecting the stream with the lake.

The men worked from dawn to dusk, hurrying to get the site ready for the skilled carpenters who were due to arrive soon. They in turn would prepare for the men who would install the steam engine that would drive the saw blade. Katy marveled at how fast the work had progressed. Rowe had divided the men into work-shifts. He had put a good man in charge of each group and given them a goal. He was a fair employer, yet he firmly demanded a full day's work for a full day's pay. The men respected him.

"Where did you learn how to do all this?"

"From Anton. He had a mill in Minnesota. I went to work as a cutter; later we went into a partnership. We figured that this was the part of the country that was going to need lumber for the next fifty years, so we sold out and came here." He gazed at her upturned face with loving dark eyes. "Fate, Nightrose. You and I were destined to meet here."

They walked on. Rowe stopped so she could

watch one of the men set a charge to blow a stump. They watched until the worker waved them back.

"Come on, honey. This is no place for you."

They headed back to town, walking quietly along the bank of the creek. Darkness falls quickly in the mountains after the sun goes down. Behind them they heard the sound of the stump being blown and the man's shout of satisfaction. They came around the bend in the creek where the willow trees were thick. A cow stood in the path calmly chewing her cud.

"Mable is loose," Katy said.

Rowe pulled her to a halt as she started forward to grasp the rope dangling from the cow's neck.

"Shhh . . ."

"What is it?" she breathed.

He heard the sound again . . . a soft thud, a low squeak. The sounds were almost inaudible save to one whose wilderness-honed hearing could distinguish the slightest unnatural noise from the soft rush of the creek water and the wind worrying the willow branches.

"Come on." Rowe placed his lips close to Katy's ear, his eyes on the willows that dangled over the running water. "Go to the cow. Talk to her . . . loudly."

Katy obeyed instantly. "What are you doing out here, Mable? You can't roam about like this. You'd make a delicious meal for a wolf pack. Come on, girl. We'd better get you back up to the shed."

Rowe moved up the hill while Katy talked to the cow, then he cut back, approaching the willows from the uphill side. With his gun in hand, he carefully parted the hanging branches and peered into the damp coolness beneath the willows.

A man lay on a woman holding her to the ground. She bucked and rolled her head trying to break free from his superior strength. Her skirt was bunched about her waist, her white legs were held in a vise between his. He held both her wrists in one hand, the other was over her mouth. Even that could not prevent the small squeaks of terror that Rowe had heard.

He reached them in two long strides, and with the strength of a madman he wrenched the man off the woman and threw him to the ground.

"You filthy son of a bitch!"

A scream tore from the woman's mouth, bringing Rowe's eyes down to her.

"Oh, my God! Katy!" he bellowed.

The man rolled to his knees in an attempt to stand. Rowe's fist lashed out knocking him back down to the ground.

"Help her," he said when Katy burst into the clearing beneath the willows. "It's Mrs. Chandler's little girl."

"Myrtle? Oh, child!" Katy knelt down beside the hysterical girl and gathered her in her arms. "Oh, honey. Oh, you poor little thing. Who — ?"

"Get on your feet, you rutting swine, before I stomp you to death." Rowe grabbed the man by the nape of the neck and hauled him to his feet. His britches fell down about his ankles. When he bent to pull them up, Rowe's big hand cupped his chin. With his fingers digging into the man's cheeks, he held him erect. "You dirty, filthy bastard! This child is no older than your own daughter!"

"Mr. Longstreet?" Katy gasped.

"Longstreet," Rowe spit out the name as if it were filth in his mouth. "I knew who it was the second I saw this fancy coat."

Lee Longstreet clamped his mouth shut and refused to say a word. But there was a sneer on his mouth when he looked down at the sobbing girl. These ignorant louts would never understand what drove a man to revenge his honor, and he'd be damned if he'd tell them. Let them do what they would. Come morning he would be long gone from this place.

"Pull up your britches and walk out of here or I'll beat you to a pulp and drag you out. If you run, I'll shoot you in both knees before I blow your rotten brains out." Rowe glanced at Katy who was helping the girl to her feet. "Is she all right, honey?"

"The poor little thing is scared to death."

"Did he rape her?"

"I don't know. She still has on her drawers, but they're torn."

"Take her to her mother. If he raped her, I'll hang him."

Katy had never heard Rowe speak with so much

venom or so much finality in his voice. With rage upon him he was like a cold stranger. Katy led the way, her arms around the sobbing girl. They walked up the path past the cow, who munched contentedly on the grass. When they reached the funerary, Rowe paused and shouted for Hank. The big man hurried out in response to the urgency in Rowe's voice. Mary followed.

"Come along, Hank. We've got some unpleasant business."

"For goodness' sake! What happened?" Mary ran a few steps to reach Katy and Myrtle.

"That lowlife son of a serpent had her down on the ground," Katy hissed.

"Who? Mr. Longstreet?"

Men along the street stopped and watched the procession that headed for the eatery. A murmur of concerned voices raced from group to group. Mrs. Chandler and Flossie, drawn by the commotion, came out onto the porch. A cry of fright came from the big, raw-boned woman when she saw the state her daughter was in. She barreled down the steps pushing everyone out of her way until she reached her. She folded the sobbing girl in her arms.

"Baby! Myrt baby —" Mrs. Chandler looked at Katy over her daughter's head. "What happened to my Myrt?" she demanded.

"Let's go inside," Katy said calmly.

"I'll be waiting, Katy. You know what I need to know." Rowe gave Lee Longstreet a shove toward the stone building.

Flossie ran after the men. "What'd he do to my sister?" she shouted. "What did that horny old bastard do to Myrt?"

Hank caught her arm. "Whatever it was, we be handlin' it. Don't get the men riled up, lass."

"If he ruined my sister, I'll kill him!" she hissed, then raised her voice and threw angry words at Longstreet's back. "If you raped my little sister, I'll cut your rotten head off!"

Flossie's words spread like embers in a brisk wind. An angry murmur came from the men who lined the street.

"Go on back, lass," Hank said firmly.

Lee Longstreet walked with his head up. He hated hard and had no regrets about the girl. He had evened the score with the Chandler woman and had enjoyed himself while doing it. He did, however, regret getting caught and regretted even more that he had been unable to penetrate the girl to the fullest. She was stronger than he had thought her to be. It had been a long time since a woman had fought him. He had merely to tell the wenches on the plantation to lie down and spread their legs. He hadn't realized how hard it was to get between a pair of thrashing thighs. He should have knocked the little bitch cold.

"Bring lanterns and light up this place," Rowe ordered.

When they reached the stone building, Rowe shoved Longstreet down on a bench attached to the front of it. Lee reached into his pocket for a cigar, struck the match on the stone wall behind him, and lit it. The group of men who ringed him were silent and staring. They wouldn't lynch him. Rowe was too civilized for that. All they could do was run him out of town and he was going to go anyway. The small gun tucked into his belt at the small of his back was a comforting weight. He had carried the gun since his riverboat-gambling days. It was effective when pressed against a man's spine.

By the time the lanterns were hung, almost everyone in town had gathered around the stone well in what was referred to as the town square. The girls from the Bee Hive and Lizzibeth stood together talking in hushed tones. The men from the bunkhouse and saloon, as well as Elias Glossberg and Laura Hillard, were there. They all stood silently staring at Longstreet, and their silence was more condemning than if they had been shouting.

After what seemed a long period of time, but could not have been more than a quarter of an hour, Katy came through the crowd, took Rowe's arm, and led him a short distance away.

"Well?" Rowe asked when she didn't say anything at first.

"There's no blood on her underdrawers, so he didn't . . . well, go deep. But he did . . . spend. It's all over her privates and up on her stomach. The poor little thing fought as hard as she could, and that kept him from completely raping her."

"You're sure?"

"Mrs. Chandler says so."

Katy could feel rage in her husband when she placed her hand on his arm. The muscles jumped beneath her fingers.

"What are you going to do?"

"Nothing that concerns you. Go on back and stay with Mary."

"But . . . what are you going to do?"

"Katy" — he looked down at her sternly — "do as I tell you and don't argue."

Stunned into silence by his curtness, Katy stood with her arms hanging limply at her sides and watched him walk to the center of the semi-circle of men in front of the stone jail.

"The girl was not completely raped, her maidenhead was not destroyed, but he did force himself on the child. Hank, Big John, Elias, Art, Lizzibeth" — he looked around and pointed to one of the lumberjacks — "and you. The seven of us will act as jury."

Rowe took one of the lanterns, waited until the people he had named came forward, then led them into the darkness behind the building.

CHAPTER
Twenty-five

Katy watched the men and the madam from the Bee Hive follow her husband. What's this? she thought. *Rowe has no authority to try the man here. Lee Longstreet should be taken to Bannack or Virginia City, or be held here until a marshal arrives.* A feeling of apprehension began to build as she waited with the crowd.

Lee sat calmly on the bench, smoked his cigar, and looked at the crowd that surrounded him. The whores from the Bee Hive were together, their legs exposed from the knees down, feathers and spangles in their frizzed hair. Vera, his wife, stood between Agnes and Taylor and stared at him. There was neither disapproval nor concern on her face. For a brief moment, Lee wondered why he had ever married her, and then it came back to him. His papa needed relief from his debts, and she had been the means to gain the brief respite. The loggers, teamsters, and miners glared at him. The lower classes always enjoyed seeing their superiors brought down. Their opinions didn't bother Lee in the least.

The "jury" returned, and Lizzabeth went to stand beside her girls. It was Rowe who spoke.

He directed his words to Lee Longstreet.

"You have violated a young, innocent girl in every sense of the word except for one. Had you accomplished what you set out to do, we want you to know that we would have hanged you without a qualm. Instead, we have decided that you should have fifty lashes."

Lee started to smile. They couldn't be serious. He looked beyond Rowe to the men; all were nodding their heads with approval. Art Ashland was coiling a long, black leather freighter's whip in his hands. Then he knew the big, dark man with his thundercloud expression *was* serious.

Still smiling, Lee reached beneath his coat for the small gun. As he brought it forward, Hank struck his arm. The pistol flew from Lee's hand. Hank picked it up, emptied the chamber, smashed it against the stone building and handed it back to Longstreet. Lee dropped it in the dirt at his feet.

"Tie him to the well post," Rowe said.

Lee whipped his head around toward Vera as he was jerked to his feet. She stood with her arms folded across her chest. Agnes slumped behind her mother, hiding her face against her back, but Taylor stood straight and looked his father in the eyes. For the first time in his life, Lee felt an emotion for his son. It was a grudging respect.

His coat was removed, his wrists were tied together and lashed to the end of the crossbeam that supported the well pulley. Through the fog that suddenly surrounded his senses, Lee couldn't believe that this was happening.

Katy couldn't believe it either. She pushed her way to Rowe's side and grabbed his arm.

"You can't," she hissed. "You have no right!"

He looked down at her with a puzzled frown on his face.

"What do you mean, 'no right'? If I had my way we'd hang the bastard. He can thank Elias and Big John for persuading the rest of us not to hang him."

"What you're doing is barbaric!"

"What he did was barbaric!"

"Let the marshal handle it."

"What marshal? They'll not bother about something they consider so piddly. They've got robbers and murderers to catch."

"I don't want you to do this!"

"It's going to be done. That man is going to suffer for what he did to that girl."

"There are other punishments. He didn't actually rape her."

"As far as she's concerned, he did. Would you rather I turn him loose to complete the job?"

"I'd rather you be civilized and turn him over to the proper authorities. You're not a feudal lord with life and death power over your subjects," she said heatedly.

"I am the proper authority here. He is guilty and will be punished."

"Why don't you cut off his hand? A public whipping is just as sadistic!"

"Go on down to Mary's or over to Mrs. Chandler's. I'll come for you when it's over."

"If you do this, don't bother. I'll not go with you!"

Rowe ignored her parting shot, strode over to Ashland, and took the whip from his hand.

"This is my job, Art."

Hank stepped forward and tore away Lee's shirt, leaving his back exposed to the light cast by the lanterns. The crowd stepped back. There was a breathless stillness before Rowe began his self-appointed task.

The lash broke across the quiet like the snapping of a dry branch. The pain caught Lee by surprise and took his breath away. After that, the lash across his back came with regularity and he set his teeth to endure it. It came to him through his agony that it was Lizzibeth, the madam from the whorehouse, who had stepped forward to count the blows in a loud, strident voice. He locked his jaws with the determination of a bulldog that had been his pet when he was a child. He'd be damned if he'd give this rabble the satisfaction of hearing him cry out. Lee centered his thoughts on what had sustained him throughout his entire life — pride and revenge. He endured the agony inflicted on his body, but he knew he would never heal from the humiliation until his tormentor was dead.

Fire! His back was on fire. *Twenty-five.* The bastard was trying to kill him! Through the agony that filled his brain an intense hatred grew.

"Twenty-six," the madam shouted.

The agony went on. The serpentine fire engulfed him. Once, he thought he couldn't endure it. Then he closed his mind, and from somewhere in the darkness he heard his papa say, "You're a Longstreet and don't you forget it."

Lee was not aware when the woman shouted, "Fifty!"

Rowe coiled the bloody leather and handed the whip back to Ashland. The crowd stood silently as Rowe cut the rope between Longstreet's bound hands, and he and Hank caught the man beneath the arms as his knees buckled. They half-carried, half-dragged him to the bench and set him down. Rowe went to where Mrs. Longstreet and her children stood on the walk in front of the hotel.

"I make no apology for what we did to your husband. He deserved every blow."

Vera nodded numbly. She looked at the man slumped on the bench. He was as far apart from her as he had always been. She gazed down at hands that had worked to raise their children, then back at the man who considered himself so far above her and his own flesh and blood.

"If someone will help him to his room, I'll . . . take care of him."

"Ma!" Taylor grabbed his mother's arm. "No! Let him take care of hisself; he won't thank you for it."

"Hush, Taylor, he's your pa. Agnes and I will look after him, Mr. Rowe."

"How can you do it, Ma, after what he did to Myrtle?" Agnes wailed.

"Because he has no one else, and because I owe him for giving me the two most precious things in my life — you and Taylor." She turned to Rowe. "I'd be obliged if you helped him to his room. And . . . Mr. Rowe?"

"Yes, ma'am?"

"The children and I want to stay on here. We'll work and pay our way. They're good children —"

"You have a place here for as long as you want it, Mrs. Longstreet. My wife and I will help you in any way we can."

Rowe turned quickly away when he saw the flood of tears come to the woman's eyes.

Katy looked at the calm, set faces of the crowd that stood silently around the well. A public whipping was something that was common fifty or a hundred years ago, not in 1874. The man should be punished, but it wasn't Rowe's place to do it and certainly not in this manner. This country would never be civilized if justice were meted out in such an offhand manner.

The ghastly *plop* made by leather hitting bare flesh jarred Katy from her thoughts and set her to trembling. She looked at the tall, dark man standing on spread feet, wielding the whip, and could not equate him with the man who had loved her so tenderly. She couldn't see his face and didn't want to. Her stomach heaved violently. She darted through the crowd just as Lizzibeth called out, "Four!"

Katy walked rapidly down the street, up the hill

past the cookshack, to the cabin where she and Rowe had lived since Mary and Hank were married. She had to be alone to absorb the dreadful revelation that her husband was less than the perfect man she had thought him to be.

For a long while she stood with her back to the door, her hands over her face. How could he do this? Her gentle, loving Rowe had in an instant turned into a cold, vengeful brute capable of stripping another man, tying him to a post, and whipping him as she had seen cruel overseers whip slaves before the war. Lee Longstreet deserved punishment; there was no doubt about that. What he did to that poor child was terrible. It was Rowe's duty to see that he was taken to the territorial capitol and brought before a judge of the court. Instead, Rowe had chosen the jury, set himself in judgment, and elected himself to mete out the punishment. *He enjoyed it.* It was as if he had reverted to being a primitive landlord of a thousand years ago.

Katy undressed in the dark and slipped her nightdress over her head. She usually unbraided her hair before she went to bed, but not tonight. She crawled into bed, turned her face to the wall, and pulled the covers up over her ears. Tears gathered in the corners of her eyes and seeped into the pillow. An ugly little serpent of bitter disappointment had slithered into her Garden of Eden.

She knew the instant Rowe's foot landed on the step stone. She also knew he would be angry that she had come up to the cabin alone. He had told her repeatedly that she was to stay with Mary or Laura if he was unable to be with her in the evenings.

A match flared, then went out. He knew she was here. She heard him drop the bar across the door, move across the room, remove his gunbelt and hang it on the peg beside the bed. She heard the chair creak when he sat down to remove his boots. When he lifted the cover to get into the bed, she moved a few inches closer to the wall.

"Katy?" His hand cupped her shoulder to turn her toward him, but she shrugged it off. She expected him to chastise her for coming to the cabin alone, but a silence followed. Then, she felt his hand on her braid. "You didn't undo your braid. You know it gives you a headache to sleep on it." His voice came softly out of the darkness even as his fingers pulled the ribbon from the end of the long rope and began to pull the strands apart.

"Leave my hair alone." She tried to pull the braid over her shoulder, but he refused to let go.

"No. I'll not allow you to sleep on the braid because you're peeved with me." He continued to loosen her hair, then rubbed gently at the nape of her neck. "Come here to me, sweetheart —"

"No. I'm not a chattel to be fondled when it pleases my lord."

"You're being ridiculous." He grasped her shoulder to turn her toward him.

Anger flared in Katy. She balled her fist and

swung. The blow caught him on the upper arm.

"Don't paw me!"

"Paw you!" A crude oath slipped from Rowe's lips. "Now, goddammit, Katy, I've had enough!" In a lightning fast move he flipped her over facing him, wrapped his arms and legs around her, and clamped her to him. Her arms were imprisoned between them; her struggles were as nothing against his strength. He held her so tightly she couldn't even butt him with her head. Anger and frustration caused her heart to pound like a hammer in her chest. She hissed and growled like an infuriated cat.

"Let go of me, damn you!"

"Now you know how that little girl felt when she couldn't move and a man was trying to go inside her. He held her just like this and she couldn't even cry out."

"What he did was no excuse for what you did."

"I did what was right. I didn't think I'd have to justify my actions to my wife of all people."

"You can't justify them. A public whipping is the ultimate humiliation."

"What that child suffered was the ultimate humiliation," he ground out angrily. "What I did was to save the worthless bastard's life."

"The court in Virginia City should have dealt with him."

"My God! You are naive. He'd not have lived to get out of town. Those men would have strung him up without a trial if not for Hank and me. Do you think I enjoyed doing what I had to do?"

After a short silence, he gritted, "You do think that!"

"Yes, I think that!"

"It was harder for me to lay the whip on him than it would have been to shoot him. I could have put a bullet in his head without batting an eye. He's a worthless piece of horseshit that his wife and kids have had to endure all these years. I didn't dare let Ashland or one of the mule skinners whip him. They would have killed him with that whip. If we had hanged him it would have set a precedent and given Trinity the reputation of a vigilante town."

"That's all you're worried about — your precious town!"

"That's not fair and you know it. You're hurt and sick because you think you're married to a cruel man. Katy, Katy, you don't know what cruelty is. That man's back will heal. His neck would not have. In a few years when little Myrtle is a bride and her husband touches her here and here," — he ran his hand caressingly over her breasts and down her belly to her soft mound — "don't you think she'll remember the first man who spilled his seed on her little body?"

"I know that," Katy began to cry. "He's a beast! I just didn't want you — it was just like I didn't know you!"

"Don't cry, sweetheart. I could see the disappointment in your eyes. I did what I thought was just and fair, and I'd do it again. If you're disappointed in me, I'll just have to live with it and

433

hope I'll not disappoint you again."

"I'm . . . sorry —" she whispered against his chin as he attempted to kiss the tears from her eyes.

"No. Don't be sorry. We're not always going to agree, but we'll face what comes together. I love you, my Nightrose. You must always believe that, even when I disappoint you." His lips sipped at the tears then moved to her mouth.

"And I love you," she whispered against his lips.

In Virginia City, Anton stood with his back to the wall of the newspaper office and watched Justin Rowe leave the hotel and walk up the street toward the alley where he would take the path through the field to the Doll House. In the week and a half since he had called on Helga and had sent the telegrams to his brother and to the nursemaid, he had noticed a drastic change in Justin's physical appearance. Rowe's brother had lost a lot of weight. He walked hurriedly as if he had only one purpose in mind, always with his head down and unsteadily, even after a day of sleep. It was plain to Anton that Justin was on the road to destruction, like a runaway train going downgrade.

It had taken longer than Anton had thought to get the answer back from his brother that the child was safe. He'd had to interrupt a telegram sent to Justin by the child's nurse. The greedy bitch wanted to make sure she was going to be compensated for the risk she was taking in hiding the child from his mother. Word had come today that little Ian Rowe was in George Hooker's keeping, and Anton was anxious to tell Helga.

Anton started for the hotel even before Justin turned the corner. A warm feeling engulfed him as he thought of the relief it could bring to Helga when she heard the news. He would help her to get her things together. Tonight she would move in with Nan Neal until he could make the arrangements to send her to his brother in Philadelphia.

Anton paused on the walk to analyze his feelings about that. Hell! He'd become so embroiled in taking care of her he didn't relish the idea of sending her to George. George just might be attracted to her and, worse than that, she to him. Holy shit! George was a good-looking man and had a lot more to offer a woman than he had. George would be ideal for Helga. With his connections, he'd be able to get her divorced from her husband; what's more, he could be just as ruthless as Justin.

"I'm getting the cart before the horse," he mumbled as he turned into the lobby of the Anaconda. The clerk nodded. Gossip about Anton Hooker and Mrs. Rowe was running rampant among the hotel help. He had been here every night within ten minutes of her husband's departure.

Anton took the stairs two at a time, eager to tell Helga the news. The door at the end of the hall opened and she stood waiting for him. He followed her into the room and closed the door.

"You've heard?" she asked.

"Yes." He couldn't keep the smile off his face. He pulled the telegram from his pocket and handed it to her.

Helga opened it with trembling fingers. Tears flooded her eyes. "Oh, Anton! Read it to me."

He shoved his handkerchief into her hands and cleared his throat.

ANTON HOOKER
VIRGINIA CITY, MONTANA TERRITORY
BOY IS HERE *stop* JUNIE IS IN HEAVEN *stop* NURSE HEADED FOR CANADA *stop* IAN IS A FINE LAD *stop* WHAT IN HELL ARE YOU UP TO? *stop*

GEORGE

"It's over, Helga," Anton said putting the telegram back into his pocket. "Ian is safe. You can leave here tonight."

"I . . . can't believe it. It's happened so fast. Oh, Anton . . ." She threw her arms around him and hugged him fiercely. "Thank you! Oh, thank you, dear, dear . . . friend!" She kissed him square on the mouth, bringing a pleasure to the vicinity of his heart, along with a pain lower down.

"I haven't been thanked so nicely in a long time." Anton's voice was raspy. He liked her arms around him and his around her. She was soft and sweet-smelling, every inch a woman. The smile on her face was beautiful. She leaned back now and looked at him.

"You'll have to read it to me again. What was that about Junie? Who is . . . Junie?"

"I can't remember a time when we didn't have Junie. She was our mother after Mamma died, our nurse, our housekeeper. She was boss of the house and we didn't dare cross her. She'll love Ian and he'll love her. You just might never get him away from her," he teased.

"He's safe? Really safe? Justin can't find him?"

"I'd bet my life on it."

"Oh, Anton. I'm going to have to kiss you again."

"I'll certainly not complain about that."

They sat down on the edge of the bed. Anton opened the telegram so she could read it for herself now.

"He *is* a fine lad, Anton," she said proudly.

"It won't be long until you'll be with him. Now what are you taking from here?"

"Everything!" Helga went to the wardrobe, opened it, and took out a valise.

"I don't have any money, Anton," she said hesitantly.

"I know that, and I told you not to worry about it. Pack your things. You'll not be coming back here."

Anton watched her fold her dresses neatly and put them in the case. She emptied the bureau drawers of her belongings, moving swiftly as if she couldn't wait to leave this place. Anton spotted the carpetbag in which Helga had told him Justin had put the letter that had upset him when they first arrived.

"Helga, I would like to see that letter you told me about. Do I have your permission to cut open that bag?"

She turned and looked at him for a long while. "You have my permission to do anything you want to do. If you want the letter, by all means break open the bag."

Anton pulled up his pant leg and removed a thin-bladed knife from a holster that fit inside his boot. He grinned at her and she laughed.

"Anton Hooker! I didn't know you carried that . . . pig sticker!"

"I never know when I'm going to have to stick a pig, Helgy."

"Helgy. No one's called me that since my papa died."

Anton placed the carpetbag on the table and cut along the metal frame until the side lay open. He drew out a handful of papers, carefully sorted them, and tossed them aside. They were stock certificates, bankbooks, and various papers. He drew out a white envelope. It's address read: Mr. Garrick Rowe, in care of Crescent Hotel, Virginia City, Montana Territory. The letter was from the Pinkerton Detective Agency. He opened it and quickly scanned the contents. He whistled, then read it again slowly.

"What is it?" Helga came to stand beside him.

He gave her the letter and watched her face as she read it.

"Oh, my goodness! No wonder he was in such a state." Suddenly she began to laugh. "All this time, he thought —" She giggled uncontrollably. "He thought —"

Anton took the letter from her hand. "We don't care what he thought. Hurry, so we can get out of here. He's going to be madder than a turpentined cat when he finds this missing. He'll know just where it will go."

"He'll go after Rowe! Oh, Anton! What have we done?"

"We'll head for Trinity at dawn. It'll take Justin a while to find someone to guide him there." Anton put the letter in his pocket, shoved the rest of the papers back in the bag and set it back on the floor of the wardrobe. "Get your shawl and let's go."

Helga went out the door without a backward look into the room where she had spent so many miserable days and nights. Anton carried her valise as they went down the hallway toward the stairs. They had just started down when the clerk came running up the stairs.

"He's coming back!"

"Oh, no!" Helga gasped. "What'll we do?"

"In here," the clerk leaped past them and unlocked the room at the top of the stairs. "Quick."

Anton shoved Helga inside and closed the door. They pressed their ears to it and could hear the clerk whistling as he went back down the stairs.

"Oh, my! I should have known it was too easy."

"I'm going to have to give that clerk a bonus." Anton grinned at her.

"How can you be so calm?" she whispered and laid her head on his shoulder. She was trembling violently. He held her tightly, loving her dependency on him.

Justin's heavy footsteps came up the stairs and down the hallway. They heard him open the door and throw it back against the wall.

"Helga!" Justin's roar could be heard on the street below.

Helga trembled violently. Anton had a fierce desire to kill Justin Rowe.

It was the first time Justin had opened that door and his wife hadn't been there. Where was the bitch? He would not have been back until morning except that he needed the gold coins he had put away in his valise. The Doll had refused to give him more than one of her potions until he paid her again. *He had to have it!* Women were greedy bitches — every damn one of them.

He jerked opened the wardrobe, his vision so blurred that he failed to notice Helga's clothes were missing. He reached down for the carpetbag. When he lifted it, the side fell open and the contents spilled out onto the floor.

His roar of rage was inaudible. Then words spewed from his mouth in an angry torment.

"Bitch! Whore! I'll kill you! I'll beat your ass till it's raw meat!" On his knees, Justin frantically searched for the letter from the Pinkerton

Agency. When he failed to find it, he staggered to the door. "Helga! Damn you for a whore. If you take that letter to him, I'll kill you!"

He charged blindly out of the room and down the hall, roaring for Helga, bouncing from one side of the wall to the other. He passed the room where Helga cringed against Anton, then raced on down the hall. Anton pressed his ear to the door listening for his footsteps going down the stairs, but he didn't hear them. Instead he heard a door slam.

Helga raised her head. "Where did he go?" she whispered fearfully.

"I don't know, unless he went down the backstairs. I'll go look. Lock yourself in here. You'll be all right."

"Anton! Don't go!"

"You'll be all right, honey." He kissed her cheek. "I've got to find out where he went. Stay here until I come back for you."

Anton let himself out and waited to hear Helga turn the key in the lock. He hurried down the stairs. The clerk and his helper were waiting.

"God! He was like a madman!" the clerk whispered in an awed voice. "He was roaring like a bull. Where did he go?"

"If he didn't come down this way, he had to go into another room."

"All the rooms are locked." The clerk scratched his head. "The door at the end of the hall wasn't —"

"Gawdamighty!" A skinny boy in overalls came

running into the lobby. "Mister! Mister! Somebody come outta that top back door and went over the rail to the rocks. I betcha if he ain't dead, he's near it!"

Anton and the clerk hurried to the back of the hotel where the floodwaters had undermined the building. Justin Rowe lay sprawled facedown on the rocks, his head smashed against a jagged stone.

"Jesus!" The clerk bent over him. "He's dead as a doornail. He must have come charging out of that door like a bull and fallen right through the rail."

Anton looked up as a piece of the broken railing fell to the ground. He looked back down at what had once been Justin Rowe and felt not an ounce of pity for the broken man who lay on the rocks.

CHAPTER
Twenty-six

A few days after Lee Longstreet had been whipped in the town square, the two drifters he had befriended, Cullen McCall and Sporty Howard, drew their pay and left town. As soon as he was able to ride, Lee left Trinity in the middle of the night and joined them in a cabin on the mountain above the town. But things were not going as Lee Longstreet had planned.

"I'll have no part in setting fire to that town," Cullen McCall said angrily. "I told you I would help steal the coal oil, but that was all."

"Are you sure we can get into the shed where the freighter stored the stuff?"

"I loosened the boards on the back side. All you have to do is lift them off. Any fool should be able to do that."

"That Ashland's a mean son of a bitch." Shorty threw his knife at a paper he had nailed on the wall and went to retrieve it.

"He is that, and Rowe's twice as mean if you get him riled, or mess with somethin' that's his. If he catches you burnin' down his town, you'll wish you were dead. He'll beat the shit out of you, then hang you for the buzzards to pick out your eyes. I've seen his kind before. He's one mean son of a bitch."

Cullen watched Longstreet carefully shuffle the playing cards. He had not said a word about what had happened in the town square, but Cullen knew he was eaten up with hate for the man who had whipped him.

"Shee . . . it! You're gettin' soft, Cullen." Sporty Howard flipped his knife into the wall again. "We get a chance to make some real money and you turn yellow-belly. Fifty dollars for a few hours' work ain't to be sneezed at. Hell! I been bustin' my arse for two dollars a day."

"Sometimes I think that all you've got between your ears is shit, Sporty. I'm not stupid enough to do another man's dirty work for a lousy fifty dollars and risk gettin' my neck stretched. If you're that stupid, go ahead and team up with Longstreet. I'm headin' for Bannack. But first I want my five dollars for gettin' in the shed and loosenin' the boards."

Lee watched the anger rise in Sporty Howard. The sneer in Cullen's voice, as well as his words, cut him deep. Lee took coins from his pocket.

"It's your decision, McCall. Stay or leave, it's up to you." He stacked the coins neatly on the table. "I'll play you for them, double or nothing."

"No, thanks." Cullen picked up the coins and shoved them in his pocket. He got up from the table and started for the door. He looked over his shoulder. "Comin', Sporty?"

"Naw. I reckon I'll stay this time."

"So long, then."

"So long."

Lee stared into Sporty's eyes. Sporty looked at Cullen, then down at the knife. When his eyes met Lee's again, the man nodded. Without hesitating Sporty drew back his arm. With a flick of his wrist the blade flew toward Cullen's back. It hit him just beneath his left shoulder and sank to the hilt. Cullen grunted once and fell.

"I was gettin' tired of his bellyachin', anyhow," Sporty said as he pulled the knife from Cullen's back and wiped it on his shirt. "He was always wantin' to go back to Laramie and see his pa. Hell! His old man warn't nothin' but a drunk." He turned the dead man over and went through his pockets. "Guess his money's mine."

"I guess it is," Lee said slowly and shuffled the cards again. "I'll take his gun."

"I guess I got me a new trailin' partner, huh, Longstreet?"

"I guess you have."

"Let's get our little fire goin', so we can get the hell outta here."

"We've got planning to do."

"Yeah." Sporty looked down at the man who had trailed with him off and on for five years as if he were looking at a stranger. "First I'll drag old Cullen out. He warn't so bad . . . at times."

Mrs. Longstreet sought out Rowe to tell him that her husband had left sometime during the night. For the first time in her life she was on her own without someone to tell her what to do and when to do it. But during the days when she had nursed her ungrateful husband, she had come to the conclusion that she would beg, plead, get down on her knees if necessary in order to break free of him and have a decent place for her children to live.

Rowe sensed her anxiety and, wanting to save her from having to ask, he asked her if she and her children would stay and run the hotel. He told her that later when the stage came through, a larger hotel would be built and the present one might as well be turned into a boardinghouse now. He told her to fix up a dining room and to buy what supplies she needed from Elias to begin serving meals.

During the days that followed, Rowe and Katy noticed that Vera had begun to take on a new air of confidence. She walked to the mercantile with a basket on her arm and greeted those she met with a smile. The biggest change was in Agnes and Taylor. Agnes offered a smile when Rowe teased her; Taylor, anxious to earn money for the family, readily accepted any small job. Katy had taken a liking to the boy and he for her. She had lent him a slate and discovered that he was very bright and eager to learn.

Things seemed to be working out very well for Vera Longstreet and her children.

It was the middle of the afternoon when Rowe, standing on the porch of the hotel talking to Vera, saw a black-topped buggy pulled by a buckskin horse round the bend and come down the street. Bareheaded as usual, he shaded his eyes with his hand and watched the buggy approach. The man was Anton, but the woman . . . My God, it was Helga Rowe, his sister-in-law! Rowe went down the steps and waited. He was not surprised to see Anton coming into town in what was obviously a buggy rented in Bannack, but he was certainly surprised to see Helga with him.

As Anton reined the horse, Rowe stepped out to fasten the lead rope to the hitching rail. Then, with a smile of welcome on his dark face, he went to the side of the buggy to offer his hand to his sister-in-law.

"Welcome to Trinity, Helga."

"Is that all you can say?" Anton shook his head in disbelief. "Couldn't you have said something like, 'My God! What the hell are you doing here?' You act like you were expecting us." Anton wound the reins about the brake handle and climbed down.

Rowe lifted Helga while grinning at his friend. "What did you expect me to do, Anton? I know you well enough to know you'll tell me in your own good time why you're here. In the meanwhile, I'm enjoying seeing Helga again."

Helga laughed. *Laughed.* Rowe didn't think he'd ever heard her laugh. She looked younger, her hair was less tidy than usual, and her eyes had a glow in them.

"Do you two always bicker like this?" Helga's eyes twinkled. "We've got a lot to tell you,

Garrick, but first I would be grateful for a drink of water. It's a long dusty ride from Virginia City."

"Come into the saloon. It's usually empty this time of day."

Rowe lifted the valises out of the buggy and set them on the porch. He called to Taylor, who had come out of the hotel when the buggy approached.

"Taylor, will you take care of the horse and buggy? The buggy can go into the lean-to beside the livery."

"Yes, sir."

Rowe reached into his pocket for a coin. "Ask your mother to prepare a room for the lady, then take her bags to it."

"Yes, sir, Mr. Rowe, but you don't have to pay me —"

"I'll pay you for this, but later we'll have a talk about putting you on a monthly salary if you're going to be handyman."

"Yes, *sir!*"

"But first, go fetch my wife. She's visiting Mrs. Chandler." Rowe took Helga's elbow and walked with her to the steps leading to the saloon/hotel. "Katy will want to welcome you too."

"Anton told me you were married. I hope you'll be happy, Garrick."

"I am, Helga. Far happier than I ever imagined a man could be." He looked down into Helga's blue eyes and said simply, "Katy's my life."

"She's a lucky woman."

The saloon was empty. Helga looked around with the curiosity of a woman who has never been in a saloon before. She was surprised to see that it looked quite ordinary. Rowe led her to a table in the corner. After she and Anton were seated, he went behind the bar and brought glasses of cool water. She took a long drink, dabbed at her mouth with her handkerchief and reached out to place her hand on Rowe's.

"Justin is dead."

Rowe looked at Anton.

"I didn't do it," Anton said quickly. "Not that I didn't want to. It was an accident."

Katy came into the saloon and headed straight for Rowe. She wore her hair in a single braid hanging to her hips. Her skirt was full, gathered on a band at her waist. With her sleeves rolled up to her elbows, she looked young, healthy, and extremely happy and carefree. She had seen the buggy come into town and was on her way to the saloon when Taylor found her. Rowe stood and put his arm around her, pulling her possessively close to his side.

"Honey, Anton and Helga have brought news that Justin met with an accident and is dead."

The smile fell from Katy's lips. She looked at the calm, clear-eyed face of Helga Rowe and was puzzled by the lack of grief she found there.

"Oh . . ." Katy glanced up at Rowe, then back to Helga. "I don't know what to say, Mrs. Rowe. I saw your husband only one time."

"You don't have to say anything, my dear. The

circumstances are not . . . the usual."

Rowe pulled a chair up close to his and Katy sat down, holding his hand in her lap.

"Hello, Anton."

"Hello, Katy. Is he treating you all right?" Anton's eyes behind the lens of his glasses took on a mischievous glitter.

"I'll just say I've learned how to handle him." A bubble of laughter burst from her lips just before she clamped her hand over her mouth. Her eyes went to Rowe's face. She was embarrassed to be laughing at a time when he had just learned his brother was dead. His dark eyes, devouring her face, were a mirror of love and pride. He gently pulled her hand from her mouth and raised it to his lips.

"We've learned how to handle each other," he said gently, lovingly, as if just to her.

Helga broke the silence that followed. "I don't think I could have endured these last few weeks without Anton." Her eyes clouded with the pain of remembering.

Anton shrugged, tried to act nonchalant and bored, but he failed. His eyes, concerned and caring, kept darting to Helga's pleading ones. Finally he reached for her hand and held it tightly, his love for her overcoming his reluctance to publicly express his affection.

"Let me tell it, Helgy."

In his slow, plodding way, Anton told every detail of the past few weeks in Virginia City right up to the night Justin went over the railing at the back of the hotel.

"It was good-thinking to get Ian to George," Rowe mused. "Justin seemed to get more unreasonable as the years went by."

"He just went crazy on whatever dope he was getting from the Doll House," Anton said. "He went downhill fast in only a few weeks' time."

"That surprises me. He never even drank much, that I know of." Rowe honestly felt regret that his brother was dead, but he couldn't feel grief. "Did you have any problem with the marshal?"

"None. The hotel clerk and his helper knew we were not near him when he went out the back door."

"We buried him on the hill," Helga added. "Anton left instructions for a marker — for Ian's sake."

Rowe nodded. "The boy should know about his father."

"Your friend, Nan Neal, was wonderful to me, Garrick. She stayed with me from the time we found Justin until after the funeral. Anton took care of everything."

"Thanks, Anton. It should have been my place to do it."

Anton shrugged.

"It's sad that a man should live forty years and have only three people attend his burial," Helga said.

"There will be the estate to settle." Rowe

placed his arm across Katy's shoulder and his hand moved up and down her arm. "Do you know if Justin had a will?"

"I don't know one thing about Justin's affairs."

"There's something else Helgy and I have to tell you, Rowe." Anton pulled an envelope out of his pocket. "Justin got hold of a letter sent to you by the Pinkerton Agency. Helgy thinks this is what set him off on the road to self-destruction. It sounds to me like it's information the agent found while he was working for Justin. For some reason known only to him, the agent mailed the report to you."

Rowe read it slowly, then read it again. The only change in his expression was a furrowing of his eyebrows. He placed the letter on the table and reached to cover Katy's hand resting on his thigh. He didn't say anything.

"Rowe?" Katy whispered. "Darling . . . what is it?"

He looked at her, lifted her hand to the table, and held it between both of his.

"He wasn't my brother. Why am I not surprised?"

"Justin's mother was already married and pregnant when she married Rowe's father," Anton explained. "Justin was born five months after they married, according to the dates recorded."

"Did Mr. Rowe know that Justin wasn't his son?" Katy asked.

"Justin's mother, Marie Englebretson, went to Rhode Island on the pretext of seeing her sick father and stayed until after Justin was born. When she came back, I expect she told Mr. Rowe that Justin was an unusually large baby."

"What about Justin's real father?" Katy asked.

"The report says he was a lobster fisherman. Marie left him for richer pastures. He still lives on the coast of Maine."

"I think father knew," Rowe said slowly. "He was never able to get close to Justin, although he did his best."

"Justin was proud of his heritage, or rather, what he thought was his heritage." Helga spoke in hushed tones. "I think it crushed his spirit when he found out he wasn't the aristocrat he thought he was and that since he wasn't really Preston Rowe's son he stood a chance of losing even his wealth. I feel sorry for him in a way."

"There was a demon in Justin," Rowe stated flatly. "He doesn't deserve your pity. He made your life a living hell, but it's over." Rowe carefully tore the letter into small pieces.

"You know what this means in a legal sense, don't you?" Anton watched as Rowe piled the scraps of paper in a tin lid used to collect cigarette butts and set a match to them. "It means that you can prove you are the only legal heir to Preston Rowe's fortune. Justin was frantic to keep this knowledge from you."

Rowe's dark eyes turned slowly to his friend. "I'll not contest Papa's will."

"I want to give back everything Ian and I will inherit from Justin's estate," Helga said quickly.

"I don't want that mansion on the Hudson. I'll not be able to manage it, or any of Justin's investments. They would be like a millstone about my neck. My son will be taught to work and to show compassion for those less fortunate than he," she added firmly.

"Besides that," Anton's hand covered Helga's, "she'll not need Justin's money."

For the first time, a smile curved Rowe's lips. "So it's like that, is it?"

"Your fault," Anton said dryly. "You told me to look after her."

"Are we invited to the wedding?" Rowe smiled at the rosy blush that covered Helga's face as she waited for Anton to answer.

"If you want to go back to Virginia City with us."

Rowe's fingers drummed on the table and he looked out the door into the bright sunshine for a long moment, his face deep in concentration. So familiar now with his moods and expressions, Katy knew the instant his decision was made. His eyes sought hers.

"Right here is everything in the world that I want." He searched her face lovingly, before he turned to Helga and Anton. "This is what I would like to do if it's agreeable with you both. Let's put the money in a trust for Ian, for any children you two may have, and for the children Katy and I will have, and we're damn sure going to have some, aren't we, sweetheart?"

Katy nodded and smiled into his eyes.

Helga looked at Anton for the answer.

"Sounds good to me," Anton said. "I'm taking Helgy back East to get her boy. We'll settle the estate while we're there and set up the trusts. Can you manage here without me until spring?"

"I think so. What do you think, Katy mine?"

"We'll miss you, Anton, but we'll manage. I know this isn't a nice thing to say at a time like this, but I'm relieved that we can get on with the building of our town and not have to worry about Justin coming here and causing trouble."

"I didn't know you were worried about him, honey." Rowe slipped his arm around her again and pulled her close.

"Of course, I was worried. Do you think I take threats against my husband lightly?"

"I told you not to worry," he said sternly.

She placed the tip of her nose against his. "I'll worry if I want to. What kind of wife would I be if I didn't worry about my husband?"

He chuckled softly. "I give up, sweetheart. Worry to your little heart's content if it will make you happy." His lips touched hers in a butterfly kiss.

"And I told you that you shouldn't kiss me in public," she scolded with laughter in her voice.

"You didn't say that!"

"You're lying again, Garrick Rowe! You know good and well I said that. What am I going to do with you?"

Anton coughed. "I thought you'd be over that lovesick, mushy stuff by now." His tone was one of disgust, but his eyes were twinkling.

"We'll never get over it." Katy pressed her cheek tightly to Rowe's and grinned at Anton saucily. "Well . . . maybe in a thousand years or so."

CHAPTER

Twenty-seven

The sound of a dog barking woke Rowe out of a sound sleep. Slipping his arms from around Katy, he raised up in bed. What in the hell had gotten into Modo? He hadn't shown that much life in months.

"Arrr-woof! Arr-woof!"

Rowe got out of bed, reached for his britches and pulled them on.

"Arrr-woof!" Modo's bark was followed by frantic scratches on the door.

Feeling his way in the dark, Rowe took his rifle off the pegs before he went to lift the bar from across the door and opened it. Instantly, the strong, tangy odor of coal oil assaulted his nostrils.

"Fire! Fire!" The shout came from down near the cookshack, followed by the clanging of the triangle bell that called the men to meals.

An icy ball of fear grew in the pit of Rowe's stomach. Light from flames flickered at the bunkhouse and Ashland's freight shed. Rowe rushed out into the yard and took a quick look around. Behind and to the right of the cabin he saw a ribbon of traveling flame. He had set enough backfires while trying to contain a forest fire to know that the fire was running along a path of fuel straight for the cabin.

"Katy!" he roared as he sprang back into the cabin. "Katy! Get up! Get your clothes!" Rowe grabbed his boots and Katy's shoes. "Fire! Hurry!" He jerked the blanket from the bed and wrapped it around her. "Let's get out of here."

They ran out the door and down the path. Sticks and rocks cut their bare feet. They were no more than fifty feet away when the traveling flame reached the cabin and the fuel-splashed walls exploded in sheets of flames.

"My God!" Rowe dragged Katy behind a thicket out of the light of the fire and helped her pull her dress down over her head. "Put on your shoes, honey." He threw himself down on the ground and rammed his feet into his boots.

All the horror of it struck Katy when she saw the angry flames leaping from the top of the cabin and lighting the sky. Rowe grabbed her hand as they ran toward the men pouring out of the bunkhouse, the cookshack, and the hotel.

"Get everyone out of the buildings," Rowe shouted. "Get everyone out, then get buckets, sacks, axes, shovels. Someone start pulling water from the well."

"What can I do?" Katy gasped.

"Get the women. Every hand will be needed to pass the buckets."

Katy raced toward the funerary, grateful that the fire had not spread to that end of town. In the flickering light from the burning buildings, she saw men pulling hames, horse collars, traces, single and double trees, and anything they could carry from Ashland's burning tack-shed. Other men were dragging empty wagons away from the building. Katy ran past Elias who was pounding on the door of the newspaper office where Laura and Julia lived. A light shone from the eatery, so she knew the Chandlers had been alerted.

The flames had set the woods afire around the cabin where she and Rowe lived, and smoke filled air made heavy by low-hanging clouds.

Hank and Mary came hurrying down the street. Hank carried Theresa; Mary a lantern.

"Thank God, you're safe!" Mary exclaimed. "We could see your cabin! Where's Rowe?"

"Rowe's up near the bunkhouse, organizing the men," Katy said breathlessly.

"Stay here, lass, so I'll know where ya be." Hank set Theresa on the bench in front of the stone jail, kissed Mary quickly, and took off running toward the group of men gathering in front of the saloon.

When Mrs. Chandler and her girls came out of the eatery and hurried across the street, Katy called to them.

"Mrs. Chandler. Over here. Can Myrtle stay here with Theresa and Julia while we women form a bucket line from the well?"

"You bet! Floss, get over there and get to drawin' water 'n' fill the horse tank. I'll fetch buckets. Elias," she yelled when the storekeeper, carrying Julia, raced up with Laura trotting along behind him. "Get all the buckets you can find."

Katy was surprised to see Art Ashland arrive with the women from the Bee Hive. He carried one of them wrapped in a blanket.

"She's got to lie down," he announced in his booming voice.

Mary was the first to react. "There's a bunk in the jail building." She led the way, carrying the lantern.

Art placed the woman on the bunk, knelt down and tucked the blanket around her.

"Who done it, Goldie? Tell me who done it 'n' I'll kill the bastard."

Goldie was the youngest of Lizzibeth's girls. She had golden hair and a delicate beauty. Now her face was bruised and broken. Blood ran from a cut that slashed her eyebrow.

"Ah . . . mercy!" Mary exclaimed when the swollen lips trembled and the girl began to cry.

"It was that no-good Howard what done it," Lizzibeth said from behind them. "He sneaked up to her room. I had Hank throw him out more'n once. He was mean, pure mean. Goldie didn't want nothin' to do with him."

"I thought he and his friend had left town," Mary said.

"Did. A couple days ago. That don't mean nothin'."

"I gotta go, girl," Art said in the softest, kindest voice Mary had ever heard him use. "I'll be back ta see about ya. Ya ain't to worry none 'bout that bastard what done this. He'll not hurt ya again."

Art left the building quickly.

"I got to bind her up a bit, Mrs. Weston," Lizzibeth said. "She might have a busted rib."

"Can I help you?" Mary asked and set the lantern on the table.

"I'll take care of her." The big red-haired woman soothed the girl's forehead with a gentle, motherly hand. "You'll be all right, Goldie. I'll tear me a strip off my petticoat 'n' wrap you good and tight. I'll tell you one thing, I'd hate to be in Howard's shoes when that big, ornery cuss that's taken such a likin' to you catches up with him."

Above the town Lee Longstreet waited and seethed. He had a notion to shoot Sporty Howard on sight. The dumb ass! He had gone to the whorehouse when he knew damn good and well it would be risky to their plan. Their only reason for coming back to town was to set it afire, not for Sporty to plow some whore who had refused him! Sporty had said he had a grudge to settle, and Lee had understood that. But when he came out of the whorehouse, Sporty had set the other fires before Lee had a chance to fire Rowe's cabin and trap him and the woman inside. He was sure they had gotten out. The damn dog had raised enough racket to waken the dead. He would have shot him, but that would have alerted everyone in town.

Looking down from the hill, Longstreet could

see the Jew drawing water from the well. The women had formed a bucket line. Vera as well as his daughter must be there, working their tails off to save something for someone who didn't care a doodle-d-shit about them. If only that damn Howard had done what he was supposed to do, the whole town would be afire by now.

The men had given up on the buildings above the town and now were trying with wet sacks to beat back the flames from the unfired buildings. There was one more thing Longstreet intended to do before he rode out. He was going to kill Rowe or his woman, whichever one he could get in his gun sight.

The woods above the town were burning. The wind was pushing the flames downward; but should the wind shift, it would trap his horse. Lee moved through the trees to where he had left the blooded animal. The one thing he prized above all others was his horse whose sire had been his papa's prize stallion.

The smoke from the green wood stung his nostrils as he hurried to where he had tied the animal. Amid the sumac bushes he stopped and looked around. He was sure this was the place. He put his fingers to his lips and whistled softly. There was no answering nicker. His eyes fell on the broken branches of the bush where he had looped the reins, the trampled grass around it, and cursed. In near panic he ran quickly to the area where the trees had been cut in preparation for a road. He paused and caught his breath before he could manage the whistle the stallion always responded to.

Then he saw his horse, a small form perched on its back, trot past the burning bunkhouse heading toward the center of town. Rage like a bubbling pot came boiling up to choke off his breath. Taylor had stolen his horse! He was the only person who could get near the big stallion besides himself. Lee jerked the pistol from his belt and held it out with both hands. Common sense told him that there was little chance of hitting the rider even as he fired two shots in rapid succession.

The bullets missed their mark, but they pinpointed Longstreet's position to Howard, who was looking for him, and to the big, angry man who was seeking Howard.

"Ya damn fool! What the hell ya shootin' at?" Sporty materialized out of the darkness to grab Lee's arm.

"My . . . horse! That goddamn little bastard took my . . . horse!" Rage had tightened Lee's throat until he could scarcely speak.

"Yore own kid? How'd he know you was here?"

"How do I know? The sneaking little son of a bitch can see in the dark like an owl. I'll break every bone in his body when I get my hands on him."

"I ain't waitin' for that. Give me my money. I'm gettin' the hell outta here —"

"The job's not done. Get down there and fire the livery."

"I've done all I'm goin' to do. I want my money."

"Where's your horse?"

"Back yonder a ways."

"We'll have to ride double."

"The hell we will. Damn you! I did what I was hired to do. Pay me or you'll get a knife like Cullen did."

"Ya ain't goin' to be needin' no money." The words came from behind Sporty and an arm like steel clamped around his neck.

The words had scarcely left Art's lips when Lee flung himself into the underbrush, got to his feet, and ran as if the devil were after him.

"What . . . what —" Sporty choked.

Art spun him around and planted a heavy fist in his nose, slamming him to the ground.

"I'm goin' ta beat ya till you'd wish ya was dead for what ya done to Goldie."

"No! It was Longstreet —"

"Then I'm goin' ta tie ya to a tree and set it afire for burning my shed!"

In desperation, Sporty tried to drag his gun from its holster, but a heavy boot struck his arm and snapped the bone. He screamed with pain.

Art hauled the man to his feet by the hair and slammed his fist into Sporty's face again and again until it was a bloody pulp. Then he loosened his grip and lifted Sporty off the ground with another blow. His head crashed into the trunk of a tree, and he sank to the ground as if he were boneless.

"Get up! I ain't through with ya!" Art yelled as he attempted to haul Sporty to his feet. The man's body sagged, his head hung at an odd angle. Art cursed. "Drizzlin' shit! I broke yore goddamn neck!" He roared with rage. "Ya dirty yellow-bellied son of a bitch. I wanted ya to hurt more!"

The words came faintly to Lee as he crouched behind the stumps where the trees had been felled to build a new cabin. One thought drummed in his head — he would never be able to get to his own horse. The damn kid would make sure of that. He had to get a horse and get out of here. Ashland would be looking for him now.

The livery hadn't caught fire as of yet, Lee reasoned. But it would. The straw used in the livery and the hay used to feed the horses had been soaked with coal oil. When the flames reached them, the flash of fire would engulf the entire livery. He was reasonably sure he had time to get down there and get Rowe's stallion, the one horse in town fast enough and strong enough to take the kind of riding he'd have to do to escape down the creek bed.

On that stallion and in the confusion, the townfolk would think he was just one of the men rescuing the horses.

Lee put his gold watch in his pants pocket and pulled off the distinctive coat and vest, that would identify him to anyone in town. After checking the load in the pistol, he tucked it into his belt and carefully made his way down to Trinity.

Katy worked alongside Helga and Laura, passing buckets of water until she thought her arms would fall off. The men fighting the fires were making headway. By beating back the flames with wet sacks and blankets they had kept the fires from reaching the hotel and the mercantile. The eatery and the funerary were saved. The newspaper office with all Laura's possessions was gone, as was the blacksmith shop, the empty assay office, and the Bee Hive. The cabins behind the town and the half-constructed homes for the workers' families were gone too.

Every once in a while Katy heard Rowe's voice shouting encouragement to the men. She glimpsed him, shirtless, his face smoked, his back and arms glistening with sweat, as he fought to save his town.

The fires had been deliberately set. Everyone realized that now. Taylor Longstreet had come riding down the hillside on his father's horse. Someone had shot at him. Vera had never been so frightened in all her life. She dropped her bucket and ran to Taylor when he slipped from the back of the huge horse.

"It was *him*, Ma. I saw him sneakin' round when I went out to pee. When the fires started, I went up the hill and whistled. Beaumont came right to me."

"Taylor! He might of killed you. He's a desperate . . . crazy man!"

"I think he tried, Ma." Taylor's young face was

frozen with hatred. "He won't get away on this horse. I'm goin' to tie him right here in front of the hotel where I can watch him."

As Katy worked she watched for a sight or a sound from Rowe. She worried for him as Mary worried for Hank and as Helga did for Anton. Laura dipped water from the horse tank near where Elias drew it from the well. She was proud of how strong he was despite his slight build. He was proud of how hard she worked to fill the buckets and pass them along the line. Myrtle stayed with the children, and Agnes and the two girls from the Bee Hive returned the empty buckets from the head of the line.

Anton came to place his hand on Helga's shoulder to let her know he was all right. Her hair hung down around her face, her dress was wet and torn. She had passed buckets until her hands were raw, but she smiled when she turned to see him standing close behind her removing his glasses to wipe away the smudges.

"Be careful. Please, Anton —" she whispered and placed her palm against his cheek.

"You too," he whispered back.

"Anton, have you seen Rowe?" Katy asked anxiously. "He was here a few minutes ago."

"He went to the livery to let the horses out. Someone told him the hay had been soaked with coal oil and the fire is going that way."

Later Katy was to wonder what it was that compelled her to go to the livery. The longer she waited, the stronger the feeling persisted until

467

apprehension was a tight knot in her chest. When she could stand it no longer, she grabbed Pearl and asked her to take her place in line. The urge to look for Rowe was so strong that she ran as if her life depended on it. She was breathless, and her heart beat like a hammer in her breast as she rounded the mercantile and ran toward the livery, slipping on the ground made slick by water flowing from the stock tank and churned into mud by the horses' hooves.

Fire had raced along the brush beneath the coral poles and was licking at the walls of the clapboard building. The double doors were open and propped back. In the flickering light from the burning cookshack across the street, she saw a man standing with his back to her, holding Apollo's reins with one hand and a gun in the other.

It was pointed at Rowe.

Katy ducked back out of sight and clamped her hand over her mouth to keep from crying out. The man's voice was unmistakably Southern and arrogant and came to her faintly through the sound of the blood pounding in her ears. She stood as still as a stone.

"I just want you to know before I kill you that a Longstreet always settles his scores. This is working out better than I hoped. I thought I'd have to go looking for you."

"You got just what you deserved. You're lucky we didn't hang you."

"You sealed your fate, Rowe, and that of the

arrogant bitch you married. When I ride out of here, I'll go by that bucket line and shoot her in the belly. It'll take her a long time to join you in hell."

"You'll never ride out of here on that horse," Rowe said calmly.

"I've not seen a horse yet that I couldn't ride."

Katy unfroze. She looked frantically about her for a weapon and spotted a long-handled shovel that was propping open one of the double doors. She grabbed it in both hands, moved toward the open doorway, and waited her chance.

"Why are you doing this?" Rowe asked, stalling for time. "Your wife and kids can stay here, and you'd be free to go."

"What the hell do I care about that peasant and her peasant brats? She's tried for fifteen years to drag me down to her level, but I've survived. A Longstreet always rises above the lower class."

"If you try to get on that horse, he'll kick you to death."

"What do you care? You'll be dead." Longstreet moved his hand to hold the reins closer to the bit so he would have more control over the horse.

Katy could wait no longer. She stepped out into the open and swung the shovel with all her strength. The metal end hit Lee alongside his head slamming it into the stall post. The gun went off and Apollo bolted past Katy knocking her against the side of the door. When she righted herself and looked for Rowe, she saw him on the ground. At that same instant the loft where the hay was stored burst into flames with a loud *pooff.* Hissing and crackling, the furious flames devoured the hay and the straw.

Rowe leaped to his feet and kicked the gun from Longstreet's hand. The man stirred and rolled to his knees struggling to get to his feet. Rowe jumped over him and grabbed Katy and pushed her out the door. They fell and rolled in the mud away from the burning building. When they looked back, the burning straw from the loft was spilling through the floor to the stalls below. They watched with horrified fascination as Lee Longstreet, with flames licking greedily at his hair and clothing, came running and screaming from the building.

"Don't run, man!" Rowe shouted to the human torch, trying to make himself heard over the man's screams of terror. "Don't run! Lie down and roll!"

In his panic, Longstreet stumbled and fell, picked himself up and ran on, a bright flame in the darkness. His screams, thin and piercing, were a sound Katy would remember to the end of her days.

Rowe and Katy sat in the mud with their arms around each other. Katy held him as though she would never let him go. It was all over . . . and she began to cry.

"Sweetheart! My brave Nightrose. Are you all right?"

"Uh-huh. I was so scared. He was going to shoot you."

"He would have, had it not been for you. I didn't see you until you swung the shovel."

"He set fire to our town," she sobbed as if that were the reason she was crying.

"The town can be rebuilt. What's important is that we're here together. Sweetheart, do you know what was in my mind when I thought he was going to shoot me? I was thinking that I'd not see my Nightrose again in this life —"

"Oh . . ." Katy wrapped her arms tightly around his waist and sobbed.

"Honey," Rowe said gently kissing her wet cheek. "Don't fold up on me now. You've got to help me get up. I've been shot."

"Shot? Oh, God! Where?" She leaned away from him to look into his face and realized the wet on the front of her dress was blood. She began to panic and couldn't draw enough air into her lungs.

"My shoulder. I don't think it's bad, but I'm bleeding like a stuck hog and I'm afraid I'll pass out."

"I'll get help! Oh, darling, hold on. Don't you die on me, Garrick Rowe. Don't you dare die on me," she choked.

"I won't. I'll not go and leave my Nightrose behind."

At the funerary Rowe lay on what had once been Katy's bed dressed only in a pair of drawers

471

borrowed from Hank. The bullet from Long-street's gun had passed through the upper part of his shoulder and nicked his shoulder blade on its way out. The wound was serious but not life-threatening. He was weak from the loss of blood. Katy had been too upset to dress the wound, so Mary, with Hank's help, had packed it with burnt alum and bandaged it. Barring infection, Hank had assured Katy, Rowe would be up and around in a few days. Now, after several hours of sleep, Rowe felt able to get up and survey the damage to his town, but Katy wouldn't hear of it.

A constant parade of visitors had been to see him since noon. Art Ashland came to tell him that he had killed Sporty Howard for what he had done to Goldie and for his part in firing the town. He said that if Rowe intended to turn him over to the marshal, he wanted to know now. He swore that he'd not be jailed for doing something that needed to be done. He said that if there was a possibility of that happening, he would pull foot for California.

"I don't see any reason to get the Territorial Law involved in our business here. Have some of the men bury Howard and we'll forget about him. How is Goldie?"

"She'll be all right, I guess," Art said dejectedly and twirled his hat around in his hand. "Lizzibeth says she's still sore at me."

"She may change her mind when she gets to thinking about it." Rowe wanted to add that he would have to change his rough ways if he wanted the love of a woman, but thought it best to leave well enough alone.

Hank came to tell him Longstreet's body had been found. It was burned beyond recognition and had been identified by the gold watch in his pocket. Complying with the wishes of Vera Longstreet, they had buried him in an unmarked grave on the spot where he was found.

Anton and Hank reported on their survey of the damage. The forest fire had been stopped in the clearing where the trees had been cut for cabins. Trees for the mill had been saved. In Trinity only the saloon/hotel, the mercantile, the eatery, the stone jail and the funerary had escaped the flames. Anton promised the men that additional help would be brought in to rebuild the homes for their families.

There had been no loss of life except for the two men who started the fires. For that everyone was thankful.

Working to save their town had drawn the residents of Trinity closer together. Mary shared clothing with Katy and Laura. Helga shared hers with the girls from the Bee Hive. Grateful to the men who worked so hard to save his store, Elias handed out blankets and supplies free to anyone who needed them. Art Ashland put his men to work alongside the loggers cleaning up the rubble.

Since the cookshack was gone with the bunkhouse, meals were served to the tired men in the eatery and the dining room of the hotel by Vera, assisted by Helga and the girls from the Bee Hive.

Few lamps were lit in Trinity that night. As dusk came on, the tired population retired to bedrolls on the floor of the saloon or two or three to a bed in the hotel. Helga, Laura, and Julia used Elias's living quarters at the back of the store and Elias slept on the countertop.

Hank arranged the long room at the funerary to give privacy to himself and Mary and to Rowe and Katy. A partition was hastily erected and a blanket hung over the door.

Katy pulled off the dress she had borrowed from Mary. She slid into bed beside Rowe wearing only her petticoat.

"How are you feeling?" she asked for the hundredth time since she discovered Longstreet's bullet had hit him.

Rowe lifted his arm so she could snuggle against his uninjured side.

"I've been resting all day while you've been wearing yourself out running around seeing to everyone, besides waiting on me."

"I wasn't shot."

"I never did ask how you happened to be at the livery. The last time I looked for you, you were in the bucket line." He placed gentle kisses on her brow.

"It was the strangest thing. It was as if strings were pulling me. When Anton told me you had gone to the livery, I was compelled to go looking for you. I thought I'd die when I saw Longstreet holding the gun on you."

"As far as I could see there was no way out. I

was hoping he'd try to mount Apollo before he shot me. That would have given me a chance. I didn't even see you until the instant before you swung the shovel. You've saved my life, sweetheart, for the second time."

Katy rubbed her palm over his cheek, rough with a day's growth of beard and pulled his mouth around to hers.

"I'm beginning to believe this yarn you've been telling me about our knowing each other in another life. But you won't convince me that those other lives were as good as this one," she whispered between kisses. "I love you."

"And I love you. You know that, don't you?"

"Uh-huh."

"We almost lost our town," he whispered between the time when his lips were not against hers.

"We'll build it back."

"It'll be a while before we can start the school and the church. Homes for the men's families come first. They're as lonesome for them as I'd be lonesome for you."

"I know. We'll have to build a new Bee Hive for Lizzibeth and her girls." The laughter that he loved so much came with her lips pressed to his neck.

"Absolutely! In the meanwhile, Lizzibeth and the girls can work in a couple of rooms at the hotel."

"No!" She lifted her head so she could look into his face to see if he were teasing. "They will not turn the hotel into a whorehouse!"

"The backroom of the mercantile?"

"No!"

"The jail building?" he'd asked hopefully.

"No!" The indignant look on her face made him wonder if his teasing had gone too far. "Why are you so interested in finding a new home for the Bee Hive?" she demanded heatedly.

"Well . . . uh . . . I just think it's an important addition to the town," he teased, his eyes shining in the near darkness, his lips twitching to keep from smiling. "I've heard the girls don't go to bed in their petticoats . . . like some married women I know." His hand captured her breast, savoring its weight and shape.

"You've only . . . heard?"

"Uh-huh." His hand moved down her thigh to the hem of the petticoat.

"Where did you pick up this valuable . . . information, Mr. Billy Goat Rowe?" It was hard to carry on a conversation when his roaming hands were causing her heart to jump out of time, her breasts to ache, and her womb to throb.

"Here and there." His hand, like a gentle thief, reached the soft down that covered the mound of her femininity and his fingers began doing wonderfully exciting things to her.

"You're not well enough for *that* tonight . . . are you?"

"Take that thing off and I'll show you," he demanded huskily. "I want to love my Night-rose." His lips, close to her ear, nipped the lobe with a gentle lover's bite.

"I want it too. But I couldn't bear it if I hurt you!"

"Heart of my heart, love of my life, you'll not hurt me."

His smile fired her with a new tenderness. She leaned over him and took his face in her hands, lowering her mouth to his for a long, sweet caress.

"You're my soul mate, my lover, my husband, my . . . everything. I love you more each day."

"I wish I could tell you, my Nightrose, what being with you is like for me —"

His mouth sought hers and kissed it with gentle reassurance and then with rising passion. His hand moved over her body, touching her with sensual, intimate caresses. Her senses reeled as they always did when he made love to her. She sighed into the sweetness of his mouth.

The magic never faded.

This was real.

This was forever . . . and beyond forever.

EPILOGUE

From the journal of Mary Stanton Weston.

Trinity, Montana Territory, July 4, 1879.
I cannot believe that five years have passed since Katy, Theresa, and I were abandoned in Trinity by Roy Stanton. As I look down from our comfortable home on the hill above the mill, I see a busy little town with three churches, a school, a bank, a stage station, and a variety of stores. Trinity has prospered due to the sawmill and logging operations and is a supply area for the ranches beyond the timber. We're preparing for a day of celebration that will equal that of Virginia City.

Most of the people who came here that fateful summer of 1874 are still here. Mrs. Chandler runs the eatery with the help of Myrtle and Agnes Longstreet. Flossie married a drummer and moved to Oregon. Myrtle grew to be a pretty girl and I think she has a serious beau. Since Agnes wants to be a teacher, the hotel man her mother married is going to send her to college in Salt Lake.

Laura and Elias married and have a boy who is the image of Elias. The difference in their religious beliefs seems to be no problem at all. Laura is running the newspaper, *The Trinity*

Gazette, with the help of Taylor Longstreet. She thinks the sun rises and sets in that young man and swears he's going to be a nationally known newspaper man someday.

After the fire, the Bee Hive was relocated in the woods at the end of town. Lizzibeth died two winters ago and Pearl took over. She runs a decent place — if you could call such a place decent.

Goldie married Art Ashland — finally. They went to Denver to make a new life and from what we've heard, Art is a reformed man. Hank says that happens sometimes when a man falls in love.

Anton and Helga live in Bozeman with Ian and their little daughter, Nannie. She is a darling child and Anton is very proud of her. On their last visit they told us that they had heard from Anton's brother, George. He had seen Nan Neal in Europe. He said that Nan was the toast of Paris. Helga said she looked for George and Nan to marry someday. George was wild about her.

Hank, my dear love, is delighted that we are expecting our third child. Theresa and Patrick fill our lives so completely that I wonder about making room for another child. I look back on the life I had before I met Hank and to me, it's a dreadful dream. My husband is the most wonderful, kindest man in the world. I am sure that Katy wouldn't agree with me.

I've saved the best for last. My dear sister, Katy, who so despised this town when we were abandoned here is its most avid supporter. She is on the school board, heads a civic committee that insisted on town meetings, and is working to bring Montana into the Union and make it the forty-first state. Rowe is busy with the mill, the mine, and his ranch. He stands back and allows Katy full rein with her projects. He loves her to distraction, and woe to the man who does not give her proper respect — even when she pushes too far.

Rowe has built Katy a fine home on the ranch. It has gables, turrets, upper and lower porches, and a gazebo all decorated with fretwork made by the most skilled carpenters. The furnishings are the finest, but Katy insists that their home be comfortable and welcoming. Rowe says he is going to fill each of the twelve rooms with little Rowes that look exactly like his Nightrose. He's got a good start, but his two black-haired boys look more like him than Katy. For all the fancy house, Katy is still the same Katy she was when she and I broke into the funerary to find a safe place to live. She still wears her hair in one long braid hanging down her back and she still rides astride.

This is my last entry in this journal. It is full. Not a single page is left. I'll close by saying that Katy and I have found love, real love, and happiness here in Trinity and we're not one bit sorry that Roy Stanton left us here in this abandoned town five years ago.

Mary Burns Weston

AUTHOR'S NOTE

The mystery of the ghost towns began with the abandoned mining towns in the West and has increased with the passage of time. Now, the Old West has given way to the New West. Today's ghost towns are shadowy remnants of a fascinating past. The settlements left empty as people followed the lure of a new gold or silver strike are like stage settings from which the actors have vanished, and the dramas of their lives are old stories passed on by descendants scattered far and wide.

Trinity, Montana Territory, is a composite of all the ghost towns I have ever visited or read about. I have often wondered why, in each case, the people moved on, leaving so much behind, and what would have happened if some of them had stayed, had dreamed new dreams, and had seen new visions.

The sketch of some of the buildings in my ghost town in the front of this book was made by my daughter-in-law, Jacky Theiss Garlock, a well-known artist here in the Midwest. She depicts them exactly as I imagined them to be.

The people in Trinity are all products of my imagination and I have tried to portray them as I think they would have been at that time. I purposely left the Indians out of this story, for to merely mention them would have not done justice to the part they played in our history.

Dorothy Garlock

The employees of G.K. Hall hope you have enjoyed this Large Print book. All our Large Print titles are designed for easy reading, and all our books are made to last. Other G.K. Hall books arc available at your library, through selected bookstores, or directly from us.

For information about titles, please call:

(800) 223-2336

To share your comments, please write:

Publisher
G.K. Hall & Co.
P.O. Box 159
Thorndike, ME 04986